SATAN'S SWORD

DEBRA DUNBAR

debra dunbar

FIENDISHLY FUN FICTION

CHAPTER 1

I stuck my index finger in the pan and watched the oil bubble up around it, searing and cooking the flesh. "It's hot enough," I said, pulling my finger out and dumping in the pancetta. It sizzled, splashing me a bit on my arm.

Candy frowned. "I wish you wouldn't do that. It really freaks me out."

Just to mess with her further, I put my finger in my mouth and pulled off the cooked bit, chewing and swallowing before creating a new fingertip. "I've got to see if the oil is hot enough before I put in the meat or it'll be all greasy." Candy looked revolted.

Wyatt came into my kitchen and planted a kiss on my lips.

Wyatt was my sexy human neighbor, and my boyfriend. We'd flirted and palled around for the two years since he moved in next door, but this summer things had gotten hot and heavy between us. He was my best friend. Everything was better with Wyatt around.

"Ewwww. I can't believe you kissed her on the mouth. She just ate her finger, you know?" Candy choked out.

Wyatt grinned. "Tastes like bacon."

Did I mention how much I liked Wyatt?

"By the way, your red light is on," he added.

Fuck. It was Dar. Again.

Dar was my foster brother. He'd been calling me and leaving messages for months now on the mirror I use as an inter-realm communication device. I always deleted them without listening because he was a pest, but the calls were becoming more frequent.

"You really should see what he wants," Wyatt said. "Otherwise he'll never leave you alone."

He was right. And I was beginning to worry a bit about the constant messages. Demons may not have the same kind of relationships as humans, but we do form attachments and care about others in our own way. Dar and I had grown up together. We'd pulled each other out of a lot of jams. Gotten each other into a lot of jams, too, but that's pretty common with demons.

"Can you just erase it?" I asked Wyatt. "I promise I'll call him after dinner."

"Units all full for the winter," Michelle announced as she entered my kitchen, raising her hand for a high five.

Michelle was my property manager, handling all of my slum rental units with great skill. I valued her expertise and made sure she had lots of bonuses under the table to keep her loyalty unswerving.

"You rented the last two then?" I asked. People didn't like to move over the winter, so it was good to have all your rentals full by mid fall. That way they stayed full until spring.

She nodded, snagging a piece of pumpkin bread from the table. Michelle did not come by her svelte figure through starvation.

"Cash, too," she mumbled with her mouth full.

Cash was good. That meant the units remained unrented as far as the IRS was concerned, and all the rental income was tax-free. Nice. Nice for Michelle, too, who got a larger-than-usual cut of cash tenants.

"Speaking of apartments, don't forget the walk-through on those canal row houses tomorrow morning," Candy interjected.

I'd wanted to buy those dilapidated properties along the canal for years. Foreclosures aren't always a good deal, but Candy was handling the sale for the bank, and I was sure she had greatly influenced them in their agreeableness.

Candy was downright demonic when it came to planning, scheming, and working events to her advantage. She was also a werewolf. She had lied to me, manipulated and blackmailed me into helping her find and take out a rogue angel this past summer. I'd almost died. I liked her. Deviousness was a trait I valued in a friend.

"Why the walk-through?" I asked, stirring the pancetta. "I already signed off on the inspections." The places really should have been condemned, but I prevailed by generously greasing an inspector's palm.

"Formality," Candy shrugged. "Hey, what do you want to do about the squatters? There is a new member of my pack that has guard training if you're looking for someone to move them out and keep them out. He enjoys that sort of thing, so the fee would be reasonable."

Squatters. Normally I'd handle them myself, but homeless people tended to have mental health problems, and my kind doesn't do well in encounters with the mentally ill. They recognize demons for who we are and refuse to leave us alone. I've had crazies follow me all over downtown, screaming at me, throwing salt on me, entreating every religious deity they know to remove me from this dimension. I

3

can't manage them, can't intimidate them, can't reason with them. They're difficult to kill, they taste bad, and are very unpleasant to Own. I'd gladly pay a werewolf to deal with these nut jobs for me. Of course, even homeless, insane people could be profited from.

"Michelle, how much should I charge squatters to live in an almost-condemned building with no running water or electricity?"

Michelle looked thoughtfully at her slice of pumpkin bread. "A dollar a day? You'd need to collect it every day since they can't save worth a darn, and any money they stockpiled would be stolen by the others."

"There's no way they can come up with a dollar a day," Wyatt chimed in. "They're homeless, Sam. Just let them stay there for free."

I ignored him. I have very strong feelings for Wyatt, but he's too generous sometimes. Which is probably why he's so poor.

"That's seven bucks a week," I protested. "I think we can charge more than that. Shit, I gave one of them five bucks to carry an air conditioning unit up three flights of stairs for me this summer."

I could have carried the air conditioning unit up myself, but it had been fun to watch the guy struggle up the stairs with it, sweating gin the whole way.

"I think you could get a buck or two a day," Candy said.

Michelle waved her hand in a dismissive gesture. "I can't handle this one for you. If there are problems, it would open up a whole can of worms with all your other properties. It would be best to do this one separate from your other investments."

I thought for a moment. "Candy, can your guy meet us for the walk-through tomorrow? Do you think he'd be interested in this kind of thing? I'd need him to collect the rent on

a daily basis, take a count of tenants, and keep the peace as a guard for maybe an hour at night, until everyone is settled in."

"Oh yeah. Reed just moved up from Georgia, and he's eager to prove his loyalty. I appreciate you considering him. He hasn't found work yet, and a wolf with idle time on his hands is never a good thing."

This could be a good thing. I hadn't planned on renovating these houses for a few years, and it would be nice to have some income out of them, no matter how small. Plus an occupied property, even by crazy homeless people, wouldn't be as likely to be gutted for copper pipes. They wouldn't sue me if the roof fell in on their heads, and a werewolf rent collector would make everything run smoothly. Wyatt wouldn't be thrilled, but he'd been more accepting of these things since learning I was a demon.

I stuck my hand into the boiling water to swirl it around a bit and pluck out a strand of fettucini to test. Breaking the noodle in half, I handed part to Candy with my scalded hand.

"I think it's done. What do you think?"

"I think I'm going to check the table setting before I'm totally turned off by my dinner."

It was ready. I fixed my hand and Wyatt helped toss the noodles with the pancetta, roasted garlic, artichoke, and sun dried tomatoes. Michelle pulled the wine out of the fridge and carried it into the dining area while Wyatt took in the pasta and made one last trip to snag the garlic bread out of the oven.

I may be a demon, but I loved these evenings with my friends, sharing food and laughing over stories. We had a lively debate concerning the prospects of favorite football teams this season, made fun of the latest Hollywood scandal, and speculated on whether there would be enough snow to warrant shelling out for season ski passes at the nearby resort. I knew Michelle skied. She'd flown out to Aspen with some friends last year for a week, and I'd bought her an expensive set of goggles she'd been eyeing as a present this past Christmas.

"I'm going to wait," Michelle said in regards to the season pass. "I'd rather go out west. The slopes are so icy here, and what little powder there is gets stacked way up on the edges. Too much corn in the middle, too. It's just not fun."

"You need to keep your edges super sharp," Wyatt told her, digging into the pasta bowl for seconds. Wyatt was a snowboarder, of course. We'd gone to the local spots quite a bit last year and I had just as much fun drooling over him at the rails and jumps as I did skiing.

"Fresh wax weekly, too, to keep the slush from sticking," Candy added.

I had all kinds of lewd comments I wanted to make about Candy's need to wax so often, no doubt because of her hairy wolf self, but I kept it clean for once.

"You ski?" I asked Candy.

"Of course."

We all stared. Candy looked mid-fifties, but I'd learned she was actually sixty-two. Werewolves lived longer than humans and tended to be fit and active right up to their end, but I just couldn't imagine her skiing. It wasn't just her age, either. Candy was not the hip and trendy type. She was meticulous, shrewd, calculating, and obsessive about control. She could have been an angel, she was such a control freak. Maybe she was more of a snow bunny, shushing the slopes in her thousand dollar parka.

"What?" she asked me. "I'll bet I'm better than you."

Wyatt snorted. "Natives from deep in the tropical jungle would ski better than Sam. She just points her tips down the fall line and barrels down the slope at a hundred miles an hour, knocking everyone out of her way. The slope looks like a war zone by the time she reaches the bottom. We almost got kicked out last winter. I had to promise them she'd take lessons. They were ready to pull her lift ticket and ban her."

I ski like I ride horses, unfortunately. "I'm fast. I'd beat everyone in a race."

"That's because unlike you, we need to reach the bottom in one piece." Michelle laughed. "You could snap every bone in your body, still finish, and repair yourself before the paramedics left the station."

"She broke two sets of skis last year," Wyatt continued. "Two! Broke them right in half. And I can't tell you the number of poles she's gone through. Not just bending them either. She throws them from the lift, like a javelin, to see if she can impale random woodland creatures."

"Hey, it's not just me," I protested. "I gave you one of my poles and we sword fought with them going down the slopes. That was your idea. And you were throwing snowballs down on the metal roof of the J-bar lift shack, totally freaking out the attendant."

"You are a bad influence on me," Wyatt scolded.

"That's my job," I told them. "Tempt you all into sin and bad behavior."

"Well, I'm forgoing the local action and heading out west with Michelle this winter where I'm less likely to get killed by a broken ski or a pole to the head." Candy commented.

"Let me know," Michelle told her. "I'm thinking Jackson Hole."

After dinner, everyone pitched in for a quick clean-up while Candy put on coffee and brought out the cheesecake.

"How are things going for you guys?" I asked Candy when we were alone in the kitchen. "Do you have a new angel supervising you yet?"

With their previous supervising angel, Althean, reduced to a pile of sand, the head enforcing angel, Gregory, had been temporarily overseeing the werewolves and their ridicu-lously strict existence contract.

I'm the only demon ever to have survived an encounter with Gregory. He'd bound me, and now I was living with his brand on the inner part of my right arm. From what I gather, it's a kind of homing beacon. It's also supposed to compel me to obey, but that part doesn't seem to work. Oh, and if I rub it I fall apart into an orgasmic mess. Very inconvenient since it's on my damned arm.

Gregory allowed me to stay alive and remain here as long as I abided by certain rules. Demons are not very good with rules, and I'll admit I'd been pushing the limits here and there to see what I could get away with. It had been eight weeks since I saw him last. That should be a good thing, but truth be told, I was a bit obsessed with him. I'd been escalating my energy usage hoping he couldn't resist coming to yell at me. I'd even taken to masturbating with the tattoo, knowing that it affects him, too. I know, annoying a powerful being that is going to eventually kill me isn't smart, but I'm a demon. It's what we do.

Candy shook her head. "No, Gregory is still our contact, but we've been told we'll have someone new by next week. He's not so bad actually. Strict. Scary beyond belief. You can't read him at all. It's difficult to know how he feels about us as a species."

Many angels thought the werewolves were Nephilim, the result of Fallen angels who bred with humans thousands of years ago. Recently, some of these angels had been taking matters into their own hands and were trying to exterminate the werewolves.

"Althean said there was a group that felt the way he did and the killings would continue," I told her, reluctant to add to her paranoia. "Plus, Gregory indicated that all is not peachy in Aaru, either, so you all may not want to relax yet."

"Aaru is their home?"

"Yeah. I've never been there since we're forbidden under the treaty between our races. I have no idea what it's like. Probably sucks. From what Gregory told me in August, they have some political unrest. I'm thinking they always have political unrest though. Can you imagine? Hundreds of thousands of those assholes in one place? Sheesh."

Candy shuddered. "Just between us, I fight the urge to expose my belly and pee every time I'm in the same room as one."

I snorted. The image of Candy sprawled naked on her back leaking urine was just hysterical.

"Yeah. I fight the urge to hump their legs every time I'm in the same room as them." Not that I was particularly attracted to angels. I'd fuck pretty much anything.

Candy rolled her eyes and headed in with the cheesecake. The others helped themselves to a sliver of the dessert and a cup of coffee while I showed everyone how I'd mastered the sin of gluttony by scarfing down three big pieces. It had caramel and pecan bits swirled through it in a gooey mess. I wanted to eat more, but I was worried I might explode.

It was nearing midnight when Candy and Michelle headed home. Candy had left the remaining half of the cheesecake for me to eat. Curse her. I'd need to run a fucking marathon to burn the calories off. Wyatt helped with the last of the dishes and took the opportunity to grab me and plant seductive kisses down my neck as I washed out the coffee pot.

"Mmmm, that's nice," I told him leaning back against his chest. "But I think I'm going to puke."

I felt him laugh, which didn't do much for my overfull stomach.

"That sexy talk turns me on so," he said. "You shouldn't have gorged yourself on all the cheesecake. If you're going to eat like that, you'll need to install a Roman-style vomitorium."

"And eat in a reclining position," I agreed. "Go put in a movie and I'll be right in."

I finished the coffee pot and looked at the drops of water in the sink. They were like tears on the sides of the stainless steel.

I'd been working on things. Back home, for the first nine-hundred-some years of my life, I had great joy throwing about blasts of destruction. Now I found myself on a strange course of continuing education. Trying to learn things that my kind would scoff at. Things like manipulation of elements. Tight, controlled, almost elegant displays of power.

Concentrating, I drew the drops of water down into the basin and together. This wasn't easy for me. I'd been trying to do this for eight weeks. I never worked so hard on something in my life. It looked so easy when he did it. That angel made everything look easy.

I had to focus all my attention on pulling the water drops and holding them into a ball in the sink basin. I held the ball there for a moment to ensure that it was perfectly round and that the hydrostatic pressure and surface tension were equalized. Then I lifted, suspending gravity in a narrow rim around the edge. The ball quivered, becoming wobbly like gelatin, before it stabilized and rose to hover above the rim of the sink. Joy flooded me at the success after so many failures and I squealed, dropping my concentration and letting the globe splashed back into the sink. I did it! Finally some progress. Nowhere near what he'd done, but progress still.

Wyatt ran in to see what the commotion was about.

"Watch this, watch."

I pulled the water together again and held the ball suspended above the sink.

"Cool." Wyatt was clearly unimpressed. "What are you

supposed to do with it? Drown your enemies? Launch it at people like a water balloon?"

That was a good idea. I'd have to remember that one.

"No, it's just practice. I'm trying to get better at my control over water. Maybe then I'll move on to air or fire."

"Well, that's very nice. Let's go watch the movie," Wyatt urged.

Humph. The angel would have been impressed. Or maybe not. He might have just made fun of me for my crappy imitation of him.

Wyatt and I spent the evening curled up on the couch watching whatever struck our fancy. I loved cuddling up with Wyatt this way. This summer, I'd nearly Owned him, come close to ripping the life right out of him to possess him forever within myself. It had shaken him badly and almost ruined our fledgling relationship. Since then I'd been careful to not show Wyatt too much of the darkness that filled me. Still, I worried. What if I lost control and killed him? What if Wyatt saw me in my terrifying, unfeeling glory? He seemed to accept the fact that I was a demon, but I lived with the nagging worry that one day it would prove too much for him. One day, he'd decide it was all too weird and walk out of my life forever.

Around two in the morning, we dozed off sprawled all over each other, only to wake up around five. Wyatt threw an afghan over me and headed back to his house while I snuggled into my couch pillows and went back to sleep. I'd forgotten to call Dar.

CHAPTER 2

I had two messages on my mirror. My foster brother Dar had called again. Ugh, he was such a pest. I was in a hurry this morning, so I planned to delete it, and vowed to call him later. The other was from my steward. He, I never ignored.

"I apologize for interrupting your vacation, Baal." My steward used the respectful term meaning "Lord" to address me. "The Low you sent has proven useful. He has also spread wild tales of how the gate guardian bowed down before you and gave control of a major gate into your hands before fleeing your wrath."

I'd been given what amounted to a free gate pass by Gregory this summer during the werewolf incident. There had been a Low trapped this side of the gate and I'd let him use my passage instead, snapping his wrist to mark him and telling him to work off the fee within my household. He'd been pretty far back during the conversation with the gate guardian, so he probably had misinterpreted it. Or he was cleverly boosting my reputation to secure a long-term place in my household.

"Obviously no one would believe a Low, even with your damage on him. I put some spin on it and looked secretive and enigmatic every time someone inquired. There are murmurings that your status is raised."

The steward sounded smug. Any increase in my status was also an increase in his.

"I took the liberty of sorting through the petitions. There is a very flattering one. So flattering that you should consider returning immediately. I've put them in a packet and sent them over. You should be receiving them in the next day or two. Please let me know your date of return and I'll put together an interview schedule."

Damned breeding petitions. I'd never escape them. Breeding wasn't just about leaving your genetic mark. It formed alliances, and confirmed status. We are a suspicious, violent, and disloyal race. An alliance with the right person could make all the difference in a demon's life.

Still, I dreaded it. Bad things happened when demons got their personal energy too close to me. I was a little worried that my breeding was going to result in someone dead. That and the whole process of reviewing petitions, negotiating, blah, blah, blah seemed to be such a pain in the ass.

The steward had nothing more to say, so I erased his message. Accidentally, I hit the one from Dar.

"Mal, you never call me back."

Dar calls me Mal Cogida, which he claims is "bad fuck" in Spanish. He Owned a human his last visit over who had taken four years of high school Spanish and he now felt he was fluent. He'd honored me with this name because in my youth, I'd had an unfortunate habit of killing my sexual partners. I have much better control now, but Dar still likes to bring it up. Endlessly. Of course, it didn't help that I'd accepted the name.

Names are like titles to my kind. We often have a dozen

names that, strung together in a particular order, identify your status. Peers can call you whatever they want, but those nicknames only become part of your official name if you allow it. I had been in a perverse mood and accepted Dar's name for me into my official list. He'e been puffed up with pride about it ever since. As if he needed any further inflation of his ego.

"I want you to get the artifact from the teeth and get it over here to me. I'll give you partial credit for retrieving it, and thirty percent of the reward."

I had no idea what the fuck he was talking about. Probably because I'd been deleting his messages for three months without even listening to them.

"They won't meet with me. I keep trying, and they won't. They said they'll meet with you. They didn't know you were there and are curious how you escaped their notice."

No idea. Not the foggiest idea what he was talking about.

"Oh, and you won't believe the rumors going around about you. One is that you beat a gate guardian with a cosmetics bag and forced her to send a Low through. Another says that you showed her your arm, and that she knelt before you swearing allegiance. The best one, though, is that you have befriended a gate guardian and meet her regularly for lunch and gossip. I'm going to explode if you don't call me back and let me know the real story here."

Well, Dar would just have to explode, I thought, erasing his message. I was busy. I'd call him later today. Or maybe tomorrow. Whenever I got a moment. Right now I needed to hurry, or I'd be late for my walk-through.

In half an hour I stood admiring what would soon be my newest acquisition, a block of twelve brick houses bordering the waterfront. This section of the canal hadn't been part of the beautification project that swept through downtown a decade ago. Just three blocks away, promenades, sculpture, and fountains transformed the flood-prone, algae-strewn canal into a tourist paradise. If you looked closer, though, you could see the cleaned-up graffiti and the broken bits of liquor-bottle glass. The civilized veneer during the day vanished after dusk, and even the gentrified areas became a haven for loitering teens, prostitutes, and drug dealers.

I was about to own a block of hovels. The brick on the row houses was broken in places, and mortar crumbled from the walls onto the pavement like pebbles and thick dust. Even the unbroken windows had plywood boarding on them.

"I took the liberty of coming down here last night and speaking with the tenants," the male werewolf beside me said. He'd been introduced to me as Reed, and I admired his initiative as much as his military good looks and melting southern drawl. "About twenty live here now, but there are probably only four or five onsite during the day. Some come and go, but the majority just use this as their storage area and night time location. They were easily convinced of the advantages of continuing to stay under the new terms and management."

I liked this werewolf. "Were you able to identify a potential representative?" I asked. It would be important to have a relatively sane individual to act as a liaison between the crazy homeless tenants and the werewolf.

He nodded. "Guy said to call him Bob. Doesn't seem to be a drug user, and has enough intelligence to know what side of his bread the butter is on. I think he's got authority issues, but I don't have a problem working around that personality trait."

That was saying a lot. I could imagine werewolves would bristle at the thought of someone not recognizing or respecting their authority. I appreciated Reed's flexibility in this matter.

"Twenty isn't a lot of people for twelve units. Think we can spread the word and fill up without having permits or the licensing authority on our heads?" Or the press. Damned press would have a field day. I'd already made the political cartoon section once this year and didn't want to see that rather truthful caricature again.

"I think we can do one-fifty. As long as the place doesn't reek of excrement, Department of Health should turn a blind eye."

I considered this. "Okay, but I'm charging more if I need to supply them with shitters. It's not my problem if they'd rather crap next to their sleeping bag than walk down to the gas station; it's not coming out of my profits."

The inside of the houses was worse than the outside. Thick dust coated the floors, disturbed only by tracks of footprints in places. There were a few sloppily cleared areas where the residents spent their time. Crates of scant belongings sat in sections of the rooms. One enterprising person had two shopping carts, stolen from the local grocery store, with an assortment of recyclable goods in them. He sat next to the carts and eyed me suspiciously, as if I planned to take them. The whole place reeked of urine and unwashed bodies.

"It's okay, dude," Reed told the shopping cart guy softly. "I told you, this is the new owner and she's just looking the place over."

"All my prayers and God has sent Satan to protect us?" The guy looked me over, tugging at his dark beard. "Evil will defeat evil, and the Ear Man will go down at the hands of the very one he worships."

I didn't exactly have a witty reply to that, so I moved on to the next house. They were all in various stages of decay with smashed drywall and attempts at artwork on floors, walls, and ceilings. One hideous room had finger paintings of animals done in shit on the walls. There were only a couple more people still in the houses. The rooms were mostly full of neatly segregated piles of unwashed, smelly belongings, reminders of the occupants' presence. Bob was in the last house. He looked at me with grim acceptance, as if I were a nasty pill he was being forced to swallow.

"I don't like this," he told Reed.

I cut Reed off before he could even reply. "It's almost winter, and it's hard to find a spot at the shelters. You'll freeze outside and all your stuff will either be ruined or stolen. I'm not telling you what to do. I'm giving you an opportunity. You can be an entrepreneur. Or you can just walk the fuck out. Either way, you're your own man."

He looked me right in the eye. "I don't work for no one; I don't take orders from no one. But if I have to, I might as well take orders from Satan. At least I know where I stand with you."

Why did these stupid humans keep calling me that? I was most definitely not Satan. The term was actually Ha-Satan, the Iblis, the Adversary, the one who tests. It was a title with all sorts of hideous responsibilities attached to it. A title no one had held since the war with the angels so long ago. A title no one wanted.

I gave Candy the thumbs up for the closing to proceed and outlined communications processes with Reed. Although he worked for Candy and would get paid through her, I made sure he knew I needed him to be in direct contact with me on any urgent issues. He seemed very efficient and I doubted I'd ever hear from him again. That done, I headed home to meet Wyatt.

CHAPTER 3

*B*y the time I got home, Wyatt had already loaded up the trailer and hitched it to my Suburban. He was the best boyfriend ever, not that I'd ever had a boyfriend before. All I needed to do was toss my clothes into the truck and load up my gelding, Piper, and off we went.

Normally, I just rode my horses around my property and the neighboring fields, but I had been convinced to enter a show. They were boring and I always came in last, so I didn't often cave to the invitations. Elsa, my sometimes riding instructor, had invited me. She was very critical of my riding skills, but was always happy to take my money. I don't know why I kept going to her. She was not respectful and I wasn't improving any. I think her verbal abuse reminded me of home and I was a bit homesick.

As we parked, I noticed that this was a huge show. Much bigger than the local ones I'd been to in the past. We were a bit early, so I left Wyatt at the trailer with Piper and explored as I made my way to the registration table. A ruckus from a big trailer caught my attention. It sounded like a horse fight, which was unusual at these shows. All the horses here were

18

regularly shown and had the routine down pat. They were typically munching from a hay bag and waiting patiently. I assumed someone's horse had gotten loose and another was taking exception to the stranger near their hay bag.

Not the case at all, I saw as I came around the corner. Tied to the corner of the big stock trailer was what appeared to be a huge gray Thoroughbred cross. And I don't mean cross in the horse-breed sense. He was a hybrid. And he'd clearly gotten more than the usual share from his sire. A demon had been across the borders, breeding with a mare. Not as unusual as you'd think, but definitely not common, either. We'll have sex with anything and can produce offspring with a female of any species if we're so inclined.

The horse was in a foul mood. He tossed his head, nostrils flaring and ears pinned as he pulled on the rope holding him to the trailer.

"Stop it," a man said to him as he came around from the back leading another horse.

The hybrid rolled his eyes and lunged at the other horse, snapping. The man went to smack its nose and narrowly missed being kicked by flying hooves as the horse spun around impossibly fast and bucked.

"Tony, come put this crazy thing back on the trailer before it breaks loose and kills someone," he shouted.

"He just kicks the trailer and makes a huge racket, scaring the other horses," a voice shouted back.

"No way are you going to be able to ride him today. Ace him and put him back on the trailer."

Ace, short for Acepromazine, was a sedative. Many riders used it in small amounts to settle nervous horses for trailering, but you needed to be clean to show. Enough of the stuff and your horse would be dozing and drooling, or even passed out.

"Is he for sale?" I asked, pointing at the horse.

DEBRA DUNBAR

The guy started, noticing my presence for the first time.

"Hundred bucks and he's yours. I'm done with this stupid beast. We trained him for steeplechase, but he gets these crazy moods and no one can stay on him. He bullies all the other horses in the pasture. It takes four ccs of Ace to take the edge off him. We can't geld him because the anesthesia doesn't work, so he's a stallion. He's dog meat at this point."

"What's steeplechase?" I asked.

"It's a race over rough terrain with jumps. The horses all run together in a field and take the jumps at speed."

Hmmm. Kind of like the elven hunts. Sounded more fun than dressage, although I had a tendency to wind up on the ground when it came to jumping.

I handed the guy a hundred dollar bill.

"I need to go register for my event. Can you keep him here and I'll be right back for him. Don't Ace him."

The guy nodded, pocketing the money and I headed for the registration table. Elsa was there and she informed me that she'd already registered Piper and me for Introductory, Level B. It would be me and the eight-year-old humans out there. You didn't even canter in Introductory Level B. Ugh.

"Sign me up for the steeplechase, too," I told her.

She looked at me with hostility. "I'd expect you'd enjoy that sort of thing, but Piper isn't suitable for that event. He's a heavy draft horse and doesn't have the speed for steeplechase. Besides, you can't manage to stay on over jumps in the arena, let alone a brush jump in the field."

That was Elsa. So full of encouragement.

"I'm riding the guy's horse over there," I pointed at the trailer. "I'll send Wyatt over with his Coggins in a moment. Just sign me up for it." I handed her a check, which she took as if it were contaminated with E-coli.

I went to collect my purchase, which was twisting his head and yanking to get free.

"I'll send my boyfriend over to get his Coggins," I told them.

Coggins was the required certificate at horse shows that indicated your animal had been tested and free from the viral disease Equine Infectious Anemia. Out-of-state shows often required additional certificates, but locally, Coggins was it. Most horse people carried a stack of copies in their trailer so they always had one handy. I wondered how on earth the vet had managed to draw a blood sample from this particular horse. He didn't look like he'd take kindly to needles.

I walked over to my new horse who flattened his ears and showed me his teeth.

"Be careful," the guy warned. "He bites. And kicks. And rears."

This horse had more of my kind in him than a Low, so I pulled up my mean and threw it at him. To humans, my mean is scary. To my own kind, my mean reveals my status. We're big on hierarchy at home.

The horse flickered his ears, and pulled his head back in surprise.

"Obey me," I whispered. I was sure he could hear and understand. "You will fucking obey me or I will take your balls off with my teeth, and without the mercy of anesthesia either."

The horse wiggled his ears nervously, but met my gaze with a steady defiance. This was going to be fun.

"What's his name?" I asked the guy.

"Diablo."

I shook my head in disbelief. What total lack of imagination. I'd live with this for now since it was the name on his Coggins certificate, but as soon as I needed to have him re-tested, I was changing his name. Maybe to something like Buttercup. Or Bunny.

I led a deceptively subdued Diablo back to Wyatt and my

trailer. Wyatt jumped to his feet, frowning with disapproval at my new acquisition.

"This is Diablo, soon to be renamed Rosebud. Or possibly Muffin. Can you run by the big trailer over there and grab his Coggins, then take it to the registration table? I'm riding him in the steeplechase."

Wyatt looked at me as if I'd gone insane. After two years, you would have thought these things wouldn't surprise him anymore.

"Sam, you are going to kill yourself. You've never ridden steeplechase before. You can barely manage second field in a fox hunt."

"I fall off all the time and I've never killed myself yet." I figured this was going to be a really short event for me.

"Well, maybe you won't kill yourself, but you'll be off him at the first fence," Wyatt said, echoing my thoughts. "Honestly, he looks like he'd enjoy nothing more than throwing you head first into a jump. He's not even gelded. You're going to ride a stallion steeplechase? It's a race, Sam. It's a flat out race, over jumps, in a field. There's a reason they call the riders jockeys in these things. It's fast. You're up on short stirrups with your rear in the air. It's close quarters. If you come off, you'll be trampled."

Wyatt looked worried. Really worried. I'm not sure why. The worst thing that could happen would be me humiliating myself three seconds into the race. He should be used to this sort of thing.

"This is going to be fun," I told him. "It will counteract the horrible boredom of the dressage test I'm doing this afternoon. Don't be a stick in the mud. Please go take care of the registration. Oh, and did you pack my jumping saddle?" I asked. It was going to really suck if I had to do field jumping with a dressage saddle.

"Yeah, I thought you might do some light stadium jumping, but not this," he protested.

He was worried. It tugged at something inside me. No one had ever worried about my safety before. Were all human boyfriends this way? I walked over to kiss him but Diablo took exception to the public display of affection and tried to bite Wyatt. No way was I putting up with that crap, so I zapped him with a small disciplinary burst of raw energy and he jumped back, looking at me appraisingly. I kissed Wyatt again, this time without interruption, lead rope firmly in hand. We stood for a moment, arms around each other, as I breathed in his warm, human scent.

"I'm going to do this Wyatt. I'll either stay on or I won't. You should video it just in case I fly off and he drags me around the field. You could post it all over YouTube, or maybe even sell it to one of those funniest video shows."

Wyatt sighed and kissed the top of my head.

"Okay. Please keep your heels down and don't get too forward on your jumps."

Wyatt went to take care of my registration and I led Diablo around to tie him next to Piper. He snapped and pawed at my big gelding, who eyed him placidly and continued to munch from his hay bag. That's my boy. Unflappable, even with some crazy animal threatening him. Steeplechase was the first event, so I put my field saddle on the gray, making sure I pulled the stirrups all the way up. It was going to be really weird riding that way. I wouldn't have much leg against the horse to hold on. Given my horrible balance, I probably would be off at the first jump. Luckily, Piper's bridle fit Diablo with some small adjustments. Piper was well-mannered, so I'd put a gentle snaffle bit on the bridle. With this monster I'd probably have chosen something like a double twist wire. I'd have to rely on my own special skills to keep him in line and not the bit. Just as well.

Elsa was always yelling at me to ride with my seat and not my hands anyway.

Before I led Diablo to the warm-up field, I needed to have a chat with him. Just to make sure we both knew who was holding the reins in this relationship. I stuck my thumb and fingers at the edge of each nostril and held him just above the lip, forcing him to meet my eyes.

"I know what you are, and I'm sure you know what I am. Life with me will be far better than with the humans. I understand what you need, and I'll allow you privileges beyond what the humans would, but I will not allow you to attack what is mine. That horse over there, he is mine and you are not to threaten him or hurt him. The human who was here, he is mine and you are to obey him as you would me. If you harm him in any way, I will not hesitate to kill you. Death by my hands will not be quick or painless. Make me angry enough to kill you and you will wish you had met your end at the slaughterhouse."

I wanted to be firm with him, but I didn't want him to think I would crush his spirit or deny him expression of who he was. It's so hard to tell with hybrids how much firmness to use and how much kindness they needed. Boomer, my Plott hound hybrid, needed a good deal of kindness and a gentle touch. I got the feeling that I would need to treat this horse more as I would a full demon.

We walked without incident over to the practice field and I scrambled into the saddle, wondering how long I'd be up there. The short stirrups felt weird, and I immediately pushed some raw energy down into the horse to help me hold myself on. Diablo danced sideways, but didn't seem displeased with the energy. It had taken me months of work with Piper before he would even let me touch him. As a hybrid, Diablo was more accepting. Eventually he would be able to tolerate quite a bit of raw energy, but this was new to him and I wasn't sure how he'd react.

More secure in my seat, we trotted and cantered about, even taking a small cross-rail jump. At this point, my only plan was to just stay on the damned horse for as much of the race as I could. I really didn't care if I came in dead last. Warm-up was uneventful, so I had high hopes as we made our way to the field. Okay, high hopes was a bit of an exaggeration. It was more like I had minimal hopes. Or desperate hopes.

My hopes were dashed at the starting line. Diablo danced around, whirling like some kind of dervish and making threatening faces at the other horses that, for the most part, ignored him. As the gun went off, he was facing backwards and had to spin around before taking off. Dead last. Luckily, Diablo had a plan. He quickly made his way into the pack where he decided the main purpose of the race was to body slam the other horses and try to bite them. My main purpose was to keep my horse between me and the ground, so I let him do whatever he wanted and concentrated on holding on for dear life.

The course was two miles, which goes surprisingly fast when you're galloping flat out. At the first fence I had a moment of anxiety. The thing was over three feet in height and looked like a hedge with a two foot tall green padded roll in front at the takeoff. Diablo didn't seem to jump high enough to clear it, and for a moment I was convinced we'd knock the fence over and go tumbling across the dirt. Instead, his hooves tore through the brushy top and I realized the solid part of the fence was much lower. Halfway through the race, I began to feel a bit more secure in my seat and I tried to urge Diablo to pull ahead. I knew he was capable of more speed, especially as I was increasing his oxygen uptake, but he didn't want to forego the joy of bullying the other horses. The field was thinning out as we made it down the last stretch, so, in a final effort, I encouraged Diablo verbally.

"You're not going to let that nutless wonder beat you, are you? Pussy."

That did it, and with a snort, Diablo surged forward. Now I truly was hanging on for dear life. I felt myself unbalance and shift to the side, but held on with my link of raw energy and grabbed his mane with my hands. I also chanted "heels down, heels down" to myself, thinking that might help. It must have since I managed to right myself as we flew past the finish line. We'd come in fifth, and if there had been another hundred yards, I may have made it to third.

Now that we were done with the race, Diablo decided to show me what he was made of. He threw his head down in preparation for what I can only imagine was the mother of all bucks. Luckily, I'd been there before. The elven horses had been bucking me off for centuries and I recognized the signs. I drove my heels into his flanks, bringing his rear forward and under him. Undeterred, he continued to canter around the field with his head firmly down between his front legs. Asshole.

After a few moments of expressing his independence, Diablo slowed down and pulled his head up to cool down. Breathing a sigh of relief, I stopped him and pulled my energy back to dismount. The bastard waited for me to drop my stirrups and shift my weight, then leapt to the side, shaking himself in a big shiver. I slid right off his side into the dirt. It had to happen sooner or later; I was just glad it was after the race was over.

As I dusted myself off, I saw the winner come toward me leading a leggy, chestnut Thoroughbred. You could tell he was the winner because he was the only one not covered with mud from the hooves of the horses in front of him.

Leading the pack had its privileges. Cleanliness was one of them.

"Congratulations," I called to him. "Nicely done."

"Nicely done on your part, too," said a voice I recognized. "Diablo was in a foul temper today. I'm surprised you stayed on him at all. Plus, you got him to pull away from the group. That's near impossible when he's in one of his moods."

He stopped beside me and reached out a hand to rub Diablo's nose. The horse glared at him, but tolerated the touch without baring his teeth or snapping.

"I'm Tony Spellious." He put out a clean hand to shake my dirty one. "I trained and rode Diablo. I'm bummed John sold him, but he's fed up with how difficult he is. Owner's privilege, but if I'd known he was mad enough to unload him for a hundred bucks, I may have bought him myself."

"Samantha Martin," I told him. "You can handle him?" I asked, indicating the nasty beast beside me.

Tony laughed. "No. But I like riding things I can't handle."

I may be dense when it comes to the subtleties of human interaction, but I know sexual innuendo when I hear it. Tony was flirting with me. That didn't happen often since humans of both genders tend to be uncomfortable around me. Before Wyatt, most sex I had was either coerced or with those too drunk to heed their instincts. I looked Tony over and liked what I saw. Lean, wiry guy. Attractive face with nice brown eyes full of spirit. Hmmm.

"Good to know." I replied. "Do you race on the track too?"

"No, I'm too big to jockey on the track," he said with regret. He was only my height, and looked to be maybe a hundred fifty pounds, so I couldn't imagine how little the track jockeys were. "I haven't seen you at steeplechase before. Do you ride other events?"

"This is my first steeplechase," I told him. "I'd like to do it again. I got talked into coming here for the dressage test, but

I don't usually do these shows. Mainly I ride in the fields around my property and sometimes fox hunt."

Tony looked surprised. "Wow, you really rock. I can't believe you did so well in your first steeplechase, especially on Diablo. You must be one heck of a rider."

"Yeah, you wouldn't say that if you saw my dressage test," I confessed.

Tony wrinkled up his nose. "Dressage is horrible. Bunch of pompous jerks and their bored horses."

Reaching to the back of his shirt, Tony ripped off his race number and proceeded to scribble on it with a pen he clearly had stolen from the registration table. No one rides with a pen in their jodhpurs, so he obviously must have thought this one out ahead of time.

"Look, I really want to talk with you more, but we've got to get the horses back and I have six I need to work with this evening. Here's my number. I'd love to ride with you some-time. Or take you to dinner, or just meet you for coffee. Whatever you want." He handed me the race number and smiled at me. "Call me?"

"Sure." I took the number. "I'll think about it."

I led Diablo back to my trailer staring at Tony's number in amazement. Wow, some guy was actually trying to pick me up. Wonders never cease.

Wyatt was sitting on the little three legged camp stool outside the trailer reading something on his cell phone. It must have been engrossing because he didn't look up as I walked to the trailer and tied Diablo. In fact, he didn't look up as I took off Diablo's saddle and bridle and brushed him down.

"Did you see me? I stayed on. Well, at least I stayed on until after the race was over. That has to be the most damned fun I've had on a horse in ages. Wyatt, I swear it's like NASCAR with horses. It's a total rush. I've got to do it again."

Wyatt finally looked up from his phone and fixed me with a cold stare. He was pissed. Why was he pissed? I didn't kill myself. Was he that mad over my racing when he didn't want me to?

"Yes, I saw you. I watched the whole race." His tone was arctic.

"Why are you mad?" I walked over to stand in front of him. I hated Wyatt being mad at me. It made me hurt in my guts. "I kept my heels down. I almost fell off at the end, but I managed to get my balance back."

Wyatt sighed and put his cell phone aside. I feared I was going to get a lecture, but as long as it ended with Wyatt not being angry any more, I'd live through it.

"Sam, if there was a girl here, and I flirted with her, got her number even, how would that make you feel?"

"Is she cute?" I didn't know how I was supposed to respond to this one. I stared at him intently trying to see if I could read his mind. "Does she like threesomes? Are you saying that you found a girl here and want to do a three-some? Because I'd totally be into that sort of thing. As long as you were, that is. But not if you're not."

Wyatt let his breath out in an exasperated puff. "That's not what I mean Sam! You were over there picking up that jockey. Right in front of me. I watched you race, waited for you, and you ignore me and go flirt with that guy."

"You want to have a threesome with the jockey?" I asked hopefully. Wyatt threw up his hands in frustration, clearly even more angry.

"What do want me to do?" I wailed, digging my hands through my helmet-flattened, sweaty hair. "Wyatt, I'm not human, and I don't understand what you mean. Just tell me what you want me to do and I'll do it."

"I don't care if you flirt with guys, but not when I'm

around. I need to be your number one guy, your only guy when you're with me," he shouted.

I grabbed the race number with Tony's phone number on it and ripped it up, throwing the bits on the ground

"He's a good rider, Wyatt. And he trained this horse. I thought he could give me some input, that's all." I walked over to him and sat, straddling him on the little camp stool. "You are my number one guy, Wyatt," I told him. "My partner in crime. You're the most important human to me ever. In over nine hundred years, you are my most favored human, ever."

To make my point, I kissed the corner of his mouth, and then trailed my lips up along the edge of his jawline. He smelled so good with the warm sunshine on his skin. He hadn't shaved this morning and the stubble scraped lightly on my lips as I worked my way up to nip at his earlobe.

"I'm a good rider, too." Wyatt's voice was husky and I caught the sexual innuendo that time also.

"Mmmm, you are. You ride me like no one ever has before," I whispered in his ear, then proceeded to run my tongue around the edge before tugging gently on his earlobe with my teeth.

That must have been the right thing to say, or possibly the right thing to do, because he crushed me tight in his arms, and buried his face in the space where my neck meets my shoulder. I shivered as he kissed me in that oh-so-sensitive spot, and decided there were activities I wanted to pursue far more than the upcoming dressage test.

Digging my fingers into his hair, I pulled his head up so I could kiss him thoroughly. He dove his hands down the back of my stretchy jodhpurs, and grabbed my ass, grinding me against him. I could feel important parts of his anatomy stirring between my legs and a thick heat wash up through me. Just as we were getting into the moment, the little camp stool crashed beneath us, dumping us flat onto the ground next to the trailer wheels. We didn't break stride and continued to kiss sprawled on the grass and dirt beside the trailer. Wyatt pulled on my shirt, popping off a button in his hurry to feel the skin underneath. I cut right to the chase and went for his belt and pants.

"Let's take this in the trailer tack room," I suggested as I unhooked the belt and yanked it in one motion from his pants with a whip-like snap.

And we did. Banging the metal door against the frame and knocking saddles off their posts in our haste. This wasn't our usual slow, thorough exploration of each other. This was fast, messy, and noisy, with torn crumpled clothing, mouths and hands all over the place. I'm not much of a screamer, but we both shouted encouragements at each other and came in a loud, sloppy, sweaty mess. I'm sure the folks with neighboring trailers were very entertained.

The tack room was trashed. Hell, we were trashed. Saddles and bridles were strewn around. The plastic tub holding the grooming and vet supplies had toppled over and colorful vet wrap had unrolled like streamers on the floor. My jodhpurs were balled up around one ankle, where they had gotten stuck on my riding boot, and my shirt dangled like a white scarf around one wrist. Wyatt's shirt had been carelessly tossed into the poop bucket, and his pants never made it past his ankles at all. We sat on the floor wrapped up in each other's arms and laughed at the wreckage.

"I don't want to put that back on," Wyatt commented looking at his shirt.

"You'll have to go shirtless," I told him tracing a line with my fingernail down his chest. Wyatt shirtless was a thing of beauty. He leaned over to kiss me and winced.

"I think I'm sitting on a hoof pick," Wyatt said shifting to pull it out from beneath his naked ass. "And you're going to be late for your dressage test if you don't hurry."

I thought about bagging the rest of the horse show and enjoying a repeat performance or two with Wyatt, but Elsa would probably come drag me off him if I was late. Reluctantly, I got up and stripped off my muddy and wrinkled shirt, hoping I'd remembered to pack an extra.

In no time at all, I was presentable with clean clothes. Wyatt was helping me with my stock tie while I tucked my hair back into a smooth pony tail covered by a net. Not a good look for me, or for anyone actually. I made it to the dressage ring just in time to head in and do my pattern of walk, trot, and stop around the ring. Piper slogged his way around with the animation of a corpse, halting crooked, and cutting his corners. As expected, I came in last, and I got the usual frothing-at-the-mouth verbal abuse from Elsa regarding lack of impulsion, lack of bend, and over-flexing. Yep, I suck.

It was midway through the afternoon by the time we got home. Wyatt stayed to help me with the horses and clean out my trashed trailer. I promised to meet him later at The Eastside Tavern, but first I had things to do. Starting with a hot shower. I'm a big fan of smelling like sex and sweaty horse, but it felt good to clean up. As I prepared to run out the door, I saw the light flash on my mirror and instinctively hit the button.

CHAPTER 4

I don't usually get a lot of calls from home, and I let most of them go to message. This was on my steward's line, so I didn't think twice before punching it.

"What?" I barked in my standard greeting.

"Mal, you fucking bitch. I can never reach you, and you never call me back. I need you to get this motherfucking thing over to me now. Like yesterday."

Dar. I didn't know if I was more incensed over him stealing my steward's call sign or his disrespectful tone.

"For someone who is trying to get me to do a favor, you're really going about it in the wrong way. You should be kissing my ass right now, not chewing it off."

"I said I'd give you credit. I said I'd share the payment with you. What the fuck do you want? I'm in trouble here, Mal. Big trouble. I'll give you the whole fucking payment if you want. You gotta help me out."

He was really upset, but that was nothing new. Dar was always getting himself in trouble. I honestly think he had more demons gunning for him than I did. Whoever he'd pissed off this time would need to get in line. A really long line.

"I'm busy," I told him. "I don't have time to bail your ass out. I'm over here on vacation, playing with the humans and having fun, and that occupies every second of my day. I'm not going to help you with some bullshit scheme you've hatched up. Call someone else."

"You owe me. Remember when that sorcerer wannabe summoned you? Who pulled your ass out of the fire then, huh?"

Yeah, Dar had come through then. Other times, too. Although sometimes he just laughed at me and left me high and dry. Still, we did have history and, stupidly, that meant something to me. I wondered how much trouble he was really in this time. I had a gnawing feeling inside, a strange urge to protect him, but I pushed it down. I really needed to cut this human sentimental crap or I'd wind up in trouble.

"Okay, okay. I'm not saying I'll do it; just tell me what you want." I knew I was going to regret this, but he was my brother.

"The teeth have an artifact that belongs to us. They don't want it. They're only holding it until we send someone to get it. I just need you to go to Baltimore, meet with them and retrieve it, then call me. I'll pop over and get it from you. Bingo. Easy money."

First things first. "Teeth? You mean the vampires? I haven't seen one in six hundred years." Ick. The last time I saw vampires they were disgusting. Dirty, smelly rats with the IQ of a fencepost. I'm not sure I'd want to touch anything they'd handled, and I'm not particularly fastidious.

"The vampires. Not those ones you saw in Venice eating plague victims. I think they might have been cast out or something. These are organized vampires. They are pretty full of themselves, but they've always been respectful. I'll give you the meeting time and location in Baltimore. Just go there and they'll hand it right over."

Yeah. Because everything Dar got himself into was that easy. And I was Mother Theresa.

"You said you were in trouble? Who is paying you? What is it? And why do you want this thing?" I asked.

"It's an artifact." Dar's tone indicated that he thought I was an idiot. He probably didn't know what this artifact thing was himself. I'll bet someone a few levels above him flattered him and promised money and status and he fell all over himself to comply. Whore.

"And? Who wants this artifact?"

"I do."

I sighed. He was such a fucking pain in the ass. "You told me earlier that you'd share the money and the credit. If it's only you that wants this thing, then there is no money to share, and whatever credit you could give me is beneath what I already have. So, I ask again, who?"

"We are peers, Mal. Peers. Don't pull this better-than-me bullshit, because it doesn't hold water. I can't believe you would even hesitate to do such a small thing for me when I help you every time you ask, when I always stand by your side, when I defend you against those who would slander your abilities and status. Ungrateful bitch."

I rolled my eyes at his dramatic rant. "Who? Tell me who, Dar, or I'm closing the line right now and you can risk your angel-bait ass to come get it yourself."

Dar paused for a moment. He'd almost gotten tagged last time over and I knew he was nervous about spending any significant amount of time here. "Haagenti," he said.

Ah, and that would be why he was in so much trouble. Haagenti wasn't just a few levels up from us. He was up. And he was old, too. No wonder he wanted someone else to do his pick-up and delivery work. Someone like him couldn't just slip over here unnoticed and do a grab-and-dash. He'd set off alarm bells the second he had a toe through the gate.

"What are you doing messing with that asshole?" I asked. "He's going to fuck you over whether you get this thing for him or not."

I felt Dar's discomfort. What had he gotten himself into this time? He knew better than to deal with the likes of Haagenti.

"I kinda have to do this, Mal," he admitted. "There was an issue, and I owe him. I've tried three times to come over myself and get the thing, but the vampires keep blowing me off and I almost got cooked by the gate guardian last time."

"And what makes you think they'll meet with me?" I asked, perplexed. I was in the same level as Dar. He was actually a few notches above me.

"They were surprised you're there, that you're living so close to them. They didn't know. I guess they're curious. Plus, Haagenti suggested it. After this last time, when I almost got dusted by that fucking gate guardian, he said I needed to get you to do it for me. He said if you did it, he'd let me off the hook. I don't know how he knew the vampires would agree to meet you."

I wished Haagenti would chance coming over himself. He was such an asshole. I'd love to sic Gregory on him. I had a moment of mental fantasy where I envisioned Gregory in all his horrifying magnificence swooping in to battle Haagenti. Haagenti in his favored lion-bull form and Gregory glowing with fire, black eyes deep as the abyss, sharp spikes of teeth and awesome sword. Gregory would shine with righteous fury and hiss as he chopped the snarling Haagenti to bits. I felt rather damp between my thighs as this all played out in my head. I could seriously masturbate to this fantasy. Mmmmm.

"Mal?" Dar asked, wondering if I was still on the line.

"Tell Haagenti to fuck off," I told him. "I'm on vacation."

"Mal, please," Dar pleaded. "I've saved your bacon so many times in the past. You know how he is. He'll stick me up to my neck in liquid nitrogen for a hundred years if I don't come through for him. It's just a pick up and drop off deal. Quick and easy. Come on. I need you."

Liquid nitrogen. Haagenti didn't fuck around. That would not be a good way to spend a century. And Dar was my brother, after all. We'd been through a lot together. That gnaw of guilt, that wiggling urge to protect Dar was back again, as was a wave of anger at Haagenti. I fucking hated that asshole.

"Okay. Tell me when and where. It better not be boring, either."

Dar gave me the info on the meeting place and time. It was on Saturday, and I had a hard time explaining to Dar that that was a week away and not tomorrow. I didn't want him hounding me all week because he couldn't keep a damned calendar.

At least it was at a food and beer festival. I was supposed to go to the Suds and Shellfish Extravaganza at the Verizon Center in DC and meet the contact at the Jolly Molly Crab Shack booth at three. Dar had no idea what the contact looked like. He (or she) was evidently going to approach me, hand me the item, and leave. I hoped they were on time or I'd have to stand there and eat crab cakes until I exploded. Luckily I did like crab, and I did like beer. Could have been worse. I told Dar I'd let him know as soon as I had the item and he'd arrange to get it from me. Hopefully I'd do this and he'd stop pestering me to death with his stupid incessant calls.

Now I was even more late. I cut Dar off as he tried to chit-chat and dashed out the door because I had something

37

really important to do before meeting Wyatt at The Eastside Tavern.

I pulled into Sharpsburg just as the sun was setting, turning the sky bright orange. Antietam Battlefield is supposed to be closed at sunset, and they make a sweep right around that time, so I was forced to park along Sharpsburg Pike and hike in. Luckily where I was headed was only a little more than half a mile from the main road.

I loved Antietam Battlefield. It was one of the main reasons I'd picked this area when I decided to live among the humans for an extended period of time. Demons are drawn to conflict, and this war had been no exception. I had fond memories of many battles, but the one at Antietam was my favorite. Of the one hundred thousand soldiers on the field, roughly twenty-three thousand were killed, wounded, or missing. In one day. It was the bloodiest day of the war. If I hadn't been a demon I would have died at least six times that day. It had been chaos. Thick smoke, the roar of the cannons, and constant gunfire filled the air. I could barely walk a few yards without being filled with lead. I'd fixed myself so much during the battle that I'd needed to bolt back through a gate that night. I hated having to miss the rest of the war, but it was better than being killed by an angel.

Grabbing a flashlight from the car, I hiked across the wide fields marked with plaques detailing the conflict. Then I hopped the rough-hewn, zig-zag fence marking Sunken Road. It had been renamed Bloody Lane after the battle. More than fifty-five hundred men had been killed or wounded in this very spot within three hours. I wanted to linger, but the place I needed to be was a bit further in, down Roulette Lane and by a copse of trees. I paused for a brief moment to remember. It had been a horrific point in the battle. Bodies everywhere, with the Mumma farm burning as a backdrop. Good times.

I walked down Roulette Lane, stepped off the dirt trail and into the woods, then stopped, seemingly in front of nothing, and looked at the gate, a jagged tear by the woods. It hadn't been here at the time of the battle. I'd discovered it one day when I'd come to reminisce.

It was a wild gate. Most gates between my home and here were created by the angels. They were big, meticulously well-crafted, stable. They were works of art. The elves back home made gates, too. Theirs were small and unobtrusive, mainly to catch unwary humans and bring them over. But there were other gates. Ones that just seemed to occur on their own. These gates were a terrible gamble. They rarely went somewhere you wanted them to go.

This summer, in a desperate attempt to get away from Gregory before he killed me, I'd taken a chance on a wild gate and almost died. Gregory had managed to find me and pull me out, but the odd thing was that he thought I'd created it. Demons must have originally known how to make gates, but we seemed to have lost the knowledge. A big to-do on my continuing education list was to learn to make gates. And I was terrified.

I must have stood there for ten minutes just staring at the thing. I'd been through the angels' gates hundreds of times in my life. I could probe them, activate and use them, but I just couldn't determine how to make one of my own. Maybe the angel gates were too complex for me to learn from. Perhaps it was like trying to understand calculus before you'd mastered basic multiplication. I was hoping that if I explored this wild gate, compared it to the more complex ones, then I'd be able to figure out how they were constructed.

I'd learned all I could with my eyes so I pulled my personal energy back safely into my core and reached out with my hand to feel the gate. It was open. The angel ones were always closed until you activated them, and were masked so humans couldn't see them. This one was small, and very hard to see. Humans would only notice a shimmer. I doubted they could fall through. The opening was narrow, like a slit, but widened as I stretched my arm toward it, as if it were welcoming me. Which didn't do anything for my racing heart.

Taking a deep breath, I stuck my arm into the gate and paused a moment, thinking it might try and suck me inside. Nope. My arm slid easily out, as if what lay on the other side was just air. No slashing, bruising, melting flesh or other alarming changes occurred to my arm. Slowly I eased my personal energy down back into the arm. It felt fine. Now for the scary part.

I placed my hand on the outline of the gate and examined its structure, felt how the energy supporting it was anchored. The outline was irregular, but surprisingly basic. Taking a deep breath, I put my hand gingerly back into the gate. I didn't feel anything particularly alarming, so I sent out a scan around the edges. The gate itself was shallow, and definitely opened up into something, although I couldn't tell what or where. The edges narrowed into a point at the top, like a triangle, but it was tall enough that a human (or a demon) wouldn't have to stoop when going through. I pulled my hand back and tried to work up the nerve to go through. Several times I stuck my hand back in and pulled it out, but couldn't bring myself to put any additional body parts in.

Finally I gave up. Chickened out. I don't have any qualms about throwing myself into unknown, potentially deadly situations, but this gate really hit a nerve with me. My instincts normally have a direct line to my moving parts, and they told me to run as far from this gate as I could. In spite of my instincts, I was still determined to get to the other side and try to figure it out. I wanted to do it without unnecessary pain and suffering though. Or death. I was coming back to try again, but not today. I needed to think about what safeguards I could put in place to ensure I didn't die in this little experiment.

I was in a bad mood as I drove to The Eastside Tavern to meet Wyatt. I'd pondered some possibilities in exploring the gate without undue risk, but I felt like a failure for walking away today. Fucking coward. I'd always just jumped into things without any thought at all about my personal safety. Why was I weak in the knees over this one?

The narrow strip of asphalt in front of The Eastside Tavern that served as a parking lot was full, as always, so I drove around back and parked by the wooded area past the dumpster. I beeped the car alarm, although at this point all the regulars knew my car and respectfully kept their sticky hands to themselves. The usual crowd of smokers was milling around the front lot and on the enclosed deck area by the door. I swung open the iron-barred glass door and wandered through the bar and dining area to see if Wyatt was already there. They'd added a coyote to their taxidermy decorations, and I patted the fellow's head as I passed by. Finally I spotted Wyatt toward the rear, sitting at one of the Formica-topped tables.

"Would you rather sit at the bar?" he asked as I plopped down beside him in the torn vinyl chair. "I can tell Brenda to bring our food and drinks up there."

"This is fine." I kissed his cheek like a normal girlfriend. "What did you order?"

"Burgers and hot wings. And your usual," he added as the waitress put down an ice cold vodka and a Bud Light in front of me.

He was the best. I sucked down the vodka appreciating that they now had my favorite, Van Gogh Espresso, in the freezer. Just for little old me.

"I need your help with something," I told him. "And do

you want to go to a beer and seafood thing with me next Saturday?"

Wyatt made a face. "I want to go, but I've got an online tournament that will probably run all day and into the evening. How late is it? I can meet you there, but it would be around seven or so."

"Nah, I hope to have things wrapped up and be back by dinner time."

I wondered about Wyatt's tournament. The only tournament I'd ever participated in had ended in disaster. I have a hard enough time staying on a horse without someone poking at me with a long pole. After my fifth time being knocked off, I got pissed and boiled my opponent in his little metal suit, which didn't go over very well. There was a cry of "witch" and "sorcery" and I'd had to make a mad dash for the closest gate. I'd barely made it through before being overrun by angry humans or nabbed by an angel. I couldn't imagine Wyatt doing that sort of thing with his computer, but people did all sorts of stuff with video games now. What a fucking boring way to spend an entire Saturday though.

"What do you need my help with?" Wyatt smiled, unaware that I was mentally deriding his life's work.

"Can you use your tablet and check all the pet stores in a twenty-mile radius to see if any of them have birds?"

Wyatt looked at me quizzically. "Don't you have enough animals already?"

"It's for a project," I told him.

"Just go to PetSmart and pick one up."

I squirmed. "They won't allow me in PetSmart anymore. Boomer was not very well behaved the last time we were there." I liked to blame it on Boomer. He made a good fall guy.

"Okay. Let's see if there's anywhere on the east coast you haven't been banned from."

Wyatt waved his fingers around the tablet's screen. "There's a place in Frederick with a nice African Grey. It knows eight words and is a steal at two thousand, although I see you as more of a raptor kind of girl. Maybe a falcon?"

"It doesn't need to talk, just breathe. Actually I want a canary," I decided. The miners always seemed to have used canaries and I didn't want to take a chance that this was a species specific kind of skill.

"How about love birds? Or doves? There are a ton of places that have doves. It's all the rage to set a bunch of them free at weddings."

"No, it's gotta be a canary."

There were no canaries to be had in Frederick except for the ones at the forbidden PetSmart, but Wyatt worked his magic and found a pet store in Glen Burnie with one.

"Do you want to go pick it up?" he asked.

I had no desire to drive to Glen Burnie so I asked him to have it delivered to my house.

"Is this canary destined to be stuffed in a bug zapper?" Wyatt asked, referring to a mouse incident this past summer.

"No, although I need it for a project." I thought for a moment. "Maybe I should get a few. Just in case things go terribly wrong."

Wyatt shook his head. "They only have the one. There's a place in Northern Virginia that has a few. I can have them ship one, but I'm not sure how fast it will get here."

I mulled the situation over. If this canary died, there was no way I was going through that gate. Maybe I'd hold off on the others until I saw what happened with one. I really didn't want to get stuck with them, and I was pretty certain that a dozen mangled, dead birds wouldn't reveal any more than one.

"Nah, let's just see what happens with this one first," I told Wyatt. It was a testament to the strength of our relationship that he didn't pester me about what the bird was for, or lecture me about torturing, and probably killing, cute, defenseless animals.

I snagged a hot wing and munched on it wondering if the buffalo sauce would be good on canary. I'd failed in my attempt to master the Sharpsburg gate today, and although the rest of my day had been wonderful, that hung over my head like a black cloud. Maybe if I tried something else I'd been working on it would cheer me up.

Looking around the bar, I thought of hot wings. I envisioned the smell, the taste, and the bite of the sauce, the texture of the crunchy, spicy skin and hot juicy meat, and the orange color. I bundled the whole experience together and sent it out into the room, pushing it gently into everyone's minds. Want. Want. Want. Then I waited.

Now, how to gauge my success? I watched the waitresses bustle around and began to count the hot wing baskets coming out of the kitchen. It was no use. I was sure I'd missed some, and I couldn't tell what the hell was on those big trays of food.

"Wyatt? Can we find out how many hot wing orders have been requested in the last twenty minutes?"

Brenda laughed when he asked her. "Is this a prank? We ran out of the things. I'll tell you almost everyone in the place ordered them, although some tables placed one order to share among themselves. There were only three people who didn't order them."

"Sam, what did you do?" Wyatt looked amused. "Is that the compulsion thing you were telling me about?"

"No, it's just a suggestion." I wished I could do compulsion. "We can influence people to do stuff that they want to do anyway, but we can't really compel people. Angels can, but we can't. Evidently I can make people want to eat hot wings. Nice skill, huh?"

"Well, it certainly has the potential for more fun than the water ball thingy," he said.

I agreed.

"Is this what the canary is for?" Wyatt asked. "Are you going to practice a kind of suggestion involving yellow birds?"

"No, that's for something different."

I thought about the gate again and a shiver ran through me. I had a feeling, deep in my core, that I wasn't supposed to go through there. I was determined to learn how to create gates though. I'd had success with the water globes and with the suggestion just now. I knew I could do this, too, if I just squashed my fear and kept at it. Still, I was glad to wait a few days until the canary arrived. Procrastination was a good thing.

CHAPTER 5

he next morning, a demon arrived with the dreaded breeding petitions. I hadn't seen her in centuries, but I immediately recognized the courier as my foster sister. I hadn't spent much time with her in my childhood. Leethu had left our sibling group when I was only about fifty. She'd been the eldest of our group, and, as a succubus, had needed to leave right at puberty for specialized training. I looked her over with curiosity and longing. She'd assumed the form of an Asian woman, Thai if I guessed correctly. It was beautifully done, and well chosen, with gorgeous dark eyes, a glistening curtain of black hair to her waist, and tawny skin. The real draw was beyond the flesh though. Succubi put out amazing pheromones, enough to overwhelm gender preferences and prejudices. Leethu was one of the best, enthralling her chosen prey but keeping them slightly at a distance and under her control. It was a skill few succubi mastered.

"Leethu." I was delighted to see her. "Did you have any trouble with the gate guardians?"

I reached forward and kissed her gently on the chin; the

traditional greeting for a younger sister to give an older one. Succubi were very fragile compared to other demons, so I could hardly welcome her like I would Dar or one of my other siblings.

"Ni-ni," she said, calling me by my childhood nickname. I felt a tingle race through my skin at her smile. "I can't stay. I just had to see you. There have been such rumors. Are you really social with that disgusting gate guardian?"

I took the packet of petitions from her and plopped them on the dining room table.

"We have an understanding," I replied. "It's not like I have her on speed dial or anything. How long are you on vacation?"

Leethu looked nervous. Succubi couldn't stay very long without attracting notice, but she had good control. She was less likely than most to cause a mass orgy.

"Not long. I just need to clear up a few quick things and then I'm back home."

"Have you heard anything about what's going on with Dar and Haagenti?" Succubi knew all the gossip. "He's trying to drag me into the middle of it, and I'm sure he's not telling me everything."

Leethu looked a bit startled. "Dar is always in trouble with someone. It's no more than usual, but I got the impression Haagenti was interested in you. It's not just the gate guardian, Ni-ni, there are rumors that you are doing crazy things here and getting away with it."

Great. I'd help Dar this once, but no more after that. I was not getting messed up with that jerk Haagenti.

"It was good seeing you." She kissed me on my forehead before turning to leave. Lust streaked through me and ached deep between my thighs. I wished she could stay.

"You too," I told her and closed the door with regret.

I spread the petitions out on my dining room table and

was amused to see that the steward had sectioned them off and ranked them according to perceived value.

The first stack held four petitions that the steward felt were my top contenders. I glanced at the first one in the pile and about choked on my coffee. Ahriman. Holy fuck, Ahriman. I didn't even realize he knew I existed. Haagenti was dog crap compared to this guy. Ahriman was one of the top five in the hierarchy. He was one of the few living who'd been around at the time of the fall. One of the oldest of our kind still alive. There had been rumors that he would become the Iblis after the war, but nothing had come of it. He had amazing power and loved nothing more than destruction and inciting humans to war. Why in all of Hel had he set his sights on me? I was still just an imp, a little cockroach. When it came to sheer raw power like Ahriman's, I was a speck of dust. Fuck, I'd never met him. I didn't even know what he looked like, what his favorite form was.

Unsettled, I looked at the rest of the petitions. The other three on the short list were flattering. Salvor was very high up the ladder, just under Haagenti's level, there was one of the Rhyx, and a well-known succubus. Oooo, the succubus would be fun!

The next pile was considerably larger and included those within a level or so of mine. Dar's was in there, as always. He had embellished his petition with cute little drawings of what appeared to be a mongoose chewing on hearts. Such the romantic. He'd been persistent in his petition since my age of adulthood and I felt like I should afford him consideration because of his loyalty and our long relationship. Plus he was a known entity. I knew his strengths and weaknesses and had a good idea of what type of offspring we'd produce. It wasn't like I needed to breed with him to solidify our relationship though. He was forward enough with me as it was.

The last pile were those below me that the steward

thought might be of interest. I glanced through them, but didn't see anything that stood out. Honestly, after seeing Ahriman's petition, I could think of little else.

I pulled it off the stack. Ahriman. Well, at least I wouldn't be as likely to kill him during the breeding process. He was probably the only one in the whole stack I could say that about with a high degree of confidence. Running a finger down the parchment, I read the petition carefully. From someone of his stature, I'd expected just a cut and dry offer. The benefit to me would be in the association alone, so the petition should be rather short and to the point without additional bribes or fringe benefits. It was rather stark, but I was surprised to see a consort clause. Basically, he would fold me and my small household under the protection of his status and I would grant him exclusive breeding rights for the next two thousand years.

I stared at the skin parchment. Why would he want exclusivity? If he thought I was going to go around spitting out offspring with every Tom, Dick, and Harriet, then why bother to petition me? And even more troublesome was the rolling in of myself and my household under his. This would propel us so fast up the hierarchy we'd all have whiplash. Why? There was no obligation to do that. How would that benefit him in any way? Because, in all honesty, if there was no benefit to him, then it wouldn't be on the table. Ahriman wasn't one to give away anything frivolously.

I called my steward.

"Ahriman?" I asked before he even had time to greet me. "What the fuck is up with that?"

"Oh Baal," he gushed. "I cannot believe the honor! You should return immediately and accept the petition."

"Why? What on earth would he gain from this association with me? "

"No idea. Maybe it was a mistake? You should return and

sign the contract before he changes his mind and withdraws the offer."

Wow. Flattering. At least he was honest. I hung up without further comment and called Dar.

"You have the artifact?" he answered eagerly. "I'll be over right away."

"No, you idiot," I replied before he could hang up and appear on my doorstep. "I don't even meet them for another six days. Can't you keep track of a calendar? I called because I need to know if there is any buzz about me. Any rumors. Anything really odd or notable."

Did Ahriman somehow know about the brand? Was there some advantage he'd gain in breeding with a bound demon? Some way to control Gregory through me? I wished I knew what the fuck this brand actually did.

"You mean the gate thing?" Dar asked.

"No. Someone high up has petitioned me with exclusive breeding rights. I find myself wondering why."

I kept the details from Dar, and especially didn't let him know about the consort clause. Dar was like a brother to me, but he'd sell me out in a heartbeat for the right price. As I would him.

There was a lengthy pause. "There was a rumor that you were bound, but no one believes it since the angels no longer bind us and all of the sorcerers are on this side of the gates."

I was bound, although it didn't seem to work very well. I still didn't see what a bound demon would have to offer someone like Ahriman. Maybe Ahriman wanted someone loyal to him who could come and go across the lines as she pleased and do his activities without fear of retribution? Of course, even though Gregory seemed to be giving me latitude on the little stuff I'd done, I think he'd probably smack my head off if I provoked a developing nation into a nuclear attack.

"Mal? Is this true?" Dar asked in almost a whisper.

"No," I lied. "Absolutely not."

I'm a terrible liar, but Dar was always a bit blind when it came to me. Thankfully he seemed to take me at my word. I really didn't want to reveal to Dar that I was bound. It was all too fantastic and unbelievable. That I had a weird, obsessive relationship with a powerful angel. That I missed him terribly and desperately wanted to see him again. That he may show up any minute and kill me. Dar would never believe me. I wasn't sure I believed it myself.

"Mal, be careful. Maybe you should come back home," Dar said with uncharacteristic concern. "As soon as you get the artifact for me." So much for the concern.

I hung up after assuring him once again I'd call him the moment I got back on Saturday, and straightened the breeding petitions in a nice, neat pile.

CHAPTER 6

The rest of the week went uneventfully. Well, by my standards anyway. My canary arrived and promptly died. I've been through four of them so far and haven't been able to keep them alive long enough to take them out to the gate in Sharpsburg. They are stupidly fragile and drop dead if you use any mean on them at all, try to feed them dog food, or squeeze them too tight. I'm running out of local pet shops, and Wyatt is getting tired of begging them to ship me yellow canaries. Hopefully, the next one would live long enough for my purpose.

Wyatt was also curious about the stack of papers on my dining room table written in bizarre script. I told him they were business stuff from back home. No way was I going to get into a detailed conversation with him concerning my breeding prospects.

Saturday came and I hoped the latest canary didn't arrive while I was running Dar's errand. It would suck to come home and find Boomer had eaten it, or it had been frightened to death by a falling leaf or something. It was a beautiful fall day for a beer and seafood festival though. I was lamenting that they hadn't held it in Baltimore. Beautiful harbor? Chesapeake Bay? What were they thinking? Still, although parking was a bitch in that area of DC, the venue was close to the museum action and not terribly far from Chinatown. I didn't want to fill up on dumplings when there were crab cakes in my future, so I headed over to the National Crime and Punishment museum to kill some time.

I'm not normally a museum person. Crime and punishment did sound interesting, although humans think of punishment in terms of being sent to your room without pudding, so I didn't have high hopes. It was awesome. I was tempted to blow off the vampire appointment and spend the whole day at the place. Yes, there was some boring shit about legislation, and I didn't see the fuss about whether death row inmates got a last meal or not, but wow, what a testimony to the sick, twisted, and creative minds these little humans had. Once again I realized how easy it was to underestimate them and how much we truly had in common.

I fell in love with Ted Bundy. Here was a guy who totally flew under the radar, appearing harmless and even injured to his potential victims. He'd whack them repeatedly over the head with a crowbar when they tried to help him load stuff into his car. Then he would rape them, sometimes adding their lopped off heads to his collection. Occasionally, he'd continue to sleep with their decomposing body. That was dedication to your art. Too bad the humans had killed Ted Bundy. I would have been honored to Own this guy in a terrible and painful way that he surely would have appreciated.

Reluctantly, I made my way back to the Verizon Center and hit up the closest booths for spicy crab balls and beer before winding my way through the crowd to the Jolly Molly

Crab Shack. Jolly Molly must indeed be jolly if she eats her own food, because it was incredible. The crab cakes had barely enough breading to hold them together. They fell apart in my mouth with a bite of Old Bay seasoning and hot mustard.

I'd forgotten my original errand when an attractive man in jeans and a t-shirt walked up to me and handed me an envelope. It looked like an embossed wedding invitation and I wondered what kind of artifact this was. I could see the humans going crazy over an ancient Roman party invite, but demons wouldn't really care about that sort of thing. I opened it up and saw that the card inside had a date, time, and meeting place. Fuck. This whole thing was supposed to be easy and now I was going to be running around on a stupid hunt. According to the lovely embossed card, I was to go to the Inner Harbor in Baltimore on Monday at noon and meet someone by the aquarium. I swore under my breath, thinking that meeting would probably leave me with a treasure map and instructions to dig at an X on Assateague Island.

I bought a box of crab cakes to take back to Wyatt, figuring he probably hadn't eaten much beyond chips and salsa during his tournament, and headed home. No surprise, there were three messages on my mirror from Dar with increasingly insulting demands that I call him and let him know where to meet me to pick up the artifact.

"The vampires are leading me on a merry chase," I told him. "All the guy gave me were directions to meet someone Monday afternoon in Baltimore. That's two days from now, Dar," I told him, trying to impress on him a sense of time.

Dar swore up a blue streak, threatening the entire vampire race with a bloody and short future. "They don't want the damned thing. They've been trying to get rid of it forever. What did the guy say to you? Why didn't he just hand it over?"

"I don't know, Dar. I'm just a fucking courier here. The guy didn't say one word to me, just handed me the envelope and vanished into the crowd like a ghost. I'll go to this meeting on Monday just because I like hanging out at the Inner Harbor, but you and Haagenti better get your fucking ducks in a row on this deal. I'm not haring all over the country playing cloak and dagger for some piece-of-crap antique."

"I'll get with Haagenti," he assured me. "I'll make sure the vampires give it to you on Monday. And Haagenti will be very grateful, Mal; he'll be very grateful."

My skin crawled at the idea of Haagenti's gratitude. I wasn't sure it would be the kind of "gratitude" I wanted. Besides, even if there were any status or money, Dar would find a way to screw me out of it. I don't know why I put up with his crap. He was not worth risking Haagenti's notice or anger. This one last time was it. No more.

Once again, I assured him that I would contact him as soon as I had the item, right after the meeting on Monday, and impressed on him that he was not to be driving me insane with calls before then.

Wyatt was grateful for the crab cakes, and his gratitude did matter to me. As I thought, he'd been so engrossed in his tournament that he'd barely eaten. I heard an exhausting amount of detail about the various competitors' strengths and weaknesses, and how Wyatt used strategy and superior skill to make it to the top five. Evidently there was some woman in Cleveland who took the top prize, beating Wyatt with ease and humiliating him with her victory. I offered to kill her for him.

"Why am I thinking you don't mean 'kill her' as in beat her at checkers?" Wyatt asked.

"No, kill her," I told him cheerfully.

I was sort of teasing. I knew humans didn't do this sort of thing. Well, maybe that Bundy guy did, but he was special. Still, I really did want to do this. It would be a wonderful gift to him. It would show him the depth of my affection, how much I appreciated him. Demons did it all the time back home. Wyatt was pretty accepting of my non-human urges, maybe I could talk him into it.

"You can easily find out her real name and address with your hacker skills, and I'll just pop out to Cleveland or wherever and kill her. That way she won't beat you anymore at your game. I'll let you choose whether I Own her or not, and how slowly and painfully you want her to die. I'll bring home a trophy for you to display so everyone will see how much I care for you." I looked around his place. "A garland with her teeth maybe, or her scalp if she has nice hair."

Wyatt made a kind of gurgling sound. "Sam. You're joking aren't you? In that weird way you do sometimes? You can't just kill her. I want to beat her at the game, not physically harm her person. I'll work on my technique and I'll win eventually."

Why would he want to do that? This idea was growing on me. What boyfriend wouldn't want a garland of teeth?

"But this is much more effective," I explained. "I don't want you losing games and being humiliated by these other humans."

"It's okay if I lose. I'll learn more that way, and eventually I'll be good enough to beat her myself. I won't get better if you just kill everyone who opposes me. Plus I won't have any fun." His voice was becoming stern. He clearly didn't understand the situation and what I was proposing.

"Everyone will wonder how I can allow my human to suffer such humiliation," I explained patiently. "Wyatt, you're my most favored human. I can't allow other humans to think they are above you. Plus, this is the sort of thing we do to show affection. I kill your enemy and bring you a trophy to display, and then everyone will know that you share a special bond with me."

"I'm not wearing a garland of human teeth as a sign of your affection." Wyatt was starting to sound pissed off. "If you do care about me, you'll humor me and let me handle this in my own way. The way humans do."

He had an overly optimistic idea of how humans handle things. "Ted Bundy didn't do things this way. He would have been on board with this. He wouldn't have insisted I stand idly by like some Low and watch my human get shown up and humiliated."

"I'm not Ted Bundy. Normal humans don't resolve conflict that way. This is a game. It's supposed to be challenging and difficult. It won't be if you just take out all my competition. I don't get this side of you. You don't massacre everyone who beats you at the dressage tests."

"Those things don't matter to me. This game matters to you. I can tell it reflects your status among the humans you respect; it provides you with a sense of where you stand in their hierarchy. I want to make it clear that you are favored, under the protection of a higher life form and that they should acknowledge your level." Besides, I could hardly slaughter a field full of eight-year-old girls in their dressage outfits and possibly hope to get away with it.

"No Sam. You are not to interfere with my work. You will not kill my opponents. I know you don't understand it, I know it goes against how you handle things back home, but you need to restrain yourself in these things."

Whatever. I would indulge him. Everyone would think I'd gone soft allowing a human to demand this of me. I was hardly a demon anymore, doting over someone so much weaker than me in this fashion. I was soft on Wyatt though. I would suffer so much if he weren't with me. I'd try to play by his rules to keep him happy. But if that woman in Cleveland got too far out of line, she was going to meet with an unfortunate accident.

CHAPTER 7

$\mathcal{I}$ was in a tank top and flannel PJs early Sunday, listening to light jazz, and getting my morning coffee. Wyatt had managed to get past his anger over my offer to kill his gaming opponent, and we'd eaten crab cakes, drank beer, and had sex for the rest of the evening. I felt all warm and happy. I was contemplating going to the gym after my coffee, to work off all the crab cakes and beer, when the doorbell rang.

There was an angel at my door.

My heart leapt. He was here. I had missed him. I envisioned showing him what I could do with the water globes and him showing me other amazing things. One look at his face and I realized he was not equally happy to see me. My joy vanished and fear replaced it. I'd pushed him too far with my crazy displays of energy and my sexual taunting, masturbating with the tattoo. This was it. I was dead. He had finally come to finish me off and he'd had the courtesy to ring my doorbell first.

"Show me your arm, cockroach" Gregory snarled.

Anger replaced the fear. How dare he show up out of the

blue, after eight weeks of nothing, and demand to see the stupid, botched-up brand he'd put on my arm. Arrogant asshole. I'd be damned if I let him order me around like this.

"No fucking way," I told him and tried to shut the door in his face. He's six-and-a-half feet tall and built like a wrestler on steroids. He put an arm in the doorway and it just bounced back off him to slam open into the wall. As he strode in, I made a mad dash for the kitchen, vaulting over the counter top that divided it from the great room. Maybe I wouldn't need to go to the gym after all.

He walked purposely across the room and stood a few feet away from the counter, watching me like a cat stalking a mouse. "Come here, cockroach" he ordered. "I'm going to fix that cursed thing or kill you. I haven't decided which option appeals the most to me right now. Either way, you've tortured me with it for the last time."

Yeah, like that was really going to make me comply. Did he seriously think I was going to actually come to him?

Instead I grabbed some knives and various kitchen utensils and threw them at him. He easily snatched the knives out of the air and plunged them into the fabric cushions of my bar stools. The spatulas and spoons he just batted away. I could have thrown a far more lethal burst of raw energy or lightning at him, but I didn't want to damage my house.

Every knife I owned was stuck in my upholstery at this point, and I was looking quickly around for pots and pans to throw next when I saw him lunge at me over the counter. I ducked down so he would go over me, and scrambled around the island. He sailed right into the cabinetry with all the force of his weight, cracking one of the doors in half.

"Damnit, you broke my cabinet!" I shouted. "They're solid hickory, a custom design. It took me months to get them special ordered. Try not to destroy my house, you asshole!"

He looked at me with interest and then put his fist

through another of my cabinet doors. "Come here," he commanded. "Or I will break every last one of them into splinters."

Fucking jerk. I ran for the open door and sensed him throwing a burst of white as he raced to beat me there. I changed course and put the huge sectional sofa between us, surprised to see how bad his aim was. That white stuff didn't come anywhere near me, and was barely strong enough to singe the door.

Gregory glanced over at me and carefully closed the big steel door, locking it, and setting the deadbolt and the chain. There was no way I could get all that crap undone and out the door before he caught me. Keeping his eyes on me, he walked through the great room to the huge glass French door sets at the rear of the house that opened up to the pool and gardens. He thoroughly locked and bolted each one. I kept the sofa between us at all times.

The angel walked over to the edge of the sofa and faced me. "Come here," he said again, this time in that soft, deep, persuasive rumble. It rolled over me in dark blue, like velvet and thunder, and I really wanted to do what that voice said.

"Come here willingly, little cockroach. Come to me and I won't hurt you. Your obedience is all I ask."

I can't begin to describe the feeling that blue put out into the room, into me. It was rich and sweet, and pulled at me deep inside. I wanted to walk over to him, to drown myself in those black eyes, to be as physically close to him as possible. If I did what he said, he'd be so pleased with me. Pleasing him, obeying him, would bring me such satisfaction and joy.

Instead I shook my head to clear the fog of blue from it, then picked up a decorative wooden candle stick and waved it at him menacingly. It wouldn't do any good in a fight against an angel, but I felt like I had to make a statement of my free will. I had to stand firm against the blue shit and its siren song.

He dashed around the sofa at me, and I ran trying to keep as much of the sofa between us as possible as I threw the candlestick at him. We did a few laps, then reversed as he tried to catch me off guard. I should have been scared that a being far more powerful than me basically had me trapped in my own home. I should have still been angry at his arrogance and attempted compulsion, but I was actually starting to have fun being chased around the house like this.

We continued the sofa laps for a while, when he suddenly leapt on the sofa and launched himself over it at me, knocking the huge heavy sectional over backwards. I was taken by surprise and shrieked as he hit me like a linebacker, knocking the breath out of my lungs. He wrapped his arms around me and twisted as we hit the ground, taking the full impact as we landed and slid across the floor, crashing into the dining room table and sending it flying. As soon as we stopped, he flipped over on top of me, pinning me to the ground. I wasn't even bruised.

I felt him take a deep breath and he looked down at me, the black bleeding through his irises to engulf his eyes entirely in their color. "Can I please see your arm?" He was obviously finding the polite word difficult to say. "I think I can fix the brand, if you'll let me try?"

I looked up at him. There was no blue stuff this time. No compulsion, no arrogant ordering me around. He actually said please. Still, I really didn't want to do this.

"I'm sorry." He sounded sincere. "I'm under a lot of stress right now, and having you constantly messing with me through the brand hasn't done much for my temper. I need to disable it. It's driving me insane, and I'm less liable to kill you if I fix it."

"Fix it? What exactly is your idea of fixing it? Making me into a mindless slave?" I asked in suspicion.

He laughed cynically. "Tempting, but I'm afraid that's way beyond even my power. I can stop it from being an erogenous zone. Anything in addition to that would be a miracle."

It would be nice not to have an orgasm every time someone grabbed my arm. It was funny at first, but now it was just annoying. Either way, this whole thing was going to be a lesson in humiliation. If I said no, he'd just force me. At least he was asking politely now, as if I had an option to refuse. Reluctantly, I raised my right arm over my head to expose the tattoo of the sword with the angel wing guards and the red, raised circle of flesh around it.

He took another deep breath, and his teeth became pointed spikes. Piranha teeth. "This isn't going to be easy." I wasn't sure if he was talking to himself or me.

I couldn't watch him when he originally put the marks on my arm since he had my head turned to face the other way and held firmly with his hand. I was determined to watch this time. I wondered if he'd bite me again. Last time it had been like a thousand hot needles in my skin. That may not sound erotic to humans, but for me it had been an incredible sensation.

Instead of his teeth, though, he took his tongue and laved the raised hickey mark with the middle part of it. I thought I was going to melt. Sensation poured through me and I arched myself against him. He ran his tongue slowly three times counter clockwise around the mark, and I thrashed against him, trying to grind my hips on his. I doubted he had a cock, or anything else down there, but I sure as hell wanted to find out.

"Try to hold still," he said thickly. He was somehow remaining enviously calm and collected while I was a mess of need.

"Can't," was all I could manage. Can't think. Certainly can't speak.

He pressed himself against me more firmly, trying to hold me immobile. It only intensified the waves of orgasm crashing through me. Three sets of this torture ensued before he finally pulled his tongue away. I hoped he was done as I was at the point of insanity from all the sensation. After-shocks were still rocking me, but the worst had to be over.

Nope. No such luck. He took the tip of his tongue and ran it around the outer edge of the hickey mark, spiraling inward at an agonizingly slow pace. I realized it wasn't his teeth that had the hot needle sensation, but the tip of his tongue. It was like jolts of pain and pleasure as the sparks spread from my skin down through the network of his red-purple deep inside me. I thought of all the things I'd love him to do with that tongue, all the parts of my body I'd like him to trace with it.

"Ohhhhhhhh," I dragged out, unable to formulate a coherent thought at this point. I wasn't rubbing all over him anymore, but before I could be grateful for small gifts, I felt the pull of my personal energy rushing to the surface.

This was really embarrassing. My kind has wild, crazy, violent sex, but the only time we allow our spirit-selves, our personal energy, to mingle is during breeding. Before you get anywhere close to an exchange there are petitions, negotiations, contracts. To have my personal energy flying to the surface, eager to leave this flesh and join with his without my thoughtful and written consent, was a grave loss of control. And at this point, I really didn't care. As I've said before, pride is not my sin.

I held my energy on the outline of my flesh, in an invitation, fully expecting nothing in return. So I was surprised when I felt the angel's red-purple energy leap up to touch the edge of mine against my skin. For the first time ever, I realized my energy had hue, orange with patches of royal blue. It swirled around and through his in an obscene splash of color, dissolving to a sharp, translucent white where it merged. Slowly, our spirit-selves blended bit by bit, turning a clear, slightly opalescent white and sending a vibration of sound deep within me. I felt more and more of our energy merge into whiteness and shuddered with the intensity of it. The process gained in speed as we rushed and swirled toward each other. Finally, there was a click of resolution and we existed as one, a translucent white, suspended between our bodies. We held there for what seemed an eternity, and then slowly bled back into our individual colors and our physical forms. Awareness returned to me and I realized that somehow we had shifted positions and I lay on top of Gregory like an overcooked noodle.

"Are you okay?" he asked after a few moments. He sounded like he was struggling to speak. Or maybe I just couldn't hear very well yet.

I was more than okay. This was the most amazing thing ever. Life altering. World shattering. Amazing. I'd never done anything like that before, hadn't realized anything like that was even possible. I was afraid to move and break the spell.

"No bones," I slurred. "Bones are gone. Can't move."

That seemed to alarm him, and he forced himself to move so he could grip my arms and chest. "I feel bones. You seem to have them. What's wrong with them? Why won't they work?"

"Metaphor." My speech was still a bit garbled. "That was epic. Can we do it again? But not now. I can't do it again right now. I need a nap first. And a roast beef sandwich. A nap and a sandwich."

"No, we can't do it again." Gregory's voice was stern. "We can never do it again."

I wanted to reply, but all I could do was lay there on him

and try to regain some control over my physical form. What the fuck had we done? It was a perfect rush of sensation that had nothing to do with organic matter. Like a moment of existence without the flesh, but without death, held together and joined with another.

I moved a bit, beginning to regain feeling in my limbs again.

"Is the brand still so sensitive?" Gregory asked. "Did I fix it at all?"

"No way I'm going to touch it right now. Give me a few moments to come back to earth, and I'll see how it goes." I rolled off him and shakily got to my feet. I had to put a hand on the tipped over sofa to steady myself.

The angel propped himself up on his elbows and looked around at the wreckage. He looked incredibly human at the moment with his hair mussed and his skin a more flesh-like texture. His teeth were no longer pointy, and the black that filled his eyes was slowly receding into his irises again. He was beautiful. Like this, or with the pointy teeth and black-filled eyes, he was beautiful. I caught my breath as I felt my personal energy stir again and a warmth run through me. So much for the nap and roast beef sandwich. I was ready to go for round two.

Gregory got up and righted the huge sectional sofa with one hand, pushing it easily back into its original spot. With that done, he walked over and began plucking knives out of my barstool cushions, placing them in the sink. I followed and began picking up spoons and spatulas from around the room.

"I'm sorry about these ripped cushions, and your cabinets, too." He glanced at the one he'd put his fist through.

"No, you're not." I laughed. "Admit it; you enjoyed tearing up my house."

Imagine my surprise when he smiled. Smiled. All the way.

Even his eyes smiled. It was devastating. He could rule the universe with that smile. He certainly could rule me with that smile. If he did that more often, he would be unstoppable.

"Okay. It was especially fun putting my fist in that cabinet there. You should have seen your face, little cockroach." The smile got bigger. I was a goner. I needed to change the subject right now before I threw myself at him like a concert groupie.

"I've wanted to show you this. Watch." I walked around the counter and turned on the sink faucet, then gathered together a globe of water.

"Very nice, little cockroach," Gregory said as I held the globe above the sink. "Can you freeze it? Vaporize it?"

"Not yet," I admitted.

He came over behind me and put his hands on top of mine. My concentration slipped with his touch and the globe wept drops into the sink basin.

"Try separating it and pulling it back together." His breath stirred the hair by my ear.

I felt him slide his power down through me, and the globe became a dozen smaller ones, hovering in a neat line above the counter. Suddenly I knew how to do it. It was as if he'd transferred the skill and the knowledge along with the stream of power. I got the feeling this was something he didn't do for just anyone. A gift. The thought made me uneasy.

He stepped in closer to me and I could feel the burn from the power he leaked. It trickled again, down through my arm, and the little balls of water became one, then shattered apart again into a thousand shards of ice, all hovering above the sink. They danced in a spiral before melting in a splash back into the basin.

"You must learn more quickly. You need to become more

than a little cockroach if you're to survive." His voice was soft, and I felt the faint hint of blue. "Stop fighting me and let me help you."

I fought off the blue, shielding myself as best as I could from his power running through me. He chuckled.

"Fine. See if you can do the ice yourself now."

He pulled his power back to a light touch, keeping his hands firmly on mine. I stared at the water and took a breath. I could do this a lot easier if he wasn't touching me. Ideally, he should be in the next room. At least twenty feet away with his back to me. Carefully, I pulled a globe of water together, raised it, and froze it from the center out, elongating the ends into a huge icicle. Pride surged through me.

"Faster," he commanded, overriding my control and returning the melted ice to the sink.

I obeyed before I could feel irritated at his tone, and a rather sloppy blob of ice hung before us.

"No. Again."

Pissed, I seized the water from the sink and transformed it straight to ice as I launched the tiny darts into my ceiling. Asshole.

He vaporized them with a poof. "Better. Again."

I looked into the empty sink.

"Create the water." Bossy angel had been replaced by the seductive one. I felt more comfortable with bossy angel.

I reached inside to grab from my store of raw energy, and was surprised when he blocked me.

"No. Pretend you're empty, desperate. Convert what you have. Fast. Now."

I reacted. Yanked the atoms from the air around me, converting them directly into a shard of ice. I spun it with a whoosh, separated it into a spiral of glittering pieces, then vaporized them one at a time with little cracks of noise, like fireworks.

"Ah, little cockroach. That was beautiful."

His physical body hadn't moved, but his personal energy reached out, rubbing along mine in a soft caress. Part of me wanted to freak. Part of me wanted to rub back. Maybe more than rub back. I needed to sit down. I needed to step away from him. It was too much, and I was confused by what I was feeling.

"Have you practiced withdrawing yourself from your physical form? So you can survive mortal damage?"

He was still holding my arms, rubbing himself along me. His power continued to pour through me, even though the water work was done. It was like being immersed in liquid fire. I struggled to remember his question.

"You mean like taking a gunshot to the head? No, I haven't worked on that."

Idiot. It's not like I could practice getting shot in the head and surviving it. There'd be no practice. I'd live or I'd die, and odds were, I'd die. Demons were more committed to their physical forms than angels. We could survive a lot of damage, but if the body died, we did, too.

"You only need something of this world to shield you, little cockroach." Gregory's lips were practically touching my ear. "What houses you doesn't have to be a living being. You can safely exist in the form of a dead corpse, a spark of fire, even a rock if you wished."

"We're not like angels," I protested. Like I'd really want to live my life as a rock anyway. "We can't do that sort of thing."

"You are angels."

Are? I thought it was "were angels," as in past tense.

"Angels who use only a tenth of their potential," he continued. "You must learn this. The day is coming when you can no longer hide under a rock, little cockroach. I would be very upset if that day came and someone squashed you under their heel."

69

I had no idea what he was talking about. "There's always a rock," I assured him.

I felt his amusement. "No. There will be no more rocks."

Before I could reply, I felt the stab of a thousand needles tracing the edge of my ear. He'd licked my ear? And he was still rubbing himself against me, in a way only beings of spirit could do. Too much. It was too much. I was going to fly apart into a million pieces, like the ice we played with. Everything blurred for a moment as I struggled to retain some kind of control.

"I'll show you how to pull back, and you can practice by having that toy of yours shoot you in the head."

He sounded like he was teasing, but I felt him reach down inside me and begin to distance me from my form. I didn't like where this was going. I didn't trust him to do this sort of thing to me. Especially not when I was so wide open and vulnerable like this. I yanked my energy away from his and frantically tried to think of something to distract him from this course of action.

"Maybe you should look at the brand and see if you fixed it or not," I said, my mouth dry. I was grasping at straws here.

"Maybe I should," he murmured against my ear in amusement.

I turned around to show him my arm, very aware that he was too close, trapping me against the sink and counter top.

"How does it look?" This was a bad idea having him this near.

"It's better." He frowned in disappointment. The distraction had worked. I felt seductive angel fade away, and analytical angel takes his place. I relaxed slightly in relief. Seductive angel scared me.

"The circle that created all the flesh sensation is more isolated and is weaker, but the brand that is supposed to bind you hasn't improved. Two parts of it never took, and the one that did is abnormally strong. And it's rooted to the wrong site, plus it...well, it's just wrong." He obviously didn't want to tell me the exact wrong nature of the thing.

He shook his head, perplexed. "I've bound thousands of demons and never had this happen. True, I haven't bound one in several millennia since we just kill you now, but it's not a skill that requires constant practice. Why did this happen?" He ran his finger over the tattoo.

I made a rather embarrassing squeaking noise and plastered myself against his chest, feeling my energy again rush toward him. I'd managed to hold back up until now, but that one touch just sent me right over the edge. Damn, I had no control at all with this guy.

He looked down at me in surprise, black flooding his eyes. Evidently his control was equally poor, or maybe he'd just been waiting for me to respond. He inhaled sharply, then grabbed me, crushing me against him, and burying his face in my hair. Yep, we did it again. It was just as incredible without the lengthy tongue foreplay. Apparently "never do this again" was only about thirty minutes. Who knew?

This time, as I began to regain control over my physical self, I realized we had pretty much collapsed into a heap where we stood.

"We can't keep doing this, little cockroach." Gregory sounded amused. Seductive angel was back, but I was too overwhelmed by what had just happened to feel uneasy. "As enjoyable as it is, we have to exist in a corporeal form in this realm. There are not the right conditions here to support a pure spirit-being. If we keep doing this, we run the risk of coming apart entirely."

He had just been telling me I could exist in a rock or a spark of fire. Those seemed just as farfetched as existing completely outside of a physical form. I wondered if there was somewhere where that rule didn't apply? Somewhere that allowed a pure spirit existence? In Hel, we needed to maintain physical forms as we did here. We were never without form, from birth to death.

"Could we ever be without physical form? Where would that be possible?"

I had this weird feeling like I wanted out of my skin. Like wanting to take an itchy sweater off and run naked. Must have been a side-effect of whatever the fuck it was we were doing.

"We could back home, in Aaru. But I can't exactly bring you there, can I?"

Aaru. I'd not heard much about it other than the fantastic tales the humans had in their worship books. They claimed it was all fluffy clouds with singing and harp playing twenty-four seven. Same song, over and over again for all eternity. Yikes. Not my idea of heaven.

I wondered what it was really like. We were forbidden entry under the treaty. Only the Iblis, the Adversary, was allowed to enter for diplomatic conference. We'd not had one for over two million years. Neither an Iblis nor a diplomatic conference. We'd pretty much severed all communication with the angels. Or maybe they had with us. It was all so long ago that no one even bothered to remember.

Gregory scooped me up in his arms and stood. I briefly envisioned us looking like the cover of a romance novel when he ruined the image by slinging me over his shoulder like a sack of potatoes. I was amazed he could stand at all, let alone do it while holding me. I could barely move my limbs yet.

He lugged me up the stairs and into my bedroom. I wasn't sure how he knew which one was mine. Then he plopped me on the bed and covered me up with a blanket. I was being tucked in by an angel. Never in my wildest imaginings had I thought of this one.

"Promise me you'll work on separating yourself from your physical form."

I looked at him blankly. Right. Like that was going to happen. Was he trying to turn me into an angel or something? Too late. About two-and-a-half-million years too late.

"Swear it." The compulsion slammed into me, then bounced off.

"Nope," I told him. "Still doesn't work."

He glared at me, his black eyes burning into mine with their intensity.

"Oh, okay. Fine. I swear on all the souls I Own that I'll work on it. Eventually."

He nodded, satisfied, then tucked the edges of the blanket around my sides as if I were a human baby.

"You must have more self control when you're around me, cockroach." I wasn't sure if I was imagining the suggestive tone or not. The whole morning had become rather surreal and I didn't really trust my senses right now.

"That's a virtue, not a sin," I told him. "So the ball is in your court with this one, baby. Of course, we both know how much you suck at that particular virtue."

He smiled. He really needed to stop doing that.

"Yes, I do seem to suck at that virtue. After so many millennia in this form, I find I'm no longer as proficient in any of the virtues as I would like."

"Good. That's not a bad thing. You should work on some sins for a while, give yourself a break."

"Take your nap, eat a sandwich," he said, not rising to the bait. "You'll be back to wreaking havoc in an hour or so."

"Wait." I was surprised when he came back and sat on the bed.

It wasn't often I saw him like this, relaxed and open to conversation. I had questions I wanted to ask him before he slammed the doors down again and turned back into asshole-angel. Plus, I really enjoyed being around him when he was like this.

"How come you're walking around like nothing happened and I'm exhausted?"

"Your form operates on a lower vibration than mine. Moving from spirit back to your physical form is a huge change in your vibration pattern. Changing that far, that fast, is tiring. I'm tired too, but I'm also a lot older than you. And I have great stamina."

That last part made me nervous. I recognized human sexual innuendo, but I wasn't sure if it was the same with angels. He reached out and slid a finger down my arm. I felt his spirit-self reach inside to hover tentatively near my store of raw energy. He needed to cut this out or I'd never get my nap and sandwich.

"I want to hold this, have it surround me." That unnerving, seductive note was back in his voice.

I looked at him in surprise. "But you said it would kill you."

"It would, unless you kept your connection and your control of it. Raw energy is nothing and everything. It's potential. It is that null space, on the verge of creation or destruction. Only your kind can hold it there. We angels can never experience it without you controlling it. Without your hold, it bursts into being and overwhelms us. A small amount we can handle. As much as you hold would kill the strongest among us. For me to experience it, I would need to have complete power and control over you, or trust that you would hold it in check. Trust you not to kill me."

"I wouldn't kill you," I told him.

He raised his eyebrows in disbelief.

"Well, I wouldn't kill you on purpose. Maybe by accident. Or possibly on purpose if I had to. But I wouldn't be happy about it."

He shook his head and pulled his hand away, dropping the shield back over himself and ending the short-lived intimacy.

"I don't trust you. I can't trust you." His smile held bitterness. "Exile has made your kind crazy, made you evil. You've devolved into something base. What you all have become, what you are, isn't something anyone can ever trust. No, if I really wanted to do this, I'd need to have absolute control over you."

I felt chilled. Hopefully he didn't really want that, because the prospect of being under his total control was terrifying.

Gregory finished tucking me in and, not surprisingly, I was asleep before he even left the room.

I woke up about an hour later feeling refreshed and made my way downstairs. He was gone, of course. I was kind of glad about that actually. Otherwise I'd have been sorely tempted to act like a one-night stand gone horribly wrong and chase him down my driveway trying to give him my phone number and imploring "Call me, call me." I needed to get a grip here.

Still, I was sorry to see that my house looked like the morning's events had never happened. Light jazz still played, furniture was in its usual place. He'd even fixed the upholstery on the bar stools, as well as my cabinets. I ran my hands over the fabric, admiring his work. I couldn't tell if he'd recreated the whole thing or patched it. Even the wood grain in the cabinets was identical to before. It was as if I'd dreamed the whole thing.

I was supposed to meet Michelle for a late lunch and a look-see at a potential commercial property, but I was starving. I wondered if I could trust myself to have only one piece of the leftover cheesecake? I opened my fridge and stared in shock. There was a sandwich. On a plate. With a pickle artfully placed beside it. He'd made me a sandwich.

An angel had tucked me in my bed and made me a sandwich.

I grabbed it off the plate, took a bite and choked, forcing myself to swallow. Definitely roast beef, but what the fuck had he put on it? Lifting off the huge slice of rye on top, I eyed the contents of my sandwich. Roast beef and cheese. That was normal. Shredded carrots, unusual, but I could go with that. Leftover tuna salad, oh my. A blob of artichoke hummus. And jelly. He'd spread a generous helping of grape jelly over the top and bottom pieces of bread.

I stared at the sandwich and wondered if this was some kind of prank, or if he really thought I'd enjoy this. I guess when a being that has never eaten food makes you a sandwich, this is what you get. It could have been worse. He could have added ketchup and ranch dressing to the mix. I ate the whole fucking thing. I somehow managed to keep it down the entire drive into the city, too.

CHAPTER 8

*M*ichelle and I had the county map spread all over our table as we planned our world domination, one rental unit at a time. Her burger and fries were holding down one corner, threatening to drip ketchup on the line representing Sottbey Street. I wasn't eating. Not after that sandwich. Typically I'd just remove it from my system, but I was allowing it to digest normally as a kind of penance. It's good to suffer sometimes; gives you perspective.

"There's where we're going after lunch." Michelle pointed at a huge square on the map. "This strip mall on the west end is for sale. It's a bigger purchase than we're used to, but I think it has potential."

The west end had fallen on hard times and although there were some popular chain restaurants there, increasing crime and low-income rentals had hit the retail industry hard. In this particular strip mall, the major grocery store had closed, leaving a big empty section surrounded by discount stores and ethnic eateries.

"What the fuck are we going to do with this big empty spot?" I pointed to the vacant grocery store building on the corner of the strip mall. It was over fifty thousand square feet. "There's already one of those big discount clothing stores in the middle, and not many businesses want a space that huge."

"Yeah, I thought about a gym, but it's really too big, even for the chain ones, and there's currently a gym over here. They have an exclusive purpose clause in their lease, too."

I pondered a moment. "Can we convert it to office space? There's enough parking. Or better yet, warehouse? There are loading docks in the rear from when it was a grocery store."

"The strip mall across the street converted their vacant grocery space into office and is leasing to Conformance Healthcare. They've had issues, though, because that kind of business doesn't enhance the volume of retail traffic needed by the smaller stores and they've had some of the stores fold with significant time on their leases. We need a retail anchor store or risk losing the other businesses, which are actually doing pretty well. Same problem with warehouse. Actually, even more of a problem, because the tractor-trailer truck volume in and out of the two entrances would deter consumer traffic."

Michelle knew her shit.

"We've got the one anchor store here." I pointed to the discount clothing chain. "How are their numbers? When is their lease up, and are they indicating whether they'd renew or not?" I wouldn't want to have two huge vacant spaces to fill.

"They've got five more years. They seem to be doing okay. I think they'd like to move to the south end where there is more high-income shopping traffic and they'd have less shrink, but they are doing well with the low income residents and the shoppers waiting for a table at the steak house."

"Do you think we could get in one of those big all-purpose outlet stores? Or a small home improvement chain? I'd suggest big office supply, but I don't know how well they'd do in this section of town."

"Party store," Michelle announced. "A huge party store chain with the costumes and piñatas. There is nothing like that on this side of town and it would work with the demographics."

I shrugged. "Let's run the numbers, float out some inquiries, and see how it looks. I don't mind retail if the income stream is there and it's not too much of a pain in the ass."

Michelle nodded and folded up the map. She was avoiding my eyes and there was an odd look to her face.

"What?" I asked.

"Nothing. I think this is a good deal, that's all."

Michelle was a worse liar than I was. "This is a crap deal. It's a huge investment, with a stupid amount of risk. It's in a horrible neighborhood that's going down the drain at the speed of light. Why are you so determined to have me buy this?"

"It's just…well, the projects were demolished downtown in the revitalization effort and all the destitute minorities got shoved out to the edges of the city and a few older developments outside of town. Everything is falling apart out here and…well…they deserve better."

Something twisted inside me when I saw her eyes, bright with unshed tears. This wasn't the tough businesswoman I knew. What was this about?

"The mall, stores, these shopping centers, they're all falling left and right. There are lots of customers, living right here, that need stores they can walk to. Plus, there needs to be decent shops and restaurants to bring the wealthier folks out. Otherwise the whole area is going to turn into a dangerous ghetto."

Her smile twisted as she looked at me. "I know it's a terrible reason to invest millions of dollars, but I was lucky enough to not grow up like this. I hate that others have to."

"You feel some sort of responsibility for these people?"

"Yes. All humanity. But especially those who are vulnerable."

I frowned. "Resources are always limited. There will be those that have and those that don't. Fate has an unsympathetic and amoral hand. That's just the way of life."

Michelle's jaw was firm. "That doesn't mean I have to sit back and do nothing. The universe may play out that way, but I'll fight it with my every breath. If I change one life, just one, then it's worth the fight."

"Well, let's go look at this strip mall then," I told her.

The old grocery store had been vacant a long time. Long enough for graffiti to decorate the walls and homeless to move in. The graffiti had been painted over, a faint outline still bleeding through the scant coat of white, and boards nailed across the broken openings. There were signs that squatters had been there at one point, but no belongings had been left behind. There was only one person, sitting propped up against the outside wall, a lump of dark green blanket against the October chill.

"We had some issues with vagrancy until a few weeks ago," the real estate agent confessed. "Nothing since then, although we still get nightly graffiti. I know it's not in a great neighborhood, and it's been missing an anchor store for a long time. It's priced accordingly."

The agent and Michelle went in while I looked at the graffiti still visible through the damp paint. There were some very ornate tags, vulgar innuendo about a man named Mike, and a crude drawing of a cat next to the entrance. I scrutinized the cat drawing. Two round circles in green with stick legs, triangle ears, and dotted eyes. The artist had taken some liberties with reality and made six legs extending from the very round torso.

"He took them one by one," a voice from the blanket pronounced. "This was his hunting ground until they all fled. He'll find them again, and kill them off. Then he'll take the children."

"Huh?" I was shocked that the lump wasn't screaming at me, trying to banish me back to Hel. Homeless people don't usually converse with me. I hesitantly walked closer. Nothing was visible beyond shabby shoes sticking from under the dark green woolen blanket. A faint smell of mildew and rotted leaves came from the lump, as if something had once been buried in it long ago.

"He kills them and takes their ears."

That sounded vaguely familiar. Where had I heard that before?

"They've come to you for protection. The Ha-Satan. The answer to their prayers."

"Huh?" I hated to be a broken record, but I had no idea what the heck she was talking about. And why did everyone keep addressing me as Satan? At least she'd gotten the name right, though.

"Your tenants. Even the ones you call homeless. They are your people, yours to keep safe. Here in your town. He kills them and takes their ears so they can no longer hear the song of God. It's your responsibility to protect them. To keep your people safe."

"I don't believe that's in our lease agreement," I told her. Was she suggesting I was under some contractual obligation to provide security for my tenants? Fuck that. Reed was there to collect rent and make sure a riot didn't break out. Other than that, these people were on their own.

"It's time for you to take up the sword of your destiny.

Time for you to claim what is yours and defend them from those who would steal them away."

Mine. The word rose unbidden from my depths, power surging across the miles.

"My Ha-Satan, my Iblis," the lump said reverentially.

Crazy nut-job. What did she think I was? Batman? The mayor? The Iblis? Not me. No way. It was bad enough I was sticking my neck out for Dar, that I'd risked myself to help the werewolves this summer. This was becoming a habit and it needed to stop right now.

"My only responsibility is to myself," I told her, feeling silly for talking to a lump of blanket.

"It's time to take your rightful place," the voice accused.

"Fuck that," I replied and went inside. Myself and Wyatt. Everyone else could rot in hell.

CHAPTER 9

$\mathcal{T}$hat evening Candy and I had a date for a fall run along the mountain trails in Gambrill park. It was a perfect October evening for a run. The air snapped with the promise of winter cold, and the wind was strong enough to sting lungs and water eyes. The path we'd mapped out was a rough cut through the woods that joined up with a portion of the Appalachian Trail. The hilly trails plus the damp fall leaves on the ground left no doubt in my mind that I'd finish with skinned knees, bruises, and muddy clothing. I'd dressed appropriately with ratty sweatpants and a stained race shirt from a 5K years ago. Candy on the other hand was a vision in her tights and long sleeve athletic shirt. Her hair was curled in its pony tail and she had makeup on.

"Seriously?" I gestured at her makeup.

She shrugged and began stretching out on an old park bench. Even her shoes looked like they'd never seen the outdoors.

"I love this time of year. It's almost full moon, too. Wish I was doing this on four legs instead of two." She flexed her hamstrings in an awe inspiring downward dog.

"Do you run in wolf form up here a lot? I thought you guys had some pretty severe restrictions on when and where you could do that."

"Yes. I still do it though. There's no angel appointed to us yet, so we remain under Gregory's supervision. Normally I wouldn't sneeze wrong with that guy in charge, but he's allowing us to hold a fall hunt. It's the first time in over fifty years we've been able to gather together in a group greater than ten and shift into our wolf forms. He's loosened a great many of the density restrictions, too. That's meant that more of us are able to mate bond and live in areas suitable to our kind."

I wondered if Gregory was actually a decent angel after all. He'd delivered justice on Althean, he seemed to be treating the werewolves with fairness, and he'd made me a sandwich. Maybe I needed to rethink my view of him.

"Not that I think he's some kind of saint though," Candy added. "I take a great chance shifting form and running out here. I don't dare hunt, and I take precautions."

She walked over to the car and, giving me a mischievous look, opened up the glove compartment, pulling out a collar. It was a dog collar. A pink, glittery dog collar covered with rhinestones and embellished with a gold tag. I walked over and noticed the tag proclaimed the animal wearing it to be "Gigi" and gave a name and phone number I didn't recognize.

"Smart. But you still would look like a wolf. A wolf with a blingy dog collar."

Candy shook her head and grinned. "These days, as long as you don't look like a pit bull, you're home free."

I handed the collar back and she secured it out of sight in the glove box before beeping the alarm on her car.

"Wyatt and I scored invitations to Bang for their

Halloween party," I mentioned to her as we walked to the trail head.

Bang was legendary in the Baltimore area. There were lines around the block to get in there on a normal weekend. Wyatt had done game testing for some bigwig and had gotten the coveted invitations as a thank you. I wished Candy had a boyfriend. She'd be fun to take to this sort of thing.

"Do you think the angels will ever allow you to mate with humans?" I asked her, abruptly changing the subject. There weren't a lot of werewolves in the area, and the existence contract kept their romantic options very limited.

"I don't know," she replied thoughtfully, setting the pace with a slow warm-up jog. "So many of the angels hold the opinion that we're Nephilim, but I get the feeling that Gregory might be in the camp that considers us a mutated form of humans. He seems to hold some influence, so I'm hopeful that there will be positive change. Although with angels it could be ten thousand years before they even think about it. The problem with immortals is they have no concept of urgency."

We'd picked up the pace considerably, and I was very impressed that Candy managed to conduct this whole conversation without even a ragged breath. I was in damned good shape, but she made me look like an overweight couch potato.

"Would you date a human if the restrictions were lifted?" I was partly teasing, but partly serious, too.

The relationship rules had been in place for thousands of years, and many werewolves just didn't feel comfortable dating humans. It had become a cultural practice over time that would be hard to break. Candy was a traditionalist, and very proud of being a werewolf. She'd been married to another wolf once, but was now divorced with grown children. I'd never seen her even look interested in a man, or woman, of any species.

We ran silently for a few moments while Candy thought about my question. Finally, she looked over at me. "I've been dating a human named Jay for a few weeks now. You've met him before; he's the CFO over at Horizon."

"So you're not only breaking the species barrier, but the race barrier, too?"

"It's sad that some backward humans still can't manage to accept a mixed-race couple, but honestly, I'm more worried about keeping it from the werewolf community that I'm breaking the species rules. So far it's been pretty easy to keep it stealthy. We're both prominent business people and neither one of us wants a lot of gossip this early in a relationship. Eventually, if we keep seeing each other, we'll need to discuss how to handle this though."

"Does he know you get furry and bite rabbits to death in your spare time?" I was amazed at this side of Candy.

"No, he knows I like the outdoors and that I hunt. I know I should tell him, but I really like him. I've been pretty lonely since the divorce, especially with the kids grown and gone. I miss being with someone who thinks I'm attractive. Jay is divorced with grown kids, too. He's athletic, enjoys bow hunting, believe it or not, loves his career, and has strong family values. He looks amazing in a suit." She looked at me and smiled mischievously. "And looks amazing out of the suit, too. He's hot. And I really have missed sex."

I burst out laughing and tripped over a root, almost sprawling face first into the dirt. "Damn, you go girl! Do you do it doggie style?"

"That you'll never know." Candy grinned then dramatically increased speed down the trail.

Conversation became impossible as we raced single file down the narrowed path. Although the trails were maintained, they were still rough with rocks and roots hiding under the damp fall leaves. We ducked under low branches and hopped mossy fallen logs blocking the trail. My shirt snagged several times on briars I could not avoid in time. The downhill grade became so steep at one point that I raced down it, out of control, hoping that I could manage to keep my feet under me. If I'd fallen, my forward momentum would have had me bouncing all the way down before I could stop. Finally, we hit the bottom and ran along what appeared to be an old creek bed. Candy led, and I felt bad knowing that I was slowing her down. On the roads, we were pretty evenly matched, but she clearly had the advantage in the woods.

We veered off the creek bed onto what was, in reality, no more than a deer track. Now the fun began as we had to squeeze through dense sapling groupings and practically crawl under briars that choked the paths. I began to feel like I was in one of the mud runs that had become so popular lately. Candy splashed her way through a freezing, rocky stream, and then led me scrambling up a shale-strewn path as we began the complicated switchbacks to the top of the mountain. My lungs were raw and my breath ragged as we broke free of the deer track and onto a more maintained, although still steep, trail. Forcing myself to speed up a bit, I managed to gain enough on Candy to jog abreast on the wider trail.

"He tucked me in bed and made me a sandwich," I wheezed at her.

"Who, Wyatt?" Candy clearly wondered why on earth this was a noteworthy event. Damn her, she wasn't even breathing hard.

"Gregory," I gasped.

There was a crash and I realized that Candy was no longer beside me. I halted and turned around, although stopping on an uphill run wasn't a good idea. It would be muscle agony trying to get my speed and rhythm back up after stopping like this. Candy was flat on her face on the trail. Actually, by the time I turned around, she had jumped to her feet, embarrassed, and was brushing the mud smears off her formerly pristine clothing.

"I must have misheard you," she said, still brushing her clothes. I was actually grateful for the short break to catch my breath a bit. "I thought you said Gregory, i.e. the angel Gregory, tucked you in bed and made you a sandwich."

"He did." I was finally able to speak now that I wasn't running flat out. "He came by to try and fix this stupid tattoo, chased me around my house for a while, then we had some weird out-of-body thing that was like sex only a million times better, then he helped me clean up my house, then we did the no-body sex thing again, then he tucked me in bed for a nap, then made me a sandwich and finished cleaning up my house before he left."

Candy stared at me open mouthed like a beached trout, our run temporarily forgotten. "Are you hallucinating? You're joking, right?"

"He was an asshole at first, but after we did the out-of-body sex thing, I swear he was coming on to me in that controlling, arrogant fashion of his. He was intense. It made me really uncomfortable, kind of scared me. I think I liked it better when he was pissed off at me and trying to kill me."

"After he had, you know, relations, with you? That's when he started coming on to you?" Candy was confused. "Because with werewolves, they usually come on to someone before they have sex with them. To persuade them. Unless… Do you think he wanted to do it again?"

"He said no, but we did anyway." I was equally confused. "I don't know angels. They hate us. Two-and-a-half-million years and the only contact we've had with them is right before our heads separate from our bodies. They hate us, they kill us. They don't angel-fuck us, talk sexy in our ears, then tuck us in bed and make us a snack. Candy, what is going on?"

"Sam, I just don't think anything good can come from this," Candy said, her voice worried. "He may feel some attraction to you, but that won't change millions of years of hate. He might find you interesting, and appealing, but in the end you're a demon and he'll overcome whatever weakness he's indulging in and kill you. You're my friend, and I will miss you, but I think you need to go home where you're safe."

I shook my head. "I'm pretty sure he can summon me from there. I'm bound to him. If he really wants to kill me, I can't escape."

"Maybe if you're home, he won't have a reason to kill you? You won't be running around here, causing trouble and rubbing his nose in it all the time. You'll be home where you're expected to do those things."

I shook my head again. "I don't want to go home. I'd rather take my chances here."

She stared at me intently, then made a sound of disbelief.

"Oh no, oh no. You cannot, hear me, cannot go falling in love with him. Just stop it right now and snap out of it. I don't care how amazing out-of-body-angel-sex is, you are not going to fall in love with an angel. Especially this angel. This is probably going to end with your death either way, but I don't want to see you die humiliated, hurt, and heartbroken, with no dignity whatsoever."

Love? Yeah right, like that was going to happen. He was no fun at all. He was a total judgmental asshole. Obsessed? Yes. Love? No.

"I know what love is. It's not an emotion we do. We just don't have the capacity for it. We crave what is new and different, to experience every combination of sensory input we can. This thing with Gregory is new, different. That's all it is."

She frowned at me. "I don't believe you. You're a really weird demon. Not that I've met a lot of demons. But you're not totally a demon anymore are you? Didn't you say that brand changed you somehow? Stuck some angel energy in you or something? Angels love. It's a strange, scary, unworldly sort of love, but it's still love."

"It didn't change me that way." I pulled up my shirt sleeve to look at the sword tattoo. "It's made me feel less... I don't know, less crazy or something. I have more patience for things, see things in greater detail, appreciate subtlety. I strategize better, can see chains of possibilities stretching out before me. But I don't feel the need to start rescuing babies and puppies. I don't feel love, kindness, a sense of duty, or guilt."

"Yes, you do," Candy said slowly. "I think you feel all those things, you just don't want to admit it."

No, she was wrong. I liked and admired Candy, but if she got plowed down by a truck, I wouldn't shed a tear. I'd miss that angel a lot, but that was only because I wouldn't have him around to teach me stuff. I didn't love him. Fuck, I didn't even like him. I only cared about myself. And Wyatt. And maybe Dar. That was it. Nobody else.

We jogged back up the trail to the cars. It was agonizing. Like trying to carry a hundred pounds of firewood on your shoulders while running uphill on jelly legs. I was looking forward to spending the night in a hot tub. Hopefully with Wyatt.

Back at the cars, Candy tossed me a chocolate bar. With a name like Candy, of course she'd carry these things around in her car. It was predestination. The candy reminded me of her comment this summer that I smelled like burnt chocolate to her werewolf nose. What a great smell. I wished I could smell myself. Of course, I'd probably binge constantly on sweets and weigh a million pounds.

"Oh, I almost forgot," Candy added, carefully putting her wrapper in the little bag-lined trash bin in her car. I'd tossed mine on the ground where the wind promptly carried it into the woods. "Reed called and let me know your units are already full of homeless. He says they are nervous about some of them who disappeared in the past week from an old, vacant grocery store they used to hole up in. Once word got out that there was space at your place at night, they were lining up to get in. Do you know there are over four hundred homeless in the city limits and you've got just over two hundred in your place?"

"Can he squeeze more in?" I wondered. "Maybe a reduced rate for those who sleep in the crawl space under the porch?"

If only I'd known about this. I could have picked up that abandoned warehouse down the street and packed them in there. Hmmm. It was owned by an out-of-town corporation. I could probably stuff it full of homeless people, collect rent from them and the owners would be none the wiser. It would be a nice little income stream.

Candy shook her head. "You're maxed out. Any more people and Reed will need to spend the whole night there. You have no idea how many fights those people get into. He's like Solomon deciding who this shopping cart belongs to, or who had first claim on the corner away from the window. You're at the tipping point where you're going to erode profits if you pack any more in."

I nodded. "Thanks. Tell Reed to call me if he needs me to help. Although I don't know how much help I can be. I tend to just upset those people and make everything worse. Still, if he needs rope or duct tape or anything to keep people in line, just have him bill me."

Candy climbed in her car. "Call me, and maybe we'll do a

mid-week run. I've been wanting to do something along the Potomac River before winter hits."

I drove home with increasing stiffness. At least the Corvette had heated seats, although that didn't help my screaming legs. I'd left a message on Wyatt's machine, but I feared I would need to soak in the tub alone. He never checked his messages when he was killing zombies, and he could be at it all night. Halfway home my phone buzzed indicating a text message. Ignoring the law, I checked it while driving, hoping it was Wyatt getting a hot tub ready. It was Candy.

"Forgot 2 tell u. Vampires own Bang. Fingers in everything. Like mafia. B careful."

Well, wasn't that interesting.

It was dark by the time I unlocked my door and threw my keys on the dining room table. Again I marveled at how my house looked. As if nothing had ever occurred this morning. Furniture all in place, knives back in the knife rack, breeding petitions picked up and neatly stacked on the table. Ice ran through me. Fuck. The breeding petitions.

When we'd knocked the dining room table across the room, they had flown everywhere. They'd been all over the floor, on the chairs, strewn across the table. Now they were in a neat pile. I stared at the pile as if it were going to transform into a monster and bite me. He'd cleaned them up, stacked them, no doubt read them. They all held fragments of my name, bits and pieces of my titles, clues as to who I was. Yes, he'd bound me, but the brand was fucked up. If he had my name, my true name, he wouldn't need to fix the brand. He'd have power over me. The power to banish. The power to compel. Knowledge of my true name to other demons held nothing but a designation of whom I was and where I stood in the hierarchy. Knowledge of my true name to humans gave them a limited ability to call and request favors and services of me, if they held enough power and skill to do so. Knowledge of my true name to an angel meant enslavement.

Forgetting about my bath, I walked over to the pile and looked carefully at the petitions. They were out of order. Of course, he wouldn't have known in what order I'd stacked them before they went flying, but he would have had a good idea of the value of each petition from the proposal it held. Instead of top down, he seemed to have put the most unworthy ones on top. I wasn't sure if I should be insulted or not. Was he implying that these were the ones I should consider? I glanced at each one carefully and my heart sank. He'd have gotten at least half of my names from these, and a good idea of my level in the hierarchy, as well as my areas of specialty. It would take time, but with some persistence he could discover all my names. Damn.

For a second, my middle felt heavy like there was a weight in my stomach, and my eyes stung. Had he orchestrated the whole thing, planned it all to be able to sneak a look at the petitions and gain control on me? Then I shook some sense into myself. That was the kind of thing that I'd do, that demons would do, not Gregory. If he'd wanted to read the petitions, he would have demanded them in that imperial tone of his. He would have taken them, even if I'd refused. He wasn't sneaky and manipulative; he was forceful, bossy, and controlling. There wasn't much I could do to stop him if he really wanted something.

And so what if he figured out my true name? He could summon me from anywhere. He could easily kill me, anytime he wanted. He seemed to be pretty good at getting me to do things, even without my being fully bound or knowing my true name. Fuck, if things kept going the way they were, he wouldn't need my true name, the brand, or even the wonderful blue shit to get me to do his bidding. I'd be eagerly slapping the shackles on myself.

I turned over the last of the petitions and stopped, staring once again in surprise. The bottom one was the one from Ahriman. Only it wasn't as I had left it. A diagonal line crossed through the entire page in black ink, so hard and deep that it dented the skin parchment, digging a chunk off midway across the page. Written across the top was lovely flowing script in the language both our races shared. It said "NEVER."

CHAPTER 10

*M*onday it rained. Not that nice, warm fall mist of a rain either. Big pelting drops of cold water whipped around the buildings in a bitter wind. The sky was a uniform dark gray, and the dampness seeped deep beneath the flesh into bone. Maryland generally has moderate weather and October is all about the pretty autumn colors and cool nights, offset by warm sunny days. It had been a bitch of a fall so far. Cold, windy, and now this damned rain. What made it worse was that this was the day I was supposed to go to Baltimore and collect Dar's artifact from the vampires. I'd envisioned a beautiful day at the Inner Harbor, and now I'd be expected to stand wet, freezing my ass off, outside the aquarium. Who knows if the vampire would even show. The guy might just look out his window, say "screw it," and go back to bed. It's what I wanted to do.

The harbor area was deserted. It was a Monday, it was October, and the weather sucked. The few people there had ducked inside Phillips or one of the other restaurants. I was shocked to find the aquarium was even open, let alone open at ten in the morning. I honestly couldn't figure out who their target audience at noon on a Monday would be until I saw the buses with their loads of school children. Ah yes, the much-anticipated field trip.

It was warm and dry inside, plus there were animals to look at. On the other hand, it was freezing and wet outside. I contemplated my options, then left a note stuck to the door saying "Dear Vampire, I am inside looking at octopuses/octopi or whatever the plural is" and went on in.

It took me a while to make my way to the octopus exhibit. I first stopped to look at the sharks. I Own a sand tiger shark and was happy to watch one of its kin swimming about the main tank. In spite of how prevalent aquatic life is here, I Own very few sea creatures. I've always been more interested in mammals with the occasional bird or reptile thrown in. The tiger shark was the only fish I Owned, and I didn't Own any aquatic mammals. I'd tried to grab a bottlenose dolphin once, but they are pretty wily and it managed to keep its distance.

I mentally made a wish list of eels, stingrays, and fish that would be fun to Own. Maybe at least one aquatic mammal, too. If I couldn't manage a dolphin, then maybe a whale. I'd really love a killer whale, an orca. It would be hard to catch these in the wild; much easier to sneak into the aquarium after hours and Own them from the small tanks here. Of course, not many places had whales or orcas. I'd need to take a road trip to Own one of them. Wyatt could help me research likely candidates. I'd just have to make sure he didn't realize what I intended to do with them.

By the time I made my way over to the octopuses, it was twenty minutes after the hour. A very irritated looking young man stood glaring at the majestic, giant pacific octopus. The irritation vanished the moment he saw me and was replaced by an expression of calm, disinterested respect. I wondered how he knew I was his contact, then realized I was the only other adult visitor in the aquarium not surrounded by dozens of squealing children.

"Baal." He addressed me with a cross between a nod and a short bow. "We are appreciative of your travel and time on this miserable day."

He handed me a rectangular box about ten inches long, seven inches wide, and two inches deep wrapped in plain brown paper. On impulse I shook it, like I would a Christmas present. It made a sound like rocks with tissue paper inside the box, and I noticed a look of anxiety flicker across the vampire's face before his features returned to bland calm. He nodded again, and wishing me a good day, turned to leave. His pace was leisurely, but I could tell from the tension in his shoulders that he really wanted to break and run.

I'm not a fool. These tissue wrapped rocks-in-a-box were not the artifact, even though I had no idea what the artifact was actually supposed to look like. The vampires had played us again. Their courier boy was terrified that I'd realize the box didn't hold what I thought it did, and that I'd take out my considerable anger on his physical being. I didn't fucking care. I didn't want this thing for myself and I was tired of Haagenti and Dar running me all over the place. I was cold, damp, and sick of all this. I didn't care what kind of trouble Dar was in, he'd have to deal with it himself. The best way to get out of something unpleasant is to be so inept and terrible at it that no one will ask you again. I'd deliver the box-of-artifact-rocks to Dar, look stupid and clueless, and then they'd leave me alone and find some other chump to do their dirty work.

My mood cheered considerably when I got home just in time to meet the delivery guy with my latest canary. He was very appealing with his bright yellow feathers, alert dark eyes and chirping noises. This one was the prettiest of those I'd received so far. I wished I'd bought another one so that I could Own one, or maybe just let it fly loose around my house. Unfortunately, I'd been rather short-sighted when I bought the thing and hadn't thought to buy a cage or food. You'd think by now, after losing four canaries, I'd be prepared, but that wasn't the case. I spread some newspapers in a cat carrier reinforced with chicken wire as a temporary home and threw in a handful of wild bird seed as food. Hopefully that would be more palatable than the dog food which had killed one of the previous canaries. I had a premonition that this bird wouldn't last long in my care and that I should put it to use right away, before I managed to kill it and had to wait again for a replacement. The rain showed no signs of clearing up, but I decided that as soon as I called Dar, I'd head to Sharpsburg.

Dar was beside himself with excitement when I called him.

"Some vampire guy met me at the aquarium and gave me a box," I told him with a twinge of guilt over what the box didn't hold.

"What does the box look like?" Okay, maybe he wasn't as dumb as I had thought.

"It's ten by seven and wrapped in brown paper."

"Ten by seven meters? Fuck, how'd you get it in your little car? How much does the damned thing weigh?"

He was a dumb as I had thought. "No, you idiot. Ten by seven inches. And no one uses metric in this country unless they are scientists or buying soda."

Dar was silent for a moment as he calculated the size of the box. "That's it? It's supposed to be able to change shape and size, so maybe it would fit in a box of that size."

I could tell he was contemplating whether to ask me to open the box and tell him what was in it. If it was something really cool looking, I'd keep it for myself and he'd need to try and pry it from my cold, dead fingers, but if it wasn't what he wanted then he'd be making a risky trip through the gate for nothing, and possibly appear a fool in front of Haagenti. I didn't offer to peek. Why make it easy for him?

"Look." I finally broke the silence. "I've got a lot to do this evening. This box doesn't appear to hold anything that's going to get up and walk away, so just come over here tomorrow sometime and retrieve it. I'll stick around all day, but if I'm away from the house when you get here just watch porn and drink beer until I get back."

I could feel Dar wavering. "Did the guy say anything to you? Anything at all?"

"He apologized for my having to drag my ass to Baltimore on such a horrible day. It fucking sucks outside. Cold rain and wind. I hope it clears up, or gets cold enough to snow soon. Oh, and he told me to have a nice day."

"Okay," Dar said reluctantly. "I'll be there tomorrow as soon as I can sneak past the gate guardian. Do you think you could prevail...?"

"No," I interrupted him. "I refuse to prevail. You want this thing, you find out a way to get it." I hung up the line abruptly. Then I opened the box.

I was curious. Dar had said whatever the artifact was it could change shape, so maybe it was something cool that I'd want to keep for myself. I took off the brown paper and saw a white shiny box with the words "Greetings from Atlantic City" across the top. Removing the cellophane covering, I peeked under the top and laughed. Well, that was just funny. Then I put the top back on and went to get my bird.

By the time I reached Sharpsburg, I was rethinking the appeal of canaries. Sixty minutes of chirping and flapping around in a cat carrier was enough to put me off birds entirely. He was pretty, though, with the deep yellow of his feathers and the structure of his wings. Back home, we all included wings in our forms. It made getting around much easier, and they had a dramatic flair. Feathers were not really practical though. Bat-type wings were flexible, structurally sound, and basic. They were easy to repair and had a nice, menacing look to them. Feathers were too frou-frou, and where some might be able to pull that off, most of us would be teased unmercifully. Angels used feathers. You don't want anyone thinking you aspired to be like them. Still, I thought, they were pretty and soft. Their intricate structure and specialized form held a fascination for me.

I'd never seen an angel's wings. The two angels I'd seen here hadn't included them in their forms. I guess it would not exactly be stealthy to walk around with big-ass wings. The humans would freak. And how would you fit inside doorways and smaller, human-sized spaces? Not very practical. I thought about my wings. I hadn't worn wings since I'd come here, over forty years ago. They were the typical bat-type wings. Rusty red-brown with mottled blue and green swirls, and talons along the ridge and at the bottom edge. It was close to dark. Maybe I'd fly a bit when I was done here. I missed flying.

I waited until the park security had done their closing sweep and left the battlefield before opening the gates and driving down toward Bloody Lane. I needed to get the car closer in, so I plowed through the fencing, four wheeling across the carefully groomed grass and along the dirt path to the wooded copse. The curators would have a fit in the morning. I'd be sure to throw a bunch of empty beer bottles around before I left so they'd blame the vandalism on drunken teens.

I pulled my supplies, including the cat cage with the canary, out of my SUV and walked the three feet to my destination. The Sharpsburg gate stood before me and I did my usual routine of sticking in my hand, etc. before carefully retrieving my bird. Closing my eyes, I plunged my fist with the canary clenched tight into the gate, counted to ten, then withdrew my hand. The bird looked at me cheerfully and chirped, seeming none the worse for wear.

Well. Now was the time to do it and die or not die. I was scared. Really scared. Gregory's words rattled around in my head. Something about how I needed to be more than an imp, and that in the future there would be a scarcity of rocks. I needed to do this.

I tied a rope to my waist and the other end to the bumper of my Suburban. Of course, the gate could disintegrate the rope, or drag the huge SUV in along with me, or kill me so my bloody remains would be found attached to a rope attached to the bumper of my car when the gate spit my mangled body out. I chose instead to pretend that it would be some kind of lifeline to help me find my way back and pull myself out of trouble. I was good at deluding myself.

Taking a deep breath, and keeping a gentle but firm grip on my canary, I stepped through the gate and to the other side. The gate itself was shallow, and I immediately found myself surrounded by nothing and everything. I'm not sure how to describe it. My eyes didn't see anything, my ears didn't hear anything. None of my human senses registered input. It was neither light nor dark. I breathed, but I didn't seem to need to. It was more out of habit.

Closing my eyes, I extended my personal energy to the limits of my form and tried to sense this place directly. Suddenly there was everything. Color, light, sound, smell. Not as a human would perceive though. Back home, the energy saturated everything making the very air feel thick, heavy, and musky. Here the energy felt clean. My mind became sharp and focused and I could see possibilities and alternatives stretching before me like threads intertwining on a three-dimensional map. My body felt slightly itchy and I wanted to remove it like an article of clothing. It was the same feeling I'd had after Gregory and I had done the angel nasty in my house.

I opened my eyes to check on my canary and make sure he hadn't croaked or anything while I was busy exploring this unknown world. He seemed fine, looking around with bright eyes. Suddenly he tweeted, the sound huge and echoing in the vast physical silence of the place. Alarmed, I loosened my grip and the bird flew out of my grasp. Great. Stupid fucking bird had possibly alerted whatever might live here of an alien presence, and now he'd escaped. I'd barely been able to grab him from the confines of the cat carrier, there was no way I could manage to catch him in this place, even though he was clearly visible, a splash of yellow in nothingness.

Panicking, I abandoned the bird and dashed back out the gate to find myself standing with a rope around my middle, a few feet from my Suburban in the dark. That was enough for one night. In fact, that was probably enough for an eternity. I'd lost my bird, and I wasn't sure if I'd be able to explore this gate in the future. What if the bird had alerted any residents of my trespass? Would they be able to follow me back through the gate to this realm? Would they be able to set up traps to catch me if I showed up again? I wish I knew where the hell it led to. An elf could probably tell me. Gregory could definitely tell me. Not that I was going to clue him in on these particular extracurricular activities.

I left the battlefield, determined to give up on this gate forever. I'd need to keep my eyes open for another one to try and examine. The whole experience made me feel depressed, like a failure. Maybe if I flew it would help my mood.

I didn't want to be caught flying around close to my house, so as I left, I drove the back way to reach Dargan's Landing. I was always surprised to see any cars at all parked down at Dargan's Landing. Most people accessed the

Potomac River and the C&O canal towpath at the major spots like Brunswick and Point of Rocks, where there was plenty of parking and easy access from the highway. To get to Dargan's Landing, you had to circle past Brunswick and along the Potomac for miles down twisty narrow country roads, then manage to see the half-hidden sign for yet another narrow wooded road that lead to the parking area. A few people were persistent about finding it, though, as there was a nice boat launch.

I loved it here. It was secluded, and on a lower traffic part of the towpath. The few people you'd see in the parking lot ignored you and minded their own business, whether it was biking, jogging, or fishing. It was an easy jog to the railroad bridge river crossing to Harpers Ferry, and there were lovely views of jagged outcroppings and the churning, muddy Potomac River. I vowed to call Candy this week and have her meet me here for our river run. Maybe we'd do it at night on four feet.

Although the rain had stopped by the time I pulled in, everything, including myself, was still wet and smelling of damp leaf mold. Normally I'd want to climb up and launch a flight from a higher area, like the cliff by the railroad bridge, but here I was sure my take off would be unobserved. I created my wings with a pop from the raw energy I held within myself, as I typically did at home, and flapped to rise majestically into the air. Flapping was all I did. Fucking gravity. This was clearly not going to work.

It took me about an hour of playing with combinations and doing mathematical calculations in my head to come up with something reasonable. The wingspan ended up being fifty feet across, even with partially hollow bones. I had to balance out the extra weight with wingspan and musculature. I also had to alter my spine angle into a curve to support the massive muscles, and extend and strengthen my breastbone to hold the additional chest muscles. I wouldn't win any beauty contests.

I'd opted to keep my arms so I could grab something if I wanted. I daydreamed for a few moments about scooping up anyone unlucky enough to be out walking tonight, like one of those flying monkeys from The Wizard of Oz. Finally satisfied that I could perform a standing take off and maintain a decent flight, I searched for a clearing large enough to accommodate my humongous wings.

Huge as they were, the wings felt glorious after so long without them. I stretched and arched them out, getting the feel for them all over again, then with a run down the boat launch I took flight. Well, I tried to take flight. Vertical takeoff is always hard, and I was carrying a lot of weight. I beat my wings furiously wishing I'd been able to catch an updraft or at least a wind to assist. Sweat beaded on my skin with effort and my feet touched the water as I slowly edged upward.

Once aloft, I was able to take advantage of gentle wind along the river and gain some altitude. The higher, the better. Up high I'd look more like a large bird. A few feet off the Potomac and people would be thinking the dinosaurs had returned. I couldn't resist a quick drop to plunge down under the bridge to Harpers Ferry though. I folded my wings tight against my body and gained speed on the descent, shooting between the bridge supports. Then used my momentum and a burst of energy to help me streak back up into the sky.

I was on my own up high. It was night, after all, and all the nocturnal flying animals were lower down catching bugs and stray rodents for dinner. It was amazing to once again feel the cold damp against my wings, hover while supported by the thermals, and to dance in the winds. I felt free, truly free. Not a bound demon, living under an angel's restrictions in a human world. Not a lowly imp, a cockroach who ran to avoid those who would squash her flat. Free. There was a sense of poignancy about it all, though, as if this were my last moment of freedom before a cage closed in upon me.

I thought about Dar and his annoying problem, that crazy lump of blanket at the abandoned grocery store, Candy, chafing under the thumb of a bunch of bigoted angels, and Gregory. That irritating, controlling asshole that fascinated me. I wondered what his wings looked like, if he ever snuck out and flew. I'd bet he was amazing to watch in the air. I would have liked to fly with him, to try and catch him.

After about an hour of playing around I found myself heading back to Dargan's Landing and my vehicle. I landed beautifully along the boat launch, not even wetting my feet, and walked toward my car with wings still extended. They brushed against tree trunks and I relished the feel of the wet jagged bark against the membranes. There was no one here, and I wanted to enjoy them as long as I could before I dispersed them. My Suburban sat quiet in the dark lot. I stood beside it a few moments then returned myself to my typical human form. It was dark and silent in the autumn night beneath the damp trees, and I felt so lonely. So empty.

CHAPTER 11

yatt and I were fairly late getting back from our ride because I'd had to switch horses midstream. Well, not literally mid-stream, although I certainly looked like I'd been in one.

On a whim, and against Wyatt's strongly worded recommendations, I had saddled up Diablo for what was supposed to be a leisurely ride through the fields. I'd been bucked off before we left the pasture. Within half an hour Diablo had bolted twice, bucked me off four times, and reared six. I'd managed to stay on through the rearing incidents, but the subsequent spinning around had me either on the ground or hanging upside down from the horse's neck. I'd stuck him full of raw energy to try and hold myself on better, but he was quickly able to overcome it and dump me on my rear. I'd been disciplining him with increasing violence and could tell that Wyatt was becoming uneasy. I really needed to force the horse into compliance or he'd become uncontrollable, but I realized the level of injury I'd need to inflict on him was beyond what Wyatt could comfortably witness. Reluctantly, I took the horse back to the stable and saddled up Piper instead.

I tried to enjoy the beautiful fall day, but I kept thinking of how I now needed to spend the afternoon bringing Diablo in line. A lot of hybrids live comfortably as their maternal animal. Maybe they'd be a little temperamental or mean, but they'd still pass. Diablo had so much more to him. He had potential, power, but it was all wasted rattling around unused in a stallion's body. He needed to learn, to explore what he could do and who he could be. Only then would he really be happy. He wasn't just a horse, and it wasn't right to let him go on living a life unrealized. Unfortunately, I'd probably need to wallop the crap out of him to get him on the correct path.

I looked over at Boomer, my hybrid Plott hound, as he trailed after us. He was the same, only he'd been raised since birth with the demons. He'd never experienced living as a dog, confounded by why he was different, trying to appease humans who didn't understand him. I watched him jog along, covering twice the miles as he traversed back and forth to catch intriguing smells. I'd had to lock him down to live here, so he'd remain undetected. It bothered me. I knew it was risky, but it wasn't fair to make him live as just a regular dog. I needed to free him. I just hadn't gotten around to it yet.

The rain had left the fields soft and muddy and I was covered from my frequent falls from Diablo. I managed to stay on Piper, but the occasions when Wyatt led on Vegas sprayed small bits of mud from the horse's hooves onto me. We were both speckled with mud by the time we rode back to the stable, but I was far worse.

I heard Diablo squeal as we dismounted and wondered what was going on. He'd be making that noise a lot this afternoon when I got a hold of him, but there wasn't anything in the barn for him to be fighting with beside the cat. I handed Piper's reigns to Wyatt, dashed in to see what Diablo was up to and saw Dar.

"Mal, this horse is very rude and needs to be taught a lesson in manners. I can't believe you tolerate this level of insubordination."

Dar was in his favorite human guise. I'd seen it before, and he sometimes even assumed it at home. His black hair was silver streaked, and deep blue eyes shone from a tanned face with a sharp nose and full lips. The original human he'd Owned to obtain this form had been portly, but Dar was too vain to walk around with a pot gut and love handles. He did keep some of the weight on the form, though, giving the impression of a powerful man, slightly past his prime and putting on a few extra pounds. Not handsome by conventional standards, but a form that conveyed power. I preferred the young Italian priest he'd picked up in the fifteenth century.

"I just got him Dar. I haven't had much time to work with him since I've been running all over the place on your stupid fucking errands."

He turned and zapped Diablo again. I let him. It would show weakness to come to my horse's defense. It would reveal that I cared enough about the horse to protect it and mean the horse could be used as leverage. It would also demean Diablo by implying that he was too weak to withstand the discipline. Out of the corner of my eye I saw Boomer poke his head in. He took one look at Dar and vanished silently. Smart dog.

"Damned animal, I'll teach you to bare your teeth at me." He readied another bolt of energy. Diablo snorted and zapped him first.

"What the fuck? You cocksucker. Mal, why didn't you tell me you had him storing energy? Fucker just shot me."

I laughed. "Stop messing with him Dar. I'm training him this afternoon and you're going to get him all fired up."

Dar walked over and grabbed a chunk of my hair, tugging at it affectionately. I missed him, too. I hadn't kept in touch with most of my other foster siblings. Dar and I always stuck around though. We kept separate households, but we both relied on each other when the need arose and we enjoyed each other's company most of the time. I felt a sudden longing to tear into him with claws and teeth, to have very violent sex with him, as my kind does. I missed him, and I missed home.

"Could use some help here, Sam," Wyatt snapped as he staggered into the stable loaded down with saddles and bridles.

"Oh, I'm sorry, honey." Out of habit I went to help him and mentally kicked myself as I saw Dar stare in astonishment.

"Mal, you have a toy! A human toy, just as disrespectful as that horse. And here you are jumping to his command. What has happened to you?"

I ignored him and gave Wyatt what I hoped was a significant look. "That's my brother Dar from back home. Just dump the tack here and go on home. I'll call you later."

Wyatt frowned at Dar, clearly not getting the message.

"Oooo Mal, he is cute. And feisty, too. I want to play with your toy." Dar took a few steps toward Wyatt and I moved to stand between them.

Crap. Hospitality with demons demanded sharing, and it was typical to pass around a human to close friends. Sometimes they didn't come back, but it wasn't any big deal. There were billions. Easy to replace a broken toy. I've never been one to share anything, though. And especially not Wyatt.

"I have every intention of welcoming you personally, as I

always do. I would never shuffle that off onto a mere human."

"But I haven't had a human in a long time Mal. He looks reasonably sturdy. I would not Own him or kill him. I won't break him beyond what you can repair. I simply want to enjoy his company for twenty minutes or so. No longer."

Wyatt, thankfully, was remaining silent.

"No Dar. You know I don't share, even with you. And you may not break him, but you'll damage him in ways I cannot fix. I like him how he is. Believe me, you will be more than satisfied with my personal welcome. I haven't been home in over forty years and I have missed my kind. I have missed you."

That seemed to have struck a chord with Dar, who was actually rather sentimental about our relationship. He turned from Wyatt and grabbed my hair again with purpose, yanking me to him.

Unfortunately, that action kicked in Wyatt's knight-in-shining-armor impulse and he reached out to intervene.

"No," I told him sharply. "This is not what you're thinking Wyatt. This is part of my culture, and it's very much a give and take. Go home and I'll call you later."

Wyatt hesitated, his jaw set in that stubborn way that foretold an argument.

"He can watch." Dar's suggestion was halfhearted. His attention was completely on me at this moment, and I intended to keep it that way.

I didn't want Wyatt to see this side of me, and I was worried that he might somehow get hurt in the fray. Demon affection was violent and collateral damage was common.

"Go home," I told Wyatt, trying to put my fledgling suggestion skills into the command. The only thing I'd been practicing was creating intense food cravings, so Wyatt promptly left to go find hot wings. I hoped he had some in his freezer or he'd be driving his rickety old truck all over the countryside to find them.

Dar and I got down to the business of welcoming each other properly with fangs, claws, tongues and bolts of energy. Diablo was a voyeur, watching from his stall, and I hoped the display would make it easier to train him this afternoon. By the time Dar and I were satiated, both of us were torn and dripping blood, saliva, and other bodily fluids. My left shoulder was literally hanging by a tendon and Dar's ribs glistened white among torn flesh. The pain and the pleasure were equal between us. We'd taken care to make this a peer-to-peer welcoming. Casual acquaintances would not have gone so far or for so long, but Dar and I had history. We both basked in the warmth of a deep friendship avowed and renewed. I felt a twinge of guilt over what I was about to do to him. I wondered how much shit he'd be in with Haagenti over this artifact.

"I take back all the derogatory things I was thinking about you, Mal," Dar teased. "I do think you've changed though. I can't tell if it's just the long time you've spent here, holding yourself tight into a human form and human behaviors, or if it's something else. You seem different."

"Trust me, the moment I'm back home, back in a more traditional form, all this will fall away," I assured him.

"And when will this homecoming be?" I could tell my extended vacation hadn't escaped his notice or curiosity.

Before I replied, I fixed myself by whole body conversion. With a crack and a pop, I flew apart all the molecules of my form, holding my personal energy and my store of raw energy close, then collapsed it back using the DNA pattern of Samantha Martin to create a totally uninjured and naked form.

Dar yelled and flung himself across the room panting and looking about wildly.

111

"What?" I stretched my arms upward to flex the muscles. I was perplexed at his reaction. We did this sort of thing all the time at home and he'd never freaked out before.

"Fucking balls, Mal! You'll bring every angel within a hundred miles with that kind of display. We've got to get out of here right now." His voice trailed off as he stared at me. Stared at a specific part of me. "What in hell is that on your arm?"

Damn. I'd forgotten about the tattoo. And I'd been so free with my energy usage the last few months that I'd forgotten how impossible that would normally be for a demon over here.

Dar was suddenly before me grabbing my arm and peering at the tattoo. "It's a brand," I told him reluctantly.

"I can see that." His voice rose with a note of panic. "You told me you weren't bound. Why would you lie about something like that? What bound you? Angels just kill us. Did a sorcerer bind you into service? How long are you to serve him, and what price did he pay? Is Owning him really worth this?"

I relaxed a bit. It would be so much better for Dar to think I'd worked out a deal with a sorcerer than him thinking I was two steps away from enslavement to an angel. I quickly thought about how to work this story, but before I could reply Dar put his finger on the tattoo and pushed his personal energy down into the red-purple.

Instantly he was across the room in a heap, smoking slightly. I, on the other hand, was shaking with anger.

"You fucking rude son of a bitch. Don't you ever assault me in that fashion again or I will kill you outright. I don't care what our relationship is; you do not put yourself inside me. Even if I accept your breeding petition, you will never be allowed that privilege. No one is ever allowed that privilege."

Actually, only the angel had been allowed that privilege to date, and I intended to keep it that way.

Dar scrambled to his feet and had the grace to look somewhat ashamed. "I do apologize Mal. I don't know what came over me to take such a liberty. I only wanted to examine the brand, not show you disrespect or violate you in any way." He paused for a moment. "I still sometimes see you as a little sister, unable to take care of herself. You take great pains to mask your ability and level. I know you can take care of yourself, and this deal you've made with a sorcerer is none of my business. I'll send over a member of my household to your steward for the next five years to compensate you for this affront."

That was very nice of him, and beyond what would have been expected. I was also glad that I'd managed to avoid the potential inquisition regarding my brand.

"I accept," I told him. "I've got the box you came for in the house. I'll get you a beer and a shirt to cover your injuries on the return trip, too."

Dar's face brightened at the thought of finally getting the artifact and I felt that twinge of guilt again. The feeling was most unpleasant. He drank a cold beer and updated me on the latest gossip while I tried to bandage him up with gauze and tape. He was going to return via the Columbia Mall gate and I doubted he'd be able to make it past mall security let alone the gate guardian ripped to shreds and bleeding all over the place. He'd managed to stop the oozing and begin basic repairs by the time I finished. I'd found duct tape worked better than the medical tape. I warned Dar that it would hurt like a bitch pulling it off, so he might want to just do a full body conversion when he returned. Or he might possibly enjoy that sort of thing.

"Then he said 'I wonder what this button does?' and pushed it launching a green fireball across the street into his residence. Blew a hole right in the side of the building and killed a third of his household!" Dar roared with laughter.

I chuckled, but wondered why it wasn't really funny? I didn't feel sorry for the dead household. It's not like I knew any of them, or cared about their lives cut short. Heck, I would have pushed the button, too. That's what buttons are for. This should have been hilarious. Maybe I was still feeling guilty about Dar's box. How much trouble would he be in with Haagenti?

Dar then went on to tell me a story about a couple of young who'd gotten caught sneaking around one of the elven woods by the high lord's scouts. They'd been dipped in honey and hung from the trees along the border of our lands. By the time they were found, they were covered in ants and other insects. One was actually being licked by a raccoon. Everyone thought it was so funny that they left them hang there for a few weeks. People took to coming out and picnicking by the spot to enjoy the view as they ate their meals. I laughed so hard at that story that tears came to my eyes. Feeling much better, more like my old self, I went to get Dar his box.

"Here." I tossed the box at him and wincing at the familiar rocks-in-tissue-paper sound it made as it flew into his hands.

"This is it?" He looked at it, doubt written all over his face.

"Yep." I watched him rip off the paper. "I hope Haagenti doesn't mind. I ate a couple of them. They actually tasted pretty fresh. Not what I'd expected from an artifact, but you know how much chemical preservatives humans put in stuff."

Dar tore off the lid that announced "Greetings from Atlantic City" with an air of doom and stared down inside the box at the colored pieces of salt water taffy.

"Try one," I urged. "They're pretty good, although I don't

know why they had to get them from Atlantic City. They make the same shit in Baltimore or even Ocean City. No need to leave the state to get decent taffy."

He looked up at me, a mixture of fury and desperation in his eyes. "You bitch! I risk myself to come here and you don't even have the artifact. Fucking bitch."

He threw the box of taffy at me. It hit me square in the face, raining the pastel pieces around me onto the floor. I laughed.

"Dar, you always underestimate me. You order me around, badger me to death about this stupid thing. You're the one who made the deal with Haagenti, not me. You don't even tell me what the artifact is, what it looks like. Do you seriously think I'm going to run all over the country like a fucking courier while these vampires laugh at me behind my back?"

"It's a sword," he fumed at me. "The artifact is a sword."

"Of course it is." I sighed. "It's never a magical macramé plant hanger, or a rice bowl of the gods. Why is it always a sword? I'm done Dar. I'm not getting your fucking sword, or Haagenti's fucking sword. The vampires clearly don't want to give it to me. Time for you to think about plan B and leave me alone."

Dar glared at me, and the trickle of guilt was back as I saw panic flash in his eyes. "You bitch, Mal. You of all people. I thought I could rely on you, and you fuck me over. Don't call me if this sorcerer ends up putting you in a bottle. I'm not helping you one bit."

With that, he turned on his heel and left, dramatically spinning tires in the driveway with his rental Honda Accord. The trickle turned into an ache. I frowned and rubbed my chest, hoping that would make it go away. It didn't. I was such a bitch. Dar needed me and once things got inconvenient, I kicked him to the curb. I looked down at the taffy pieces scattered on the floor. It didn't seem so funny now. I felt ashamed. What would Haagenti do to him? Dar seemed tough, but he wasn't really. Not tough enough to hold up to Haagenti's torture.

No. I refused to feel guilty about this. It was his fault, not mine. I'm not responsible for his bad choices and the repercussions of those choices. I'm here to enjoy myself and have fun, not pull his ass out of the fire. Fuck him, fuck Haagenti, fuck the vampires. And fuck that stupid sword, too.

Wyatt was just as pissed. I found him in his house surrounded by take-out boxes with buffalo sauce smudged around his mouth. He glared silently at me. I stifled a laugh because the glare looked really funny with the hot sauce-covered lips. Laughing at Wyatt right now would be a really bad thing.

"I'm so sorry honey." I mopped at him with a napkin. "You don't understand how things get with my kind, and Dar had taken a liking to you. It was easier to deal with him and send him on his way without you there to distract him."

"I ate three dozen hot wings," Wyatt thundered. "It's bad enough that you dismiss me like I'm some flunky, like some toy, but I drove to three different places to get different styles of hot wings, then came back here to eat them. I still want more. There is no way I can possibly fit more in my stomach, but I can't shake this need to eat more of them."

I must have put too much into it. Maybe when someone cared about you and was open to pleasing you, there didn't have to be such force behind the suggestion. I wondered if I could have driven him to eat himself to death. I think it was possible to do that. I think I saw it in a CSI episode once.

"I'm sorry, Wyatt. I was trying to get you out of there as quickly as possible so you'd be safe. You don't know what Dar is capable of."

That made him pause. "Are you okay, Sam?" He looked

me over for damage. "Is he so much more powerful that you need to let him rape you to keep him from killing you or me?"

I snorted, unable to hold back a laugh at that one. "No, we're fairly even on the power scale. It's not rape, Wyatt. It's like when you kiss or hug close friends and family to greet them after you haven't seen them in a while."

Wyatt looked disgusted. "I don't greet my sister by yanking on her hair and having sex with her. That's... It's just gross. I know he's probably not your genetic brother, but you guys still grew up together."

"Our relationships are very different. I don't expect you to understand, or approve, but you need to know when to get out of the way for your own safety. We get caught up in things, and you are very fragile."

Wyatt clearly didn't like the idea that I regarded him as "fragile," but too fucking bad. He needed to take this seriously. Humans might be hesitant to kill, Ted Bundy aside, but my kind wouldn't bat an eyelid. They'd rip him to shreds with great glee.

"I'm sorry I did this to you, treated you this way," I murmured, gathering him close. "Let me show you how sorry I am."

Wyatt stiffened, and not in a good way. I pulled back to look at him and saw a mix of revulsion and anger on his face.

"No, Sam. I'm still mad at you. You do this all the time to me, shunt me off to the side with some excuse of how fragile I am. I'm sick of it." He pushed me away.

"You are fragile," I protested. "One blast, one rake of a claw and you'd be dead. I can't stand the thought of losing you. You have no idea how horrible it is to worry about someone's safety all the time. It's not very demonic of me. It's very unsettling. I have this terrible need to make sure you're not killed."

117

Wyatt stared at me for a moment. I could see the anger draining from him, but the sadness that took its place didn't make me feel any better.

"Sam, I do know what it's like to worry about someone all the time. I worry about you. I did all through the incident with the werewolves this summer and I still do. It's what happens when you care about someone. It doesn't mean I try to wrap you up in cotton and protect you from life. I trust that you're competent enough to take care of yourself. I wish you felt the same about me."

I didn't know how to reply to that. I had a bad feeling things weren't good between us right now and it scared the piss out of me.

"Go home, Sam." Wyatt ran a sauce-smeared hand through his hair. "It's okay. Really. I'll catch up with you tomorrow sometime."

I went home, feeling shitty. I just wanted to crawl into bed, but there was a horse to train.

At least the training with Diablo went well. My other two horses were grazing in the pasture where Wyatt had turned them out prior to walking in on Dar and me. Diablo still stood in his stall. He eyed me nervously as I came in. I ignored him for a while, cleaning and putting away the tack from our morning ride, then cleaning out the other stalls, placing fresh hay and water in each. By the time I finished, Diablo was staring at me intently, following my every move with his gaze. I walked over to him and placed a hand on his nose, letting my energy trickle through him in a caress.

"I'm proud you stuck up for yourself with Dar," I told him. "Dar likes to mess with mine. It makes him feel like he has a closer tie to me than those in my own household. See how Boomer took off? He knows better than to stay around and let Dar torment him. You could hardly have avoided him, trapped in this stall. In cases like this it's acceptable to use as much force as you need to defend yourself. I'll jump in to bail you out if you truly need it."

Diablo flicked his ears and pushed his nose against my hand.

"You need to learn though. There are bigger demons than Dar, and they won't hesitate to rip you apart one tiny piece at a time. You can go back to the way you were before, a nasty horse destined for slaughter at human hands, or you can put yourself in my household and be so much more."

The horse swished his tail. I could see he was nervous, that he didn't trust easy. I didn't blame him, it was hard to trust a demon, even with a household bond.

"I will reward your loyalty. If you don't show me loyalty then I won't be there for you when you need me most. You don't mean that much to me right now. Show me loyalty, show me how amazing you really are, and I may begin to care. Over time, I may care a lot."

The horse's eyes registered comprehension. He nudged my hand again with his nose.

"Good. Let's get to work then. I need you to know what I expect from you."

By early evening I was beginning to think Diablo was a valuable acquisition. I'd lunged him and he'd proven to be sound in all his paces as expected. Then I saddled up, hoping Wyatt didn't see me riding this monster out alone, and headed through the fields. Diablo was easy to stay balanced on with the chunks of raw energy driven into him. He shifted their anchor points as we moved, ensuring that I remained in optimal position during the ride.

We flew over coops and downed trees, launched over four foot fences, and rocketed through the countryside. Diablo's hooves tore up huge chunks of the wet ground, but he never slipped once. He was sure-footed as we raced through the leaf-strewn woods, and pivoted around trees. I suddenly knew how the Elves must feel, so connected and at one with their horses. I'd spent so much time falling off, that I never realized how wonderful the experience of riding could be. True, I Owned a horse and it was very enjoyable to race around on four hooves, but being carried was amazing. It was a kind of sharing that I hadn't experienced before.

Done with the equine part of Diablo's evaluation, I began putting raw energy into him to store. He gladly accepted it, but didn't seem to know what to do with the stuff. Reaching in, I showed him how to increase his muscle mass, change his physical self for optimal speed. I could feel his joy at his increased ability.

Heading out of the woods, I urged Diablo to use the energy I'd put in him. "Let's blow something up." I gently guided the energy he held into a blast that exploded a nearby boulder. He leapt to the side in momentary panic as chunks of pulverized rock filled the air. In seconds I was on the ground and my horse was gone. Vanished. I must have momentarily blacked out, because I didn't remember him running anywhere. It was like he just disappeared.

I looked up at the sky for a moment, wondering how many miles I'd need to walk to get home, when a nose appeared before my face. I really must have hit harder than I thought. I hadn't even heard him coming back. I was grateful that I wouldn't have to hoof it back on my own though.

It took me a few moments to find another rock to stand on so I could climb back in the saddle, which gave Diablo a chance to calm down. He took some convincing before he was willing to accept that the rocks were not going to suddenly explode, and that the destructive energy was something he could control. I helped him blow up a few small rocks, then urged him to do it on his own, thinking that the log ahead of us would be a good target.

The horse shot out a bolt of energy, but instead of incinerating the log, he arched it around a tree and exploded a hiding buck. Deer bits flew everywhere. I laughed and patted Diablo with approval. At least this part of my day had gone well. I could leave Diablo with a small store of raw energy, in case he needed to defend himself. Hopefully he wouldn't blow up the barn with it.

It was dusk by the time we returned to the barn. I gave Diablo a good rub down and some extra grain in his bucket, then brought in the other two horses for the evening. My improved mood was fading with the day's light. This was the first time I'd done the barn chores in months. Wyatt had always done them for me, but he was nowhere to be seen. I wondered how long he would avoid me. I hated when we fought. Hated him being mad at me. I felt guilty about Wyatt, guilty about Dar, and all the amazing demon horses in the world couldn't erase that guilt.

CHAPTER 12

The plumber grunted like an irritated pig. I didn't blame him since the bathroom was rather small and he was balled up on his side, wedged in the tiny space between the toilet and the sink. I watched from the hall along with three other sets of interested eyes. There was more grunting, and the guy wiggled on the floor like a fat caterpillar, his buttocks and crack bursting from his pants in a stereotypical fashion. Mrs. Perez winced. I wasn't sure if she was wincing because of the unavoidable eyeful of ass she and two of her four children were receiving, or if she was contemplating the doubtful cleanliness of her floor. With four boys living in the house, I was sure the plumber was squirming around on at least a few days buildup of urine from careless aiming.

"I'm so sorry to bother you with this Ms. Martin," she apologized again. "I kept plunging and even snaked it out, but it just isn't flushing properly. This is our only toilet and with the kids, well, you know." Her voice trailed off, embarrassed.

Yes, I'm sure the kids shit blocks of cement. Kids do.

122

There was a bent hanger strategically placed beside the plunger next to the toilet to assist in reducing excrement to a manageable size and forcing it down the sewage system. As much a fan as I was of modern plumbing, things were easier when everyone just crapped in a hole in the ground. At least you were sure the shit was going down. Now you had to eyeball it and do quick mathematical calculations to determine whether it was going to narrowly squeeze through the toilet opening, foolishly designed for rabbit turds, or spill out all over your floor in a flood of sewage while you frantically tried to turn the fucking water off.

"Batman clogged the toilet," the youngest child told me confidently. He'd made this claim several times. He looked to be about five or six. I wondered if Batman was a nickname for one of the older boys or his imaginary friend.

"Shut up Angelo," said the older boy. "I think it was Miguel," he told me, referring to one of his older, teenaged brothers. "He never eats his vegetables, and Mama told him this would happen."

Mrs. Perez looked mortified and hastily sent the boy into the kitchen on an errand. She and the four boys had lived in this two-bedroom apartment for five years now. When she'd first moved in there had been a husband. The adults had slept on a fold-out bed in the living room and the kids doubled up in the tiny bedrooms. The husband had been gone for a few years now. I wasn't sure if he was in jail, deported, or just run off to escape the responsibility of four growing children. The matriarch of the family didn't seem to even notice his absence. I knew she worked three jobs, and although she was occasionally late on her rent, she always caught up quickly and paid the fees. I rather liked her and her gutsy children. Especially this little one who looked at me with such bold, dark eyes.

"Spiderman can't keep us safe from the bad man who cuts

off ears," he told me somberly, waving the plastic superhero he clutched in his hand. "The green cat with six legs captured Batman and is torturing him, but there is no one to protect us from the ear man."

"I don't know what Miguel has been letting him watch on TV," Mrs. Perez lamented. It's no wonder he's waking up with nightmares, all this talk about ears being cut off and torturing."

"I will keep you safe," I assured the little boy. "I won't let anyone cut off your ears. Ear man quakes in fear at the mention of my name. You tell him I'm coming for him." Maybe that would help this cute little kid sleep at night.

The plumber struggled to his feet and heaved the toilet from the floor, laying it on its side in the tiny bathroom. The smell of raw sewage wafted up from the exposed pipe. Shining a flashlight, he peered down into the depths.

"The ear man took Patsy. He took Pancake Joe. Soon he'll start taking us, too."

"Angelo," Mrs. Perez scolded.

She shook her head at me. "A couple of the local homeless have gone missing. It happens. They wind up in jail, their families stick them in rehab, or they find another spot and move. I don't know where he is getting this fantastic story of someone nabbing them and cutting off their ears."

"The cat told me," Angelo insisted. "The green cat with six legs. She sees everything. She is a ghost."

A ghost cat. And an ear-obsessed serial killer that would put Ted Bundy to shame. Human children had the best imaginations.

Angelo turned to me. "Will you really protect us? Protect me? I don't want him to cut off my ears." Faith shone from his dark eyes.

Something roared from deep inside me and the world narrowed to nothing but the trust in those dark eyes. His life was in my hands. I'd just vowed it. Mine. He was mine and I trembled with fury at the thought that another would dare try and take what I claimed.

I shook my head to try and rid myself of the feeling. I'd lied so he'd feel safe and not have nightmares. It was a lie, not a vow. I was a demon. It's not like I was going to start beating up playground bullies all over town, let alone go chasing down a ghost and some guy with an ear fetish.

"A-ha," exclaimed the plumber triumphantly, forestalling any further conversation on this intriguing serial killer, the extra-limbed feline ghost, and my personal responsibility to defend the city.

The plumber was bent over the toilet, flashing us at least fifty percent of his posterior as he yanked on something stuck within the labyrinth depths of the porcelain bowl. Finally, with a large amount of jiggling flesh, he withdrew a twisted black object.

"I do not want to piss off the six-legged, green cat ghost if this is her idea of torture," I commented, staring at the mangled plastic Batman figure.

Angelo squealed and rushed to grab the toy. "You saved him! Batman has escaped."

"Oh no!" His mother held him back by his shirt collar. "We are throwing that thing away. Unfortunately, Batman did not survive his torture of being drowned in pee and poop."

Her pronouncement triggered a flood of tears from Angelo who threw himself on the ground, devastated at the tragic loss of such a heroic character. Faced with such inconsolable grief, Mrs. Perez had the plumber place Batman in an old saucepan where he would be hopefully boiled clean. Or perhaps forgotten long enough to obtain a replacement.

Pale with the thought of the cost, Mrs. Perez assured me she would pay for the plumbing fee since this clearly fell under her lease as a repair she was liable for. I had no intention of sending her the bill. Such entertainment was well worth the money. I even slipped Angelo a twenty to assist with the costs of Batman's recovery. He'd certainly need a good therapist after that ordeal.

I was so happy to see Wyatt in my kitchen when I'd arrived home. He wrinkled his nose at me when I went to greet him.

"Sorry. Batman lodged in a toilet. Very fragrant rescue."

"Do you want to grab a shower?" He sounded funny, like he had a secret and was trying to be casual so as to not give it away. I didn't care; I was thrilled to see him after our argument. "I brought some lunch over for us. And your brother has been ringing your mirror off the wall."

Sure enough the red light was frantically blinking. A nagging worry chewed in my gut as I pushed the button.

"Mal, will you try again to get this artifact for me? Haagenti scheduled another meeting. It's in Atlantic City, and we'll arrange a nice hotel for you and some comps. You and your toy can go and have fun fucking and gambling, so it won't be a waste of your time. I really need this favor. Call me back."

Dar sounded subdued. It bothered me.

"Atlantic City?" Wyatt put Styrofoam containers on my table. "There's a gaming tournament there next week I was thinking of doing. Maybe we can combine the two trips? It could be fun."

I ran up to take a shower and think about it. Wyatt seemed amenable, and I really wanted to get back into his good graces.

"When is your tournament?" I asked as I came downstairs from my shower. "I do want to go. We can drive up in the Corvette and enjoy the comps and nice luxury hotel suite.

You can do your tournament, and I'll get business done, and we'll have some fun, too."

Wyatt told me the dates, and, with a sly smile, handed me a plate. It was loaded with hot wings.

"I love hot wings." I laughed.

"Good thing since it will probably take me a week to get over this craving you've forced on me. I figured if I was going to have a steady diet of them, you should share in my misery."

I looked at the table. He had buffalo style, a dry rub selection, barbeque, and one that looked like it had a Thai sauce on it. Nothing else. Just hot wings. I grabbed him and kissed him, trying to balance my plate in the one hand, relieved that he was seeing the humor in this. I appreciated that he never stayed mad at me long, never held a grudge, always came back. He was my favorite human. Ever. I loved Wyatt. No, no I didn't. Demons don't love. It was probably just gas or something.

We ate the wings and discussed the tournament in Atlantic City. This one involved a military shooting game with aliens. I hoped Wyatt wouldn't be at a disadvantage since he primarily only killed zombies. We packed the leftover wings in the fridge, and I told Wyatt that I liked the dry rub ones so much I would eat them cold for breakfast the next morning.

Then I called Dar.

"Mal." The relief in his voice was palpable. "The meeting is in Atlantic City this Saturday."

"Nope, it's not." I could actually feel his panic through the distance at my words. "I have plans this weekend." I gave him the dates for Wyatt's gaming tournament and told him to let Haagenti know that the meeting would need to be rescheduled for one of those two days. "And there is a price. There are two things I want beyond the hotel room and the comps if I'm to do this."

"I'll ask Haagenti, but I can't speak for him." Dar was very nervous and it definitely worried me.

"What I want has nothing to do with Haagenti. First, I want you to place your household underneath mine for the next two hundred years. Effective immediately."

There was silence. I knew I'd insulted him. To put his household under the control of mine would be to announce to all demons that he considered me significantly above him in the hierarchy. He would, in effect, be bowing down before me in subservience. Normally this kind of bold request would have Dar frothing at the mouth, screaming obscenities at me, and threatening me with bodily harm. The silence on the line meant that he was far enough up shit creek that he was weighing the benefit of my protection against the humiliation this action would cause him.

Folding his household under mine would mean that Haagenti would need to go through me before pummeling Dar. Not that I would be much deterrent to one of Haagenti's level, but it would be a distraction and possibly buy Dar time to pull his ass out of the fire. Besides, I was over here indefinitely, and Haagenti could do little but verbally harass me and mine until I returned. Or he could come here and beat my ass. I was betting that he wouldn't cross the lines to come get me. And if he did, I was betting that I could run and hide behind an angel. If the fucker would bother to come to my rescue.

"Mal, I…" Dar hesitated.

"Immediately," I interrupted him. "And tell Haagenti that any future requests he makes of you need to be made to me through my steward. It's appropriate protocol. Also tell him if he has a problem, he can come over here and kiss my lily-white ass."

"I hate you, Mal." There was relief in Dar's voice. "I hate you."

"I hate you too, Dar," I told him affectionately.

"Cut the fucking love fest and let me know what your other demand is," Dar ordered in a more cheerful tone.

"I want a hunt. I want permission from the vampires to hunt in their territory without reprisal."

I had desperately needed to kill something for a long time. I was longing to Own again too, but the urge to kill was strongest right now. The hunt for Althean this summer had been fun, but rather unsatisfactory since I hadn't gotten to kill him myself. Gregory had forbidden me to kill as part of the price I paid for remaining here, so I hadn't done anything since then. The need had been gnawing on me for months and was beginning to occupy more than its usual share of my thoughts. If I didn't hunt soon, I'd be more liable to kill someone accidentally on purpose. I'd heard the vampires were willing to orchestrate a kill and carefully cover it up. There was probably a price. I'd let Haagenti pay the price.

"I don't think that will be a problem, as long as you limit the number. They are probably not going to give the nod to you collapsing a building on three hundred people, but they'll be okay with a targeted kill of their choosing."

"Tell them no fish in a barrel, and no sheep." I didn't want an easy, boring kill. I needed something that would fight back.

"Got it." Dar signed off, and I turned to see Wyatt looking at me warmly. I was really feeling the love today.

"He's in trouble, and you're protecting him. I'd expect a demon to refuse to help, to abandon him and even laugh at his plight."

"Dar has been a good ally in the past. Having his household in mine will bring increased status to me, and they'll be very useful. I'm not being altruistic here. Besides, Haagenti is a total ass. Even though he'll mop the floor with me when I eventually return, I'll really enjoy taunting him from over here."

"Don't give me that." Wyatt smiled. "You were outraged this summer over how the angels were treating the were-wolves, and now you've jumped into the line of fire to protect your brother from this Haagenti bully. You're the demon hero, Sam."

I wasn't sure whether he was teasing me or not. All I knew was that I was not hero material. Ick.

"Are you going to let me help?" Wyatt asked. "Am I just going to be eye candy in Atlantic City, or do I get play too?"

"It's not just the vampires, Wyatt," I told him. "It's demons, too. What I just did is going to cause a shit storm of trouble. Haagenti is going to send people to get me, and they won't care if you get killed. In fact, they might deliberately kill you or use you as a hostage to get me to go with them."

"I shot an angel for you, Sam. What do I need to do to prove myself to you?" Wyatt was getting angry. Here we go again.

"Yeah, and I admire the balls it took to do that, but what mistakes did you make? What should you have done?"

Wyatt looked at me in surprise and considered the question.

"Well, I should have had more distance between us, so he couldn't grab me, although I'll bet he's pretty fast, so I'm not sure how much distance. It's not like I could use a sniper rifle from a mile away in that situation."

"And?" I prompted.

Wyatt sighed. "I should have unloaded the weapon on him. I just shot once and paused to see if it was enough."

"Not just unloaded the weapon. You needed to beat the fucking shit out of him with the empty gun, grabbed what-ever was nearby without turning your back on him and kept going until he was a smear of red. Then thrown salt on the smear and burned it." I had no idea if that would work. I was just trying to impress on him the need for extreme force."

"You're right," Wyatt admitted. "You'd think with all the zombies I've killed I'd know this by now."

"Okay. Let's say you're home and Dar knocks on your door. He's looking for me and I'm not home. What do you do?"

"I call you and tell you that your brother is looking for you?"

"He makes you feel uncomfortable, but he smiles and asks to wait inside your house for me. You might let him in. You sit here now and say 'no way,' but you were brought up to be polite and he's my brother so you might let him in. You might let him get so close that it's too late to do anything when he grabs you. I come home to you broken on the floor, and Dar so sorry that he got carried away."

"What should I do, Sam? Just shoot him on the doorstep?" Wyatt's tone was sarcastic, but he was right.

"Yes, exactly. Have your gun when you answer the door and shoot him. Tell him to go back to my house and wait or you'll blow his head off. He'll whine and you'll feel guilty, but you'll be alive."

"Seriously?"

"Seriously. Demons don't like to take too much damage over here because fixing it sends out an energy signature that alerts angels of their presence. He'll weigh the risks of taking huge damage and being dusted by an angel against the enjoyment of taking you apart and decide it's not worth it. But you can't just threaten. You've got to show that you are able and willing to carry it out by shooting him first."

Wyatt nodded. "What else do I need to know?"

"We'll talk more about plans and scenarios this week before we go," I told him. "The good news for me is that

Haagenti's goons won't be going for my death unless they feel they are in mortal danger, so the key is to avoid capture and annihilate them quickly before they decide they need to kill or be killed."

"So are we partners?" Wyatt smiled.

He was going to get killed. He was a cute, smart, gutsy human with weapons, and he was going to get killed.

"Partners," I affirmed.

Wyatt walked over and kissed me thoroughly, wrapping his hands around my waist and pulling me against him. "Weren't you going to apologize to me in a very special way for making me gorge myself on chicken wings? I'm ready for that apology now."

I apologized for a good hour. It was the best apology I'd ever delivered, if I may say so myself. Wyatt seemed to think so, too.

CHAPTER 13

*H*ere I was, once again, wandering Columbia Mall. Dar had not had an easy time returning home after our encounter and begged me to help him get through the gate this trip so he could deliver a bribe for the vampires. It seems Haagenti hadn't originally been thorough in his research, and vampire custom required a gift be given in exchange for handing over the artifact. I wasn't convinced the lack of gift was the reason they'd been running me all over the place, but was intrigued to see what Haagenti's idea of a suitable present would be. Dar was to deliver this gift to me, I was to take it up to Atlantic City, attend a meeting with some bigwig vampire, exchange the bribe/gift for the artifact they supposedly didn't want and were eager to unload, then return home and await pick-up from either Dar or one of Haagenti's minions.

I was contemplating refusing to allow Haagenti to use Dar to pick up the sword. It would be great fun to have Haagenti tear around at the last moment trying to find a courier willing to cross the lines for him, one that he could trust not to snag the sword and run for the hills. He'd probably also want to find one sufficiently high enough up to smack me around a bit while over here. He was furious that I'd protected Dar from him, and absolutely livid that I kept insisting he direct all his communication through my steward. That was the sort of thing for those below, and Haagenti was far above me in the hierarchy. Normal protocol would have him delivering messages via his flunkies straight to me, not him personally dealing with my steward.

Although my steward was enjoying all the drama, he'd warned me that I was in for a bad time of it as soon as I returned. He strongly advised I immediately take Ahriman up on his offer in the breeding petition, not only to protect myself and my household, but to further put Haagenti's nose out of joint. I'd thought with satisfaction of Ahriman's petition, defaced with the dark ink and an angel's vehement opinion. I'd just have to endure Haagenti's wrath upon my return because I didn't plan on accepting Ahriman's offer. Of course, I didn't tell my steward that. It's always good to keep an alternative on the back burner, just in case things get desperate.

I'd parked in the deck this trip and meandered my way around the mall enjoying some shopping time while Dar anxiously cooled his heels. After adding a few items to my shopping stash, I finally found the gate. It was in the shoe section of Nordstrom's. I checked out the fall boots and pumps while I looked for the gate guardian. The shoe section was always packed, so it wasn't easy to pick her out. I was thinking of trying on an awesome pair of royal blue leather platform pumps when I spotted her.

Instead of the gaudily dressed old lady, this time she was a twenty-something professional with a nicely tailored gray pants suit and white tank top. As I walked toward her, she swiveled, identifying my race, and honed in for the kill. Checking herself before she'd taken two steps, she paused and frowned in exasperation, then continued to walk toward me at a more leisurely pace, looking me over, top to bottom.

"Go ahead." She waved toward the gate. "I have no idea if this was supposed to be a onetime thing or not. Typical with these high ups. They give me vague instructions, and I am never sure exactly what they mean. I'm just going to assume you have an eternal pass at this gate to come and go as you please. No more worms though. Just you."

"I'm not going through." I showed her the shopping bags. "I'm picking up a few things, and thought I'd stop and see if you wanted lunch."

She looked at me as if I were insane.

"You stopped by while shopping to ask me to lunch?"

"You do get a lunch break, don't you? I know your boss is a total slave-driving asshole, but I assume you still get occasional breaks. If not, then you need to think about organizing. There really should be a gate guardian's union. I'll bet the Teamsters would fold you guys into their group. Their roles are getting kind of light lately."

"You want me to go to lunch with you? Accompany you somewhere and join you in consuming food?"

"Sweet and sour pork?" I had a feeling that might be the magic word. Or magic set of words.

The guardian looked hungrily at me. Actually, she looked like a junkie about to score. Glancing around, she nodded.

"Okay, but I can't be long."

I followed her out of the Nordstrom entrance and into the mall, weaving around the racks of shirts and pants. Once into the mall, I moved up to walk abreast so we could chat.

"Do you always assume female forms?" I asked her as we walked through the mall toward the food court at the opposite end. "I've never seen you as a man."

"Trust me," she replied. "It is so much easier to be female when guarding a gate in a shopping mall. If you're a male and the gate is in the little girls' clothing section, or lingerie, or worse, by the kiddy carousel, then mall security is busting you before noon. They all think you're some kind of pedophile. Heck, even if the gate is in the men's section, they think you're a pervert looking to score. It's so much easier as a female. Females buy stuff for everyone in their family, boyfriends, brothers, kids. Women can spend all day at a mall and no one will suspect them of anything illegal or immoral. No one thinks you're going to snatch their kid, or peep at them trying on jeans if you're a female."

"Makes sense."

"Yeah, well I had to learn it the hard way. Angels don't pay any attention to these kinds of subtle details, so we go into these assignments blind and have to stumble around until we learn enough to do our job. The whole time, the Ruling Council reps are down our throats, threatening us every time something goes wrong or a demon gets through. We don't get to train our replacements either. They switch us around on gates or yank us home and slap a new guardian in here to make the same mistakes all over again."

"Have you said anything to your boss about this?" I felt sorry for her. No wonder we managed to pop back and forth with relative ease. Fucking management disaster.

"Yeah, my boss is such a warm, benevolent, caring type," she replied, her voice sarcastic. "He's part of the Ruling Council. He doesn't give two cents about my difficulties. I'm just supposed to do my job perfectly, and if I can't, that's my fault."

"He is an arrogant asshole." I might be obsessed with the guy, but I did recognize his failings.

We walked all the way through the mall to the food court, and stepped up to the vendor selling thick, goopy messes of American-style Chinese food. I got a couple egg rolls and ordered the sweet and sour pork for the guardian. The guy behind the counter frowned at my companion.

"No. I'm not giving you extra sauce. I'm not giving you sweet and sour pork either. You can have fried rice."

The guardian looked like she were about to vault the counter and perform a smack-down on the guy. I've been here over forty years though and I know how to handle these kinds of things. Taking out a fifty, I tossed it at him.

"Give us our order and three sauces and you can keep the fifty as a tip. She's with me."

The guy shoved the fifty in his pocket and promptly served up the food as the guardian danced in glee. It was rather disconcerting to see a professional business woman hopping around like that.

We sat down and the gate guardian proceeded to slurp sauce from one of the pint sized soup containers the guy had put it in. The stuff looked disgusting. It was that semi-gelatinous red stuff that is all to do with sweet and nothing to do with sour. Yuck. Sweet and sour sauce was so much better in China where it was brown and actually sour. Now that was something I missed. I hadn't been in China in over fifty years.

"Gregory tried to fix the brand mark," I mentioned casually. I really wanted her opinion on it.

She looked confused for a moment. "Oh you mean my boss? His name's not really Gregory." She continued to slurp the red sauce, ignoring the chicken nugget looking bits of pork that were supposed to accompany it. "Grigori is what he's in charge of. He runs the cleanup operation; he's in charge of the Watchers."

"What is the Grigori?"

She paused a moment, wiping the red from around her mouth and licking it off of her fingers before stuffing her face into the container again. I reached for a pork nugget and she smacked my hand, flashing her pointy teeth at me. Okay then.

"The original Grigori, the Watchers, were composed mostly the tenth choir of Angels. They were to deliver the gifts of Aaru to the humans so they could begin their evolution toward perfection."

Tenth choir? The angels had nine orders, also known as choirs just as we had nine orders or Circles. When was there ever a tenth one?

"The elves had evolved in accordance with their gifts. We'd considered vampires, but it was decided that they were not worthy. The angels thought that humans would achieve more and be more pure than even the elves were.

I stifled a laugh. The elves were far from pure.

"Of course, you demons disagreed and hadn't wanted the humans to have the gifts of Aaru. That disagreement plus your vulgar insistence on experiencing a corporeal form to every degree fueled the war. You demons wallow like pigs in the physical, reveling in every filthy nuance of it. You claim that is the way toward enlightenment."

She shuddered in disgust even as she reveled in the filthy delights of her sauce.

"After the war with the demons ended and you were banished from Aaru, the plan went forward to deliver the gifts to the humans. Two high angels were sent along to supervise the Tenth choir. One was a Seraph. A Seraph," she told me as if I should share in appreciation of this fact that one from the highest order was supervising the event.

She started in on the second container of sauce, glancing around and leaning in as if to impart juicy gossip.

"In order to exist here, we must all assume a corporeal form, but the longer we are flesh, the more we are subject to temptation and sin. Back then, everyone assumed the angels were too strong to fall."

Her face disappeared for a moment into the container, only to emerge with thick red sauce smeared around her mouth and nose. I think she was getting drunk on the stuff. Her eyes were not focusing well and she was being pretty free with information.

"Disaster." She slurped a mouthful from the container. "The Watchers were corrupted by the flesh. They revealed secrets of Aaru far beyond what they should have, driving human evolution at a greater speed than they can handle. Plus they took human sexual partners and produced hybrid offspring – the Nephilim."

She looked disgusted. As if she had room to condemn with her gluttonous consumption of sweet and sour sauce. Then she leaned in even further, looking around as if we might be overheard by someone who cared.

"It went unnoticed for a very long time because the two high ones had also fallen into ways of the flesh. Once all this came to light, the situation had disintegrated to the point that the Ruling Council had the Angels of Vengeance step in."

She started on the third container after running her tongue around the inside of the second to ensure it was squeaky clean.

"The biggest problem was that the knowledge given to the humans could not be recalled. They are ruined. Maybe they never should have been offered gifts from Aaru at all. Their spirit is too much imbedded in their flesh, and they cannot be expected to rise above it. We should have left them as animals. It's too late now to do anything about that, so I personally think we should just destroy them all and start over."

That was pretty harsh. They were the ones who fucked it all up after all. Maybe there should be a clean sweep in Aaru instead. Assholes.

"So where does your boss come in?"

"He is in charge of those who are here trying to correct the problem. The second Grigori. So basically, he is the head Grigori. They watch the evolution of the humans. They normally don't interfere, but if the humans get too far off their proper evolutionary path, he and the Watchers will wipe them all out."

I felt chilled. No one should have that kind of authority. Who was he, or this stupid Ruling Council, to judge an entire race of beings? I really wanted to continue this conversation, but her eyes were so unfocused that if she didn't weigh in on my brand soon, she wouldn't be able to even see it.

I slid my arm out of my jacket and showed her the tattoo. She looked at it closely and dissolved in laughter. I thought red stuff might come out her nose.

"Oh, that must irritate him so much, that pious, high and mighty, judgmental snob. To have bound himself to a demon. What a total disaster. Such irony." She smacked her forehead on the table, laughing.

What? He wasn't the one with the tattoo. What did she mean? She must be totally drunk off gooey sauce and not thinking clearly.

"What does it do? I know what it was intended to do, but what does it really do?"

The only answer was snoring. She'd passed out face down with empty containers of sweet and sour sauce scattered around her. Crap. Should I just leave her here?

I went up to the Chinese food guy. "What do you guys do with her when she does this?" I handed him another fifty.

He sighed pocketing the money. "I'll let her sleep it off and get her a few liters of Mountain Dew for when she wakes up. That's why we don't let her have extra sauce. This happens every time."

I thought it was funny that he recognized her no matter what form she took, and that her changing appearance didn't seem to bother him. I guess the long-term workers here at the mall had just learned to accept these things. I thanked the guy, apologized for the inconvenience, then walked back to the gate at Nordstrom's.

"What took you so long?" Dar snarled. He looked rather out of place milling about the women's shoe section. I totally understood what the gate guardian had been saying about males in the mall.

"I was having lunch with the gate guardian. It would have been very rude to run out in the middle of our conversation."

Dar stared. "I knew it."

He thrust a small flat box at me. "Use this in exchange for the artifact. Only give it to the master vampire. Don't waste it on some flunky, or sell it on eBay."

Dar was getting a bit bossy. He must be stressed, even with the umbrella of my protection. I opened the box. Little vials of blood nestled in silk were neatly lined up in a row.

"Where the fuck did you get elf blood?" I looked closely at one of the vials. "No, forget I asked. I don't want to know."

I couldn't see any elf volunteering to be a blood donor, and I really didn't want to know if he or Haagenti had assaulted or killed one. They didn't take that kind of thing lightly and I didn't want to be in a position where I'd need to choose between my relationship with a high lord and Dar. He might be a shit, but he was my foster brother and we'd been through a lot together.

"Try to stay out of Haagenti's way. I'll contact you when I get back from Atlantic City – which is not this weekend." I emphasized the timeline so he didn't bug the crap out of me when I hadn't even left yet.

Dar turned to go and paused for a second. "I don't know what is going on with you, Mal, with this sorcerer, and the gate guardian, and your unbelievably ballsy taunting of Haagenti. I hope you know what you're doing. I hope when all the shit you've thrown up in the air lands, it lands in some beneficial fashion."

"Thanks Dar," I said as he popped through the gate.

I glanced longingly at the blue platform pumps, but I had a box of elf blood in my purse, and I really wanted to get in a jog and think about what the gate guardian had told me before Michelle came over tonight for our pre-Halloween girls' night in. The pumps would have to wait.

CHAPTER 14

J was about three miles into my jog when out of nowhere I was slammed against a tree by my shoulders and held there. I had no idea what hit me, so I instinctively shot a bolt of lightning into the thing grabbing me. The only reaction I got was to be banged against the tree trunk a few times.

"There is a dead bird in the fourth circle." Gregory's voice was ominous.

I didn't have to feign surprise. What the hell was he talking about? Was this some secret agent code? Should I respond cryptically that the brown bull tap dances in May? Instead I just looked at him blankly and wondered why he was so angry?

He banged me against the tree a few more times, as if he was trying to smack the answer out of me.

"So we're back to violence now, are we?" I asked him. "What happened to Make-Me-A-Sandwich Angel? I liked him better."

That bought me a whack against the tree that practically

knocked me unconscious. For a moment, there were two of him in my vision. Not a reassuring sight.

"Why a dead bird? What does it mean and how did you get it there?"

I still had no idea what the fuck he was talking about. And I told him so.

More bouncing me off the tree ensued. This was getting annoying so I zapped him hard.

"Will you stop for a second and just tell me what the fuck you are talking about?"

He did stop. And he did take a deep breath.

"There is a dead canary in the fourth circle of Aaru. How did you manage to get a dead bird there? And why? Is that supposed to mean something; is it symbolic of something? Is it a personal message? Are you threatening me?"

A canary. Well, now I knew where the wild gate in Sharpsburg went. Which was an exciting bit of knowledge I wasn't going to share with the angels. Why was the canary dead though? It should have been flying around, pooping on their heads. Although a dead bird was kind of cool. What a great idea to sneak into one of the circles of heaven and leave a dead bird on their doorstep. Wish I'd thought of it.

"Are you prophesying the broken link of the divine? The de-evolution of angels as symbolized by a dead bird? Or perhaps because the bird is yellow, you're implying that the mightiest of the angels will fall? Are you? The yellow canary is often a metaphor for a spy. Is there an informer in Aaru that will be discovered and die?"

Holy crap, he was seriously over-thinking this whole thing. Were all angels this crazy? It was just a damned bird. Sometimes a cigar is just a cigar.

"It wasn't me," I lied. "Sometimes starlings fly down my chimney and get in the house. One broke its neck trying to fly out through the French doors last winter. I'll bet that's what happened."

He stared at me with those black filled eyes as though he was thinking of doing far more than smacking me against the tree.

"We don't have chimneys. Only angels can gate there. So how did you manage to get a dead bird there? And why? Why did you come there? How did you know to come to the fourth circle? What is the bird supposed to signify?"

"Maybe one of your angel friends brought it there? As a snack maybe?"

His fingers dug into my shoulders, as he held me firmly against the tree. Then he leaned down with his mouth right in front of my ear. I clenched my teeth together, fighting conflicting emotions of fear and anticipation, and fighting my eager personal energy that didn't seem to recognize the seriousness of the situation at hand.

"I know your energy signature as if it were my own. Your presence there lingered behind and I could feel you on the dead bird, too. I will only ask you one more time. How did you get that bird there, and what is its purpose?"

I held there a few moments, savoring the threat in his voice, enjoying the fissure of fear shivering through me. Because that's how we roll.

"I have no idea what you're talking about," I lied.

He actually put his mouth against my skin. On my neck right under my ear. I could feel his breath against my skin. My own breath came in fast, shallow little bits and I waited to feel those pointed teeth. Or the hot needles in the tip of his tongue. I was terrified. And I was so turned on. One scrape of those teeth and I'd be in ecstasy. And then I'd probably be dead. The fact that he was willing to risk his own life and a chunk of the county in killing me and releasing the

145

huge amount of raw energy I held indicated how enraged he really was. Oddly enough, I hoped he survived the explosion.

Instead, he pulled away from me and let go of my shoulders, obviously struggling for control.

"I'm busy." He backed away to a respectable distance. "I don't have time for your childish antics. I cannot concentrate on what I need to do with you pulling impish pranks and throwing your energy around. I thought this would end when I fixed the brand, but it didn't. I should just take you back to Aaru and put you in a cage."

"I've been good. I haven't broken any of your rules. I haven't Owned anything, I haven't killed any human, haven't started any plagues or global weather events. I'm not even masturbating with the brand anymore. What am I doing that is so annoying?"

He glared at me. "I told you no conversion. There is a green cat with six legs walking around downtown."

I couldn't resist the cat. The whole story had been so intriguing. "That was just a little tiny conversion, nothing big. Nothing that should bother you. It shouldn't count."

"Flying down the Potomac River? That's not a little conversion. I'm going to drag you to Aaru and put you on a leash as punishment." He sounded as if the prospect of me leashed in Aaru held great appeal for him.

I looked at him with big, sad eyes. "You'd forbid me my wings? Deny me flight?"

He winced. It was a low blow. Angels were particularly fond of their wings.

"I don't have time for this. Who knows what you'll do next?"

"Fair warning, I think the gate guardians are going to unionize. You didn't forbid me from encouraging fair labor practices, so you should overlook that one."

He motioned with his hands, as if he were trying to restrain himself from tearing me limb from limb.

"You are driving me insane. What am I supposed to do with you? You have got to be the worst, most disruptive thing that has ever happened to me in all my life."

"Just ignore me," I told him. "I was here more than forty years before you recognized me; it's not going to be the end of the world if you just let me do my thing."

"I can't ignore you. You have a part of me lodged inside yourself. I honestly think you're doing this stuff on purpose to irritate me. It's like having someone constantly pestering you, poking you, yanking on your hair for attention."

"Well you're the stupid idiot who put a chunk of yourself inside a demon. I know you were angry, blah, blah, blah, but you're smart enough to know that you were giving me a portion of your spirit. This whole thing is your fault, not mine."

He stared at me in disbelief. "I didn't give a part of myself to you, you took it. I blaze a trail into your spirit to create the bind, and then pull back. I've done it thousands of times without ever having this happen. I didn't think it was even possible. You seized hold and kept that portion. There was no way I could remove it."

He had to be lying. I'll admit I've grabbed some demons before, when they've gotten their personal energy too close. I devoured them, killed them. I didn't break off a piece and imbed it in an awkward network throughout myself. He fucked up, and he was blaming it on me.

"I've been trying ever since to take it back, but you won't let it go. I'm older than you by billions of years, I'm infinitely more powerful, but I can't seem to break myself free from you. A lowly, inept, baby demon. Nothing but a dirty, nasty, foul, despised cockroach."

I knew he didn't exactly have a high opinion of my status and power, but this was really insulting and it stung. I didn't want this shit inside me. He was welcome to it. If he was going to be mean, he could just fuck off. Let him pretend I was some greedy bitch, snatching his spirit and hogging it to myself. Whatever. Asshole.

I shrugged my shoulders. "So sorry your ineptitude in binding me caused all this trouble. If I'm so lowly and foul, then how could I possibly seize a portion of a majestic, god-like creature such as yourself?"

He inhaled sharply, but I wasn't done yet. "Know what? I don't want your shit. It's a stupid color, it doesn't compliment my own hue one bit, and I hate lugging it around. It stinks, too. Now fuck off and let me finish my run."

I pushed away from the tree to move past him only to be slammed against it again as his mouth covered mine. Normally, I'd be all up for a little nookie against a tree, but it was clear right away that this was not a kiss of passion. I felt a sharp painful ripping inside me, more agonizing than anything I'd felt before. The fucker was trying to kill me.

I blasted him as hard as I could. Threw a stream of raw energy at him that should have burned him all the way through. It didn't disintegrate him, but it did knock him backward a few feet, safely away from me.

"I'll fight you with every last thing I've got if you try that again," I told him. "Even if you succeed in killing me, the amount of raw energy I have will explode out of me with a vengeance. I hope it fucking kills you, too, you asshole."

He glared at me in silence.

"Let me know if you think up anything to get this shit out of me. Anything that doesn't involve killing me, that is. I want it out of me worse than you do. I want it out and gone. In the meantime, just go the fuck away."

I jogged past him and down the road which was getting

blurry before my eyes. He'd tried to kill me. Really kill me. After that morning in my house, after the tucking into bed and the sandwich, I thought... Ah, it didn't matter what I'd thought. Candy was right, I needed to stop this now and stay away from him.

CHAPTER 15

*M*ichelle came over late that evening to help me figure out an appropriate Halloween costume for Wyatt's and my big night at Bang. I wasn't into it, but didn't have the heart to cancel on her. She was so psyched and had brought over Chinese takeout.

Hunan bean curd usually brightened any mood, but I kept mulling over my day, mulling over all the shit I'd thrown up in the air, as Dar had said. Dar's dilemma, Haagenti's inevitable punishment, the damned sword I was supposed to retrieve. Spending a fortune on a money-pit shopping center. The humans insisting that I needed to save them from a killer. A little boy's dark eyes popped up from my memory and I quickly banished the image. Stupid humans.

Then there was the conversation with the gate guardian, the vials of elf blood on my bedroom dresser, Gregory trying to kill me. Was he really bound to me? Between that and the part of him permanently lodged inside me, no wonder he was homicidal. Not that I had any idea how to utilize a bound angel. We didn't bind other beings, we Owned them. Angels bound.

"Are you okay?" Michelle asked as I displayed various skin colors and horn types for her critique. "You seem distracted. Did you and Wyatt have a fight?"

"No, for once Wyatt and I are fine. My brother from back home is in a bit of trouble and I'm trying to bail him out."

Michelle nodded knowingly. "I've got five siblings. I know how wrapped up you can get in their problems. Still, family is family and it's important to be there for them."

"Yeah, but I'm going to get the shit beat out of me for protecting him. I'm not looking forward to that," I told her. "What about these horns?"

"I like the ram-type ones that curled down better. I think you're less likely to snag them on the decorations." She walked around me to see them from the back. "My brothers were always taking the fall for each other. I think it's nice that you're sticking up for him. I didn't expect a demon to do that."

Me either.

"Had an angel try to kill me today, too. That sort of ruined my mood. How about a tail?"

Michelle didn't seem fazed by my announcement. "Yeah, that would bum me out, too." She looked at the tail. "Try shorter."

"Then I somehow got roped into protecting that little kid in the apartment on Clive Street from a ghostly cat that shoves his actions figures in the toilet and some guy that wants to cut off his ears."

"The little Perez boy? He is awfully cute. Wait," she looked up, a frown on her face. "They're not supposed to have pets in that unit. Did you say they had a cat?"

"It's a ghost. Don't get your panties in a knot."

Reassured that no one was violating the pet clause in their lease, Michelle turned her attention back to my tail. "How about really short? So it won't drag on the ground?"

"I don't do a tail at home, so I'm not used to it. I'm afraid I'm going to get it stepped on or whack someone with it. Maybe I'll skip the tail and go with the wings and horns instead?"

Michelle considered the tail again. "Yeah, and the spikes at the end are probably not a good idea at a crowded party anyway. Let's see the wings."

Wings. I'd already gotten in trouble doing wings. Might as well have a repeat performance.

"How about these?" I manifested the huge bat wings and odd body structure I'd used to fly down the Potomac River. It was suddenly cramped in my living room. I shifted a few inches and knocked over a lamp.

Michelle looked horrified. "Sweet Mary and Joseph, you look hideously deformed. Can you make your body look more normal, and reduce the size of your wings by maybe ninety percent? You'll never fit in the doorway with those things."

"But if I reduce them and change my torso back I won't be able to get off the ground," I complained. "All those paintings and statues? They're bullshit. No way could those creatures even glide down safely from a cliff. Physics doesn't work that way."

"You don't need to actually fly. You're going to be at a party. Think of them more as accessories. Like a handbag or earrings."

I shifted the accessories in question, knocking another lamp over. It rolled off the end table and onto the floor.

"I'm philosophically opposed to wearing non-functional wings. What if I need to make a quick getaway? Or someone throws me off the roof?"

"Wyatt is going to puke if you look like that." Michelle picked up the lamp and tucked it safely under the table. "And even if you fold them, you're not going to fit in the room with those things the size they are. Come on Sam, it's just a costume. For a party. You can fly around with your freakishly deformed body afterward if it makes you feel any better."

"Fine." I reduced the wings and returning my body to its previous human shape.

"What do you think?" I modeled the form. I was a latte color with curved ram's horns, red eyes with slitted pupils, furry lower half with goats legs and hooves, and my beautiful bat-like wings.

"Are you okay walking upright with your legs and feet like that?" Michelle scrutinized the odd angle.

"Yeah, I've used these legs at home."

"Do you look like this there?"

"No, this would be pretty boring in Hel," I confessed. "It's not like I can do my first form or anything dramatic here and get away with it. Plus, I really wouldn't be able to drive in most of the forms I use at home. As it is, I'll need to do the wings and feet when I get there."

"Wyatt could drive," Michelle suggested.

"Nope. No one is allowed to drive my car." Wyatt had once this past summer, but only because Gregory threw him the keys and gated me away before I could protest. It would take a real emergency for me to turn over the keys to my Corvette.

"What does your first form look like?" Michelle asked. "Can you show it to me?"

I popped quickly into the shape. It felt so familiar and comfortable. When we are created, we are gifted a form from the parent shaping us. We immediately assume this form since we must always have a corporeal shape to exist. Our first hundred years are spent like that, until we have the skill to modify it significantly or assume another.

153

"Wow." Michelle circled me to get the full effect. "Can I touch you?"

"You can touch the scales, but not the spikes. They're poisonous," I told her wordlessly.

Michelle gasped and held her head. "I didn't know you could do telepathy."

"I can't read your thoughts, and you lack the skill to speak to me without your voice. This is the only way I can speak to you in this form though." I laughed and the sound came out a raspy click.

Michelle ran her hands over the scales, avoiding the spikes and small tufts of hair that dotted my form. She worked her way around to my front and looked at my three heads, touching the scales on one cheek and gently running a finger down a fang.

"So smooth, so sharp," she mused. "The scales are such a pretty red-orange."

"Wow," I heard from the doorway. I swiveled one of my giant heads around to see Wyatt, open mouthed, his eyes roving down my long form. "Is that what you're going as? I'll need to strap you to the top of the Suburban like a dead deer. I don't even think you'll fit into the horse trailer."

"No, I'm going as something more manageable. Michelle wanted to see my first form."

Wyatt approached with an amazed look on his face. He didn't seem to notice that I'd spoken to him without using a voice. He reached out a hand and I cautioned him silently about the spikes.

"Which head should I talk to?" He looked from one head to the other.

"It doesn't matter, they're all me. Of course, when in doubt, you should always choose the middle one."

He rubbed me all over, tugging slightly at the tufts of fur. His caresses felt good. I wanted to purr.

"Your scales are smooth like glass," he admired. "They're reddish in places, too. And I really like the furry tufts."

He traced a scale with his finger. "You're beautiful like this, Sam."

His words hit me hard and I suddenly felt like I couldn't breathe. He thought I was beautiful like this? A three-headed, scaled monster, with stubby legs, and bits of blue fur? This was the form I'd been given at birth. The form I'd worn for hundreds of years. A human thought me beautiful. My human thought me beautiful.

They both stepped back and I popped into the shape that was to be my Halloween costume.

"This is what I'm going as for Halloween," I told Wyatt. "Do you want me to try anything different?"

"No, I like it a lot." He looked me over.

"Wanna hit that furry ass?" I teased, wiggling my rear at him. He laughed.

"I'd want to shave it first. Maybe I should stock up on razors for after the party. It's likely to take more than one to get through that."

"You may need clippers," I warned him.

Michelle gathered up her belongings.

"I'm outta here girlfriend," she told me. "My work here is done. Score one for the Halloween costume."

"Thanks for helping me." I gave her a hug. My ram horns whacked her in the head, and she clearly didn't know how to hug me in return, with the wings occupying most of my back.

"Thank you for sharing your magic with me, Sam. I never thought in my life I'd be helping a demon with a Halloween costume, petting her scales, and eating Lo Mein."

Michelle headed out and I popped back into my Samantha Martin shape. Which, of course, was naked, from my conversion.

Wyatt helped himself to the leftover Lo Mein and bean curd. "Amber is going to be so jealous. She's wanted to go to the Halloween party at Bang for years. I'll have to send her pictures."

"What's she like, your sister?" I asked on impulse.

He had told me a few things here and there about his family, but not much. It was hard to relate, and honestly I never cared about human childhoods or family relationships. They were complicated and boring. I suddenly wanted to know more about Wyatt's family. What was he like when he was little? Did his sister steal his toys, melt them, and hang them from the rafters? Did she impale durfts on his spikes where he couldn't reach them? Or leave him in the woods for a week tied to a log?

Wyatt looked surprised at the unexpected question and sat down on a chair at the dining table.

"She's smart. People think she's reserved and distant, but she's not that way with her friends and family. Don't get me wrong, people are drawn to her. She has a way with them. When someone's pissed off or difficult, she can manage to totally turn the situation around. But even so, there's a distance she keeps." He paused a moment and traced the wood grain on the table with his finger.

"Remember I told you my father died when I was ten? He was electrocuted putting a two-twenty line in the garage? Well, Amber and I had been in the garage just before. Dad and I had been fighting. He could be really mean when he was drunk, or angry, or frustrated, and he was having a hard time with the electric line. Anyway, we'd had a big fight and I'd stormed out. Amber stayed there with him. I left, and Amber stayed and saw him die. She saw him electrocuted. She was only five and it really messed her up to see that. She was in such shock that she didn't even run into the house to get help. Mom found her there, just staring at Dad, when she went out to see how things were going."

Wyatt looked up at me and I could see the impact of this terrible tragedy in his eyes. "Amber was in therapy for years and years. She was convinced she'd killed Dad. The therapists said this was normal. That kids think their feelings of anger toward parents result in their death. I'm amazed she turned into a normal teen, a normal young woman. She saw Dad die in a horrible way. I don't think I'd ever have been able to break free from that kind of thing."

I'd seen a lot of beings die through electrocution. Heck, I'd killed a lot of beings that way myself. Personally, I thought it was funny, but I could imagine how terrible it would be for a human to witness it. Especially someone you loved, a member of your family. I hated seeing Wyatt with that look in his eyes. It made me hurt, too.

"What did you guys do together growing up?" I asked, shifting the conversation to hopefully a lighter, more pleasant memory. "Were you close? Did you fight? Did she melt your toys and hang them from the rafters?"

Wyatt gave me an odd look. "We didn't have a lot of money for toys. If we'd destroyed each other's stuff, my Mother would have beaten our butts. We were close, but with five years apart we had different sets of friends and different interests. She didn't get in as much trouble as I did, but then Amber has always been good at sweet talking her way out of trouble. Mom says it's a Lowrey trait, that Dad was the same way."

"You're good at sweet talking, too," I told him in admiration. "I wish I had that talent."

"Hmmm, maybe, but Amber makes me look like an amateur. Anyway, as we got older, we'd do stuff together occasionally. See a band, go to the beach with a group of friends, camp out." He laughed. "All my friends wanted to date her. They were always pestering me to set them up with her."

I could imagine so. If she'd gotten half the looks that Wyatt had, she probably attracted quite a bit of attention.

Wyatt pushed the stack of breeding petitions aside to reach for the egg rolls. "Did you have a lot of brothers and sisters growing up? Besides Dar, I mean?"

"Oh yeah." I laughed. "There are hundreds in a group at a time. The home I was raised in was pretty selective, though, and I only had two hundred siblings. Sixty made it to adulthood."

"You lost seventy percent of your family?" Wyatt asked, looking at me in sympathy. "What happened?"

"Oh, that's an impressive number," I assured him. "There are a lot of accidents with young demons. That's one of the reasons we have so many offspring."

I looked over at the stack of papers beside him and made a decision. If I was going to start treating Wyatt as more of a partner, I needed to include him in more of my life.

I motioned toward the stack. "Those are breeding petitions. Other demons requesting that I sire a child. I'll probably accept one of them. I don't think I'd actually want to form a child; be the one receiving the energy and arranging for its upbringing. I may change my mind eventually, but it's not something I feel any urge to do right now." I didn't feel any urge to sire a child either, but probably would do it just to solidify an alliance. Especially with Haagenti breathing down my neck. Hopefully, I wouldn't kill anyone in the process.

Wyatt pulled the stack over to him. "Any top contenders?" He didn't seem bothered by the idea of my producing offspring.

"This one is very flattering." I pulled out the one from

Ahriman. "And these three are noteworthy also. Here's the one from Dar."

Wyatt looked at the petition from Dar with its drawings, and then looked at the others. I know he couldn't read the script, but appreciated his attention to them.

"If he's your top contender, then why is there a black ink line drawn on the paper?" He indicated Ahriman's petition.

I had a feeling it was time for honesty. I was a terrible liar anyway. "Gregory put that there. His writing at the top tells me that he does not approve and that I should decline this petition."

Wyatt looked confused. "Does he need to approve of your choice? Do you have to run these kinds of things by him now? Is this part of the binding?"

"No. He was over a few days ago trying to fix the brand and accidentally saw the petitions. You know what an asshole control freak he is. This particular demon is old. I'm sure Gregory knows him from the wars and has a personal dislike of him."

He put down the petition and looked up at me.

"I don't like you dealing with that angel, Sam. I worry that he'll lose his temper and kill you. And I'm jealous, too. I see how you are with him. I can't compete." He sighed. "Not that I expect this thing between us to last long. One day, when you and I have worked our way through the Kama Sutra, you're going to grow bored with me and toss me aside for someone else, like that jockey. We humans will always be just toys to you."

"No, Wyatt." I moved over to him. "I'll admit I'm fascinated by Gregory, but that doesn't lessen at all what I feel for you. You're not a toy to me. You never were, and you never will be."

He reached over and pulled me onto his lap, squeezing

me tight. The tension cleared and I suddenly felt that all was well between us. Better than well.

"Good," he grinned. "Now tell me what kinky things your beautiful demon-self wants to do tonight. All the details."

"Well," I hesitated. He looked at me approvingly, nodding for me to go on.

"Okay, I would love to have sex in the tub."

"Sounds fun." His hands moved slowly over my skin.

I was encouraged by how he'd accepted my first form, by how quickly he'd accepted my assurances of what he meant to me. So I let it all out with uncharacteristic honesty.

"A tub filled with blood. I can strangle you right before you orgasm. Not kill you, just suffocate you enough to give it that great edge. With a noose made of intestines. Maybe I'll gnaw on the other end." My voice trailed off as I imagined it all. I was so turned on.

Wyatt made a noise that sounded like a cross between a laugh and a cough.

"Now, I'm not saying 'no' here, but maybe we can use wine instead of the blood and hold off on the auto-erotic asphyxiation and the noose of entrails. Save that for a special occasion in the very distant future."

He didn't run for the hills. He'd seen my first form, had a glimpse of who I really was deep down, and he didn't run. Maybe this could work after all. Everything tightened, then I felt as if something cracked inside me. Warmth ran through my core. Maybe Wyatt was more than my best friend, more than a boyfriend. I held him tight, feeling his skin against mine, breathing in his special smell, then I got up and headed for the kitchen.

"I'll have to see if I have enough wine," I told him.

CHAPTER 16

*T*here was frost coating the stubble in the fields as I pulled my car into the empty ice cream shop parking lot. Originally the plan was a night time run along the C&O canal towpath, but we'd found out the path would be absolutely deserted on a weekday morning in October. It was a perfect opportunity for a daylight run. The train station parking lot at Point of Rocks where I normally would have parked was packed with commuters, so Candy had suggested we park a few miles down the road at this creamery. She knew the owners. I eyed the closed sign, wishing they were open, but I guess not many people ate ice cream early morning on a weekday with frost on the ground.

"Gossip," Candy announced pulling a bag from her car.

"Bring it on," I encouraged.

"We have a new angel." She had the air of one delivering the news of royal birth. She paused a moment for maximum impact, and to allow my curiosity to skyrocket. She definitely had my undivided attention.

"His name is Naromi. He goes primarily in male form, although he is still fairly androgynous. He's supposed to be a

temporary assignment until Gregory gets us a more perma-
nent one. Gossip mill says Gregory has big fires to put out
and can't deal with us right now."

She crossed her arms in front of her and gave me what I
can only assume was supposed to be a significant look. I
stared back at her.

"Well," she prodded.

"Well what?" I tried to look innocent.

"What have you done to set heaven on its ear? I'm
assuming you're the one causing these big fires?" She was
clearly not going to give up.

"I haven't done anything. Life is pretty much going along
as normal," I lied. Did the dead bird really cause that much
grief? Maybe there was a good reason for all the holy fury
Gregory had delivered on my head.

"You're banging an angel, whatever that entails, and I
don't want to know specifics," she added hastily. "I figured
you'd be privy to their doings now."

"We don't exactly have political discussions. I don't get a
state of the union address on the few occasions I see him. He
usually spends most of our time together threatening my
person."

Candy frowned at me for a moment. "I wonder if
someone up there found out he was getting intimate with
you. That's got to be against the rules. I can't imagine they'd
look kindly on romantic entanglements between your kind."

Worry crossed her face. "I hope he's not in trouble. I hope
they don't call him back home to reform him and stick
someone else in his place. We're actually building a decent
relationship with the guy. Who knows what jerk we might
end up with."

Her worry wormed its way inside me. Could he really be
in trouble? He'd bound a demon instead of killing it. And
here I was, running amok, getting away with all sorts of

crazy behavior that would have ended any other demon's life five times over. I was sneaking into Aaru and pretty much thumbing my nose at them by leaving items. All this, and Gregory still refused to kill me to date. Plus he was angel-fucking me. And the cherry on top of it all — he'd killed Althean, another angel. Damn. They were probably going to grab him and slice his wings off, stuff him in prison for all this. This probably amounted to treason.

"I'm sure it's nothing. A fight over who gets to precede whom at a state dinner or something stupid like that. Tell me more about Naromi. Here we are running in the daylight today. Is he okay with this sort of thing?" I wanted to switch the subject back to a less explosive topic. A topic I hoped wouldn't end up with me blamed for the woes of the entire werewolf race.

"It's too early to know how he stands on the issues or how much leeway we'll be given, but I get the feeling he follows Gregory's instruction to the letter."

I got the feeling everyone followed Gregory's instructions to the letter. Everyone except me, that is.

I pulled a dog collar out of my car. "I'll need to change first so you can put this on me, otherwise I'll just blow it to bits when I convert."

"Put your clothes in here." Candy pointed to what looked to be saddlebags. "We can change, put on clothes, and get a bite to eat and some coffee somewhere. Maybe Williamsport, or Hancock if we get that far."

I had to hand it to her, the wolf could plan. I balled my clothes up and stuffed them in the bag as Candy cringed, no doubt contemplating the wrinkled mess I'd be at the coffee shop. Handing her the collar, I popped into the only domestic canine form I Owned. Candy sucked in her breath.

"Wow, you are adorable!"

I shook myself, floppy ears flying, and dashed over to hump her leg enthusiastically.

"Okay, not so adorable now." She pulled me off by the scruff of my neck and snapped the collar on. I wiggled and licked her hand. It tasted like cocoa butter lotion with a bite of antibacterial gel.

"Do you Own anything bigger than a beagle? Will you be able to keep up?"

I gave her what I hoped was a scathing look, and bounced on all four legs. The collar jingled merrily.

"At least no one will think I'm a menace running with a beagle," she commented, removing her clothing and placing it carefully and neatly in the pack. She put her blingy collar around her neck and strapped the pack loosely around her waist, dropping to all fours so it wouldn't slide off as she changed.

It took a good fifteen minutes. Muscles and bones rolled around in a contorted mess under her skin. I watched for a moment, fascinated at the horror. I'd need to do this at home sometime to freak everyone out. Of course it would hurt like fuck to take that long to convert my form. After a few minutes, I left Candy to change in peace and wandered around the parking lot, my nose glued to the ground.

The world was a cornucopia of smells to a canine nose. Dozens of humans had been through here in the past few weeks. I could sort them all, tell in what order and when they'd arrived, how long they'd stayed, when they'd left. On the more recent ones, I could smell faint traces of where they'd been before arriving, the food they'd been around, the pets they had, their family members, whether their car had an oil leak, or if they'd pumped gas before arriving. I differentiated the owners as the most frequent smells, the ones who remained the longest before leaving. I identified their employees; noticed that one teenage girl had been indulging in intercourse prior to her shift. I sniffed around the lot and found the used condom. In the parking lot, too. Hmmm.

Candy came up beside me, glancing down at the condom then looking up at me and rolling her eyes. It was a funny thing to see on a wolf. I laughed and the sound came out as a wheezy bark. The pack fit Candy surprisingly well, with a fuzzy shearling cover on the strap to prevent chafing. I wondered if she had it custom made. Reaching behind her, she grabbed the strap with her teeth and tugged outward, tightening the apparatus. Then with a swing of her head, she took off toward the road.

We trotted down the street, and followed the railroad tracks across from the steel girder plant to the river and the towpath. This was a tiny industrial area outside the small town of Point of Rocks, and the morning air was filled with the sounds of forklifts and skid loaders. A few voices shouted instructions to each other, but everyone ignored two dogs jogging along the train tracks.

In no time at all, we were on the packed dirt of the towpath and tearing top speed along its length. The cold breeze brought a flood of woodland and animal scents to my nose as the miles passed. The tree-lined trail widened out at Brunswick, revealing the large railroad station and a series of small camping cottages. The canal to our right had mostly become a grass and tree-filled ditch, but there was an occasional swampy area, a nod to its original purpose. I wanted to go down and sniff around, but I was having a hard time keeping up with Candy. As a wolf, her legs were longer, and she was definitely in better shape. Racing down the path, I could see Harpers Ferry ahead, across from us on the West Virginia side of the river. There was the railroad bridge I dove under with wings so recently, the tunnel in the mountain to our right, and the ruins that had been the Salty Dog Tavern.

Candy pulled further ahead past the shell of the tavern. I lost sight of her as she wove around the twisty turns of the towpath. My breath was ragged and my little legs pumped to carry me past another ruin, and the bridge overlooking the rocky falls of the Potomac. I could see her up ahead. I wondered if I should soldier on and try to keep up, or bark out for her to wait. Just before the parking lot where I'd begun my flying excursion, she skidded to a halt, practically digging a trench with her rump, and stared into the woods. A rabbit? I felt a rush of excitement and ran harder to catch up. Oh, I hoped it was a rabbit.

Candy looked intently into the woods, ears and nose twitching, cocking her head to one side in curiosity and shaking the dust off her rump. It wasn't the look of a predator spotting a kill. What did she see? I slowed down to a more manageable pace, since a rabbit was clearly not in my immediate future, and tried to catch my breath as I trotted nearer. Not sparing me a glance, Candy walked with calm curiosity to the wooded area that once was the canal and vanished.

I sprinted again. There was no sign of her in the woods. I couldn't see her, I couldn't hear her. It's not like she'd be hidden by vegetation either, this late in the fall when everything was brown and dead. I slid to a stop dramatically by the place I'd last seen her on the path and stuck my nose to the ground. Here, and here. Then over here. Then she moved down here to this tree. I stopped and looked up to see if I could spot what attracted her attention and yipped in surprise. There appeared to be a child sitting down by a tree. A small human child, about three years old, with a tear-stained face and dirty clothing. The child looked at me pleadingly, convincingly, but I could smell nothing except the woodland scents and Candy's signature werewolf odor. I recognized it right away. An elf trap.

Elves stole human babies, but they also stole adult humans. Since they never left our home realm, they used humans, not just as servants, but as informants and traders to come and go through the gates. Adult humans who fell into this clever trap would be sold off, trained, and perhaps eventually entrusted to return here and run errands. Mostly, they remained servants for the remainder of their lifespan. Slaves actually, although the elves did seem to treat them fairly. Better than they would have fared in our hands, anyway.

I got a good running start and plunged full speed through the gate, plowing into a solid furry object on the other side. Candy snarled and snapped, missing me by a hair when she realized who had knocked her flat. I batted her on the nose with a paw and looked up to see two elves with drawn arrows trained on us. With a pop, I converted back into my Samantha Martin form. This alarmed Candy to no end, and she thrashed about to find me naked and sprawled on top of her. The elves lowered their bows.

"Calm down, I'm getting off you. Just give me a second here," I scolded her.

The elves exchanged looks and waited for me to address them. Nice manners. Even though they were hunter scouts and I outranked them, this was clearly their territory and I had no permission to be here. By all rights they should have shot me and dragged me off to teach me a lesson about the folly of trespass.

"I'm so sorry to invade your territory like this," I said scrambling inelegantly to my feet. "The werewolf is part of my household and stumbled into your trap before I could warn her. We're leaving now. With your permission, of course."

I grabbed Candy by the collar and hoped she'd cooperate.

She looked around in bewilderment, and then up at me, her eyes full of questions.

One of the elves nodded at me. "You may pass, Azi-Baal," he said, addressing me by one of my names and my status title.

I'd been trying to peek at their clothing to see if I could determine where we were. The fact that he'd recognized me and called me Az as opposed to one of my other names clued me in. I'd done favors for this high lord before. Fate was truly smiling on me. A few of the other high lords would have been happy to see me skinned and hanging in their hall. I bowed at the elves and reached out a hand to activate the gate. The trap was one way. A human, or a werewolf evidently, could just walk right in, but they would never be able to return without the skill to trigger the gate. Talented elves and demons had that skill. And, of course, angels.

I dragged an unresisting Candy through the gate and walked her down to the parking lot before letting go of her collar.

"That was a close one," I told her.

She looked intently at me with big eyes, and jutted her muzzle toward me. Clearly a request for explanation.

"Elves." I made a face. "They have territories in our realm and use these gates as traps to snare humans to serve them."

Candy looked horrified.

"It's not a bad life. The elves seem to treat them well. They don't beat them or torture them or have sex with them. The humans work and they have food, clothing, and shelter. Talented humans are provided instruction in the arts. Some can become sorcerers if they have the skill, although adult humans don't have the time to perfect such an art. The human babies they take make much better sorcerers."

Candy looked even more horrified. She made a choking noise.

"What a stupid fucking trap. A toddler? In the woods on a weekday morning in October? Of course a human could never resist a lost little kid in the woods, no matter how improbable the scenario. Humans are such suckers." I looked at Candy. "Werewolves are evidently suckers, too."

She gave me a scathing look that was, no doubt, intended to wither me where I stood. She had a very expressive face in wolf form.

"We're lucky those guys are on good terms with me. Their territories are divided into kingdoms and nobody recognizes anyone else as an equal. I've done a favor for this particular high lord. I went and retrieved one of his sorcerers that went rogue a few centuries back. It actually didn't turn out very well at first. There was a misunderstanding. A failure to communicate. Evidently, I was supposed to bring the sorcerer back to them alive and not in so many pieces. I was on their shit list for a while until the high lord realized that the whole deal had been an effective deterrent. His humans toe the line now, terrified that he'll sic me on them if they stray. So we're good. I'm not in such good standing with most of the other ones though."

Candy sighed and shook her head. She looked me up and down, and then peered down the trail, waving a paw toward the path.

"Yeah, let's keep going. I exploded my collar, though, so if we get hauled into the doggie pokey, can your friend vouch for me?"

She nodded.

The rest of the run to Williamsport was uneventful, although I noticed Candy tended to keep a shorter distance between us. While she changed shape I nosed around as beagle. There was a discarded candy wrapper with some chocolate still smeared on it that I entertained myself with when I was done identifying all the other dog visitors by their urine marks. I checked to see if Candy was finished, then popped into my human form and put on my clothing so we could head in for breakfast.

Candy looked with despair at the wrinkled mess of my clothing. We'd found a little diner in Williamsport and were enjoying coffee and a huge spread of food. Candy was the only one bothered by my disheveled appearance. None of the wait staff seemed to mind. In fact, our waitress was beyond pleased to have a table of hearty eaters on a weekday morning.

"Did you and Michelle get your costume worked out for Halloween?" Candy asked, eyeing the packets of jelly on the next table. I got up and retrieved them.

"Yeah. It's not that dramatic compared to what I do back home, but it looks good."

"Be careful with the vampires, Sam," Candy warned. "They see everyone else as food and are very protective of their secrets. They isolate themselves from all the other species and they don't mingle with humans unless they are hunting. I suspect that this event is where they pick their prey."

I shrugged. "I've seen a few vampires recently. They are always super polite and pretty expressionless. I can't imagine they'd attack me."

"I'm sure the ones you've seen are their young. The old ones don't come out during the day. I've never met an old vampire, but I know they are ruthless. I'm not sure how they'd feel to have a demon at their hunting party. You know how territorial you get about others infringing on your property, driving your car? They are that way, too."

"You guys are territorial," I said in amusement. "Everyone is. Even the humans. I've seen them get terribly bent out of shape if someone walks on their lawn."

"Yes, but most species will defer to a bigger threat. We

don't like them, and we'll try to drive them out if we can, but werecats are tolerated in our territories. Demons are definitely tolerated in our territories. And, of course, we have to abide by our existence contract where the vampires do not."

"Why don't the vampires have an existence contract? They have an angel assigned to them." I didn't see how these vampires could be as much of a threat as Candy was making them out to be. Pain in the ass, maybe. Liable to do me harm? Nope.

"Vampires existed as a race before the humans, so they're clearly not Nephilim. Their angel is more of a diplomatic advisor. They don't want the angels to be irritated enough with them to try to stamp them out, but they don't fall under their control. They were never granted heavenly gifts like the humans. They stole them. Ninety-nine percent of the vampires were human once, so it's not like it was hard to steal the gifts and use them for their own gain."

"Ninety-nine percent? I thought all the vampires were humans once. You know, bitten and transformed into creatures of the night?" I said the last bit with a dramatic, spooky voice.

Candy wasn't amused. "They're an actual separate species. They reproduce, although rarely. Those ones are called 'Born' as opposed to the humans they turn into vampires, which they call 'Made'. If they didn't have the ability to transform humans, there would probably be only a hundred or so worldwide. They're really picky about who they choose to turn. And the process is long. It takes half a millennium until a human is a vampire with more than minimal skills and abilities, and thousands of years before they are truly old and at full power."

"And you know this how?" I teased. "Did you perhaps personally interview Dracula? Aside from the few I've seen recently, the last time I saw vampires was six hundred years ago. Those ones were eating dying diseased people, living like rats, with the cognitive ability of a piece of drywall. You've been watching too many late night movies."

"Fine." Candy glared at me. "I hope they bite you."

The air around our table turned frosty as Candy gave all her attention to her omelet.

"Mmmm, I hope so, too." I teased, unable to resist pissing her off even further.

We ate in silence for a while. I stole a glance at Candy, who was pointedly ignoring me. She had a lot on her plate right now, and I didn't mean the omelet. Her whole race was at the mercy of angels, many of whom were voting for their extinction. She was breaking rules left and right that could result in her death. She'd just about gotten turned into a pincushion by elves, and now I was antagonizing her. Those elves would have killed her, too. If not right there, then after they'd taken her somewhere and "examined" her. They have no use for werewolves.

"Look, I'm sorry I made you angry," I told her. "Let's just change the subject. How is Reed doing with my smelly tenants? Are they giving him any trouble?"

"No, things are going smoothly," she replied, as if she were undecided whether to stay mad at me or not.

"Still at full occupancy?" I prodded, hoping to push her out of sullenness and into a conversation. "Any good stories? Fights? Overdoses? Orgies?"

"There have been some words tossed around, but no fights. Werewolves are very good at keeping order. It's gotten to the point where he's only there an hour at check in, to get everyone settled and collect rent, then again in the morning." Candy laughed suddenly. "Oh, he told me he'd seen a mutant cat with extra legs that someone must have dyed green. I told him to lay off the Jack Daniels."

"That's my doing," I told her cheerfully. "Did he like it?

The extra legs aren't functional. It was a pretty good trans-formation though. I'm fairly proud of it. Usually when I attempt anything with other creatures I end up killing them. Piece of cake to do stuff to myself, very tricky to do it to someone else though."

"I'll have to tell him that." She chuckled. "He thought it was one of those birth defects like you see in side shows at the carnivals. He figured the thing had survived this long only to have sadistic teenagers catch it and coat it with green Manic Panic hair dye."

"No, just a demon having fun with some stray kitty." I was glad the cat was making such an impression. "Let me know if he finds the ear-man though. I'd love to meet him."

Candy looked startled for a moment then grinned. "Oh you've heard that story, too? Reed says he's the homeless people's boogie man. The legendary ear-man snags them in the dark, when they are cold and alone, then slices off their ears and dumps their bodies in the pit. The psychologists would have a field day with all that symbolism."

"Ghost stories," I agreed.

"Yeah, the homeless people say he's moved on to killing little kids." She shrugged. "Maybe he needs smaller ears for his collection."

I'd gone cold. Angelo. Little Angelo Perez with his dark eyes so trusting as he'd looked up at me. He'd said he was in danger, and now I heard this. I didn't care if it was a ghost story, my skin was crawling right up my back in panic. I scrambled for my cell phone and realized that I didn't have any of my tenants' numbers. Maybe Michelle did.

"What's wrong?" Candy asked, noticing my face. "It's just a story, Sam."

"Are you sure? Homeless people go missing and no one even notices. Maybe little kids are missing, too. Kids from poor families that no one cares about. There's a little boy, one of my tenants, and I need him to be safe."

"Sam, it's fine. Really," she assured me. "Even kids from poor families don't just vanish. There are AMBER alerts and all sorts of special emergency procedures if a child goes missing. I promise you, none of your tenants' children have disappeared. I'd know about it. Everyone would know about it."

I took a deep breath and relaxed. She was right. This was a stupid myth. The kid wasn't in any danger. What was wrong with me, freaking out like that?

We finished breakfast, and then headed back to the towpath for our return run. Candy protested my stuffing food into the pack, but I couldn't resist the irony of asking the waitress for a doggie bag. I made sure I put it in my side of the pack. Candy would never forgive me if I got ketchup on her clothing.

The run back was exhilarating. Candy once again stayed fairly close, becoming pinned to my side and keeping me between herself and the elf trap as we passed it. With that safely behind us, she gradually pulled ahead to lead me by about twenty feet. I loved my beagle form with its floppy ears and big paws, but I was seriously considering Owning something with longer legs. Candy was easily out pacing me, and I was running furiously just trying to keep her in sight.

As we rounded the corner by Brunswick, I saw the back of a figure walking ahead of us. The man appeared to be a hiker, loaded down with a huge backpack and a walking stick. Candy dropped to a trot, to keep from startling him, and glanced behind at me questioning. I closed on her and gave a joyful beagle howl as I passed. The man turned, startled, but quickly relaxed when he saw me bounding up with wagging tail and wiggling body.

"Hi boy." He knelt down to run his hands over me. "Wow, you are just the cutest thing I've ever seen."

I don't know what it is about dogs that makes grown humans talk in baby talk. He scratched me behind my ears and I just about had an orgasm in ecstasy. I seriously needed to have Wyatt do this sometime. I encouraged him to continue by licking his hands and squirming around. Candy approached slowly, trying to look non-threatening, by wagging her tail and panting with tongue extended. Still, I could tell the moment the hiker saw her from the way he stiffened and caught his breath.

To ease the tension, I ran back to Candy and jumped at her face, licking her muzzle and pulling playfully at her ears with my teeth. She went along with the act, doing a play bow, and shaking her head so the blingy collar jingled its tags. Evidently, I'm a better actress in doggie form, because the hiker relaxed and even patted us on the heads as we passed. It had definitely been an awesome run. I made a mental note to do this one again, without the adventure through the elf trap, and, hopefully, with longer legs next time.

CHAPTER 17

"I hope they don't card me," I told Wyatt as I surveyed my Halloween form in the car rear view mirror. "The only place I have to stick my license is up my ass."

We'd managed to find an out-of-the-way place to park where I felt reasonably safe leaving my Corvette, and I'd been able to create the large, unwieldy portions of my costume uninterrupted. It had taken a while. Wyatt was irritated. He seemed to be cheering up now that we were parked and the prospect of a beverage was within his reach.

"I have a man-purse I can put it in." Wyatt eyed the pouch-looking bag with amusement. He was dressed as an elf. Not one of the Keebler elves. More like the Orlando Bloom, Lord of the Rings, kind of elf. I'd just about passed out laughing when I saw his costume. From what I could gather, the vampires and the elves hated each other. Wyatt going to their party dressed as an elf would be like going to a Bar Mitzvah in a Hitler costume. Of course the irony was lost on Wyatt, who couldn't figure out what was so funny about the outfit. I'd explained what little I knew about vampires to him, and had managed to tell him how gloriously inappropriate his costume would be before I dissolved into another fit of laughter. Wyatt had offered to change, but I insisted it was brilliant, and I wouldn't have him wear anything different.

"Good idea," I told him as I stuffed my license, some money and my car keys into the bag. "Better not run off on me with some hot-looking Lady Godiva, you've got my car keys."

We walked the five blocks up the road to the club while I goosed Wyatt with my tail. I'd changed my mind about the tail thing. It felt weird. It wasn't an appendage I normally wore, but it was growing on me. I'd made it furry like my lower half, and jointed it considerably so I could swish it around like a cat, making sure to put tiny joints in the end so it acted as a finger. I foresaw an evening of fun with that tail.

We attracted a lot of attention just walking up the street, although honestly most of the attention was on me. I heard people speculating how I got my legs to bend in the manner of a goat with the little hooves, and much admiration on my wings. In response, I stretched out a wing behind Wyatt, arching and rustling it a bit. The "Ooooo" noises were very gratifying.

Once we reached the doorman at the club, suddenly all the attention was on Wyatt. The vampire at the door stiffened, like someone had put a rod up his ass, and glared at my elf.

"Is this your idea of a joke?" he asked, incensed. "I don't care if you're invited; you're not getting in dressed like that."

"What a shame," I replied. "And we were so looking forward to the party."

The doorman noticed me for the first time and his eyes bugged out before that placid dull mask they all seemed to wear slipped over him. He glanced rapidly back and forth from the guest list to my face.

"Wyatt Lowrey and guest," I told him helpfully. "I'm the guest. I hope that's okay."

"I thought you said these people were polite, with excellent hospitality, Sam." Wyatt put an arm around my waist. Smooth move, since my waist was mostly hidden by wing.

"I've only had pleasant experiences with them so far, sweetie. This is very disappointing." I pouted.

At that time another vampire came out the door, her eyes also bugging as she saw me. She elbowed the doorman sharply in the side, and gave him a furious glance before turning to me with that look of bland neutrality.

"Baal, I am so sorry you have been made to wait outside. Please come right on in." She glanced at Wyatt and winced. "Both of you, please come in."

I paused as we walked through the door and did a quick scan. The place was packed. Lights were dim with flashes of neon from the dance floor, the music pounded a bass heavy beat, and tables loaded down with food and huge, fantastic ice sculptures were off to the side. A bar, modern in chrome and black granite, serpentined around the entire left side of the huge room.

Wyatt had shown me his hacked list of the guests, so I wasn't surprised to see local and state politicians, a few notable news anchors and morning shock jocks, and some recognizable celebrities. Nobody A-list, but not community theater either. Others must have been local businessmen and women from the way they were working the room.

The vampires were easy for me to recognize. There was just something about them that clearly identified them as non-human, although Wyatt and the other humans couldn't seem to see this difference. There looked to be about ten vampires in the room, with varying degrees of power. Oddly enough, they were either clustered together or lined awkwardly against the wall, like social outcasts as a high school dance. They eyed the humans with a kind of nervous longing, as it were beyond their skills to engage them in small talk. I found the whole thing terribly amusing.

Our female escort parked us at the bar and exchanged a quick glance with the bartender before wishing us a lovely evening. The bartender was human, but unlike the rest of the humans in the room, he seemed to recognize the vampires and be able to tell their social ranking. He glanced at Wyatt's costume in surprise, hiding a quick grin. This human clearly understood how his bosses might react to an elf, and found it rather funny.

"Can I get you a drink, Baal and companion?" he asked, with warmth that had been lacking in our interaction with the vampire staff.

"The Companion will have whatever you've got on tap." Wyatt was having as much fun as I was with this whole thing. "My Evil Mistress would like your best vodka."

A few of the humans sidled up to me and began admiring my wings. A rather well known Baltimore journalist asked if she could touch them. I assented and watched one of the vampires along the wall clench his fists in frustration as she fawned over them. Clearly, I owed Candy a big apology. I should never doubt her. This party was just a big gift basket of goodies for the vampires, who were picking out their snacks for the evening. Wyatt's outfit had gone unnoticed so far, as we were hidden in a mob of humans pawing my wings and furry ass. I hadn't gotten this felt up in, well, in forever. Happy to reciprocate, I used my tail to grope the crotches around me, and heard quite a few squeals and laughs. The vampires along the wall were now glaring at me.

The bartender delivered our drinks, biting back a smile and trying to mimic the bland expression the vampires habitually assumed when they interacted with me. I glanced down at the glass of vodka and hoped those lessons with Gregory hadn't deserted me.

"Stand back," I warned the bartender, "I saw this in a cartoon once and I think I can do it." Taking the glass of vodka in my hand, I froze it. It was supposed to cover the glass with lovely frosty etchings and chill the vodka. Instead the glass shattered, sending shards and frozen vodka through the air and onto the humans. A bit overkill, but I had been practicing ice and not chill. The bartender had been smart enough to heed my warning, but a human next to me shrieked and grabbed a napkin to staunch the blood from her cut arm.

"I think the vodka will sterilize the cut," I told her. "You may want to retain a lawyer though. Cheap fucking glasses in this place. You're probably permanently maimed. You might need amputation."

A man beside the injured woman offered to take her for stitches. They left and I instructed the bartender that everyone should receive a vodka shot. He'd just lined up a row of shots when I saw a male vampire coming toward me with a rather pinched expression on his face. Such an expression ruined the looks of what was probably a rather handsome vampire of Latino descent. Pity.

"Baal, we do have cold vodka," he told me, wringing his hands. "We certainly don't expect our guests to have to chill their own beverages."

I waved my hands around in my best imitation of a magician and grinned at him. "No, I can do this. Really. I've been working on it at home. My angel has informed me that it's important to master this skill, so I need to take every opportunity to practice."

I managed to chill five out of eight glasses. Two burst in a spray of icy vodka and glass, and the other cracked down the middle. I made a show of licking vodka off the bar with a long forked tongue while the humans applauded in delight. By this point, I'd attracted the entire club. The vampires glared from their spots, the placid expression finally slipping from their faces. Just to add to the fun, I chewed up one of the shot glasses and swallowed the chunks, dribbling blood out of my mouth and onto the floor.

"Do you do shows?" a human dressed as Osama Bin Laden asked. "I'd love to book you for our sales convention this year."

"Aren't you in that Gwar band?" another asked.

"No, idiot." His friend, whose Batman costume left a lot to be desired, punched him. "She's in Hollywood special effects."

"Let's dance," I told Wyatt and led him onto the dance floor.

This brought Wyatt out into the open from the huddled crowd of humans and to the attention of the line of vampires. I felt angry energy like a whip coming off them. There wasn't a placid face in the crowd. It was nice to know they could be jolted into revealing emotion.

Wyatt and I danced as the humans slowly migrated to the dance floor and to us again. I was having fun stroking him all over with my tail. I couldn't wait until tonight. There were all kinds of things I wanted to do with this tail. I hoped Wyatt was up for some kinky experimentation.

"Sam, if you don't calm down with that tail, we're going to need to find a room," he laughed. "Either that or I'm going to be spending the evening with a big wet spot on my elf pants."

I reluctantly pulled the tail away, and extended its length a few feet so I could molest nearby dancers. Flexing a wing, I knocked over a gargoyle ice sculpture and broke the head off.

"Oops." I bent over to pick up the ice and smacked my

horns on the table, sending a tray of carrot sticks flying and spilling a bottle of sparkling water across the damask table-cloth. I also knocked one of the guests flat onto the floor with my outstretched wing. This party was clearly not set up to accommodate demons.

"No, no, Baal, let me," said the Latino vampire who'd offered the chilled vodka earlier. He'd been following me around, watching me with a flutter of anxiety on his pinched face. "Maybe you and your companion would like a private area for a while?"

"Oooo, you have one of those chocolate fountains," I said as I stood up. Unfortunately my horns were hooked on the tablecloth and food trays slid off the table. "Sorry about that. Damned horns," I told him as I ripped myself free from the cloth and proceeded to the fountain, dangling a torn section of tablecloth from one of my horns.

I stepped over the guy sprawled on the floor, who was nursing bloody nose, and eyed the chocolate fountain. I'd always wanted to buy one of these. It would make a great Christmas gift for Candy, who was a raging chocoholic. There was an assortment of goodies to dip in the pouring dark stream. Pineapple, apples, pound cake, strawberries, cheeses, and pretzel rods. No orange slices though. Nothing is better than chocolate and orange. Nothing.

I skewered some fruit and cheese onto a pretzel stick and coated it with chocolate. Not bad. My finger coated with chocolate was just as good. Not that I ate the finger, although that did seem like something I'd want to try in the future.

"Come here Wyatt," I called. "I'll bet this chocolate is just as good on your fingers, too. Mmmm, I am getting an inspiration here. This could possibly be one of the best sex toys ever. I wonder if I can convince the vampires to give it to us?"

"It would never fit in your Corvette." Wyatt looked at the

huge basin of chocolate. "Even if it disassembled, it would be too big. Plus, you'd get chocolate all over your car seats. You know how you get about stuff on your car seats. I think we're better off hitting up Bed Bath and Beyond in the morning."

The Latino vampire had escorted the bloody nosed man to the door and made it back to my side in an inhuman burst of speed. I'd given up on fingers and stuck my long, forked tongue into the chocolate. Unfortunately the tongue wasn't shaped for optimal conveyance of chocolate, so I put my mouth into the stream and slurped it like a water fountain.

"This fucking rocks," I told the vampire, noticing that several of the other humans were heading to the door.

"I can put it in a private room for you to enjoy," the vampire suggested in a tone of desperation.

"I wish I could take it home," I told him.

"I will personally drive it to your house right now." He sounded on the verge of panic.

"Juan, why don't you see to our other guests," a smooth, soft, male voice said. I could actually feel the energy, the power, from this guy. It was soft and soothing, like a warm, fuzzy electric blanket that comforts you right before it shocks you in the leg. It was about time the boss man got here.

So this is what the real vampires look like I thought, eyeing the guy over and thinking this must be one of the old ones that Candy was talking about. Funny, because he didn't look old. Maybe early thirties in human years tops. He was an attractive guy with dark hair, gelled and tousled, and gray eyes. His mouth turned up at the edges slightly, as if the humor of the world were too much for him to keep bottled up inside. His eyes belied the faint smile though. They were hard, calculating, ruthless, and right now they looked pissed in his bland, mild, expressionless face. I got the feeling that he was pissed at others besides me.

"Whoa, where did you come from sweet cheeks?" I put a chocolate smeared hand on the sleeve of his dove gray, cashmere jacket. I'll give the guy credit, he didn't flinch, didn't grimace, didn't even look down at the ruined, expensive fabric.

"Baal, my name is Kyle Fournier and my staff and I respectfully welcome you here to Bang. We're honored by your presence here with your companion." He choked a bit on the companion part as he saw Wyatt and his costume. "Your companion. I'd like to speak to you privately to convey a special privilege to you and to present you with a token of our esteem."

Well, Kyle did know his stuff. Demons love gifts, and anything described as a "special privilege" was something I wanted to know about. I wondered if this was like those timeshare meetings I always got suckered into where I'd need to invest in his high rise in order to get the fruit basket and commemorative charm bracelet. I hoped not. That would be terribly disappointing.

"Wyatt, why don't you dance with that nice woman over there?" I indicated one of the vampire women lined up against the wall. She looked at me in alarm. "Those poor women have been ignored all night. She looks like she could use a little male attention."

Wyatt headed toward the woman who looked beseechingly at Kyle. He nodded at her, and she took Wyatt's proffered arm as if it were contaminated, and walked with him to the dance floor. I really wanted to stay and watch them dance, but I had a gift in the offering, so I motioned to Kyle and followed him into an office behind the bar.

The room was a typical manager's office. There was an old desk and swivel chair, two chairs that looked like they had previously gone with a restaurant table, and several filing cabinets. The desk had stacks of papers on it, and the huge Towson Custom Motorcycles calendar behind the chair had scribbled notes on each of the days. A few cases of beer sat along the wall beside the door. I plopped down on one of them and yanked the scrap of tablecloth off my horns, wiping the chocolate off my face as best as I could. I had a feeling this would become a serious conversation, and I had a hard enough time being taken seriously without a white flag flapping from my head.

"I want to assure you that your human will be treated with care," Kyle said with sincerity. "We respect your owner-ship mark on him."

"Oh, I'm not worried about Wyatt." I laughed. "He shot an angel in the head this past summer. Big fucking caliber, too. I'm sure he can handle a bitey vampire if he needs to."

"Well, he won't need to." Kyle obviously didn't believe me about Wyatt shooting an angel or his ability to take care of himself. "I want to offer you your choice of any human in the club tonight. Any. We have a room downstairs you can enjoy them in, or you can take them with you, or I can have them delivered to your home. We'll take care of the inquiries and the paper trail. Totally off the record. You can do whatever you like to them, make it last as long as you want and we'll cover it up. Just pick out who you want, and you can take them right away."

Ahhh. Basically I could rape and dismember a human of my choice without fear of discovery as long as I got the hell out of his club right stinking now.

"But I already have a human. And I'm very satisfied with his services. Can I have a vampire instead? Wyatt seems to like that nice young lady he's dancing with." I watched a muscle twitch in his jaw. This was fun.

"We would never insult you by offering you a lowly vampire. The humans here are all handpicked; they are all

185

well known individuals. Perhaps two would be more to your liking?"

I got off the stack of beer cases and walked over to the vampire. "What about you, Kyle Fournier?" I ran a chocolate covered finger down the front of his jacket. "Are you on the offer list? I could spend some time with you and be quite happy." In reality, I suspected he'd probably kick my ass.

The vampire looked down at me and I saw something flicker deep in those gray eyes. Behind the ruthlessness there was a flash of humor and a grudging acknowledgement. He clearly realized he was being backed into a corner.

"Okay, let's cut to the chase here." He dropped the bland expression and looked at me like a fellow predator should. "What do you really want? Because I doubt frolicking with a vampire is that high on your to-do list."

It was about fucking time. If these vampires lost all the polite, smoothing, bullshit and got down to business, they'd get a lot more done.

"You certainly understand how frustrating it is for me to run all over the metro area following a trail of bread crumbs to nothing?" I sat back down on the beer cases and Kyle relaxed a bit, half sitting on the desk with one foot dangling. "I've got bosses riding my ass, threatening to impale me on a stake if I don't make progress. I'm under immense pressure to deliver this artifact thingy, and I'm not feeling the cooperation here. Just hand the damned thing over, and I'll go away."

Kyle looked mildly sympathetic. "I can appreciate the difficulty of your position, but you should also understand that we get a ridiculous number of your kind trying to lay claim to this object. We suffer from an equal frustration, being run around at every demon's beck and call only to find out they are not able to possess it. Obviously, we'd regard anyone wanting to claim the object with suspicion at this point."

He gave me a look that clearly said he had grave doubts I'd be able to possess the object. That he strongly believed I was another one wasting their time.

"Look, I don't want the fucking thing, some asshole back home does. At this point, I want to just deliver it to him, or tell him you guys sold it to the Russians, or something."

Kyle sighed. "The artifact has to be collected in person. If this 'asshole back home' wants it, he needs to come get it himself. It won't go to a courier. Can you just inform him of this fact? We've had this same conversation with thousands of other demons. Don't you guys communicate?"

"We're not big on information sharing," I admitted. "I've kind of pissed the guy off at this point, too. I doubt he'd believe me."

"No! You? How could that possibly be?" Kyle said, his voice thick with sarcasm. I rather liked vampires when they took off that dull boring mask and let their emotions out. I wondered if they were all like this guy underneath that horribly bland façade.

"I'm supposed to go up to Atlantic City next weekend, and I have a very unpleasant suspicion that I'll meet with another flunky who will give me a bag of ketchup packets and tell me I need to go to Pittsburgh for another meeting. My crystal ball predicts I won't be happy. In fact, in order to overcome my severe depression from the incident, I'll be forced to spend a lot of time in this club. I'll also need to spend a lot of time in all your various clubs, casinos, manufacturing plants, distribution centers. As a form of therapy, you realize. It may take me centuries to get over this funk."

"You'll be dispatched into the afterlife by the end of the evening with all the energy you're throwing around," Kyle sneered, thinking to call me on a bluff. "You should be thinking more about how you're going to avoid the angel descending on your head and less about blackmailing me and my family."

I showed him the reddish purple sword on the inside of my arm. It had always garnered such a dramatic reaction from everyone else that I was disappointed to see him look at it blankly.

"Nice tattoo. And that means?" he asked.

"I'm bound. Your angel? His boss put it there. He's very smitten with me and is greatly amused by my antics," I lied. Hopefully vampires had horrible lie-radar. "He'd not mind in the least my devoted attention to your establishments."

"Yes, yes. The angels all adore you. I'm sure you're very special," he said, again with the sarcasm. "I think I'll take my chances."

"No, seriously." I'd never had this problem before. Damn. "Ask your angel about me. Ask him about the cockroach."

"Yeah, I'll definitely do that." He smirked. "Back to the issue at hand here, we can't just turn this thing over to you. We could duct tape it to your backside, and it's not going with you if you're not the right demon. There is no sense in continuing to waste everyone's time with these games. Just tell the 'asshole back home' to set up his own meeting and we'll talk."

"All I want is to go to Atlantic City next weekend and actually meet with your head honcho. I can sense your power levels, so don't try to dress someone up and pass them off as the big guy because it won't work. I have a very nice gift, something I know he'll appreciate, so the meeting won't be a total drag for him. We'll sit, have a pleasant conversation, then part ways. I'll tell the 'asshole back home' that I tried, that it was a bust, and everyone will go on about their business."

Kyle frowned and ran a finger over the chipped desk. "I

can't speak for The Master. I can convey your request to him, but I don't have the authority to commit him to this meeting."

How hard was it to get an audience with this guy? It would be easier to get in to see the Pope for fuck's sake. I threw up my hands.

"Throw me a bone here, buddy! I can't just walk away from this thing. Let's find a mutually acceptable compromise."

The vampire continued to frown and examine the desk. I could sense him thinking, rather than stalling. Threats hadn't worked, maybe a bribe? Maybe vampires were more motivated by the carrot than the stick?

"I could perhaps offer you a future service? I'm very good at blowing stuff up. Possibly demolition work or assassination? I'm sure you have enemies somewhere to be harried and intimidated. Nothing intimidates quite like a demon."

"We're pretty good at handling that sort of thing ourselves."

"Okay, your turn. Suggest something. Before I get bored. You wouldn't like me when I'm bored."

He shifted on the desk and examined a piece of paper. "There may be a rotation of staff in the near future. Some personnel changes could occur. I would hate for these to disturb you."

I stared at him. What the fuck was he talking about? He met my stare knowingly, as if I was supposed to understand this cryptic statement. I shook my head in bewilderment.

"Personnel changes," he prompted. "A terrible shame if these disturbed you, caused you upset, and led you to feel the need to express your views."

"Am I supposed to be disturbed or not?" I asked in total confusion. "And what am I supposed to do or not do if I'm disturbed or not disturbed? And exactly what is disturbing me? Are you hiring a new barkeep and firing the old one?"

Kyle gritted his teeth in frustration. He wasn't the only one frustrated here. Could the guy just fucking talk plain and simple English?

"Changes more involved than a new barkeep. We would deeply regret if these bothered you in any way and caused you to be displeased, to go on a rampage in your displeasure."

"So you want me to ignore the fact that you shuffle your staff around and not lose any sleep over it?" Sounded good to me. It's not like I'd even be aware of any of their staff changes. Crap, I hadn't even known they existed here, with their little empire, up until this month. No big deal to continue ignoring their existence and going on about my life.

Kyle pounded a fist on the desk. He actually cracked the oak with the first blow. I had no idea vampires were that strong. Impressive.

"There is likely to be a coup soon in the area," the vampire said through clenched teeth. "I would like your oath that you will support me, back me personally, and make it difficult for those who oppose me. In return I will guarantee you an audience with The Master."

Well, I guess he could speak for this master guy, or at least influence him enough to guarantee his compliance. Not a bad guy to know, this Kyle. He seriously needed to learn from the elves' mistakes and communicate in a clear and straightforward manner with us though. Otherwise he was going to end up with a sorcerer in a bag when he wanted a walking, talking one.

"Sounds like fun. I'm to take it that your master fellow won't be giving you his blessing?"

"Doubtful," Kyle said warily. "Is that a deal breaker?"

"Nope. Nothing I like better than pissing off the big dogs."

He slid off the desk and motioned toward the door. "As a

gesture of goodwill, will you and your companion leave my club now without further incident, and not return?"

He learned fast. "Sure, although I may reconsider my future patronage if events do not turn out as foreseen." Ha! See? I could talk cryptically, too.

I walked out and was amused to see Wyatt herding his vampire dance partner all over the floor by the force of personal space. He'd narrow the distance between them, she'd back up, and then he'd do it again. Finally her back hit the table and she looked at Wyatt in alarm as he moved in close and placed a hand on her waist.

"Hey sweetie, cutting in here," I told her. Wyatt pivoted to dance with me and I saw the vampire actually sag against the table in relief.

"Did you have a nice talk with Mr. Expensive Suit?" Wyatt was clearly having a good time.

"Yes, but I'm afraid we need to leave now. I'm sorry. I can see you're having fun."

He grinned. "I've had a wonderful time, Sam. Wonderful times with you usually entail getting kicked out of somewhere, though, so I'm not surprised. It was well worth the eviction."

"I'll make it up to you, baby," I told him, making free with my tail on his body.

"I could possibly get drunk enough to overlook the fur and the tail," he said, eyeing me. "But the wings and horns have got to go."

"Deal," I told him as we made our way to the door. I drove home very fast. And yes, the tail was very useful appendage. I highly recommend it.

CHAPTER 18

The week went by, relaxing and uneventful. Wyatt and I rode horses, ate hot wings, curled up together and watched movies until we fell asleep. He'd been practicing killing aliens instead of zombies and I even spent a few mind-numbing hours watching him wave a chunk of plastic around at a television screen and shout in triumph. I was looking forward to a long weekend of fun in Atlantic City, gambling and clubbing. I'd have my stupid meeting, walk away empty-handed, and then Wyatt and I could celebrate the destruction of aliens with a bottle of vodka.

In the back of my mind, I was pretty sure it wouldn't be that peaceful. Haagenti would probably have his people poised and ready to grab me the moment I left the vampires. It was probably for the best. Peaceful always sounded good, but in reality it was very boring. I was looking forward to a few good fights, as long as Wyatt didn't get hurt.

Reed called on Thursday night, right as I was finishing up with my packing. Part of me really wanted to send him to voice mail. It's a wicked twist of fate that something always goes wrong with rental properties right before you need to leave town. Always. And it always requires your immediate presence, often resulting in airline cancellation fees or late arrivals. It was never anything that could be handled by others. I reluctantly answered his call. If I didn't, he'd call Candy and she'd track me down and make me deal with it anyway.

"Wassup?" I greeted him.

"Ms. Martin, I hate to call you directly like this but we've got a problem here that I think you need to deal with personally."

Of course! I'm going to Atlantic City for the weekend, so it has to be something I need to deal with personally.

"When the first one went missing I didn't really think anything about it, but the second one, and now a third one, well I'm worried here."

Whoa, that was really jumping into a topic. What went missing? Was someone ripping copper piping out of my properties? I'd heard crackheads did that and sold the scrap metal to garner drug money.

"It's just not normal for three to be gone like that."

"Wait, wait," I interrupted. "Three of what is missing?"

"Three tenants are missing. These spots in your houses are coveted, so when the first disappeared, I thought someone paid him to leave so they could have his spot. But two more are gone."

He was calling me in a panic over a turnover of three tenants? "So, what's the problem here? Just give their spots to other people."

"We're not so popular anymore, Ms. Martin. Some are packing their things to leave. They're saying that you were supposed to protect them, and if you can't, they are going to run and try to hide."

Huh? Hide from whom? And just because three tenants bail on me, now the rest want to go?

"The missing guys were there in the early evening to secure their spot, and then they were gone by morning. One each night. Vanished. Kitty says she knows what happened."

"Wait, back up a moment here. Who do they need to hide from? And a cat is talking to you? Is this the six-legged green cat? Because I didn't give it the power of speech." Even if I could do that, it probably wouldn't say anything but "feed me" or "pet me." Cats were not great conversationalists.

"She says the three missing ones were murdered. I did find some blood out by the creek promenade, and it is strange that they'd leave willingly, without their belongings."

"And the cat knows what happened to the missing tenants?" Maybe as a werewolf Reed could talk with cats?

"Kitty. She's one of the homeless people, but she doesn't stay here. They all know her. I think she's been around the area for a long time, although I've never seen her before the tenants started disappearing. She says the murderer is usurping your right."

I was flabbergasted. There is no way a homeless person used the word "usurp." It wasn't a word you commonly heard. I doubted Reed knew that word either. Maybe I'd misunderstood him.

"You mean slurp? A man is 'slurping U-right' which must be street slang for taking someone else's stash?" Maybe she was referring to "The Man." Humans blamed everything on "The Man." I'll bet he did a lot of slurping, whoever he was.

"No, usurp." Reed sounded rather awed. "I kid you not, that is exactly what she said. She's one of the more lucid that I've met, and I'm sure I heard her right."

"Reed, I am leaving for Atlantic City in the morning. This will have to wait. The murderer is only taking one per night, right? So I can wait until Monday and I'll lose a max of four people. That's not too bad."

There was a disapproving silence from the phone. I could tell that Reed was one of those who felt duty came before fun, and that four lives outweighed a gambling weekend in his opinion. I let the silence drag on, determined to wait him out, but werewolves are made of strong stuff.

"Okay, fine! I'll be right down, but there might not be a whole lot I can do until I get back."

This sucked. I wasn't about to postpone my trip, but the prospect of having my homeless tenants snatched and "The Man" chipping away at my cash flow wasn't really all that appealing either. Somehow, I doubted I could get this all wrapped up in twenty-four hours though.

Reed was waiting for me at the darkened row houses with a person I can only assume was Kitty. The woman appeared to be genderless in her bulky layers of clothing. It was impossible to tell if she was stocky or if she just had on fifteen shirts under her dark, hunter green jacket. A knit cap hid her hair, and mismatched gloves covered her hands. The oddest thing in her appearance was the very long scarf that merged her head into her shoulders, vanished under her coat, and appeared in two long strips from under the bottom of the coat to dangle down between her legs, like extra vestigial limbs. It was hard to keep my eyes from the scarf ends swinging from her crotch.

"This is Kitty." Reed motioned to me, "Kitty, this is Ms. Martin. She owns these buildings and she really wants to hear all you know about this man who is murdering her tenants."

Kitty eyed me up and down. I wondered if she was thinking about stealing my clothing to add yet one more layer. Finally satisfied, she nodded.

"The man takes people, kills them, and cuts off their ears."

Oh great. The homeless boogie man again. Reed dragged me all the way down here to hear a fairly tale. I glared at him.

Kitty shook her head. "He is in your territory, killing your people. And now he has the nerve to walk right into your house and take them." She looked me up and down again. "You have a responsibility to protect them. They prayed for help, and you, their Ha-Satan, must answer their pleas."

What the hell? She sounded like that lump of blanket outside the vacant grocery store. Even if I was the Iblis, I wouldn't be running around answering human prayers. What Bible was this woman reading?

"I didn't come down here to hear a ghost story. I don't care about some Ted Bundy with an ear fetish. Do you know why my tenants are leaving or not?"

"You should care," she replied in an equally irritated tone. "He's hunting in your territory. He's killing what belongs to you. He's trying to take your place, usurping your rights."

There was that usurp word again. I'd heard it with my own ears. And speaking of ears.

"So you think this guy, this murderer, is snatching homeless people, killing them, and making trophies out of their ears? He's doing this to rub my nose in it? As a deliberate challenge because he wants to be the devil?"

Kitty shifted from foot to foot. "I don't think he's doing it deliberately to piss you off. You should be pissed off though. I'm pissed off. I can only watch him. I can't kill him, but you can."

I looked over at Reed for confirmation. He nodded.

"I don't know anything about ears, or this slurping business, but I do think someone is killing off your tenants one by one," the werewolf said.

I sighed. I guessed I was going to have to find this guy and take him out. I'd rather let the police deal with it, but he was costing me, taking rent money out of my pocket, so to speak.

And he was hunting in my territory, poaching. Plus, he might do as the rumors said and start killing children. If that fucker so much as looked at Angelo Perez, I'd rip his own ears off. Other body parts, too.

"Do you have his name and address? Please tell me you at least know more about this guy beyond his fascination with ears."

The woman shook her head. "I don't know that. I know where he goes, where he likes to frequent. You can track him from there."

I turned to Reed. "If we had an address, I'd just run by there now and blow him the fuck up. I don't have time to do a tracking job tonight though. I've got to leave for Atlantic City in the morning and I'll be there all weekend."

Reed stiffened, disappointment in his eyes. Having a werewolf look at me like that was pretty horrible. It was worse than when Boomer gave me that look.

"I can't postpone this trip. Seriously. I've got to meet with a guy there, and he's like the fucking Pope to try and get an appointment with. There's no way he'll ever let me reschedule. Can you pull some guard duty till then? At least people will feel safe here and hopefully we can fill the open spots with new tenants."

"I can do that." I knew Reed would do his absolute best to keep the people safe, but he still had that look in his eyes, as if I'd let him down.

"One more thing. I need someone to keep an eye on this boy." I scribbled the Perez's address on a scrap of paper. "The little one. He's about five, I think. If you think he's in any danger, step it up and do full security on him. If you need helpers, go ahead and bring them in. Just bill me."

"Sure. You'll be back on Monday?"

"Sunday. I'll come back immediately after my meeting and call you as soon as I'm in town."

I wasn't sure how I was going to fit in a hunt for this murderer when I'd probably have a horde of demons breathing down my neck. Heck, I wasn't even sure I'd be returning from Atlantic City. If not, no one would see me on this side of the gates for at least a century. Reed and the werewolves may end up needing to handle this one solo.

CHAPTER 19

*W*e were up early, cramming duffle bags into my little Corvette trunk. I refused to drive all the way to Atlantic City in the huge Suburban, so we packed extra light. Honestly, it was mostly my stuff. Wyatt intended to be fighting off aliens for the weekend and didn't expect to need much in the way of clothing changes. I'm pretty sure all he had in his duffle bag were a couple pairs of underwear and a toothbrush. I'm not normally much of a clothes horse, but I didn't know what my much anticipated hunt would entail. In addition to jeans, I'd thrown in a couple of dresses and heels, fully expecting that they'd be so trashed I wouldn't return with them.

Wyatt slept until we were north of Baltimore, which didn't make for an entertaining drive. Aside from a few traffic snarls, we moved along pretty well. I had to restrain myself from drawing on Wyatt's snoring face with a sharpie or stuffing Doritos up his nose though. Finally, I turned on the radio to distract myself and put my favorite soft rock station on. Wyatt stirred and pulled his coat up over his head.

I had a lot to think about anyway. Haagenti was going to

be on me like flies on shit as soon as I left Atlantic City. He wouldn't trust me to turn the artifact over if some miracle occurred and I actually did manage to retrieve it. He'd have someone up there to watch me, to follow me home, to snatch it from me, and grab me, too. Plus, I was sure by now he knew that I wasn't going to succeed. Either way, his efforts to punish me for my insolence would be tenfold after this weekend.

I thought about voluntarily going home and taking my lumps. The longer I waited, the more my household would suffer his assaults. I glanced over at Wyatt. He'd be in danger, too. If Haagenti had any sense whatsoever, he'd quickly realize my affection for Wyatt and threaten him. If I left, though, I'd probably never see Wyatt or any of my human friends again. They'd all be dead by the time Haagenti finished with me. I thought about Candy and the werewolf issues, Michelle and our dreams of rental-world domination, of Reed and this killer picking off my tenants. All that would have to go on without me if I was being dipped in liquid nitrogen or pulled apart on a rack for a hundred years or so.

I thought of Gregory. He wouldn't care if Haagenti grabbed me. A few centuries of my being tortured wouldn't put a crease in his plans. Besides, if he needed me for anything, he could just summon me right out from under Haagenti's nose. The whole scenario would probably amuse him. Somehow, the thought was comforting. He was my one constant. He wouldn't age and die in a mere century. He wouldn't change. I'd come out of the ordeal, and he'd still be the same fascinating, enthralling asshole he was now.

I glanced over and saw Wyatt glaring at me. Journey's "Lovin' Touchin', Squeezin'" was playing on the radio.

"What?" I asked.

"You secretly hate me, don't you." He gestured toward the radio. "You can't stand the thought of me taking a much needed nap and leaving you to drive without conversation. You're torturing me with this sappy stuff."

"It's Journey. I love this song."

Wyatt mumbled something under his breath, picked up the CD case, and started looking through it. He paused with a choked noise, his eyes growing huge.

"You're joking, Sam. Justin Bieber? What are you, a twelve-year old girl?"

One Less Lonely Girl. I sang the song in my head. That was a great song. How could he not like that song? Still, I squirmed a bit in embarrassment.

"A twelve-year old girl gave me that CD," I lied. "For my birthday."

Wyatt snorted. "It's a good thing you're a terrible liar. Otherwise, I'd be horrified at the thought that a demon has been hanging out with a bunch of giggling pre-teens."

He continued to thumb through the CDs. "Air Supply Greatest Hits? No, no, I'm wrong here. It's an Air Supply cover band in Spanish." He waved the offending CD in my face. "Sam, what on earth are you thinking? How did you even get this thing?"

"Some tenant left it behind," I told him. "We evicted him, and there were all these CDs. Most were in Spanish, but I've got a Barry Manilow in there, too. That one's in English."

Wyatt looked at me a moment, and with the fastest movement I've ever seen, rolled down the window and tossed the case of CDs out onto the highway. It barely hit the road before a semi plowed over it.

I was pissed. "You asshole. I liked those CDs. I don't come over to your house and trash your video games, or drive over your controllers. If you think that will make me listen to that Dubstep crap for the next two hours, then you better fucking think again."

"I'm sorry Sam, but it's past time for a musical intervention here. You can't keep listening to this stuff. It wasn't even remotely good when it was popular, and it certainly hasn't gained anything over time. You need to pull yourself together and try to expand your musical interests a bit. You're on a downward spiral, and if you keep this up, you'll find yourself friendless, living in a box in a back alley, stinking of your own excrement, and covered in track marks."

I looked at him in surprise. I had no idea Air Supply led to lack of bowel control and hard core drug usage. I wondered if it was something subliminal, a kind of compulsion programmed into the lyrics. Was Russell Hitchcock a sorcerer? He didn't look that menacing to me, but sorcerers were pretty sneaky. Even so, I was sure Justin Bieber was okay. As soon as we hit a rest stop, I was ordering a replacement from my iPhone. The Barry Manilow one, too.

Wyatt took out a little USB stick and waved it at me.

"I made a playlist before we left. See? This is the sort of thoughtful thing boyfriends do for their girlfriends. I promise no Dubstep. Just some songs I thought you'd like that won't drive me bonkers. I'll put it on your stereo and hopefully continue my nap while you enjoy music that reasonably hip people might listen to." He popped the USB stick into a slot on my stereo and a rap song filled the car.

Wyatt dozed back off, and I was entertained by his musical selections. The collection he'd chosen was eclectic. A few stereotypical Rob Zombie songs, but the rest were a pleasant surprise. Within an hour, I'd become a fan of Prodigy, Eminem, and some band named Sick Puppies.

We were past Aberdeen and fairly close to the section where Maryland, Delaware, Pennsylvania, and New Jersey all meet in a rush of inlets and waterways when I pulled over and woke Wyatt up for a pit stop.

"We're almost to the Delaware border. We've got another

hour and a half or so until we get there, so I thought we'd grab some coffee."

Wyatt nodded, looking at the map on his cell phone. He'd printed out the directions he wanted me to take before we'd left the house, and for once, I didn't disagree. We'd cross the Memorial Bridge and drive a bit on the New Jersey Turnpike, which I detested, then veer off onto some lesser traveled roads into Atlantic City.

"I think there's a ferry from Cape May into Delaware," he said with interest. "On the way back, let's do the ferry and the scenic route along the ocean. We can cross the Bay Bridge in Maryland. Of course, that all depends on if the vampires are running us out of the state on a rail, or if your demon buddy is after you with a blow torch."

Wyatt and I had strategized for days on what we'd possibly face during and after this trip. It would be good to have another set of eyes checking on the vampire motives and looking out for other demons. Plus, he needed to be aware of the situation so he could avoid getting killed if things got really violent.

Wyatt looked around the rest area with its selection of fast food stands. "Do you think they're following us? Are there any here?"

"Haagenti's crew wouldn't bother," I told him. "They'll be at the casino to make sure I show up and have the meeting, but they're not going to waste time following me around on my way there. I'm hoping to have a couple of days for Haagenti to see if I'm going to deliver the artifact to him, then all hell is going to rain down on my head."

"Somehow, I don't think you're going to get a few days," Wyatt commented grimly. "I'm thinking they're going to jump the gun and grab you right in the hotel, maybe even before your meeting."

It was a possibility, but I expected that Haagenti would

want to wait to see if I actually came up with the sword. And he was probably paying these guys well enough that they'd hold back, no matter how tempting a smackdown on me might be.

"It's the vampires I'm more worried about right now," I said. "I'm not sure what kind of reception I'm going to get. I get the impression they are the sneaky cloak-and-dagger kind. So they may be very nice and polite to my face and try to stick a poisoned dart in my back, just to make sure I don't run around screwing up their businesses."

Wyatt made a face. "I wish we knew more about them. I have no idea if I'm supposed to be packing holy water, crucifixes, or a jar of minced garlic. I brought my DE, although it might just piss them off. Not like it did a whole lot of good against your angel friend."

"I think vampires might be more susceptible to a .50-caliber bullet to the head than an angel. At least it should slow them down enough for you to run for it. I'd advise heading for a populated area. They seem to prefer to keep things low profile. And always trust your instincts. Sometimes the stupidest shit is the shit that saves your life."

I saw over a dozen casino resorts in the town as we pulled in, and I wondered how profitable they were. Atlantic City is cool and all, but it's no Las Vegas. It had that tired look, like a famous hooker past her prime. Fine in soft lighting, rather disturbing in the harsh glare of daylight. Right off the main strip, the city faded into a ghetto of boarded up stores, pawnshops, and convenience marts. Thankfully, most patrons didn't seem to be out during the unflinching noon hours. Aside from the business crowd and locals, visitors remained sheltered in the comforting embrace of the casinos.

Our resort was one of the newer ones, just down the street from the Trump resort. I was tempted to pop over there and see if I could luck out and have a Donald sighting.

There wasn't a demon alive that wouldn't give their six arms to Own Donald Trump. No one had been so coveted since Elvis. The guy was rumored to have spent a fortune on protection. So far no demon had been able to grab him, but I would hate to find out he was here in Atlantic City the same time as I was and I didn't make an attempt.

The man at the check-in desk was human and very polite. He pulled my name up on his screen and muttered something under his breath as he glanced rapidly from the screen to me and back again. Frantically he looked around the reception area, presumably for an actual vampire to take over.

"Just a moment, Baal," he sputtered. "We didn't expect you this early, and had wanted to greet you in a more ostentatious fashion."

"I'm pooped." I yawned. "Let's skip the ostentation for now. I drove the whole way up here, while my companion slept." I shot Wyatt a teasing frown. "He was no help, no entertainment whatsoever. And he snores. Right now I just want to raid the mini bar and see if I can find Donald Trump."

"He's not in town," the desk clerk interjected. I got the feeling he repeated this phrase a lot. I wondered how many demons availed themselves of this casino's hospitality in the hopes of snagging The Donald? No wonder they were annoyed.

"Ah well. Just give us our keys and we'll go entertain ourselves." I put my hand out.

"But, the Casino Manager, she really wanted to welcome you. And you have a meeting scheduled, and some proposed activities to review." He looked around frantically again. I reached over the counter and snatched the key cards from his hand.

"Your Casino Manager can catch up with me later.

Honestly, it's not a big deal. You really don't want me waiting around here in your lobby. I might get bored. You wouldn't like me when I'm bored."

That seemed to alarm him even further. After practically shoving a terrified bellhop down our throats, he scurried off, no doubt in search of the Casino Manager.

The bellhop was human, too. He kept shooting nervous glances at me and sympathetic ones at Wyatt. I'm sure he was imagining a horrible, bloody fate for him. Wyatt grinned up at the elevator numbers and pinched my ass. I heard the bellhop gasp in alarm.

The elevator opened onto our floor and Wyatt continued to fondle my butt as I lead the way out. "Refreshed from your nap, I take it? Forget looking for The Donald; let's order room service and fuck for a couple of hours."

"I've got to check in for my tournament," Wyatt said as I unlocked the room. "I can probably spare an hour or two though."

I tipped the red-faced bellhop. "You can just forget about that tournament tonight because I'm planning to tear you up. By the time I finish with you, you won't be able to walk. Take a nap while I'm driving, will you? I'm going to shove one of those mini-bar wines up your ass for that one."

The poor guy raced through the door. Wyatt and I dissolved in laughter.

"You do realize that they are all appalled at my lack of worshipful respect toward you?" Wyatt laughed. "I guess I'm supposed to be shackled, crawling behind you on all fours, licking your feet and speaking only when spoken to?"

"Oh wow. We totally have to do that sometime Wyatt!" I was serious. "Then you can shackle me and I'll pretend to be your pet demon. You'll be the mighty sorcerer who has me in a sacred circle and is making me do all kinds of kinky things to pleasure him. Oh wow."

That little mischievous gleam flashed in Wyatt's eyes. "I'll definitely put that one on my to-do list. Let me run down to the registration table and get all that out of the way. It shouldn't take more than an hour. I'll text you when I'm done and we'll have the whole evening free to shackle each other and empty the mini bar."

Wyatt headed down to do his thing and I unpacked my small bag and explored the room. It was a nice suite, high up in the resort, and overlooking the ocean from a spacious balcony. The bed was a dark, four-poster with a deep red brocade bedspread and throw pillows. Matching pillows were scattered artfully on the couch and chairs. An elegant desk and modern office chair sat off to the side of the sitting area with a full range of internet hookups. A massive flat-screen TV dominated the far wall, and I was happy to see the remote was not chained to it. Surround sound speakers were strategically placed throughout the room. Wyatt would definitely approve of the electronics options.

The bathroom was a work of art. Double sinks against a wall of mirrors were illuminated by recessed lights. A huge spa tub in beige and gold marble flanked an enormous glass walled shower with double heads and cushioned marble bench seats. The most amazing part about the whole bathroom was the televisions. A small flat-screen TV was mounted between the sinks against the mirrored wall. Another was in the little closet that held the toilet. A third was on the wall facing the tub, and a fourth actually inside the shower enclosure. I examined it closely, amazed that it could function with all the water and steam of the shower. Each set was numbered, and the two remotes showed the TV numbers on them so you could have a different show on each set and control them with the one remote. Even though I'd showered this morning, I took another one just to experience the joy of lathering up while watching Rachel Ray drizzle sweet potato fries with balsamic vinegar.

I was just starting to get bored when a human knocked on my door with a bottle of wine. He wasn't dressed like one of the hotel employees, but I let him in anyway. I'm not a huge fan of wine, but it's impossible for me to turn down a gift of any kind. He glanced briefly around the room and handed me the bottle, showcasing the pretty label of gold swirls on a cream background. I recognized it right away. It was elf wine.

My mind raced. Elves don't cross the gates, and even though I'd pissed off a few of the high lords, I doubted they were angry enough to send someone over here to take me out. And they probably wouldn't be presenting me with gifts before they killed me. This human didn't appear to be a sorcerer, just one of their messengers. I wondered briefly if this was about the incident with Candy and the trap.

"Baal," the messenger said. "Lord Taullian would like to respectfully request your services in a matter of personal importance to him. He has heard of your recent troubles and can offer assistance as an added incentive."

Taullian? That wasn't the guy I helped with the sorcerer. At least I didn't think so. There were so many of them; they were all lords, too. I looked at the human in confusion, hoping he'd help me out here.

"The Western Red Forest? By Maugan Swamp?" the messenger prompted helpfully.

That was where I'd grown up. I'd spent my childhood playing in that forest. The elf children would shoot at us with their arrows, tease us, and try to drive us from the woods. We'd reciprocate, but they were so fast, and we'd been warned not to kill them. Fond memories.

"I'm honored His Lordship would consider me, but I'm

rather occupied right now." I tried to convey an appropriate amount of regret.

"This isn't a matter that requires your immediate attention," he assured me. "Once you have a free moment in your schedule, Lord Taullian would greatly appreciate it if you would attend him and hear his request. And, of course, if your current situation becomes problematic, please don't hesitate to ask his assistance."

That was a strange offer. Usually the elves didn't interfere with demon matters. And they certainly didn't offer assistance without a signed contract. This was definitely something to keep in my back pocket. If things got too hot with Haagenti, it was nice to know I had options.

"It could be months," I warned. "I don't know how this whole thing is going to work out. It might be a while before I have any free time."

"Lord Taullian understands, Baal. If we don't hear from you in a few months, we will respectfully remind you of our request." He bowed and let himself out.

That sounded menacing, but it wasn't. It was actually very prudent to schedule a reminder like this. Demons often forgot commitments, and I was very interested in what this guy had in mind.

Wyatt called to tell me he'd been longer than he thought down in registration. There was a briefing he had to attend, then a social networking event. He'd also been roped into a dinner that night. I was bummed that I couldn't spend time with him as planned, but he had his own life and hobbies. It wasn't often he got to hang out with a group of gamers from all over the country, and it was understandable that he'd want to make the most of the event. I told him to be careful, to shoot first and ask questions later, and then headed down to see what I could find to entertain myself.

As I soon discovered, there were four restaurants and a host of high-end shops in the resort, all surrounding the flashy din of the casino. Signs everywhere welcomed the gamers, and also advertised a comedy act that was enthusiastically billed as the best outside of Vegas. The whole thing seemed flat, kind of forced, like no one's heart was really in it. Everything was very well organized, carefully displayed, and meticulously run in a terribly soulless manner. I played around with a couple of the slot machines and then headed to the bar.

The bartender, wearing a name tag proclaiming him to be "Scott," was the first non-human I'd met so far in the place, although from the look of him and absolute absence of any kind of energy, he had to have been a fairly recent turn. He wasn't what you'd expect a vampire to look like. He was overweight, with eyes like a basset hound and a big round nose. I wondered if vampires got better looking with age. This guy certainly was proof that they didn't select their candidates primarily on looks. He glanced up at me as I sat down and smiled a welcome with his mouth. His eyes looked right through me, as if I weren't even there, as if I didn't matter one bit, didn't register at all on his scale of importance. I could have been a gnat.

"What can I get you?" His voice friendly, his eyes looking right through me.

It was weird. The vampires had always been cloying, obsequious, and polite. He wasn't disrespectful, there was just something empty in his attitude. It was as if he were on auto-pilot.

"Bud Light," I told him. I just wasn't in the mood for vodka right now. "How long have you been here, Scott?"

"Couple of months," he said in that cheerful, empty voice. "Moved here from New York. Are you in town for the gaming tournament?"

I picked up the beer he'd placed in front of me and took a

swig. Samantha Martin was a nondescript middle-aged female. Not the usual competitive gamer. Maybe he thought I was here chaperoning my geeky teenager?

"My boyfriend is. I've got a brief meeting, but I'm mainly just trying to enjoy myself." I smiled at him. "What do you do for fun around here?" I wondered if there were vampire-only clubs and parties, if they went grocery shopping and watched Pay-Per-View like the rest of the world.

"Well, the beach is pretty deserted this time of year, but it's still nice to walk along the boardwalk and check out the shops. You can pretty much find any kind of entertainment, live music, comedy shows, acrobatics, and theatrical presentations. Lots of dance clubs. And, of course, everyone enjoys the gambling. Is there a particular game you play? Blackjack? Poker?" He was so friendly and chatty. Was I the only one who noticed how off it all seemed?

I handed him my room key to charge the beer and took a plunge.

"How long have you been a vampire, Scott?" I asked.

He looked at me quizzically. I almost believed him.

"Wow, maybe I shouldn't have given you that beer. You're sounding like you've had quite enough already." He laughed in a genial manner. "I've never had anyone mistake me for Dracula before." He gestured at his round belly. "Not exactly the tall-dark-handsome-with-a-cape type."

He swiped my card and froze, what little color he had draining out of him in a dramatic sweep. He actually had to steady himself with a hand on the electronic register as he stared at the screen.

"Baal. I... I... I'm so sorry. I didn't recognize you, what you are. I meant no disrespect. I'm so sorry." He shook slightly and stared at the spot just below my eyes. Poor guy was terrified. What were they teaching these vampires about us?

"Dude, it's okay" I reassured him in what I hoped was a friendly manner. "Seriously. I've been living as a human for over forty years and hardly anyone recognizes me. I'd have been insulted if you did know what I was at a glance. We're good. Really."

He looked up at me, curiosity getting the better of him.

"Forty years? Honestly? I see your kind in here a lot, but I don't think they stay longer than a couple of days."

"I had to really control myself, to hold back a lot to remain undetected," I told him. "I'm proud to say I had an angel within twenty feet of me once and he didn't even recognize me. So don't feel bad. Even the vampires down in Baltimore didn't know, and I've been practically camped out on their doorstep. Your boss can hardly fault you."

He grimaced. "Oh yes, she can. Actions are what matters. Results, intentions, circumstances are all of little importance."

He recited this like it was something he'd memorized from a vampire training manual. I wasn't sure if he was too young to have perfected the polite distance that all of the other vampires had with me, or if the shock of finding out I was a demon had blown his composure clean away. Either way, I planned on taking advantage of his chattiness.

"I've heard 'the end justifies the means,' but this whole 'means above all' doesn't seem very productive. How the hell do you guys get anything done?"

He hesitated for a moment, glancing around. "The code of behavior has loopholes, but only the very old are skilled enough to take advantage of them. It's better for the rest of us to follow the letter of the law."

Before I could reply, an out-of-breath woman dashed through the bar to my side, obviously awaiting my attention. I turned and looked at her obligingly. This must be that Casino Manager who everyone had been insisting I meet.

"Baal, we welcome you here," she gasped. I wonder how far she'd run to make sure I didn't disappear before she managed to finally speak with me. "My name is Kelly and I manage the casino. I'd like to introduce you to Mario who will be your liaison during your stay."

Mario must not run as fast, since he hadn't yet arrived. I wondered if he looked like the video game Mario. Kelly did not look like a video game character. She was a vampire, not as young as Scott the bartender, but not old enough to be putting out any kind of power signature. She looked to be in her mid-twenties, although with vampires it was impossible to tell. She was tiny. Barely over five feet and slight of frame, probably a hundred pounds max. She looked to be of Mediterranean descent. Her skin tone light, her eyes as dark as her hair, her face an adorable heart shape with high cheek-bones and a tiny, pert, turned-up nose. All her features pointed toward a fragile, delicate woman, but the way she carried herself, the authority in her every movement, spoke otherwise. This was a woman who'd had to fight a stereotype every step of the way to be taken seriously. Maybe because of that her emotions were closer to the surface, covered by only a thin crust of polite distance, as opposed to the miles of concrete that surrounded the other vampires I'd met. Besides Scott, that is.

"If there is anything you need, anything at all, please don't hesitate to let Mario or me know. Mario will always be at hand to serve you, and I'll give you my cell phone number in case you need to reach me directly."

I realized that Mario was going to be my minder. He'd make sure I didn't cause too much trouble, steer me in the appropriate direction, let the higher-ups know if I was getting out of hand. I wondered if they did this with all the demons, or if Kyle had ratted me out as particularly trou-blesome.

"Your meeting with The Master is scheduled for Sunday morning. We have a hunt scheduled for you Saturday night. I have several targets for you to choose from, and I took the liberty of noting their schedules for that night so that you may save time and effort in locating your chosen prey."

Ahhh. My meeting right after the hunt. That way I don't get so carried away killing things that I run out of control. I'd have a tight time window to keep to. If I got over excited and missed my meeting, well then I'd certainly not be granted another. They'd been told I was under pressure to deliver this thing, so this schedule would assure I'd keep my killing within parameters. I'd be willing to bet Kelly wouldn't even discuss potential prey until tomorrow, just in case I was tempted to start early. Plus, they'd scoped out the schedules of the victims to keep me from enlarging my kill numbers as I looked for them. Very smart folk, these vampires.

"I'm afraid we're still nailing down those schedules, so I won't be able to discuss the potential prey until late tomorrow afternoon," she apologized. Just as I'd thought. "I can offer you several choices of entertainment for tonight and tomorrow though. Perhaps you would like a snack?" She said this with a significant look. Not this again. I assumed I needed to guess what the fuck she meant.

"Snack like burger bites?" I asked. "Or snack like something bipedal that would scream a lot and beg for mercy?"

"The latter." She smiled, as if she'd just offered me a pretzel. "I was told that you brought a human toy for enjoyment, but I thought perhaps you might like something additional? I'm assuming you may have already used up the one you brought with you."

Sheesh, these vampires were worse than we were.

"Wyatt is my companion, my most favored human. He's not a toy. I don't intend to break him or use him up. He's going to be occupied with the gaming tournament for most of the weekend, so I'll probably do the tourist thing, gamble a bit, see if I can find The Donald and Own him."

A brief look of frustration crossed Kelly's face. I'm sure she would have preferred I locked myself in my room and devoured humans for the weekend. If I was out and about, Mario would have his hands full keeping me in line. Too bad.

"I don't believe Mr. Trump is in town. Mario will be thrilled to show you the highlights of Atlantic City and our fair casino though."

Yeah, I bet he'd be thrilled. Hope they were paying this guy a lot of money.

"So you're in charge of this whole resort? Impressive." I thought I'd butter her up a bit and see if I could get any useful information from her. It worked. She practically glowed with pride.

"Oh no. I report directly to the General Manager though. I'm in charge of the casino and the VIP services. Stephen is in charge of the hotel, dining, and facilities. With VIP guests such as yourself, I have primary responsibility for their entire experience."

She said this with a smug look lurking under the polite, generic smile, indicating that this function put her a notch above Stephen in the chain of command. We demons understand the importance of these little things, since knowing where you stood in a hierarchy was a big part of our lives. It was either a big part of vampire lives too, or Kelly just had an axe to grind with Stephen and liked rubbing his nose in the fact that she was a smidgen more important. I nodded and looked at her as if her status pleased me.

"Can you let me know if there are any other demons in the resort, and where their current locations are?" If she'd tell me, it would save me time. I didn't really feel like spending the afternoon combing the resort looking for Haagenti's goons.

215

Kelly looked suspicious. I knew she was well aware of every "VIP" in her resort and probably had minders tracking their every breath. I could see her wondering why I wanted this information and if it would be detrimental to her if she gave it to me. We don't usually work in groups, so it wasn't likely that I'd gather a posse and trash the casino. Still, I'm sure she was wary of my intentions.

"There are three," she said grudgingly. "Two are in male form, the other in female form. They don't appear to be together. One male is currently at the spa getting a pedicure, of all things. The female is at the ten dollar blackjack table, although she is making some noise about being hungry. The other is in his room. He is scheduled to leave tonight."

Wow. I was really liking this Kelly woman. She was obviously stretched thin with four of us here at one time, but still knew exactly where we each were.

"You're good," I told her, not shy about giving praise when it was due. "Why did it take you so long to track me down? You should have had a tag in my ear the moment I stepped through the doorway."

I could see the aloof mask getting thinner.

"We didn't expect you so early. In our experience, demons usually don't get up before noon, and we knew you had a good drive to get here. After you got here, none of us seemed to be able to identify you easily. The reservations desk had only a vague description."

She paused and her eyes ran over me in admiration.

"You have the most convincing human form I've ever seen. You don't leak energy. Even your actions are those of a human. If you hadn't used your room key to pay for your drink, you would probably still be wandering around here unnoticed, until you started counting cards at blackjack or manipulating the roulette wheel, that is."

"Or exploding glasses of vodka while trying to freeze

them," I added. I was sure she'd heard about the fracas at Bang.

She couldn't hide a quick grin, and the mask evaporated.

"I know the most successful predators are those that blend in, appear other than what they are, but..." She paused, deciding how to phrase her question. "But does it bother you when others underestimate you, think you're just a weak human?"

This was clearly something she experienced all the time. And it bothered her.

"It's a decision you have to make," I told her honestly. "Personally, I like to say 'fuck it.' Let them underestimate me. Means they're more surprised when I drive a pike through their face."

Kelly looked doubtful. "But don't you demons put huge stock in your place in the hierarchy? If you're underestimated, doesn't that affect your rank?"

I shrugged. "Yes, but I don't really care."

"Doesn't it hurt your pride? Isn't it insulting when someone thinks you're a nobody, thinks you're not worthy of respect?" she asked.

Like when someone thinks you're an insignificant, worthless cockroach. I winced. It had never bothered me before, but I was starting to care what that stupid angel thought about me.

"Pride has a terrible price," I told her. "People with pride are so easy to defeat. They never see it coming. A little cockroach takes down the mighty giant. Of course, it's best to make it look like a fluke, an accident, and run and hide as quickly as you can."

Kelly looked doubtful. "But then no one knows you've done it. They still won't respect you. How can you advance, live up to your potential, and take your rightful place in the world if you hide in the woodwork like a cockroach?"

I was feeling really uncomfortable with her logic. All this talk of respect was bullshit. She wasn't getting my point here.

"There's a reason pride is a sin," I told her. "The inner strength you feel is deceptive. It actually creates enormous vulnerability, sets you up for a fall of your own making."

I made a quick decision. Heck, it worked with the gate guardian in Columbia, might work with vampires, too.

"I'd really like it if you'd join me for dinner. Wyatt will be busy with his gaming friends, and eating alone is boring. You do eat, don't you? You guys consume more than blood, right?" I hoped so, otherwise it might be an awkward dinner.

She looked surprised and a little nervous. "Yes, I eat solid food. I actually eat a lot. Very fast metabolism, you see."

I smiled. "Why don't you pick the place, make the reservations, since you know the restaurants. I'll put myself in your capable hands. Mario can let me know when and where." I pointed to a large, bouncer-looking man with a Bluetooth prominently attached to one ear. "I assume that's Mario."

Kelly nodded and gestured the man over. Mario most definitely did not look like the video game Mario. He was a vampire, a huge black guy with a shaved head and not a bushy mustache in sight.

"Mario, this is our honored guest. Please ensure she enjoys her visit by being attentive to her every need."

"Call me Sam," I told him.

"Of course, Baal." I got the feeling that he would never call me Sam.

"All righty then. Come on Mario, let's go get ourselves a pedicure." I said, gesturing for him to lead the way toward the day spa and demon number one.

The demon was picking out pink nail polish. Idiot. I watched him a few seconds to see if I could determine who he was. He wasn't leaking quite as much power as most, so it took me a moment. Finally, I realized with a sinking heart that it was Sobronoy.

Sobronoy is a hit-man. For a fee, he'll knock down the targeted demon and numb them physically, confusing their thoughts enough to incapacitate them, and deliver them to whoever paid him for the job. He was good. It was looking like I would soon be up close and personal with Haagenti.

I walked up to him and handed him some blue polish. "Here. Pink is so last year."

He tensed, finally realizing who I was, and turned to fix me with a cold gaze.

"Nice form." His eyes moved slowly down to my feet and back up. "Should be great fun to peel the flesh off you one strip at a time. Maybe Haagenti will let me watch."

I felt slightly ill. This wasn't going to be the enjoyable kind of torture.

"You better hope you get this thing, and that you have the good sense to turn it over to Haagenti. Maybe he'll be so pleased with the object that he'll take it easy on you. Otherwise you're going to be in for a difficult couple of centuries. Either way, you're not leaving this casino on Sunday, so you better get your affairs in order."

There wasn't a gate within a hundred miles of the casino, so his comment could only mean one thing. He had a button. The thought chilled me even further. Buttons were created by the elves, and sold by them at substantial cost. Haagenti wanted to ensure my return enough that he'd bought one, or possibly more, and given them to his staff. All Sobronoy had to do was grab me, activate the portable gate, and we'd probably be standing right in front of Haagenti. Damn.

"Either way, I'm trying to ensure you don't make a terrible fashion mistake." I pushed the blue polish into his hand. "I'm not going home accompanied by a demon wearing pink polish."

I turned and strolled out of the spa. I was good until Sunday. Not sure what I intended to do from that point on though.

"Where is the other one?" I asked Mario.

He spoke quietly, little more than a whisper into his tiny headset.

"Dice."

We walked over toward the dice table and I saw her right away. She was around my level, although her form was somewhat odd with too-thin, bent legs and a nose that looked more like a beak. She had a huge platter of calamari, and her vampire minder was desperately trying to keep her from placing it on the felt of the game table. Maybe she would have played better betting calamari rings. She certainly couldn't do worse from the ever-decreasing pile of chips by her side. Demons are usually very good at gambling. We can count cards with the skill of a computer, run the odds, and, when that fails, weight the dice slightly or rig the slot machine. She must not have understood the game rules to be losing so badly. That or she was distracted by the calamari.

I strolled up beside her, took a piece of calamari and ate it, not looking directly at her. She stiffened, recognizing me, and then looked down at the fried squid. I took another piece and ate it, licking my fingers. Mario made a strangled noise, and I could feel him tense. No doubt he thought walking up to some unknown being and eating their food uninvited was picking a fight. Not with demons. Stealing food, especially in this blatant way, was a social thing. Stealing anything else would result in immediate retaliation, but not food.

"Are you enjoying your vacation?" She offered me more of the calamari. Mario's eyes widened and he released the breath he'd been holding for far too long.

She was Labisi, I finally realized. It took me a while since

Labisi didn't normally go in female form. She was one of Amaimon's servants. I wondered if Haagenti had borrowed her or if he'd been owed a service. He and Amaimon were in the same peer group.

"Yes." I took another calamari ring. "Although I assume by your and Sobronoy's presence that my vacation is coming to an end." A nasty, bloody end, probably.

She smiled cruelly, eating a couple of the rings herself and wiping her hands on the table felt, much to the annoyance of her minder and the dealer.

"Yes, I'm here as back-up. Although given Sobronoy's reputation, I doubt my services will be needed."

Lovely. Labisi wasn't as good a retriever as Sobronoy, but she was still formidable.

"My meeting isn't until Sunday. Hopefully I'll get the artifact and Haagenti will be less pissed off at me when you guys reel me in."

She shrugged. "Doesn't matter to me. I'm enjoying myself, and I get paid whether Sobronoy brings you in or I do."

I nodded, and stuffing another calamari ring into my mouth, walked away. Mario followed me closely, even as I left the casino and headed up to my room. I needed to think and plan before my dinner with Kelly.

The third demon was waiting for me by my door. Mario stood attentively by the elevator and watched as I approached the guy. This one I didn't recognize.

"Let me guess. You have a witty speech about how doomed I am, and how the moment this meeting is over you're going to snatch me and present me with a bow to Haagenti for my well-deserved punishment."

He was amused. "No, I'm here to make you an offer."

I looked at him with suspicion.

"The offer from Ahriman still stands," he said. "One word and all this goes away."

Ahriman. The breeding contract. Gregory would fucking kill me if I accepted that offer.

"Why me?" I asked him. "Wasn't Ahriman alive during the wars? He's ancient, powerful. What would he want with a troublesome imp?"

"He finds you interesting. You are the first thing since the war to jolt him from boredom. He thinks you will contribute to amazing offspring, that you will be an enjoyable partner."

I stared at him in amazement. "Does he know that I take? That I devour?"

Bad things happened when demons got their personal energy too close to mine. I hoped I'd be able to breed without killing a demon, but I'd begun to wonder. If I'd really snatched part of Gregory and kept it, a powerful angel, what would I do to a demon? Even one as strong as Ahriman.

"Ahriman finds that an admirable trait in a partner."

I stood for a moment, considering that statement.

"I'm rather occupied right now." I repeated what I'd said to the elf's messenger. "I will consider the offer though."

He nodded. "He is ready to assist if you need."

The demon turned and left as I went into my room and shut the door firmly behind me. That elf lord, and now Ahriman. Offers of protection with strings attached all around me. I wondered if Gregory would show up with a similar offer. Something inside me lurched a bit at the thought. It would never happen though. He'd probably be happy if Haagenti took me off his hands. He'd probably think I deserved the punishment. He'd probably laugh at the whole situation.

CHAPTER 20

$\mathcal{I}$ was surprised to be meeting Kelly that night in one of the resort's Italian restaurants.

"Really?" I asked once we'd ordered. "I thought you guys didn't do the garlic thing."

We'd decided on a basket of garlic bread, and angel-hair pasta with clams and some butter-white wine-garlic sauce. Poor Wyatt wouldn't want to be within five miles of me tonight.

Kelly looked annoyed at what was clearly a stereotype. "I love garlic. No one accuses humans of being allergic to garlic if they don't want it on their ice cream or in their milk. I don't understand why everyone thinks that just because some of us don't want garlicky flavored blood that we'll run shrieking every time we're within two feet of a plate of pasta."

"Believe me, I totally understand," I told her. "Humans are always throwing salt at me. Helloooo? Didn't you just see me eat that bag of potato chips? What am I, a slug or something?"

Salt could actually be a problem, but only with the right

ritual and a witch or sorcerer with a decent degree of power. Hardly anyone knew the appropriate ritual to summon one of us anymore, let alone trap us in a circle of salt. The inquisition had wiped out most everyone with those skills centuries ago. Of course, the elves could do it. I winced slightly with the memory.

Kelly nodded. "Yes, I've heard that salt thing with you guys, too. And how many times does someone have to throw holy water at us? Ruins my make-up and pisses me off. Doesn't make me melt into a pile of goo."

"Yeah, and I've clearly seen you guys out and about during the day," I commented.

"Well, we are nocturnal," Kelly admitted. "But that doesn't mean I'll burn to dust if I have to drag myself through a day shift."

"And the religious symbol thing?" I rolled my eyes.

"Well I was brained in the head once with a ten pound brass crucifix." Kelly laughed. "Thing almost killed me, so maybe there is something in that legend."

Our waiter came by at that moment and attempted to remove my wine glass.

"Oh no, you don't." I grabbed the stem. "I want wine."

"Yes, I know you ordered wine. I'm taking this glass though."

His tone was very patronizing. I really didn't care about the man's snobby attitude, but I did love to mess with the humans whenever I could.

"Why is this glass here if it's not for wine? Why did you bother to put it on the table, just to take it away five minutes later? I want wine, and I want it in a wine glass."

The waiter attempted a tug of war with me. "Yes, I'll bring you your wine in a wine glass. This isn't the right glass. I need to bring you the wine in the appropriate glass."

I didn't let go. In fact, I yanked hard, practically hauling the waiter face first onto our table.

"But this is a wine glass! Why do you bother putting it on the table if you don't use it?"

"This is a red wine glass," the waiter said, tugging firmly and ignoring the furious looks Kelly was giving him. "It's not the correct one for the wine you're ordering."

We'd already had an argument about my insistence on red wine with the clam pasta. I gave in on that one. I wasn't giving in on this.

"I don't care. I want my wine in this fucking glass. It's here, and I want to use it, dammit."

Kelly reached over with a blur of speed and pinched the waiter's arm, ruining my fun. He jumped and looked at her, paling suddenly as he realized what he'd done. I saw red spreading on his white shirt sleeve and thought how strong she must be to break his skin with just a pinch.

"There is no need to remove the glass, Jeffrey." Her tone was friendly, but her eyes did not look friendly. Jeffrey nodded and dashed off to the kitchen. Before I could begin to complain about her interrupting what was promising to become a brawl of epic proportions, Kelly wiggled a finger. In a shot, another vampire was at our table.

"Stephen," Kelly said in that scary, friendly voice. "Jeffrey has proven himself to be an unacceptable waiter. Please take care of the situation."

Ah, so this was the rival Stephen. No wonder he looked so pissed. She'd caught one of his staff behaving badly and it reflected on him personally. Plus now Kelly could rub his nose in shit even more. I had a strong feeling that Jeffrey would not live to see the light of day.

"Now, where were we?" Kelly asked with an apologetic smile.

"I take it Jeffrey is a dead man?" I didn't really care about

Jeffrey's fate, but I was very curious about how vampires ran their society.

Kelly's eyebrows raised. "Would you have tolerated that sort of behavior?"

"Oh, we behave like that all the time. Yeah, we punish, but that's more because we enjoy punishing than because of any need to enforce rules or standards of etiquette. It's just an excuse to have fun with someone." Not that we normally needed an excuse.

"With vampires, rules and codes are inflexible." She smoothed her napkin. "If you get caught, that is. If you're stupid enough to get caught, then you deserve whatever punishment is deemed appropriate. Even death."

"What about Old ones? I can't see anyone telling your master that he's going to be staked because he flipped someone the bird."

"Of course not," she smiled. "Old ones, especially the Born, make the rules and are free to change them at will. If you're on the top rung of the ladder, then you get to do whatever you want."

I got the distinct feeling that Kelly had that top rung in her sights, that in a matter of centuries she'd be knocking others off that ladder right and left on her ascent. Forget Kyle Fournier. Did their master realize what a viper he was harboring in his bosom with this girl? She'd bide her time and not hesitate to slide a sharp stake into his back when the moment arose. Born or not.

"And that Stephen? How embarrassing for him to have this happen with one of his staff," I commented.

Kelly's chin rose and a light sparkled deep in her eyes. "Stephen won't be here long."

Yeah, he'd probably be in the bottom of a ditch. I looked at Kelly again. Pride. Ah well. She had such promise, too. Sad to see talent like this go to waste.

"So, are you Born?" I asked.

I was relatively sure she wasn't a Born. The reminder might jar her back to reality. I thought that maybe if I put a little pin hole in that rapidly inflating ego, she'd come back from the edge before it was too late. Kelly winced.

"No," she said, her voice flat.

"Isn't that a hindrance?"

She squirmed a bit. "There aren't many Born. A few Made hold territories and have families."

"Hmmm." I chewed thoughtfully on a hunk of garlic bread. "Is that Kyle guy down in Baltimore a Born? He's not a bad looking dude and I think he's got some power. Maybe you can hitch your wagon to him and have him pull you up the ladder a bit."

Kelly sat ramrod straight and shot me a furious look.

"I do not need to hitch myself to anyone, Born or otherwise, to advance."

Our meal arrived then and we ate in frosty silence. I was sorry that I'd smashed our budding friendship. I liked this Kelly. Liked her enough to try to put her on the right path. I may be a cockroach. I may fuck up a lot, but I'm still almost a thousand years old. I hate to see a promising vampire bite off far more than she can chew.

CHAPTER 21

I took off my clothes and surveyed myself in front of the full-length mirror. If Kelly didn't hate me after our conversation at dinner, she'd definitely hate me after the activities I'd planned for tonight. With a pop of energy, I assumed the shape I had in mind. Instantly a tall, thin Scandinavian woman peered back at me. I'd Owned this woman a few hundred years ago. She'd been in her eighties when I Owned her, and I'd been pleased to see how much of a knockout she had been in her youth. If she'd been a human in current times, she'd have been a supermodel. Six feet tall with long legs and an elegant frame, she had naturally pale blonde hair, ice blue eyes, and cheekbones sculptors dreamt about.

Assuming forms is a skill with varying degrees of talent. When we Own a being, we have access to all the information necessary to replicate their flesh and house ourselves in it. Some demons struggle to put together a convincing human form, no matter how many they Own. There are always slight errors, off parts.

Others can hold a human form, but only exactly as it was

when they Owned it. So if they Owned a man in his nineties who was unable to walk, had erectile dysfunction, and wrinkles like a bulldog, then that is the only way they could put the form together. That's why most demons tended to Own healthy, attractive, young people. It was good for them to be old enough to have a lot of life experience, but not so old that they had chronic incontinence or arthritis.

It took special skill to be able to assimilate the information from those that you Owned and choose how to present their form. I had this skill. I'd taken Samantha Martin when she was twenty. Younger than my preference, but I couldn't pass up the opportunity. I could create her form as an eight year old, or as an eighty year old, even though she'd never lived to be that age. I could create her form without scars, correct injuries and genetic abnormalities, even modify the form within some parameters.

Looking at the blonde woman in the mirror, I enlarged her breasts. I didn't want them to be ridiculous, but today's fashion demanded a larger bosom than this woman's genetics allowed for. Satisfied, I walked naked into the main room of the suite to grab a beer from the mini bar.

I was just pulling out a bottle when the door rattled and Wyatt walked in.

"I've got that bag with the timeshare stuff you wanted." He turned to close the door behind him. "I sincerely hope you're not going to make me sit through one of those four-hour meetings just so you can score a fruit basket."

Spinning around, he stared open-mouthed as he saw a tall, gorgeous, naked blonde grabbing a beer out of the mini bar. The look on his face was priceless. Embarrassment, appreciation, confusion.

"Oh, sorry. Wrong room." He looked around, obviously confused as to why his key worked and why this did indeed appear to be his room. I laughed.

"It's me silly." I put my arms above my head and modeled the form with a swing of my hips. "You like?"

"Sam? Is that new? Where have you been hiding that? Not exactly stealthy, you realize. Everyone who sees you is going to remember you."

I pouted slightly and gave Wyatt a sultry look. His eyes went from my mouth down to the boobs and further. Clearly his mind was detouring rapidly.

"I don't plan on walking through the lobby naked, you know. In fact, I don't plan on walking through the lobby like this at all," I told him.

"I'm hoping you don't plan on leaving the room," Wyatt said, his voice husky with desire. "At least for an hour or two."

I walked over to him and kissed him lightly, pushing away the hands that grabbed to pull me close. "Later," I teased. "Can you stay in the room for the night and cover for me while I give my minder the slip? I know you've got an early morning, maybe you can get caught up on some sleep?"

"I don't think I'm going to be able to get to sleep at all tonight." He ran a hand through his hair. "Five minutes, Sam. That's all I'm asking here is five minutes."

"Later." I bent over to pick up the canvas bag of timeshare materials he'd tossed on the floor, making sure to give him a full view just to taunt him further. I hadn't realized how much human men enjoyed diversity in physical form. I'd need to let Wyatt fuck me as all my Owned females. It would take years.

"So you really think you can ditch your minder?" he asked me, still eying my breasts. "There's a rather large guy, a vampire I'd guess, lurking around our room in the hallway. I can't imagine you'd give him the slip no matter what form you assumed. Plus this place is covered in cameras. None in our room, but there's one right outside pointed at the door."

"Our escape plans hinge on me being able to somehow sneak out. I don't know how things are going to go down with the vampires, and there are two demons here determined to grab me right after my meeting on Sunday."

"Wouldn't it be better to confront the demons here? If we run, they're more likely to ambush us. I thought you'd want to take the offensive?" Wyatt asked.

"I could probably only take out one before I lost the element of surprise. I'm not sure who the vampires would support if I attacked a demon and we blew up part of their business interest. Having them gunning for me would seriously hurt my chances. Plus, one of the demons is very strong, with a lot of experience in bringing in captives. I'd rather face him at home with Boomer and Diablo to back us up."

Wyatt nodded thoughtfully, watching me as I pulled some clothes out of the dresser drawer.

"Hey, those are my clothes," Wyatt protested. "I didn't pack those"

Humans were so slow on the uptake.

"I grabbed them from your closet back home. If I lose them or ruin them, I promise I'll replace them." I'd replace them with better clothes than the stained t-shirt and worn jeans I'd grabbed.

"I like those jeans," Wyatt warned. "And there's no way they'd fit you, either in your regular form or the one you've got on right now. Which is totally hot, by the way," he added, his eyes roving over me.

I looked at Wyatt and with a grin, quickly popped out of my tall, blonde female form and into one that was as close as I could come to Wyatt's without actually Owning him. He stared at me in shock.

"I didn't think you could do that unless you Owned someone? Did you kill me and I don't remember it?"

"No, no," I reassured him. "You're still alive."

I'd explored so much of him, touched and held so much of his genetic composition, that I was pretty confident in my ability to fake an imitation. It was far from perfect. Without his memories, his emotions, his personality, it would only be a cheap copy.

He looked at me carefully, walking around the naked copy of his flesh. "I think I need to work out more."

"You're perfect." I kissed him. He recoiled. I guess it wasn't very sexy to be kissing yourself.

"Vampires don't give humans a second glance, they are just an animated dinner as far as they are concerned. I'm betting Mario won't follow me at all if he thinks you're the one who has left the room. I'll pack a change of clothes and some makeup and heels in the timeshare bag he saw you come in with and change form in another casino. Hopefully they'll never know I've left."

Understanding sparked in Wyatt's eyes. "What do you plan on doing with your night out on the town?"

I shrugged. "I'm thinking of smacking the bee's nest with a big stick and seeing what happens."

Wyatt grinned. "I'd guess that bees are going to come out and sting you rather painfully."

"Yep." I stuffed heels, a dress, and a small make-up bag into the canvas sack. "But a few stings might be worth it. If I'm going to get out of here in one piece, I need to know all I can about how they handle things. Especially how they handle an unruly demon."

"Okay." He backed up as I went to kiss him again. "I'll stay here for the night, safely out of sight in the room, but you seriously need to have sex with me as that blonde woman. Deal?"

"Deal," I told him, heading out the door.

Mario glanced at me as I passed as if I were just another

random guest. I wondered if he even recognized Wyatt as my human, or if they all looked the same to him at this point.

Grinning to myself, I took the elevator down and strolled right out the front door, past all the staff, past the bell hops, past the doormen. Home free. I walked a few doors down, slipped into another casino, bought a drink, and then strolled into the men's bathroom casually holding my canvas time-share bag like a tourist out for an evening stroll. I peed in the urinal, just to enjoying urinating while standing, then disintegrated the screws holding the cover on the air conditioning vent. I left the vent cover on, went into a stall, and stripped, quickly popping into the tall blonde form that Wyatt had so admired. A tube-like, skin-tight dress slipped over my lithe body, and I stepped out of the stall. I was putting on make-up in the mirror when a man walked in, doing a double take as he caught sight of me.

"Oh, sorry. I thought this was the men's room." He looked at the open door in confusion. It clearly said "Men." I giggled like I'd had too much to drink and faked a thick accent.

"Oh no. I am not so good at reading right now." I batted my long, mascara-dark lashes at him and tossed my waist-length, blonde hair. "It's okay for you to be here. I want to finish my make-up."

He looked me over slowly, still holding the door open in indecision, his brain working through the alternatives. He could try to pee in front of me, or he could go into a stall. Or he could stay and chat me up. Fear and insecurity won over, and, making his apologies, he left the bathroom. Human men were so strange sometimes.

Finishing my make-up, I stashed the canvas bag with Wyatt's clothes, along with the cosmetics, in the air conditioning vent, making sure to seal it back up. Then I strutted out of the men's room. Every eye in the place swiveled to follow me as I made my way across the floor.

After a couple hands of blackjack, quite a few people had begun to follow me as I meandered around the casino, and I ensured the security cameras caught me on their tape. Then I headed out and asked a doorman to hail me a cab to the club Wyatt had indicated was the latest hot spot.

Bon Chance was tucked away in the warehouse district in an old import/export wholesaler's building. The exterior was chipped cement block with sprayed graffiti announcing the club's name. It looked like it was about to collapse down on the patrons' heads. There was a line a block long snaking between the side of the building and a ratty velvet rope. I stepped out of the cab and walked right up to the bouncer, who promptly moved the rope and let me in. No one protested. Evidently six foot tall, blonde supermodels got to line bust. Inside, everything shocked the senses. The outside was dilapidated, but on the interior, no expense was spared. Lights flashed across the huge dance floor which sat nestled partially under a raised dais. Off to the side behind glass was the DJ, barely visible in contrast with the sensory overload of the rest of the club.

Two bars ran the span of the converted warehouse on either side of the dance floor. Mahogany and gilded marble covered the bar, the walls, the floor. It was a strange mix of modern and classic, of rich natural materials and steel girders. Everything jarred visually in a dizzying confusion.

I strolled with confidence up to the center of one of the bars and pointedly ignored the bartender. He immediately raced over to take my order. As he went to get my chilled, herb-infused vodka, I eyed the other patrons. The women nearby were trying hard not to stare at me. They'd glance and then turn back to their companions whispering. A few eyed me boldly. The men were even more amusing. They stared with a combination of lust and fear on their faces. I wondered if I'd overdone it in choosing this form. Maybe it was just too intimidating? Beyond reach of most humans' confidence?

Picking up my drink, I meandered around the club, noticing how the humans carefully stepped away from me and then followed me with their eyes. I wasn't sure what trouble I could get into. I didn't think that making them all want hot wings would attract the vampires' attention. I could try making them all want sex, but that wouldn't be out of place in a club like this. An orgy was beyond my skill. I wasn't exactly a succubus. A brawl? Or maybe I could throw some electricity around and explode all the light fixtures in a shower of deadly sparks. Lost in my thoughts, I screeched to a halt and stared as I noticed the man about ten feet away dancing with a dark-haired beauty. He looked like Wyatt. He looked a lot like Wyatt.

Suddenly the predator in me reared after years of careful control. I wanted Wyatt, had wanted to Own him ever since I'd met him, but I'd restrained myself. I couldn't allow myself to Own Wyatt. I knew that destroying his physical form and gathering his being within me would be a hollow pleasure. I cared for Wyatt so much that having him constantly with me, but not individual, not autonomous, would destroy me.

I needed to Own. It's what we demons do. I hadn't Owned a human in so long; the craving was almost as painful as the craving to kill, to devour. This man right in front of me looked so much like Wyatt that he might make a good substitute. Might ease that aching hole of need inside me, not just to Own Wyatt, but to Own any human I could. And it would certainly piss off the vampires, throw them into a tizzy. It was perfect.

But Owning was on Gregory's forbidden-things list. The vampires should be able to cover up my planned kill tomorrow night, but they might not be able to cover up an Own. Plus, I wasn't sure how much Gregory could sense with all this fucking shit of his networked throughout me. Reluctantly, I turned and walked away. I made it five steps.

Fuck it. I'm a demon. And getting the crap beat out of me by Gregory and the angels was probably a whole lot better than what Haagenti had in mind for me. This guy was mine.

I sent out the suggestion, light and airy into the room. Others around me caught the ambient effects and began to look at the humans beside them with a hunger, with an interest. I pulled and the man who looked like Wyatt turned to me. Want, want, want, I called silently. I tried to keep it gentle, tried to keep it subtle. The man excused himself from his dance partner and approached me.

It was so easy. So simple. I danced with the man, let him buy me a few drinks, let him take me to his place. Owned him. Killed him. I made it pleasant for him; one of the best sensory experiences he'd ever had. I'd kissed and fondled him, letting him do the same to me. I'd carefully sent tendrils of my energy in and heightened an orgasm through the lovely bundle of nerves in his genitals. He'd looked at me unseeing, with the glazed look of ecstasy, as I pulled and firmly ripped him from his very cells and into my being. I don't think he even realized I had him; ever realized that he was dead.

I should have been satisfied. I felt worse, collapsing on the floor, overcome by the empty ache I had never in my whole life been able to fill. This was a terrible mistake. It made me long for Wyatt even more. It made me feel strangely guilty for betraying the promise I'd made to Gregory. I felt hungry, unfulfilled, ashamed.

After some time, I managed to pull myself together and gather my thoughts. I could easily cover this up. I Owned the man. I could assume his form, let the security cameras see me leaving the room, go pick up some other person and allow the security cameras to record him or her leaving alone, framing them for the murder. But then the vampires wouldn't know I'd done it. Plus, I just didn't care. I left the room as the tall blonde and went right out the door of the secure apartment building. It's not like the humans could do anything to me. I was going to be in a shitload of trouble with the vampires though. And Gregory. He'd forbidden me, and here I'd just done it. Maybe he wouldn't know. There were three other demons in town. I could blame it on one of them.

Going to a nearby casino, I stripped in the bathroom, tossing my dress and popping into a small, familiar shape. Scurrying along the walls, I made my way outside and hugged the building fronts, heading toward the casino where I had transformed from my Wyatt look-alike into the blonde woman. It was dicey going through the revolving doors without being smashed, and I was momentarily concerned when one of the resort workers looked pointedly at me, as if considering whether to squash me with his shoe or not.

"Stan," the guy called out instead, turning from me. "Those cockroaches are back. You need to get pest control in here again pronto."

It wouldn't do much good. I could feel the pesticide from the spray a week ago and it was the wrong kind. It burned slightly, but wouldn't harm a real roach, let alone me. Making my way to the bathroom, I popped into the naked Wyatt-look-alike and promptly locked the door hinges. I didn't want anyone walking in on me naked while I retrieved Wyatt's clothing from the air vent and dressed. No one even attempted the door, and moments later I strolled out, looking just like Wyatt without the timeshare bag.

"This wasn't the way the evening was supposed to turn out," I thought as I walked casually back through the casino and up the elevator to my room. What the fuck was wrong with me? I'd snuck out and stuck it to the vampires. I'd caused chaos on their watch. And I'd Owned someone. I hadn't been able to do that since Samantha Martin. I should feel good. Why was Owning not as satisfying as it had always been? What in the world would I do to ease that horrible need within me if Owning no longer did?

The strange gnawing in me continued unabated. I hadn't felt this way since I was a child. I'd put all that desperate need, that broken feeling behind me long ago. I was a demon, one with skills, one who had a promising future. Maybe demons were not meant to live this way, as humans with human feelings and emotions. Maybe the last forty years were taking a toll on me and I really did need to go home.

I opened the door to the room and saw Wyatt sitting half dressed on the bed with his laptop. A surge of very un-demon-like feeling swept through me. Seeing him there on the bed took my mind off the terrible, hollow feeling inside me. I removed Wyatt's clothes and quickly popped into my Samantha Martin form.

"Oh, sorry," I said, remembering too late. "You wanted me to be the tall blonde woman tonight, didn't you? Does it bother you that I Owned her when she was eighty-six though? I thought I better ask before you got too wrapped up in lust."

"Sam," he interrupted. "You're busted. That vampire woman came by here. I tried to stall her, make up some story about how I went out and came back and that their cameras must not have seen me, but she didn't buy it. She'll probably be here any moment."

Sure enough, there was a knock on the door. It was Kelly with the cold mask firmly in place.

"Baal, I hope you had an enjoyable evening, although Mario could have directed you to some of the better spots in town had you given him the chance. It saddens me that you

didn't turn to him or me if you felt the need for entertainment."

She was good. I didn't see a spark of anger at all in her
stance, in her eyes, although I'm sure she was pissed as all
hell at me.

"What do you mean? I haven't left the room all evening," I
lied. She wouldn't believe me, but it was still worth an effort.

I watched as Kelly opened the large purse and pulled out
a series of pictures, laying them in sequence on the table.
One of Wyatt coming into the room, one of me/him leaving,
one of me/him entering the bathroom of the other casino,
one of me as the tall blonde leaving, one of the tall blonde in
the club with my victim, one of us in the elevator at his
apartment, one of me leaving, one of me/Wyatt leaving the
bathroom of the other casino, and one of me just a few
moments ago, as Wyatt, entering my room. That one was still
warm, as if she'd ripped it right off the printer in the security
room and ran up here. Fuck, she must be fast.

"Very impressive control of the human form, Baal. Especially your toy here. I've never heard of a demon who could
assume a form that he or she didn't Own."

Kelly looked at me with that friendly politeness that
didn't reach her eyes.

"We do not want to curtail your enjoyment or impose on
you in any way, Baal. We only want to provide the highest
degree of service to you, and we can't do that if you don't
allow us. Luckily, I was personally watching security footage,
and noticed you leaving your room in your toy's form. We
carefully followed you, not to interfere, but to ensure your
safety. The human snack you enjoyed this evening was a
rather notable local businessman, but we have disposed of
the remains and provided necessary false leads for the
human law enforcement."

Silence stretched on as I looked at the photos with interest. So they had followed me the entire time? I hadn't realized that. This Kelly woman was good. These vampires were possibly going to be more of a problem than I had hoped.

"Angels can't help but notice the activity tonight," Kelly said. "Covering up your actions from the inept humans isn't the difficulty here; it's ensuring the angels don't catch you. We pride ourselves that we've never lost one of our guests; I'd hate to have that perfect record broken, especially on my watch."

"Yes, it would really suck if I were taken out by an angel." I thought of Gregory. I probably was going to be taken out by one eventually, just not the one she was imagining.

"We only wish to serve you, Baal. We only wish to earn your gratitude."

I got the message. I'd slipped their minder, been a bad girl, but they'd cover for me, overlook it if I behaved from now on. Right. Not likely.

"I am grateful." I grabbed her in an enthusiastic hug. She stiffened with alarm, but tolerated it and promptly left.

"Sam?" Wyatt asked, looking down at the photos. "Why does the dead guy look like me?"

Fuck.

CHAPTER 22

I kept things low-key the next day, although I was interested to note that Mario either did not swim or did not relish a frigid dip in the ocean. He watched me with anxiety from the shore, trying to keep me in his sight. I was tempted to assume my tiger shark form and give him the slip, just to watch him freak out. I wondered if Kelly had punished him for his inattention last night. I doubted she'd be forgiving if he lost me again.

Kelly met me early that evening to go over my choices of prey. No doubt the candidates were individuals who had offended the vampires, fallen behind on "contributions" or refused to sell businesses to them. There were two individuals who were heads of a local drug business, and the CEO of a waste management company. At least the drug dealers would probably be armed and pose some challenge. I didn't think the CEO would be much fun.

"You can select one of them." Kelly showed me a page of profile information along with pictures. One? That sucked.

I picked one at random and Kelly began to go over the

241

guy's schedule and detail exactly when and how I was to take him down. This was going to be no fun at all. I was regretting that I'd arranged it. I should have just gone solo. I would be in enough shit when Gregory found out about last night though. One human dead and Owned. He'd have me in Aaru so fast my head would spin. This kill might be boring, but at least it was safe with the vampires covering it up.

I was supposed to walk into the guy's house and rip him to bits. Then I would walk right out. Everyone else would be carefully busy elsewhere. I'm sure the dead guy would be a good example of who not to piss off to the rest of the gang, and his vampire-picked successor. This was all to take place at exactly eight o'clock this evening, two hours from now. Boring.

"Can I at least stalk him a bit first?" I complained. "Or possibly kill his dog? There's not much satisfaction in just killing something, you know."

Kelly looked surprised. "I thought that's all you demons wanted."

She looked at her notes briefly and I could see her struggling between the desire to provide fulfilling entertainment for me and the risk I'd pose if I deviated from their plan.

"Maybe you could go there thirty minutes early, although he'll probably just be watching TV. I don't see that he has a dog."

"I'll be there at eight. Am I to assume one of your guys is going to come along and watch?"

Kelly shuddered. "No. Mario will meet you later. Is an hour enough time? We'll send in a clean-up crew, too."

I agreed and told her I'd meet Mario in the casino at nine.

The dealer was indeed watching TV when I arrived. I unlocked his back door using my special skills and snuck quietly through his house, yelling "Surprise!" and jumping into the room like I was at a birthday party. He shot me, which, honestly, was the highlight of my day to that point.

It was a good shot, right into the gut. Hurt like fuck. I was very impressed. What guy watches Friends reruns with a loaded pistol in his lap? A paranoid drug dealer, I guess. He was paranoid enough not to trust the shot to take me down, either. Diving behind a rather solid looking coffee table, he upended it like a shield, then fired another shot that ricocheted off a metal wall hanging and imbedded harmlessly in the drywall.

I ripped the ugly metal object off the wall and held it in front of me. We were fairly close in this living room and I really didn't want to take a chance that he'd blow my head off. He popped off another shot at me and I bounced it off the decoration. My arm vibrated with the force of the bullet, going slightly numb. Fixing the gut wound, I thought about a plan of attack. This was turning out to be a far more interesting evening than I had thought.

The next shot managed to snake through the gaps in my improvised shield and tear through my shoulder. Four shots? Or was it three? I couldn't remember and it really didn't matter. I had no idea what type of gun he had and what the clip held. Wyatt could tell me. Wyatt could sneak a millisecond glance at a portion of the gun and tell me exactly what type it was, what year it was manufactured, what caliber and how many bullets the clip held, as well as what movies the gun had been used in and what the various state laws were concerning the firearm. I felt a sudden surge of admiration for my human, but he wasn't here right now and I had a drug dealer to disembowel.

The guy popped his head above the coffee table to better take aim at me and fired off a series of fast shots. I took advantage of the target and flung the wall decoration at him like a huge metal Frisbee. It would have taken his head clean off, but it bounced slightly on the edge of the coffee table and flipped upright, smacking him in the forehead and dropping him backwards. I ignored the two additional shots in my chest and dove over the table, landing on him with all my weight.

He was prepared and managed to punch several more bullets into my chest. I actually felt the heat of the gun muzzle burning into my flesh. Grabbing his shoulders, I flipped us over so he sprawled on top of me. In an effort to balance himself, he pulled the gun from my gut and reached out to brace against the floor with both hands. Mistake. I hooked one of his legs with mine and shot an arm across the front of his neck to grab his shirt at the shoulder. Scissoring my legs, I flipped him again, straddled him, and put weight on my forearm across his neck. With his attention on my choke hold, I grabbed his hand and, with a flash of energy, snapped his wrist. The gun fell to the floor with a thud from his limp, useless hand.

"It wasn't me, it wasn't me, you stupid bloodsuckers," he gasped. I put pressure on his neck, using it as leverage to pull myself more upright while still straddling him.

"I really don't care what you've done or not done." I slowly extended horns from my head and let red fill my eyes. "You're paying the price, regardless of how blameless a life you've lived. And somehow I doubt your life has been all that blameless."

He looked at the horns and my inhuman eyes with a sudden flash of knowledge. This guy knew about vampires, and he knew about demons. I wondered what he'd done to piss them off. Not that it mattered, but curiosity gnawed at me.

"It wasn't me," he insisted. "She set me up. If you spare me, I'll let you know who really pulled the deal off and you can go get them. That's who the vampires really want. There are four of them. Why kill just one of me when you can kill four humans and let the vampires know they have a traitor among them?"

I paused. She? Could it be that minx Kelly that set him up? Oh, she was good! And four? I hadn't had a kill like that in a century.

"Talk to me," I encouraged, still straddling the guy.

"Uh uh." He shook his head. "You have to promise to spare my life and then I'll tell you."

Easy enough. "I'll not kill you," I told him with a hand upraised. "Scouts honor."

"Jack Hennet, Brad and Phil Johnson, and Abel Mallory," he said, promptly ratting out his buddies. "They worked with that pretty female vampire, Kelly, to divert the shipment and fake the manifest, cutting the other vampires out of the deal. They made it look like I'd arranged a break in to the warehouse and took the goods myself. All the drugs in this region come into an import/export warehouse which acts as a front for the operation."

Wow. This was good stuff. Kelly screwing over her own family and, no doubt, intending to do the same to her human accomplices. She would have rocked as a demon.

"Abel will be at the warehouse all night. He's the leader, and his office is the last one on the right after you come through the door."

He went on to give me the address for the operation. They'd be armed and nervous after their embezzlement. I foresaw an amazing evening of violence ahead of me.

"The others should be in and out tonight for the month-end audit bonuses. You can grab them all if you're patient and hang around long enough."

"Thank you," I was truly grateful. I began to send energy deep within him. This would hurt, but I wouldn't prolong it.

I had other places to be before the vampires caught up with me and cut my fun short.

"You promised," he screamed. "You said you wouldn't kill me, you promised!"

"Yes," I said with pity. "But demons lie."

CHAPTER 23

I surveyed my kills with satisfaction. This night just kept getting better and better. I'd wrapped up my original, sanctioned kill in record time and raced over to the warehouse. I was well aware that I'd passed my meeting time with Mario three hours ago. I figured that I'd just keep on killing until they eventually caught up with me. No one had shown up so far, and I had plenty of time until my morning meeting with the head guy. Plenty of time to have more fun.

Four bodies. I was inspired to create a lovely tableau and started prepping by removing limbs and stacking them neatly in piles, while formulating a vision of sculpture in my head. Wyatt would be at his game all night and this was more fun than spending the evening at a blackjack table. I contemplated removing teeth, but opted to leave them in and do eyes instead. And maybe tongues, too. I had just completed separating and organizing all the parts for my artwork when I heard a noise. Turning, I saw a man at the edge of the warehouse. In spite of his obvious shock, his instincts were good and he bolted. I took off after him.

The warehouse was a warren of stacked boxes, forklifts,

and shelving racks. The bay doors were locked down tight and I'd be on him before he could wrestle them open. Unlike most warehouses, the human-sized doors were not beside the bays, but clear across the building and down a hall flanked by offices. There were only two doors and they were placed to keep any visitor contained and shielded from what they shouldn't see. The guy had to have recently come in through one of those doors. If he'd been here before, in one of the offices, he would have heard all the screaming and made a quiet exit. No doubt he was here to pick up supply and walked in on my evening's entertainment.

I assumed the guy was heading back to the door. He'd need to weave around the shelving units a bit. I had a clearer path and should get to the hallway in about the same time. There, I could disable him and enjoy a fifth kill tonight. Kind of like dessert.

I paused when I got to the hallway. There was no sign of the guy. Had he beaten me here? I made my way down the long hall toward the door, checking each office briefly as I passed. I would have heard the echo of the heavy steel door if he'd fled the building. If he'd left, ah well. If he was still here, he was going to remain here until I found him. I'd start by searching each of these offices thoroughly on my way back to the warehouse.

As I turned around, I saw the guy standing at the warehouse end of the hallway. Smart. He had me trapped at the end of a hallway, drastically limiting my movement and increasing his chances of hitting me with a bullet. Raising his arm, I saw a flash, heard a roar, and felt a bullet slam into my chest, followed by another.

Wyatt had told me that in spite of what you see in the movies, it's very difficult to get in a head shot, or even a limb shot, on a moving and unpredictable target. When you need it to go down, you aim for the biggest area you can, the torso.

I also knew that no matter how skilled they were, humans became terrible shots when they were stressed and scared. This man had punctured me with two of the four bullets he'd shot. Not a bad success rate.

This would barely slow me down, though. I began to rapidly recreate flesh, raining the shattered bits of bullets from my body and coughing out blood from my lungs as I shuffled toward him. All the blood loss would have been more dramatic if I hadn't been already soaked with it from my victims.

The guy held his ground and continued to shoot, pumping bullets into me so fast I lost count. I longed for the days of the six shooter. Who knows how many bullets this guy had in his clip, or if he had another clip to snap in before I could reach him. I concentrated on removing the bullets and healing the flesh as quickly as he pumped them in. One blast hit my hip spinning me off balance to land on my rear.

I rolled over and got up, fixing the shattered bone for stability before repairing the flesh. He dropped the empty clip and tried unsuccessfully to slap in another as I straightened and kept moving forward. I wasn't in mortal danger, and continuing to walk toward him riddled with bullets was freaking him out in a very satisfying way. His hands shook and he dropped both the empty clip and the full one. At that point, he realized that even if he did manage to load the gun, it wasn't going to do any good. So he ran.

I chased after him, letting him stay just a bit ahead of me as we weaved in and out of the warehouse rows. A few times I let him get far enough ahead to try and hide, then I'd carefully flush him out to run again. It was fun, dangling hope before him that he might escape, that he might elude me. That false hope thrilled me, and it would be even sweeter when I caught him and saw it die desperately in his eyes.

I herded him slowly toward the others, aware that he was

tiring and becoming frantic. Finally he broke into the open and paused, unable to stop himself from gagging at my neat piles of body parts and organs.

"That will be you too," I told him. "Immortalized in a work of art I'm going to create. It will bring meaning and beauty to your death. Five is a far more auspicious number than four. You'll lift the piece up; bring it nobility through the addition of your flesh."

He looked at me in horror and backed away slowly, as if he finally realized that there was no chance of escape. There wasn't. I walked casually toward him.

"I won't promise you a painless death, because that's no fun at all. You'll scream, you'll cry, you'll beg, but at the end of it all, you will die. I do promise that. There will eventually be a release from the pain. I'm very turned on by all this chasing, too, so I may lose control and kill you quicker than I would like. You can take comfort in that."

He slipped in a smear of blood, landing heavily on his rear and narrowly missing the intestines roped in coils beside him. Scooting on his butt, he kept his eyes fixed on me, but not fixed in a way that I could lock him in and hold him with my gaze. Pity. I approached and stood over him. Mmmm, what to do, what to do? So many options.

"I challenge you to a contest," he said, his voice wavering a bit. "If you win, you can have my soul. If I win, I get to leave here unharmed and safe from you forever."

I laughed. What an interesting man this was.

"Your soul? I could take that; I could Own you without your consent. I don't even know if I want to Own you. So many humans are boring and dull. There's probably nothing you have that would be a suitable bribe. I admire your fortitude, though, and your ability to think so quickly on your feet. Or on your ass."

"There must be something I can offer you," he said with

surprising calm. "And the challenge of a contest itself should be entertaining."

I wondered how this man knew so much about my kind. He must have a relative who had taught him some things in his childhood. A granny witch maybe.

"I do enjoy a challenge." I mused over his proposal for a moment. I had enough time. Curiosity wiggled through me. What did he have in mind?

"Okay, I'm game. What kind of challenge? A feat of strength or agility? A task we must complete? Like perhaps who can find the most beautiful ring? Although we'd need someone impartial to judge that contest and all your friends here are dead."

He shook his head, remaining seated on the ground and carefully not looking at me. "Not strength or agility. I know I couldn't win that."

"A riddling game? Or a musical contest? Not violin though," I added hastily. That Daniels guy had cleaned my clock a few decades back and I didn't want to suffer such embarrassment again.

"I don't play an instrument. And I'm not good at riddles."

Fuck, what was the guy good at? I'd probably win anyway, but it would be a lot more fun if he felt like he had a chance in it.

"Beer bongs? Belching? Or you could take out your phone and we could play Words With Friends for your soul." I was losing my patience with this guy. He was no longer holding my interest. Time to start dismembering.

"Angry Birds."

"I was fucking joking!" I yelled in frustration.

"Angry Birds it is. If I win, you let me leave unharmed, unhurt and guarantee I live out my normal lifespan free from you or any of your kinds' torment. If you win, you get to do with me whatever you want, including taking my soul. You can also have all of my immediate family."

"You either really hate your family or you're really confident in your ability to play Angry Birds," I commented.

"Deal?" he asked.

"In order to make you safe from other demons, I need to mark you," I warned. "It's the only way. Otherwise they won't know to keep their hands off."

He thought for a moment. "Okay"

"Deal then."

We stared at each other for an awkward moment.

"Do you have it on your phone?" I prompted.

He pulled out a flip phone and showed it to me.

"Oh, wonderful." I dug around in my pants pockets for my phone. I obviously hadn't brought a purse to a hunt and had almost left the phone behind. I hoped it hadn't gotten smashed during the evening's fun activities.

"The devil has an iPhone?" the guy asked in amazement as I pulled it out and examined it for damage. It started right up.

"How else am I going to call my boyfriend and tell him I'm running late?" I replied.

I scrolled through the huge list of apps that Wyatt had helpfully downloaded onto my phone. I didn't even know what half of them did. What the fuck was Qwerty anyway? Under games I had Solitaire, Mahjong, Words with Friends, Bejeweled, and Zombie Dash. No Angry Birds.

"This better be a free app," I told the guy as I scrolled through the online store. "I'm gonna be really pissed if I have to pay a dollar ninety-nine for this thing."

I'd seen the Angry Birds merchandising and got the general idea that the player catapulted fat, red birds at various structures in an attempt to smash everything and kill the equally fat green pigs. I loaded the game and the cheerful, catchy tune blasted full volume through my phone speakers.

It was the kind of tune that would be stuck in my head for days.

"How should we do this? It seems to be single player. Should we compare high scores? Best two out of three?" I asked my opponent.

"Scoring is by level. You unlock the next highest level by killing all the pigs before you run out of birds, regardless of your score. Maybe a combination of highest level achieved and highest score on any level?"

"That can be the number we compare to determine the winner." I said, shifting the pile of legs so I could sit down on the bloody floor. "If you fail a level three times, then your round is over, and we do three rounds? Top overall score out of three rounds wins?"

He thought about it for a moment then nodded.

"I'll go first," I offered, feeling generous. "That way you have an idea what score you need to beat."

I hit the play button and shrank the images so I could see the bird catapult and my scaffolding target all on the screen. The bird launched with a vindictive squawk and promptly smashed the wooden structure and killed the pig. I cleared level one with a score of twenty-eight thousand, thirty. Why was that only worth one star? I killed the fucking pig with one shot, damn it. I got ten thousand more points on the next level, but still only one star. Fuck this game. I managed to work my way through nine levels with declining scores. I could only hope that flip-phone guy sucked worse than I did.

"Three hundred forty-two thousand, two hundred seventy." I told him, passing the phone over. He'd been peering over my shoulder watching me play, torn between wanting to see and keeping as far from me as possible.

He looked at me in suspicion and tried to do the math in his head.

"My high score times level nine."

He continued to work the numbers unsuccessfully.

"Oh, for fuck's sake," I said, sticking my finger in a cold, congealed pool of blood. If we didn't resolve this soon, I'd need to do my sculpture with stiff body parts.

Finding a somewhat clean space I wrote out the formula and showed him the math. He nodded his consent.

I had no such qualms about personal space, so I hovered inches from him, breathing across his ear and feeling the tension roll off him. He only cleared level five, but had a higher score than me, bringing his total score to slightly below mine. I snatched the phone from his shaking hands and smiled at him with satisfaction. Two more rounds and I'd have warm, soft flesh to go with the cold. I still only cleared nine levels, but significantly improved my top score.

"Five hundred twenty-two thousand, two hundred seventy," I told him smugly, then went to write it in blood on the floor. It was starting to look kind of cool, all these numbers and math formulas written in blood on the warehouse floor. I'd put circles and triangles around it and totally freak out the human who discovered it. Maybe I'd carve some prime numbers on the torsos of my sculpture, too. It would tie everything together nicely.

I breathed down my opponent's neck again and watched as he worked his way through nine levels. His scores were pretty close to mine at this point. I'd been unable to beat the tenth level and leaned in even closer to see if he'd provide a clue.

"Do you mind giving me a little more space?" he asked with an odd combination of irritation and fear. "You're practically in my lap. Worse than my kids."

"I can't get past the tenth level and I'm trying to see if you can. The structure the pigs are in isn't wood anymore. I use up all my birds hammering at the thing only to have the pigs safe and doing that mocking grunting noise at me. I hate these fucking pigs."

"You need to tap on the screen when they are close to their target on this one so they break into more birds and get extra oomph. Didn't you pay attention to the directions? The game showed you that when you reached the level."

No, I didn't. I don't read directions, even in graphic form. I like to just wing it. I watched him carefully as he made it to level eleven and pulled ahead of me in top score. Last round.

I made it to level twelve this time, but couldn't manage to kill the big fat pig sheltered in pillars of concrete on either side.

"Seven hundred twenty thousand, forty-nine," I told him. That put me back into the lead. This was his last chance to save his life and his hands shook as he took the phone from me. I could hear his heart pounding, smell the sweat, thick and rancid on his skin.

Twice he failed level twelve, having the same problem with the big fat pig as I had. On his last attempt, his last bird, the thing managed to break through the glass ceiling and squash the pig from above.

He'd already won, but I knew he couldn't do the math in his head, so I let him continue to play and sweat it out while I leaned over him, blowing in his ear and rubbing myself seductively on his back. If I was going to let him go, I might as well have some fun first.

He finished out at level fifteen and tried, to no avail, to do the math in his head. I made him write it out himself in blood on the floor. He shook like an epileptic the whole time. His bloody numbers were practically undecipherable.

"Eight hundred ninety-six thousand, two hundred eighty," he told me, his voice catching on a sob. Then he vomited all over the numbers. I stood and watched him, panting on all fours, threads of spit extending from his mouth to the pool of puke.

"It seems you've won your freedom. Of course, it would be the ultimate in irony if you were to be hit by a bus on your way home this morning."

"Mark me so I'm safe," he panted as he glanced up at me, still not directly meeting my eyes. "I want to get out of here."

There are lots of ways to mark someone as mine. I could damage him in some fashion. Even though the wound or broken bone would heal, the signature would remain, forever evident to my kind. I could fuck him, although it usually took several times for the energy to hold tight. I thought about the angel tattoos, the little brownish angel wing marks they left on the foreheads of those they killed. Their "forgiveness mark," showing that the dead had paid their dues and were ready for whatever judgment the afterlife brought. Those marks were small and subtle, hidden along the hairline.

I'd do a tattoo in a more visible spot, I decided. Of course, all the demon symbols that would have terrified the humans a few hundred years ago were cool now. It was common to see even businessmen sporting bloody skulls, winged beasts, or corpses on their bodies. The stuff of nightmares was now stylish. Inspired, I placed a thumb on his cheek and sent my energy into it. He balled up his fists, but withstood the pain. When I finished, I pulled my thumb away to see a fat green pig on his cheek.

"There. Other demons who see you will know you are mine and they should keep their hands off. Of course, if someone's really pissed and gunning for me, they might decide to torture or kill you to taunt me. That's unavoidable."

"How likely is it that you're going to piss someone off and they'll take it out on me?" His voice quivered in fear.

"Oh I piss a lot of people off. That's pretty likely. But

you're not one of my household. I have humans around me I care much more about. It's a pretty slim chance that someone would bother with you when they have so many other beings whose injury or death would cause me pain."

I looked at the tattoo with a critical eye. I think my perspective was a bit off, but it looked pretty good if I might say so myself.

"The vampires probably won't mess with you. You may want to avoid angels though. A demon-marked human isn't going to win any mercy from them. Of course, your current profession probably wouldn't have won you mercy from them anyway."

"Vampires?" he asked.

I shooed him away. "The door is welded shut. I really want to finish up here, so if you could just go somewhere and hide, I'll allow my creative genius rein. I'll be sure to open the door for you when I leave. Feel free to watch if you want."

He clearly didn't want. He took off into the recesses of the warehouse where I'm sure he was hiding behind a box or under a desk in an office. I wondered how he'd feel when he saw his new tattoo. He'd probably be wearing a Band-Aid over his cheek for the rest of his life.

I'd just completed my work of art and un-welded the door when I felt a blast knock me to the ground, burning a hole through my hip. It couldn't be Gregory, he would have had much better aim, I thought as I scrambled on my back to face the angel.

He was slim and androgynous as they all seemed to be. All except mine anyway. I rolled to avoid a second blast and scooted on the floor, dragging a leg slightly from the damage to my hip, narrowly missing a third blast. Didn't the fucker know I was off limits? Or maybe my special status had been revoked since I'd last seen Gregory. Just in case, I threw a huge wave of energy at him, knocking him through the wooden side of a crate.

"Is that all you've got?" I shouted and set the box on fire. It was pretty impressive to see the angel burst from the burning crate, wreathed in fire but undamaged, like a legendary phoenix.

He smiled. "The vampires cannot protect you now. They'll probably be grateful to have such a troublesome guest exterminated."

I dodged another blast and launched myself at the angel, knocking him back across the floor with me on top of him. Before he could react, I drove a burst of energy into him and enhanced it with a sonic boom, like the one that had so injured Althean this summer. His eyes grew big.

"Wait, wait. I didn't realize you were Tsith's bound demon. Hold off your attack. I'm in his choir, I can't battle you, it is forbidden. Hold off."

I stood and let him get up. Tsith? He'd called Gregory Tsith? Tsith wasn't a name, or even a title, it was a term of endearment. A rather embarrassing term of endearment, in my opinion. It was like calling him sweetie pie, or lovey muffin. Ick.

The angel stood and looked me over, then, with a shimmer of light, transformed into a decidedly female form. A very beautiful female form with white hair cascading in a fine sheet to her shoulders, and bright blue eyes framed with long, gold-tipped lashes. Her pale pink lips puckered with consideration as she continued to assess me. I wondered what she was thinking.

"I'm Samantha Martin." I put out my hand. Might as well introduce myself. I wasn't sure which of my names Gregory knew, what he called me. Besides cockroach, that was. I felt a fierceness inside me at the thought of this angel calling me cockroach. I'd kill her if she called me that name. Only my angel could call me that.

"I'm Eloa." She refused my outstretched fingers.

Eloa meant pity, mercy. It was an odd choice of angels to be a liaison to the vampires. Although I was sure the angel's idea of mercy and pity wasn't the same as everyone else's. There wasn't a lot of pity in her eyes as she examined every inch of me. Curiosity, excitement, uneasy wonder, and faint disgust was written clear as could be on her face.

"Um. You don't think we could possibly keep this thing between you and me, do you?" I asked, gesturing at the stack of body parts. "There's no need to tell your boss that I've been a bad girl. I can make it worth your while."

She gave me a rather nasty smile, and continued to look me over. Gregory was going to fucking kill me over this weekend's events.

"I guess that's a yes? A maybe?"

She examined me further, ignoring my question.

"Why are you staring at me? Do I have bits of human in my teeth or something?" I was feeling like a zoo animal about to be poked, prodded, and catalogued. Plus, I was getting the odd notion that she was assessing me as a rival.

That perfect bow of a mouth turned up in an innocent smile. "You have no idea the uproar you've caused among the angelic host. Tsith binding you is pretty notable since he hasn't bound a demon in thousands of years. He always just kills them."

She said the last bit with pride, and let her eyes once again wander over me, this time in open scorn. I wished she'd stop calling him that name. It was creeping me out.

"Some theorized that Tsith was planning to infiltrate your realm and use you to destroy the demons once and for all, but when you managed to gate into Aaru and drop a dead bird there, a virtual panic ensued. No demon can get into

Aaru, none. Scholars will debate for tens of thousands of years on how you managed that one. Then you sneak in again and leave a pile of smoldering excrement."

I felt a little guilty at that one. I'd been so furious at Gregory, and a flaming bag of dog poop seemed like the perfect gift.

"No one is sure what Tsith's intentions are, what he plans to do with you, but a few have dared question his ability to keep you under control."

She said this as though she personally wanted to do away with these doubters.

"What do you think?" I asked, curious of her reaction as well as her answer. I wasn't let down.

"It is not my place to wonder about my Tsith's intentions. He is old, powerful. His knowledge and purity allow him an omnipotence others can only dream of. I live only to serve him."

Yikes. She was really on a roll here. And now she was referring to him as "my Tsith." As if he would be remotely interested in a boring sycophant like her. I frowned at the angel, but she was oblivious to my irritation.

"Every time someone mentions ending your existence, Tsith gets furious and commands that no one is allowed to harm or kill you. That only he has that privilege."

How nice that he was saving me for himself. I wondered how much time I had left. I was hoping that I could somehow manage to kill this nauseating angel before he did me in. I was beginning to hate her.

"And it is his privilege." Clearly the humans weren't the only ones who worshiped my angel. "You are bound to him, you are his property, and no one should presume to touch what he claims."

Fuck her. I might be bound, but it wasn't as if I were an inanimate possession, a rug or a chair. I realized she'd be happy if I were a trophy on his wall though. Gritting my teeth, I pushed down my detest for her, with her floaty white hair and pouty little mouth. I needed information, and she was hardly going to give it to me if she thought I was a threat, or if she thought I was a rival for her Tsith's affections. Blech.

"Don't get your halo in a knot or anything," I reassured her. "I think whatever usefulness I pose is coming to an end, and it's clear, based on our last encounter, that he won't hesitate to kill me when he's ready."

She looked at me, no doubt trying to decide if I was the equivalent of a chair or not.

"Seriously," I insisted. "I'm nothing but an annoyance to him."

I saw her relax slightly.

"Let's go get a drink, or maybe some nachos, and chat," I suggested casually. Then I sealed the deal.

"He talks about you all the time, you know," I said with a tinge of sad regret, as if I longed for him to speak that way about me. "It's always Eloa this, Eloa that. The only one he can trust to really get the job done, his right hand."

I saw her glow and nod in agreement.

CHAPTER 24

*T*he bar was a bit of an issue. It seems humans don't want to serve drinks to someone covered in blood and gore with bullet holes riddling their clothing. Eloa had to wave her delicate little hands around and pout a bit to get them to ignore my existence. Of course, that now meant she had to order the drinks.

"Get me a vodka," I ordered. "Tell them I want it cold. And not the cheap shit, either."

I was beginning to wish she'd go back to her androgynous male form. The Marilyn Monroe thing was grating on me big-time.

Eloa ordered two vodkas, and with a little smirk pulled something out of her pocket. I couldn't believe it. A joint. The angel seriously had a joint of marijuana on her. Completely ignoring human, and probably angelic, laws, she lit it up and offered it to me after taking a puff. I didn't hesitate. After all, I am a demon.

"Hot damn, this is nice," I said passing the joint back to her. Maybe Marilyn Monroe wasn't so bad after all.

"Yes, it's one of the more palatable things of this world."

She took a puff, her pink lips framing the joint in languid seduction.

"Try the vodka. That stuff rocks, too. It's so much better than that crappy wine the elves are always foisting on us."

She threw down the shot and held up the empty glass, raising an eyebrow in speculation. "It goes well with this burning weed wrapped in paper."

Okay, this angel was growing on me. I'll admit I liked the gate guardian with her snarky humor and her gluttonous cravings for sweet and sour sauce, but an angel that liked pot and vodka was like a kindred spirit. Why couldn't Gregory be more like this? We'd have a total blast together if I could get him to enjoy alcohol and drugs.

"You seem pretty cool, the gate guardian seems pretty cool. Why does your Tsith have such a massive stick up his ass?"

The word stuck a bit in my mouth. I can't believe I actually called Gregory "Tsith." Eloa stiffened, no doubt offended that I'd think an angel had a stick up his ass. Still, I was curious why he wasn't like the other angels I'd met to date.

"You can't really expect him to be friendly and loving after what went down during the war."

They'd all been through the war. They were all really stinking old. That couldn't be the reason, unless there was something specific that happened during the war that I was unaware of. I expected that they'd all be less than friendly and loving after the war, not hanging out with me in a bar drinking vodka and getting high.

"I don't really know what happened," I confessed. "I'm not even a thousand years old, and we don't really talk about it. I would have thought all you guys would have been thrilled to be done with us though."

"The war took a toll on us." Eloa paused to take a drag on the joint and pass it back. "Our two races may have differences, but a total split like this was painful. Friends, families broken apart, entire choirs fractured. We don't even know what happened to those we knew before the war. There has been no communication since that point. Are they dead? Do they care anymore? Have they descended so far into evil that we wouldn't recognize them if we saw them?"

The bartender sat two more vodkas in front of her. She pushed one over to me with a slightly distracted look on her face.

"Some wonder if the things that broke us apart were worth it. You all got exile, but I think we probably got the worse end of the stick. Aaru is not the same. It's stagnant there. Our evolution has dropped to a crawl."

"Do you think your Tsith regrets the war, wishes things had gone down differently?" I held my breath. Her answer meant a lot to me.

"Tsith led the charge into battle. He commanded the army, was one of those who advocated holding firm on our morals and values, who insisted that the demons either repent or die. He lost his youngest brother in the war, his favorite."

Fuck. I remembered him telling me about his youngest brother. The one he'd played in the lightning with, the one he loved the most. Dead. Something tightened up inside me at the thought.

"He was in hand-to-hand combat with the Iblis that final battle of the war. They nearly killed each other. He sliced the Iblis practically in half but not before he'd had his wings torn to shreds, almost cut off."

I winced. Wings for us are just an appendage. For angels, they are their most vulnerable spot. They seldom display them in corporeal form if they can avoid it.

Eloa shuddered. "You don't normally survive losing your wings. He still has terrible scars."

I wasn't sure if she meant scars on his wings, or other scars. Probably both. My heart sank further. He wouldn't regret what happened between our races. Not if he was one of the main drivers of the war. He'd lost his brother in the war, had his wings nearly severed. He'd never feel anything but hate for me. He'd never see me as anything more than an abomination, never anything more than a lowly cockroach.

"It's been two-and-a-half-million years and there hasn't been any attempt at reconciliation?" Gregory might never forgive or forget, but surely the other angels wouldn't have such wounds.

"There is no Iblis. Right after the exile, the title was lost and no one bears it. Who would we contact? The Iblis is the sole demon who is allowed access into Aaru. The Iblis has a seat on the Ruling Council. The entire treaty was set up to allow some form of contact and mutual cooperation in matters concerning us both, but instead there has been a total split. The seat on the council remains empty, and increasingly there are those that think total separation is best and the seat for the Iblis should be wiped from the treaty."

I drank the vodka and stared at the bar. I thought of Gregory, his dead brother at his feet, his wings in tatters, meting out fury upon a horned, scaled Iblis. Images of war were normally pleasant, but this one churned my stomach. The whole conversation was making me depressed. And I'd had such a good evening, too. Stupid fucking angel with her stories of the war.

"Well, it's been nice chatting with you." I abruptly rose and threw a twenty on the bar. I needed to get away from here, away from her, away from the sick feeling in my middle. She looked at me in surprise. I could feel her eyes on me as I left the bar.

Kelly was waiting for me at the hotel lobby. The polite

mask was on her face, but she was clearly furious. The sight cheered me up considerably.

"Baal, we are so glad you are safe." Her tone didn't sound glad. "When you did not return after your hunt, we tracked you and were quite concerned when we saw the carnage in the warehouse."

"I'm good," I assured her. "Hey do you guys have any Nacho Cheese Doritos? I seriously need some Nacho Cheese Doritos right now."

The muscle in her jaw twitched. In fact, even her eye twitched a bit at the edge.

"We had an understanding," she hissed. "One kill. One. You've destabilized the power structure of a major drug operation, one that makes us a lot of money. It will be nigh impossible to prop them up before a rival group jumps in. We had control, we had cooperation, and you've destroyed all that. One night, and you've destroyed a decade's worth of work."

Yeah, and I knew her secret, too. Little traitor. Little snake in the grass. Embezzler, siphoning funds from her family's interests. I admired her, but she was reaching too far, too fast.

"How about Cool Ranch? If you don't have Nacho Cheese Doritos, then maybe Cool Ranch will do."

"And that freakish, sick thing you did with the bodies? I had to send in vampires to deal with it. It was too much for my humans to handle. Now other vampires know. They know that I allowed you to get out of control. I'll be blamed for this whole fiasco." Her smile was downright frightening at this point. An insane looking grimace on her heart-shaped face.

"It was a work of art," I said, with a flourish of my hand. "I hope they enjoyed it, appreciated how much of myself I put into it."

"An angel was there. Eloa probably. I have never lost a guest to an angel. The only saving event this evening is that he didn't catch up with you or you'd be dead and my reputation would be in even greater shambles."

"Oh, but he did. Or she did," I corrected myself. "He looked like a pouty Marilyn Monroe. We went out to a bar, drank vodka, and smoked pot."

Kelly audibly ground her teeth. At least that macabre smile was gone from her face.

"Are you sure you don't have any Nacho Cheese Doritos?" I asked again. "I think I saw some in one of the vending machines if you don't."

Kelly snapped. Fangs shot down so fast that they actually cut her lip.

"I am going to shove Doritos so far up your rear that you'll be coughing them up for a week," she shouted, punctuating her words with a finger on my chest. Vampires were strong; I could feel her finger actually bruising me.

"I am going to cram Doritos in every hole. I'll jam them clean up through your sinuses and into your brain. I'll make new holes in your body to stuff them. You screwed me. You totally screwed me."

At this point, every two-legged being in the lobby had stopped and was staring at Kelly. I noticed Stephen with a smug look on his face. Guess that promotion was looking better for him.

"Sounds like fun," I said. "Just send the Doritos up to my room and meet me up there. Wyatt might be interested in some Doritos-in-the-ass action, too. I don't want to leave him out."

I walked out of the silent lobby and headed straight to my room. Things were probably going to go down real fast from this point forward, and I needed to find Wyatt and tell him the score.

Wyatt was a big lump of covers in the bed as I walked in. I seriously needed to talk to him about his sleeping habits. He slept so soundly that an explosion wasn't likely to wake him. He was going to get himself killed if he didn't alter that habit. To help make my point, I ran across the room and launched myself on top of him, finding only a pile of pillows and blankets. Maybe he wouldn't get himself killed after all. I swung my head upside down over the edge of the bed to look under it, suspecting he might be sleeping there. Thankfully he wasn't. It looked like no one had cleaned under the bed in months. I'd need to talk to Kelly about this. If Kelly was still alive, that is.

"Sam? It's about time you got back," Wyatt's groggy voice said from the closet. "I got bumped out of the tournament fairly early on. Looks like you had a good night," he added seeing my blood and gore stained clothing.

"I had such a good night that we are going to need to put our sneak-out plan into action." I walked over to kiss him.

"Whoa, you really did have a good night. You reek of pot. Was that part of the spoils of war?"

"Nope. So don't try to hit me up for any. I shared a joint with an angel after killing off most of the management of a local drug empire. There was a bit of a scene downstairs with that Kelly girl, so I strongly suspect they'll move up my meeting with the master guy and kick us out before daybreak."

Wyatt looked regretfully around at our clothing. "Ah. Just the essentials in a bag as we planned?"

"Yeah, except I'm going to try and walk out the door as the tall blonde. There's no way Haagenti's people are going to let me leave this casino, so I'm going to see if I can sneak out."

Wyatt looked concerned. "Won't they sense your energy? I thought you guys all recognized each other?"

"I don't leak," I told him. "And my physical form is damned near perfect. It's probably a fifty-fifty chance that they won't recognize me, but it's the best I've got."

I grabbed a pair of jeans and a bright red oxford shirt, throwing another pair of jeans and a plain white t-shirt in Wyatt's small duffle with my license, cash, cell phone, and the box of elf blood. Then I raced for the shower. I wanted to be clean for my meeting. I was towel drying my hair when I heard Wyatt answer the door.

"Ten minutes, Sam," he hollered, throwing a bag of Doritos in the bathroom door at me. Nacho Cheese.

I ignored the Doritos and put on my clothes, piling the wet hair in a pony tail and forgoing make-up. It's not like I needed to impress this guy. The whole meeting was just a formality. He says "Hi," I hand over elf blood, we make small talk for two minutes, and then off I go, empty handed.

I grabbed my duffle and tossed Wyatt the car keys.

"You need to take good care of my Corvette. No scratches, I don't even want to see drool on the steering wheel. If I'm not there in one hour, go ahead like we planned."

He met me at the door and kissed me. It was one of those kisses like someone's afraid they won't see you again.

"Stop it," I told him. "I'm a cockroach and we must have a dozen lives or something. Don't get all soppy on me, I'll be there."

"You better be," he said, his voice husky. "Otherwise I'm going to drop your car into the Chesapeake Bay. On purpose."

That was proper motivation. I gave him a quick kiss and followed Mario into the elevator.

CHAPTER 25

*M*ario led me into what appeared to be a long, narrow study. The door where we entered was at one end. At the other was a large, ornate, dark wood desk with an equally ornate chair behind it. The wall behind the desk was bare, no doubt so there was nothing to distract your attention from the man in the chair. A couple of guest seats were angled in front of the desk. To the left, a couch sat with a coffee table in front of it. To the right, a series of built-in bookshelves, filled with books, pictures, and knickknacks. Mario and I were the only ones in the room.

"So what do I call this guy?" I asked Mario. "I'm assuming he has a name. Bob? Phil?"

"You can call him Master," Mario said definitively.

Yeah, like that was going to happen. I looked around, and was rather surprised when Mario left. He actually left me alone here to wait for this guy? Shouldn't he be worried that I'd take off with the silver, or go through the desk drawers or something?

It was absolutely silent in the room. I was starting to get bored, so I went and looked over the items on the bookshelf.

There was an eclectic mix of books. Some beautiful leather-bound classics. Philosophy, a very old Bible, and an equally old copy of Pilgrim's Progress. A handful of modern paper-backs and some worn children's picture books. These books had been read, and I assumed they meant something to their owner.

The pictures were equally intriguing. A beautiful black-and-white of cliffs overlooking the ocean, and one of fields of wheat, bent in the breeze. One of a little boy with dark hair and gray eyes, his mouth turned slightly up at the edges like he found life infinitely amusing. It had to have been Kyle as a child; the resemblance was too striking to have been otherwise. There was only one reason I could think of for a man to have a picture of a little boy in his personal study. Yes, Kyle is a bad, bad boy, I thought with amusement.

My host had still not arrived, so I turned my attention to the knickknacks on the shelves. Beautiful woven rush baskets, so tiny they fit on my fingertips like little thimbles, were next to the old Bible. Beside the picture of Kyle was an old wooden top, its string frayed and its paint chipped. I handled a piece of hemp rope with wonder. What signifi-cance could it hold for the owner? These were clearly all very personal objects with great meaning. What an intriguing man to have so much of himself out on display like this, even if it was his personal study. Did he needed reminders of his past? Something to anchor him to lost humanity in a very long vampire life? But then, this man was born a vampire. There were no roots of humanity to remember. Perhaps they were to remind him of what he'd never had.

I was just about to turn away when I saw the egg. I've seen a lot of eggs in my years. Intricate jeweled ones, sugar ones with little edible scenes inside their hollowed-out shells, and actual bird eggs, warm and colorful. This was the most beautiful egg ever. I caught my breath and picked it up, running my fingers across its surface. It was a kind of metal. I couldn't tell what, and I probed it with all my might. The surface was covered with little symbols and letters, none of which combined to form any language I was aware of. A metal egg with raised symbols shouldn't hold this much fascination for me, but it was hard to put it down. I desperately wanted to stick it in my pocket and steal it. It would be kind of obvious walking out of here with a huge bulge in my jeans pocket so I reluctantly put it back on the shelf and sat down on the couch. There was a glass candy dish with what appeared to be bits of beef jerky in it, so I helped myself.

As usual, I had my mouth stuffed full of jerky when my host walked in. I could feel him the moment he opened the door, his power rolling before him like a wave. I jumped up and vaulted the coffee table to shake his hand, swallowing the poorly chewed stuff and choking slightly.

"I'm so glad to finally meet you Mr. Master. I'm Samantha Martin. You can call me Sam."

My host looked at me with the same placid, bored look as the rest of his crew. Unlike his crew, though, there wasn't much beyond the surface that appeared human. Kyle was Born, but he still looked like all the other vampires. This one didn't, and I wasn't sure if it was his age or his power or a combination of them both that set him apart. He wasn't good looking in the conventional sense of the word. Thin, almost gaunt, with sharp angles everywhere, and eyes that seemed glassy and feverish. His skin was a grayish color. If he'd been human, I would have thought he was in the late stages of cancer or some wasting sort of disease. He even smelled like something that hadn't been exposed to fresh air for centuries. In spite of that, he had a sort of aristocratic air about him that made me feel like I was a poorly educated, naughty child. This was going to be a long five minutes. I wiped the drool from the corner of my mouth with the back of my hand.

"Excellent jerky you've got there," I said, by way of conversation.

A ghost of a smile crossed his face. "Yes, we made it ourselves."

Clearly this was an inside joke. I wondered if the jerky was some poor sap that'd lost big at blackjack. I'd eaten human before, so it didn't exactly faze me.

"Please sit." My host motioned toward the guest chairs as he moved to sit behind the desk. I plopped myself down on the couch and he frowned, changing direction and turning around one of the guest chairs to face me. Clearly this was a lot more informal than he'd planned. Too bad.

"I'd like to start by apologizing for the incident in the lobby with my former Casino Manager," he said smoothly. "We don't tolerate that kind of behavior, and I'm hoping you don't hold her disrespect against our family."

"I'm terribly affronted that she didn't actually show up to shove Doritos up my ass. That would have been epic." I shrugged. "I totally understand if you needed to kill her. Shame, though. You're missing some spunk like that in your ranks. Of course, if you're worried that her power might rival yours, then you should definitely off her. Taking out strong rivals under the guise of keeping behavioral standards is a good way to prop up a tottering empire."

His dull skin glowed somewhat, a silvery gray. He knew what I was doing, but the implication that he was old, weak, and outdated still stung.

"You do realize that we cannot just hand this artifact over to you? That it chooses who it goes to and isn't likely to go to a courier?" He ignored my comments.

"Oh yeah, your son told me that already." I was amused to see him start as I referred to Kyle as his son. "I just thought we'd chat a bit before I go home and get my ass soundly beat."

He looked at me with some curiosity. "Why go to all this trouble to get a meeting if you know you won't be able to retrieve the artifact?"

"And miss out on a few days of gambling and killing at some other demon's expense? I never pass up a freebie."

His eyes brightened slightly. "Surely that isn't your only reason?"

I was hardly going to tell him I was hoping to mitigate my smack-down from Haagenti a bit by putting in an effort.

"No. My boyfriend had a computer game tournament up here and I wanted to come along to make sure you vampires didn't end up making jerky out of him."

That was a horribly insulting thing to say, but my host wasn't paying attention to me. He wasn't even looking at me. Instead he was frowning at something on the coffee table. I looked down and saw the egg sitting there, right next to my hand. Fuck. I thought I had put it back on the bookshelf. It wouldn't be the first time I'd stolen something and not really been conscious of it, though.

"I'm sorry." I picked up the egg and replaced it on the bookshelf. "I was admiring some of your decorations, and didn't realize that I'd not put that one back."

This really didn't look good. I didn't want the head of the entire northeast region of vampires thinking I was stealing his personal items. Hastily, I dug in the little duffle bag and pulled out the box that held my gift. Well, Dar's gift, actually.

"Here." I tossed the box at him. He caught it in a quick, smooth motion, and raised his eyebrows at me. "A gift. I was told I was to present a gift to you."

He looked at the box suspiciously then opened it. A soft gasp escaped him as he looked at the tiny vials, and he ran a finger lovingly over them. Dar clearly did something right here.

"I cannot accept this, Baal. This gift is precious beyond words, and I cannot reciprocate by giving you the artifact."

I waved my hand at him. "Keep it. Otherwise I'll sell it on eBay and it will end up collecting dust on the shelf of a forty year old fat man living in his parents' basement. There are only so many people interested in buying elf blood, you know."

He nodded, and giving the vials one last caress, closed the box and placed it on his desk.

"So, what else should we discuss? The weather, perhaps? Or your favorite sports team?"

"Nope. I should probably head out," I said, making to rise.

He halted me with an upraised hand and frowned at my bag. "Is there something else in your satchel, Baal?"

"Just a change of clothes," I replied, checking quickly. My face reddened and I pulled out a metal egg. I was so fucked. No amount of elf blood was going to make this one right. And he'd caught me stealing it, too; otherwise how would he have known it was in my bag?

I got up to put the egg back once again. Suddenly, it flashed and morphed, and instinctively I threw it across the room. In a panic, I jumped up on the couch as if it were a mouse and shielded myself with a couch cushion.

"Get down, it's gonna blow," I shouted.

After a few seconds of silence, I peeked around the couch cushion to see the egg lying on the coffee table once again. A chunk of the bookcase had broken into splinters on the floor where the egg had impacted.

"Perhaps if you held onto it, rather than hurling it across the room, you'd figure out what it is," my host said sarcastically.

I reached out tentatively and picked up the egg, still

holding onto the cushion with my other hand, just in case. In a flash, it became a sword. It was rather plain, with a braided hilt and round knob pommel.

"So this is what all the fuss is about?" I asked. The master guy nodded.

"Well, it's very nice," I lied. "Should I stick it back on your bookcase, or is there somewhere else you keep it?"

"It appears to want to go with you," my host said.

Wow, this was a lucky turn of events. I could give the sword to Haagenti after all and maybe be back here before Wyatt died of old age.

"You cannot give it away. It will remain with you until it decides otherwise."

"I have no use for a sword," I said in frustration. "I don't know how to use it. I don't fight with a sword. What the fuck am I supposed to do with this thing?"

He shrugged, looking like he might start to laugh at any moment. "It can change shape to whatever you want. A knife? A staff perhaps? Or an egg? At this juncture, it's mainly ceremonial, although if you need, it can be a powerful weapon for you."

"What sort of ceremonies?" I asked. I couldn't recall any demon ceremonies off the top of my head, let alone one that included using a sword.

"At Council meetings, or if someone questions your authority. Or you could always just chop off an angel's wings with it," he added, his eyes glittering in amusement.

I looked at the sword with a growing sense of doom. Now I really didn't want the damned thing. Not if it was what I thought it was. As if Gregory didn't hate me enough right now. He'd destroy me if he saw me with it.

"It's the Sword of the Iblis, Ha-Satan." He sounded rather sympathetic. "Surely you didn't think you were coming to retrieve Excalibur, did you?"

Of course. But why would Haagenti have wanted such a thing? Yeah, I could see him drooling at the prospect of chopping angel wings off, but I didn't envision him wanting to be the Iblis. Nobody wanted to be the Iblis. I certainly didn't want to be the Iblis.

"Can I give it back? Maybe you vampires can hold onto it until some other sucker, I mean demon, comes along?"

He shook his head. "It's a sentient object, Ha-Satan. I have no control over it."

What the fuck was I supposed to do with this thing? Maybe I could hide it and no one would know. Stick it under my bed or something.

Well, there was nothing to be done about this right now. I needed to leave pronto and sneak out of this hotel or I wouldn't make my rendezvous with Wyatt. Of course, it was going to be hard sneaking out of a casino with a big sword in tow. I concentrated on the sword, begging it silently to turn into something useful, like a Gucci bag or a pair of Ferragamos. There was a flash, and a gold barrette in the shape of a feather lay in my palm. Oh, the irony.

"Well, thank you very much for your hospitality." I clipped my hair back with my newest accessory. "I wish you the best of luck in quelling the upcoming rebellion."

He shot me a shrewd look as he rose to shake my hand.

"I'm hoping I can count on your continued support and friendship, Ha-Satan."

"Oh absolutely," I lied, grabbing my duffle and heading out the door. "I'm totally in your corner on this one."

Time was running out. I raced for the elevator, and jumped in, smacking the button for the lobby. The hotel was not tall, and I only had a few floors to go, so I dropped the duffle bag and quickly popped my form into the tall blonde, blowing apart every stitch of clothing I had on. In a moment of panic, I grabbed at my hair thinking I'd blown apart the

Barrette of the Iblis along with my clothing, but I was relieved to find it there undamaged. I'd never live it down if I managed to destroy a priceless demon artifact within five minutes of taking possession of it. Scrambling, I threw on the jeans and white t-shirt from the duffle bag, going commando for speed in dressing, and shoving my ID, money, and my cell phone into a pocket. Just as I was pulling on a pair of wedge pumps, the elevator dinged and I stepped out, leaving the duffle behind.

I meandered around the casino for a bit, searching for either Sobronoy or Labisi. They both knew my meeting was this morning, but I'm sure they assumed later. Maybe they weren't going to bother staking the place out until lunchtime? I headed toward the hotel lobby area and stopped dead as I caught sight of Mario. He'd most likely seen the footage from before and might recognize me as this tall blonde woman. It was too late to backtrack without bringing notice to myself, so I casually kept walking, hoping he'd not see me. Nope. He glanced up and froze, staring intently at me. Fuck. I slowed down and looked at him, wondering what to do. He was clearly wondering what to do, too. How tight was he with the late Kelly that I'd screwed over? He knew both Sobronoy and Labisi were going to grab me. Would he rat me out to them?

Our eyes met for a brief second, and I saw him smile. Walking with an inhuman speed toward the door, he touched the sleeve of a man there. Sobronoy, I thought as I saw him turn. Fuck, Mario was going to hand me over. I did not want to have a knockdown, drag out fight with Sobronoy in this hotel lobby, but there was no way I was going down easy. I took a breath, ready to pull my energy up, but something made me hold back. Sobronoy walked away, with Mario following him. I sighed with relief and saw Mario give me the peace sign behind his back. That vampire was on my good list. I owned him one. Anytime Mario, I thought. Anytime.

Feeling like escape was within my reach, I walked out the revolving doors and grabbed a cab. Within ten minutes, I was outside the city limits and happily walking into an IHOP and Wyatt's arms. Home free. Almost.

CHAPTER 26

I was followed," Wyatt whispered into my neck as he hugged me. I was actually taller than him in this form.

"Is she here?" It had to be Labisi.

He shook his head. "In the parking lot. Sam, I'm not sure how we're going to get out of here. Maybe if you stay like this, she'll think I'm cheating on you. Then we can go to a rent by the hour motel, and hopefully she'll give up and head back to the casino."

She might, but I thought she'd probably continue to follow Wyatt until Sobronoy told her he had me in his grubby little hands. Soon enough Sobronoy would figure out that I'd slipped out of the casino, and she'd connect the dots.

"I think our best bet is to act like you're flying the coop with me. We'll head home as fast as we can and if she comes after us I'll deal with it."

"They know where we live, don't they? Even if we get away from them, they'll eventually show up at your house to grab you. Wouldn't it be easier to deal with them here?"

I shook my head. "At home I've got Boomer and even

Diablo to help out. You have no idea how amazing Boomer can be if I turn him loose, and I know Diablo will be happy for the opportunity to kill something. He blew a deer apart the other week. He's pretty impressive. I know he'd love to help me kill a demon."

Wyatt looked surprised. "I thought you all didn't kill each other?"

"Well, not in the normal course of things, but I'm not going home and the only way I can send a strong message about this is to kill every single demon Haagenti sends to collect me."

Wyatt nodded and we walked out the door like two illicit lovers, got into the Corvette, and drove off. I was driving, so if Labisi came after us I could take off like a maniac. I hoped she was stupid, because there would be no way Wyatt would just hand over the Corvette to some random hot chick. The moment I got into the driver's seat, she should have been on us.

Clearly she was stupid, because we pulled out onto the highway with her a respectable distance behind. We'd made it all the way into Delaware when she must have gotten the phone call from Sobronoy. I saw the gray Honda weave around traffic and speed up. She was fast and rather reckless, clipping other cars to catch up, but I'd been living as a human for forty years and my driving experience far outclassed hers. I'd pulled away and put about a quarter mile between us when she began to catch up. Fuck.

I wasn't taking any chances and kept looking in my rearview mirror, so I actually saw her coming up behind us. I was going to need to deal with this right here. Otherwise I'd be stuck in a defensive position while she blasted away at my car. I needed to get out and confront her where I'd have room to move, duck, and dodge and have an opportunity to take her head off.

"Give me your belt," I told Wyatt. "I'm going to yank over to the shoulder here and confront her. When I hop out, you scoot over and take the wheel so you can drive."

"I'm not driving off and leaving you, Sam," Wyatt protested.

I looked at him in surprise. "Of course not. I want you to mow her down if you get the chance."

Wyatt grinned. "Will do."

We pulled over to the shoulder and I looped Wyatt's belt loosely around my waist.

"Try to make sure she doesn't notice you, so you can surprise her. And be careful," I instructed as I jumped out of the car to face Labisi.

She pulled over behind our car about fifty feet and got out, putting her hands out to her sides in supplication.

"Come with me, little imp, and no one will be hurt. If you refuse, I'll fight you. I don't care how much energy I use. I can take you down and be out of here before the angels arrive."

I looked at her and saw the edges of the disk in her hand. Great. She had one of the damned elf buttons, too. How much had Haagenti spent to make sure I came back to face his wrath?

I walked forward with my head down in a submissive posture. I was only an imp, a little cockroach. She surely didn't expect me to fight. Taking the feather barrette out of my hair, I shook it loose from the pony tail and made as if I were going to toss the ornament aside, only to swing it in an arc and wish like hell it was a sword again. There was a flash and a sword appeared. Unfortunately I hadn't figured in the time it took for the object to transform and it missed her head, assuming its deadly shape on the downward stroke.

Labisi shrieked and yanked her head backward, throwing her arms forward for balance, which put her right limb squarely in the path of the descending sword. Well, at least I did some damage, I thought as the sword cleanly sliced through her arm and sent the limb tumbling to the pavement. Labisi shot a bolt of energy toward me with the remaining hand and I hit the ground and rolled, avoiding the blast that knocked the sword loose from my hand. The energy slammed into a Nissan and launched it onto its side into the median as the occupants screamed.

My sword clattered to the ground, and then shot into traffic as another of Labisi's bolts of energy hit it. Bitch was trying to destroy my sword! Didn't she know what it was? I rolled after it as it slid across the road and under a pickup truck, narrowly avoiding a car that swerved to miss the sword and almost creamed me instead. Cars were honking, people screaming, and I'd rolled my way through a particularly nasty patch of oil some vehicle had spilled in the roadway.

Everyone on the road was in a panic and the pickup truck sped up, driving right over top of the sword. I winced thinking I clearly wasn't a good choice of guardian for this thing. I'll bet Thor never had his hammer run over by a truck. I hadn't even been the Iblis for twenty-four hours and I already sucked.

Figuring I'd deal with traffic better on my feet, I lurched upright and tried to grab the sword, narrowly avoiding being mowed down by a sedan. A second blast of energy took a chunk of flesh off my leg and blew pulverized bits of asphalt into the air. Labisi was now filling the pavement full of holes with shotgun-like blasts. Fuck, she was not kidding here. I wondered if the edict from Haagenti was "dead or alive" after all.

At this point, cars were recklessly speeding past our scene of chaos. A few idiots slowed down to rubber-neck. One car was soundly rear-ended and pushed right on top of my sword. I'd be lucky if the damned thing worked at all after this kind of abuse. I tried once more to dart around the traffic and grab it, but a blast from Labisi hit a few feet from me, digging another chunk out of the road. Fuck the sword. I needed to take this demon out fast before she actually hit me with one of those shots.

I ran and ducked, putting the rear-ended car between the pair of us. Labisi screamed in frustration and raced toward me, shooting a blast that sent the car blocking me up and over the car in back of it. At this point the oncoming traffic had stopped, blocked in by drivers too smart to drive into explosions and flying vehicles. It was just us and the screaming humans.

I thought of how pissed Gregory was going to be at me. Weird, I know, to think about that sort of thing in the middle of a fight, but I did. I'd Owned a human, killed six, and now this. He was going to beat me senseless and drag me back to Aaru. Aaru... Hel... Two beings trying to haul me places I didn't want to be. I didn't know how I was going to get out of either of these situations.

I was running as I thought, trying to get behind another car when Labisi grabbed me by the wrist. She was strong and I struggled hard against her, feeling my wrist bones begin to snap and crumble.

"I've got you, you fucking piece of shit," she announced in triumph.

Yep, she had me, but she didn't have her button. I'd sliced off the hand with the portable gate and the realization dawned on her as she looked down at a stump of an arm. I seized on her moment of inattention and grabbed the antenna of the squashed car beside me, intending to snap it off and beat her with it. The antenna was on tighter than I thought and my hand was slippery with oil from the spill I'd rolled in. It snapped loose from my grasp and, like a whip, cracked Labisi in the face. She screamed as blood poured from the vertical gash, and let go of my wrist. I bolted.

A blast of energy streaked past, melting the front end of the car before me. She wasn't holding back at all. I might have to use energy to take her out instead of trying to do it the human way. I was in so much shit with Gregory that blowing up a section of the interstate and a bunch of humans shouldn't make much difference, but first I had to find that damned button before she did.

Scrambling and dodging, I looked for it. Another blast clipped me, tearing flesh and bone from my hip, sending me sliding face first along the blacktop and partially under a pickup truck, where I found my nose firmly against an arm. Her grip must have loosened when her arm separated from her body, because the button was up under the front tire. Luckily, the truck was jacked up a bit and I scooted toward the button.

A hand grabbed my leg and tugged painfully. I had to get that fucking button, so I held onto the truck's frame with one hand and whipped off Wyatt's belt. I felt my hip begin to dislocate as I tossed the buckle end at the button, trying to drag it to me. I missed with the first toss, and I wasn't sure my leg would hold out long enough to hook the portable gate. Just as I was about to give up and turn my attention to Labisi, I heard a squishy thunk, and my leg was released.

I felt it. In a fraction of a second, I felt her store of raw energy pour out of her. Wyatt. All the humans. My beloved car. She didn't have as much as I did, but it was still enough to blow a huge hole in the interstate and kill everyone in the area. Mine, I thought, with as much intent and power as I could put behind the word. Then I pulled the raw energy inside me. I took. I devoured. In an instant, I possessed it all, every last speck.

Scrambling forward, I grabbed the button, and scooted

out the other side of the truck. There was Wyatt, in my Corvette, driving back and forth over a pulp of Labisi. I winced thinking what this was doing to my precious car. He pulled the car off her, and got out, his gun half hidden in his waistband, to look down at the chunks of flesh and bone on the road.

"Do you think she's dead, or should I shoot her a few times just to make sure? I don't want to shoot her unless I have to. You'll be visiting me in jail for a long time if I discharge a weapon on the highway."

"Uh, no. She's dead." I limped over.

Demons can take a huge amount of damage, but, Gregory's assurances aside, total destruction of our physical form kills us. There was no way she'd survived this one, but I reached down and ran my energy over the flesh just to make sure. Yep. Dead. I quickly fixed my hip and other injuries and looked at the elf button. Normally I'd want to keep something so expensive and cool, but I could hardly cart this pile of gore home in my car, and I needed to send a message.

I put the button on what remained of Labisi and activated the portable gate. "*Glah ham, shoceacan.*"

The flesh and bone vanished in a flash, leaving only a smear of blood on the pavement.

"Are you okay, Sam?" Wyatt asked, his voice concerned as his eyes roamed over my tattered clothing and newly healed flesh.

"Yes, thanks to your bulldozer imitation with my car," I replied. There was a pretty good sized dent in the bumper, but given the wreckage around us, the Corvette had fared well.

Wyatt smiled at me, his eyes warm, and he put his arm around my shoulder. "Happy to be of service."

I motioned toward the car. "We've got to get out of here.

I'm expecting Sobronoy at any moment, and he's going to be much harder to fight than Labisi."

It wasn't just Sobronoy I was worried about. Gregory would probably arrive soon and I was hoping to avoid that confrontation for as long as possible.

It took us a while to weave around the broken and abandoned cars and make our way back into traffic. I wondered about the fallout from this little incident. Someone was bound to have videoed the whole thing on their cell phone, possibly even taken down our license plate number as we left. Would state police come calling? Was I going to have to deal with the nightmare of a human legal system in addition to pissed off angels and demons? I glanced over at Wyatt, deciding to see whether he could hack our way out of this one. Maybe he could switch my car plate number and registration records at the DMV with some other poor sap.

Wyatt navigated using his cell phone, and we tore down back roads in record time. Sobronoy was nowhere to be found. I had been worried that he'd be waiting for us at the house, but we seemed to make it there before him. I pulled in Wyatt's driveway and let him out.

"Go inside and get all your defenses set," I told him. "I think we've got at least a few hours before Sobronoy gets here. I'm going to go get Boomer and Diablo and take care of things and my house, and then I'll call you."

He kissed me and hopped out.

CHAPTER 27

J parked by the back of my house and ran out to the barn in order to find Boomer and unlock his magnificent hellhound self. Usually he was snoozing in the barn all day, but not today. I checked the usual spots, and then headed out to the field to look for him. There was a huge groundhog hole at the edge of the woods, and he liked to shove his head in it and nap. He wasn't there, but a demon was.

Oh, not Boomer, I thought in panic. How long had this demon been here, waiting for me? What had she done with Boomer? With Diablo? They were both nowhere to be found. What if Candy or Michelle had come by? Had the demon killed them all? I'd halted in shock to see the demon there, by the groundhog hole. She'd seen me and was smiling, with a smug look on her face as she motioned me closer.

I recognized her right away. Busyasta. She was so high in level that she didn't even bother with a human form. She just didn't give a shit. Her long claws clacked as they rapped on the rocky ground, her skin stretched tight over bones and golden yellow in the sunshine. A stench of rot wafted over to me on the breeze. I hoped it was her that smelled so bad, and not the remains of my friends. That bastard Haagenti was covering all the bases if he had a demon waiting here at home for me, in case I escaped the two in Atlantic City.

"Where's Boomer?" I asked, my heart in my mouth. At least Diablo has some means of defense. Boomer didn't. Why did I leave my dog locked down so tight he couldn't fight back? I swore that no matter how many corpses he dug up and ate, I was never doing this to him again. Ever.

Busyasta looked confused for a second. "The groundhog?" She smiled. "I killed it and ate it. Thing put up quite a fight. It would be nice if you did, too. It's so disappointing when they come easy."

I relaxed. She'd killed the groundhog. If she'd taken out a hellhound or a demon horse, she would be rubbing their deaths in my face. They had to be alive. Somewhere.

I reached for my barrette and panicked as I felt my loose hair. I'd left the sword under a car back in Delaware. It's not like I'm used to carrying a big ass sword around with me. I mentally kicked myself. So worthy of the Sword of the Iblis that I'd forgotten it under a car. I'll bet no warrior in the history of the universe had ever done that. I'll bet Thor never left his hammer behind after a battle. I was going to lose against Busyasta big time. I was going home in a body bag if I had to fight her with only my energy. Taking the initiative, I shot a blast at her and dove, picking up a couple stones as I rolled back to my feet some distance away.

Busyasta laughed. I'd missed her completely. I'd been living as a human for so long, trying to lay low, that I'd lost some skill. This wasn't going to turn out well, being forced to fight with energy like the demon I was.

"You suck," Busyasta commented, climbing down from the groundhog mound. "I'm going to need to ratchet this down big time if I want to have any fun at all with you."

I threw my rocks at her and was thrilled to see them impact with her face. She laughed again as blood ran in streaks down her forehead and cheek.

"Little imp, you fight like a human." She launched a stream of energy at me.

I dove and rolled, shooting out a blast of my own as the edge of hers hit my leg. Oddly enough, my leg didn't blow apart in a gory mess, it just went numb. The bitch was taking it easy on me, playing with me. I shot another blast at her, and as she avoided it, ran at her as fast as my one numb leg could go. She fell backward with my tackle right on top of the groundhog mound and I shot energy into her at close range.

She deflected the energy with a grunt. Fuck. She'd actually converted the blast I'd thrown at her. Our foster parents used that skill to break up fights, but few demons managed to cultivate it. I'd need to either overwhelm her defense with an overload of energy or take out her physical form in a more unconventional, human manner. Backing up, I looked around for a weapon. Damn, I wish Boomer or Diablo was around to help me take her down. She couldn't shoot at all three of us.

Busyasta struggled a little, her rear stuck down into the sizable groundhog hole, and I took advantage of the opening to shoot her again with a blast of energy. She twisted, pulling free of the hole and my shot clipped her, ripping flesh down to bone on her back.

"Bitch," she said and shot me square in my stomach, throwing me a few feet and onto my back. I rolled as the world spun in a blur before my eyes. I was tingling numb in all my extremities and I couldn't see straight. My only hope was to wait until she came close to grab me, then empty everything I had in her, hoping to overwhelm her defenses.

She continued to blast at me as she came closer, obviously

making sure I didn't shake off my numbness before she could secure me and gate me back to Haagenti. This was it. I had only one chance to try and take her as she grabbed me. Once she activated the elf button, I'd be in Hel. Then I wouldn't just have her to kill; I'd have Haagenti and his entire household.

I saw a shadow come towards me and I shook my head, desperately trying to regain control of my senses. My legs didn't work properly, and I scooted on my rear trying to evade what I thought was Busyasta, and prepared my blast. Just as things came into focus, I saw a head rolling to stop a few inches from my feet. Busyasta's head.

Looking up in amazement I saw a shadowy form wiping his hands on his pants, a pile of sand at his feet. I knew who it was even before he finally came into focus. Gregory. I sat, still sprawled on the ground, and stared at him, my mouth wide open. Oh holy shit, I was in for it now. I didn't expect to have to deal with him this soon.

"What?" he asked, noticing my expression. "I came to talk with you about your recent infractions and got tired of watching you play patty-cake with this thing. I'm busy. I don't have all day to hang around, waiting for you to finally kill her."

I made a garbled, unintelligible response.

"Besides, with the body count you've racked up this weekend, you can hardly deny me one lousy kill," he added.

That was true. I looked down at the head at my feet and wondered if I would be next. Gregory followed my glance.

"You can keep that if you want." He said this as if he were a suitor for my affections, handing me a bouquet of flowers.

"Are you sure?" I asked in a strangled voice. "Maybe you'd like to add it to your extensive collection of trophies?"

"I gave up on my collection a long time ago. There were too many, and they were taking up too much space.

Besides, flesh doesn't last long in Aaru. Trophies just disintegrate."

Ugh. I picked up the head by the hair and turned it to face me. Busyasta looked surprised. As if she didn't see this one coming.

"Of course, since I'm taking you back to Aaru with me, you'll have the same problem." Gregory walked over and sat next to me in the dirt. "You can leave it here for your toy to keep for you, or take it with you and hang it on the wall of your cell to enjoy while it lasts."

Great. I'd escaped the threat of one prison only to land in another.

"That bitch of an angel ratted me out," I complained.

He smiled. "Yes, Eloa did. But I don't need someone to rat you out, I sense this stuff. Maybe you should have thought of that little problem before you latched on and kept my energy. Let's see. We've got six human kills, one Own, and a real mess on the highway up in Delaware. I had to send someone in to make sure that didn't come to light."

I sat beside him dejected. I wasn't sure which alternative was worse, him banishing me to Hel and facing Haagenti or stuffing me in a prison in Aaru. I wondered if he'd still teach me things, spend any time with me at all, or if I'd just be left to rot in a cage. No globes of water, no more angel fucking. Just boring Aaru and nasty, mean angels poking at me.

"Don't worry, little cockroach." His voice was affectionate. "I will take very good care of you. You'll grow to enjoy being in Aaru with me, and I'll work to reform you. Maybe eventually you'll repent enough to be allowed some freedom."

I was reassured he'd actually spend time with me, but what was this reforming business? That had an ominous ring to it. I'd rather just stay here. Wasn't there an option that would let me stay here? Door number three, perhaps?

Gregory reached over and rubbed a strand of my hair between his fingers, sending his energy into it with a possessive caress. I felt that pull, that attraction to him. Maybe there would be angel fucking after all. That might make this whole reformation thing tolerable. I couldn't help but extend my own energy out to meet his, the edges touching in a song of white. He went to push farther in, only to jerk away in a sharp, painful withdrawal.

Gregory stared strangely at my hair. I ran a hand over my head and felt the hard metal of the feather-shaped barrette. Son of a bitch. I could have used it earlier, but I guess that was my punishment for leaving the thing under a truck in Delaware. I wondered if Gregory would let me keep it in Aaru, if he even had the ability to take it away from me. I unclipped it and ran my thumb over the ridges before offering it to Gregory.

"Do you want to see it?" I asked.

"No, no, no." He waved it away.

Too late I remembered this was the sword that had nearly cut his wings off. Yeah, he wouldn't want to see it. He was going to probably find a way to keep it out of Aaru, too. Guess it would be going back to the vampires for another million years or so. I turned it over in my hand. It was just as fascinatingly beautiful as when it was an egg.

"I know I should be shocked out of my mind that you have the Sword of the Iblis," Gregory said. "But I'm far more surprised that you somehow convinced a powerful, sentient object to become a hair decoration."

I shrugged. "I was trying for designer shoes or a nice purse, but this is a good compromise."

"Little cockroach is the Iblis." He rubbed his face with his hands. "The Ruling Council is going to go crazy over this one. The Creator must truly have a wicked sense of humor, or perhaps we are all being punished."

He looked over at me, actually smiling. "I hope you like meetings and paperwork and hearings."

I was a bit panicked at the thought of meetings, paperwork, and hearings.

"I don't want to be the Iblis. This thing just followed me home and I can't get rid of it. Maybe we can pretend I don't have it? Don't tell anyone, okay?"

Guess it wasn't going to stay under my bed. Fuck, I'd left it on a highway in Delaware, under a truck, and it still managed to find me. I didn't have much hope of ditching the thing.

"Too late," he said with a grin that was completely out of place on an ancient angel. "I'll be popping by all the time with lengthy documents for you to read, kill reports to sign."

"So, you're not taking me back to Aaru and putting me in a cage for punishment?"

"Oh no," he assured me. "It would be bad form to drag the Iblis back by her hair and stuff her in a cage. Besides, this is shaping up to be a far more entertaining prospect. I think I'll wait on your punishment a while and see how this goes down instead."

"Okay." I wasn't sure which of the three futures before me were worse: Haagenti's torture, Gregory's punishment, or meetings and paperwork.

"I'll need to put you on the agenda for the next Council meeting," he said, barely getting the words out as he laughed. "Gate you into Aaru for it. Oh, I can just see their faces," he gasped before dissolving in laughter.

I didn't see what was so funny. I had no desire to attend Ruling Council meetings. I'd been to Aaru and wasn't impressed. Admittedly, I only jumped in through the wild gate enough to leave random objects, but it still didn't strike me as a place I'd like to spend any amount of time. He struggled to regain some semblance of control. Finally, he wiped his eyes and took a calming breath.

"You take care of that head, and I'll be back tomorrow with this week's kill report." He chuckled again, then got to his feet and gated away.

I looked down at the head. Wyatt and I needed to get this back to Hel somehow to show Haagenti how futile it was to face me. Unfortunately, Gregory had dusted the elf button along with Busyasta's form, so I had no quick and easy way to send the head back. I'd need to send it through a gate. I also needed to call Reed and check on my other looming problem. But first, I had to find my dog and my horse.

I headed back to the barn and stopped in amazement. There was Diablo. Right where I'd left him in his side pasture. I know I wasn't hallucinating. He hadn't been there earlier, and now he stood before me with a sheepish look on his face. Had he learned to latch and unlatch the gate? Without opposable thumbs? How the hell had he gotten out? And how the hell had he gotten back in? Putting the mystery aside for another day, I walked up and patted him on the neck, letting him know how glad I was that he was okay. He rubbed the top of my head with his nose. I think it was affection, but with horses I'm never really sure. He could have just had an itchy nose.

I searched the barn for Boomer with growing concern and was relieved to find him hiding under the boxwood bushes by the pool. He'd dug himself a huge hole and practically buried himself in it. He, too, looked rather sheepish, but I didn't care. I grabbed him, hugging him and planting affectionate kisses across his gritty, dirt-covered head. He licked me and his breath reeked of death. He must have been snacking on road kill before he'd gone to ground to hide from Busyasta.

"Stick around, Buddy," I told him. "I'll need you in a few hours when I get back."

Next on my list: call Reed.

There was a text from Candy that I'd missed in the chaos of my last twelve hours.

Reed shot. Need you back now or he's going after the guy himself.

Fuck. What else could go down in a twenty-four-hour period? I'd hoped I'd at least be able to get a few hours sleep before having to deal with this. I texted Candy back.

On it.

Then I called Reed.

"I'm back. I need to take care of something first, then I'll be right over. Give me a couple of hours."

"That cur shot me. I caught him taking one of the tenants last night, and he shot me." I could feel Reed's fury through the phone. "If you're not here by midnight, I'm going after this mongrel myself. No one takes a human I'm protecting, shoots me, and gets away with it."

Yikes. Candy was right. I was sure she'd used her authority as pack leader to hold him in check this long, but he wasn't going to wait much longer. I felt for Reed, but sympathy wasn't going to cut it in this instance, authority was.

"I will handle this," I snarled at him. "You stand down. These are my people, you are my employee. I will take this fucker down myself. Do you understand?"

I felt him bristle, but back down he did.

"Is the little boy okay? The one I asked you to look after?" Worry clenched my gut.

"Yeah, he's fine," Reed said, his voice still gruff. "I've got a friend keeping an eye on him since I can't be two places at once. This guy seems more interested in your homeless tenants right now."

"Good. I've got to go to Columbia, then I'll come straight back. Wait for me."

I hung up the phone and turned to Busyasta's head.

"Come on, bitch. We've got to hurry."

Wyatt and I made it to Columbia Mall in record time and dispatched Busyasta's head, with a note stapled to her forehead, through the gate as the guardian watched grimly. Thankfully, the gate was in the parking garage at the moment, so no shopping humans witnessed me drop kicking a head through. I briefed Wyatt on the way home and hoped he could protect himself until I took care of this asshole snagging my tenants. Sobronoy could show up at any moment, but after that it would hopefully be at least a day before Haagenti sent another crew of demons after me. I had that long to think of something long-term to protect Wyatt since I couldn't always be around. Right now, I had a serial killer to deal with.

CHAPTER 28

I looked down at Boomer. I'd locked him down so tight that he was practically powerless here. He had so little self-control that I'd been worried he'd attract angelic attention unless I put a damper on his powers. I'd been allowed pretty much free reign by Gregory, and I'd thought many times about loosening up the restrictions on Boomer, but I'd never done so. It had just been easier to control him and his actions like this. It had been eating at me though. That stupid guilt I'd been feeling more and more lately.

Boomer grinned up at me and wagged his tail expectantly. He knew something was in the works and was eager to participate. The guilt dug in deep. I was just as bad as the damned angels. I hated how they controlled the werewolves, restricting their activities and lives to the point that they were practically human. They were barely allowed to do any wolf-like activities, nothing that would allow them to live the life their birth dictated. I thought of Candy, unable to run free, live where she wanted, date, and breed in accordance with her own desires. Boomer, too. He was a hellhound and

I'd reduced him to a neutered, submissive canine. Yeah, he'd probably get himself, and possibly me, killed with his actions, but that was the life he'd been born into. Who was I to clamp him down to fit my desires?

I put my hands on his head and his tail wagged furiously, anticipating a good scratching. Rubbing the velvety hound ears, I untied the knots restricting him and set him free. He panted in happiness, still retaining his Plott hound form.

"I know you're going to dump me in all sorts of hot water. But I can't exactly cast stones. Just try not to get yourself killed. I've become rather fond of you."

Boomer sneezed in agreement and shook himself, flapping his ears wildly around his head.

"We've got someone we need to track down." He perked his ears and tilted his head expectantly.

"Some guy has been hunting in my territory, killing my human property." Boomer looked outraged.

"He's human, and there will be a lot of competing scents to sort through. I'll need you to use your special skills to pull out the human who has killed recently. It probably won't have been an emotional kill, or heat of the moment. He doesn't know his victims. He may feel a sense of joy and excitement at killing them, or he may feel nothing at all. I doubt he feels angry, but he might be driven by an impersonal, generalized anger. We might need to check out a couple trails until we find the right one. I know you'll be able to find this guy for me."

Boomer wiggled his whole body in excitement. He loved this sort of thing, and I again felt a twinge of guilt that for decades he'd been reduced to chasing rabbits and foxes. I might let Boomer make the kill. He'd enjoy that.

It was dark as we pulled up to the row houses. Reed waited outside with his arm in a sling. I was pretty sure the gunshot wound had healed by this point. Candy said werewolves healed at a remarkable rate. The sling was a good touch though. If the guy came back, he'd expect Reed to be wounded and at less than his best. He'd be wrong.

"I kinda hope you don't catch him and he comes back here so I can have a shot at him." Anger radiated like waves from Reed. "I like to take care of my own business, you know. I don't like to call you in like this."

I could feel his frustration. Reed was more than capable of handling this guy. He could probably track the guy better than Boomer, since he'd had a good smell on him. I'd be chafing, too. I remember how irritating it was this past summer when I hadn't been allowed to kill Althean, when Gregory had effectively leashed me.

"I don't want you running afoul of your contract," I warned Reed. "Trust me, if I wasn't worried about you winding up dead with angel wings on your forehead, I'd sic you on the guy. It's personal for you, and I hate taking this kill out from under you, but Candy would never forgive me if I let you do this."

"Even if you didn't have a special dispensation, you'd still go after this guy," Reed complained. "You'd take the risk and give the angels the finger. You wouldn't put up with their nonsense, not when someone attacked you. Not when someone snatched a human you were supposed to guard and then rubbed your nose in it. I can't stand sitting on my paws like this. I'm a werewolf. I need to act like a werewolf."

"I'm sorry, Reed," I told him. I meant it. "Believe me, I understand. Now is not the time to be giving the angels the finger. Wait until it's something really worth dying for. Until then, just stay under the radar."

Reed didn't look convinced. I needed to talk to Candy about him. I was all for rebellion, but he really shouldn't throw his life away on a stupid human who was foolish enough to shoot him.

"Kitty is waiting for us around the side by the canal," Reed said.

He led Boomer and me around the block of row houses to the canal side. Sure enough, there was Kitty, shapeless in her huge green coat with the disturbing scarf ends dangling like wasted legs from her crotch. She looked me over as she had before, then performed the same level of scrutiny on Boomer.

"Sniff here." She pointed to a corner of the eroded cement walkway along the canal.

Boomer went to where she indicated and sniffed in a loud snuffling way as he swung his head back and forth. He padded around in a square grid, widening out from the central point and sorting through the scents. He looked up at me and pawed the ground.

"Three people who have killed have been here within the last twenty-four hours," I translated for the others.

Boomer did a complicated paw, head shake and whine combination.

"The first killed with hate in his heart," I told Reed and Kitty. "We'll track him first since his is the strongest scent." I looked at Reed. "There's a two in three chance we're wrong. Can you stay here? If he comes back, you've got full license to defend yourself. And I define "defend" pretty much any way you want to define it."

Reed seemed satisfied with that possible scenario and stayed at the row houses as Kitty and I followed Boomer. We walked a few blocks and around the back of an old cannery where a tent was set up. Boomer looked up at me, and I motioned for him to catch and hold the man. My hound tore through the tent like it was butter and we heard a man's shriek, then silence. Walking up, I pulled aside the torn tent piece to see Boomer in partial form with massive head and shoulders, hackles raised, and long beads of spittle dropping from his bared fangs. He had the man locked in place with his yellow eyed stare.

The man looked terrified. I couldn't tell if he regularly wet his pants, or if he'd done so in response to Boomer's snarling appearance. He was tall and unexpectedly well-fed for a man living in a tent behind an abandoned cannery. His personal hygiene left a lot to be desired though. His beard and hair were matted and streaked with gray amid the dirt. His hands were practically black. The only clean things were the whites of his eyes.

"Hold him Boomer. Good boy." He wagged his tail, which looked odd with his ferocious front half. "Is this him?" I asked Kitty.

She peered at the man. "Can I touch him?"

I nodded, and Kitty went over to run her hand down his cheek and across his mouth. Her hands blurred slightly as they touched his skin, becoming slightly transparent and disappearing when she pushed against his matted hair.

"Cold," he said, shuddering slightly. Softly, she chanted something, then again ran her hand over his face.

"No." She shook her head with regret. "This man has murdered. He killed a man in the group he used to camp with. The man slandered him, stole his belongings, and would set traps to hurt him and make him look foolish in front of the others. He planned for many weeks and killed the man, leaving his body in the woods and taking his belongings before he left. He has only killed the one man."

I sensed the man's alarm at this revelation of his darkest secret. I'm sure he thought he would soon be dead. I didn't care about his crime. It wasn't my problem. I wasn't an angel of justice. Let someone else deal with the dude's actions.

"Okay. Sorry about your tent buddy," I told the man. "Boomer, let him go. Let's try again."

The guy collapsed against the floor and this time he did

pee his pants as Boomer let him free. We walked out and headed back to the row houses, making sure we flagged down Reed, telling him that we'd hit a dead end.

"Two more to go."

Boomer once again sniffed the ground. He'd reverted to his regular Plott hound form as we left the cannery. He was a fierce looking hellhound and very attractive, in a horrifying way, when he was in partial form, but I really admired his glossy brindle coat and lean athletic form as a dog. His thin tail swung like a whip back and forth, and his jowls puffed in and out as he inhaled the scents. I hoped he continued to choose this form now that he had the freedom to change. I rather liked it.

Boomer looked up and did the complicated head and foot movements again.

"This one killed with no emotion at all." I translated for the others.

I didn't tell them everything though. Boomer had indicated that this murderer somehow felt it was his right to take life at will. As if he were entitled. I remembered Kitty's words from before and felt a chill of anticipation. This had to be our guy.

"I don't think this is the guy," I lied. "But we should follow it up anyway. Reed, can you stay here again?"

Reed looked suspicious. I was a terrible liar. He nodded, though, and headed back to the front of the building to make his security rounds. Kitty grinned at me.

"I thought you guys were supposed to be good at lying?"

"With all the practice I've had you'd think I'd be good at it. Unfortunately, I truly suck."

We followed Boomer as he trailed along, nose to the ground, in a convoluted pattern throughout downtown and across the park. At the end of the street, Boomer indicated that the guy had gotten into a car.

"Are we at a dead end?" I asked him, frustrated.

Boomer grinned and shook his head. In a blink, a two-headed hellhound stood in front of me. Drool dangled in long threads from shiny fangs and his yellow eyes glowed. He was so beautiful with his sharp rough spikes of brindled fur and massive shoulder and hip joints. His paws were the size of dinner plates and his heads came to my shoulder. One head sniffed the air and the other sniffed the ground. It sounded like a freight train. I looked over at Kitty. She was unfazed at Boomer's new appearance.

Boomer began trotting and I broke into a jog to follow. I wasn't sure how Kitty managed to keep up with her voluminous layers of clothing, but she managed, almost floating above the ground as she ran. I made sure I kept Boomer on the inside of the traffic, where his interesting appearance would be partially screened, but I wasn't terribly concerned. Internet videos of a two-headed dog jogging in the night weren't high on my list of worries right now.

We trotted past the military base, past several new subdivisions, and outside the city limits before Boomer turned up a side road into the mountains. The road wound around the wooded properties and became gravel. Finally, the hellhound stopped and looked up an obscured path. There was an area on the side of the road where the brush had been cleared and tire tracks indicated a regular parking area. It was empty of car or truck.

"I think the guy might not be home," I told Kitty, pointing at the tire tracks. "It is his normal hunting hour. We might have a long wait ahead of us." She nodded and we both followed Boomer up the narrow path.

I'd expected to see an old trailer, or a tent, or some dilapidated shack. I was surprised, though, when the path opened out onto a nicely mowed lawn and an attractive brick rancher. There may have been a driveway at one point, as indicated by the small garage attached to the house, but the asphalt had been ripped out long ago and nothing marred the green lawn and woods surrounding the house. This dirt path appeared to be the only access.

Boomer did quick surveillance while Kitty and I remained out of sight at the wooded edge of the lawn. He returned and indicated that our guy wasn't home.

"I'm going to break into his place and wait for him inside," I told Kitty. "You may want to stay hidden. I'm not sure what we're going to find in there, or what will happen when he gets home and finds us inside."

Kitty nodded.

"Of course, since you're already dead, he can't exactly kill you." I was taking a guess here. I'd never met a ghost before, and wasn't exactly sure.

She grinned at me in confirmation, her teeth jagged and blackened. Then she turned and vanished into the trees, fading away to nothing at the edge of the woods. It was an impressive trick, especially for a homeless woman in a huge coat, even if she was a ghost.

Boomer and I walked right up to the front door. There were four locks on it. The standard handle lock, two dead-bolt locks, and a sliding bar lock. Gritting my teeth, I sent tendrils of awareness in and around the door to explore further.

This summer, I'd had my hand melted and come rather close to death from touching a hex. The experience left me rather wary of sticking my personal energy into houses and doorways. Still, it was the best way to examine the entrance. I'd assumed the guy was just a human, but I wanted to make sure. No sense in stumbling in to find a witch, a sorcerer, or another demon had put unexpected traps on the entrance. I felt nothing but the physical barriers and proceeded to unlock them. It would have been quicker to just melt the locks, convert the mechanisms into putty or dust, or to blast the door open, but it would have ruined the lovely surprise I was planning.

I was so excited. Would he be like Ted Bundy? A genius killer with the soul of a poet? Would there be heads in the freezer, or bodies buried under the crawl space? What amazing things would I find behind the door?

Once inside, I carefully set the locks back in place and surveyed the house as best as I could in the dark. The guy had left no lights on at all. With the neighbors so far away, any light I turned on would shine like a beacon.

The house was unremarkable, but I kept looking, sure there would be a freakish lair somewhere. I peered at the pictures and books on the shelves beside the wood stove. Some popular mystery paperbacks and a few romances. A Bible, various magazines, and puzzle books. The pictures showed an older aged man and woman, one of a black Labrador, and a rather nice sunset on the beach. Maybe Boomer was wrong? This didn't look like the house of a killer.

I picked up the phone and called Wyatt. "Hey, Sam," he said. "How's your hunt going? Is Reed okay?"

"Yeah, he's just pissed that he's stuck behind while I'm doing the hunting," I told him in a hushed voice. "Any sign of Sobronoy?"

"None so far. I've got everything locked down tight and a camera on the road coming in."

Good. Maybe we had some time. This back-to-back killing was starting to wear me down a bit.

"Hey, do me a favor and check out this house? Boomer says this is it, but it just looks too normal." I gave him the address and heard him tapping in the background.

"It's not in the city limits, is it?" Wyatt said, half to himself. "If you went out past the army base, it's got to be closer to Yellow Springs. But there's nothing with that house number on that road. Let me try the roads branching from there and see if maybe the name changed at one point."

Wyatt chattered on in one part of my mind, while another looked at the dining room and the kitchen. A silk floral arrangement was on the table, along with a decent amount of food in the cabinets. I grabbed a beer out of the fridge and tossed the cap into the trash. Might as well indulge while Wyatt was checking things for me.

"Okay, I'm looking at satellite images now, and I can see the house, but it doesn't appear to be on the postal registry. Let me overlay the satellite images with older street maps and check the last twenty years of census and tax records and see what I can find."

The master bedroom was a little less pristine, with the comforter hastily thrown over the bed sheets and dirty socks on the floor beside the hamper. The sheets under the comforter were reasonably clean. Nothing was under the bed or in the closet beyond dust bunnies and clothing. The bathroom was unremarkable with a blob of toothpaste in the sink and a crumpled towel on the floor. Nothing in this house stood out at all beyond the weird removal of the driveway and the excessive locks on the door. I didn't even see the expected rifle or shotgun anywhere. What the fuck? I was so disappointed. Where was the psycho stuff? Where was the snuff porn, explosives, heads in the freezer?

"Got it. Mr and Mrs. Wratzler. They've owned the house since 1970. Place was built in 1968. I show them as the current owners."

The second bedroom looked untouched. The bed was carefully made, and there were knickknacks artfully arranged on the dresser and the bed stands. No dust. I pounded on the bed and didn't see any dust rise from it. Whoever this guy was, he was a neat mother fucker.

"Mr. Wratzler was a civilian vet tech over at the base until his retirement in '86. His wife got Grand Champion for needlework at the county fair in '83. They pay their taxes regularly. Mrs. Wratzler died in '95. Looks like cancer from the 'in lieu of flowers' notation on the obit. Absolutely nothing on Mr. Wratzler since then."

"Thanks, I'll see you soon," I told him and hung up.

If the wife was dead, could the husband have gone crazy and begun killing homeless people? It's not like he'd be avenging his wife's death from cancer by killing vagrants. All this clean neatness was not what I'd expected either. He'd have to be really fucking old, too. Did he clean all day, and go chop off ears at night? He must be really fit to grab someone off the street, wrestle them to the ground, kill them, and drag the body off somewhere. None of this made sense.

A more likely scenario was that a younger man knocked off Mr. Wratzler, who would have been easy pickings as a reclusive widower. Then he'd have a home base to organize his killings. I motioned for Boomer to come with me and headed down to the basement. It was either the garage or the basement, and I was banking on the basement.

I flicked on the light and headed down the stairs. There was a nice finished section with carpet, a TV, comfy chairs, and a table. There was even a mini kitchen set up. On the dining room table was a sculpture of what were clearly human ears. After the sterile weirdness of the upstairs, this area was a breath of fresh air. I could feel his personality down here. I envisioned him watching TV in the recliner, dozing off late at night, comforted by the presence of his trophies, knowing that the house upstairs would shield him from a hostile and misunderstanding world. Finally, something interesting about this guy.

Ears. It was an odd choice.

Usually it was eyes. Eyes were the organ of perception, of

vision, and awareness. Taking a victim's eyes meant their judgment couldn't be reflected back. The judgment of God, condemning a killer for an act beyond the scope of humanity. It robbed their power of perception and stole it for a killer's own use. Tongues were also popular. The dead could not accuse without their tongues.

Ears were weird though. It was a theft of spiritual perception. They had once been a common Egyptian and Far Eastern theme, but not one seen much in the modern world. Ears connected a person to the soft, subtle sounds of life, of death, to the sound of the divine word. I looked at the sculpture carefully. It was composed of both right and left ears. This guy at least was balanced in his duality, preserving both that which hears the whisper of birth and the whisper of death. Personally, I would have made a hanging mobile from the ears, so they could move in the air and freely receive sounds on the wind. It would have been more artistic, more poetic than this odd, lumpy collage.

The ears had been dried in a relatively professional manner to preserve them from decay. I reached out and felt one. They were fairly leathery. Not dried to the point of jerky. It was a fine line. Not enough drying and they'd still be soft, but mold and mildew over time. Too much drying and they'd be difficult to work with and susceptible to crumbling.

He'd taken armature wire and pierced the ears, probably using a bead reamer from a craft store. It would have gone through the dried ear easily. The lowest ears were wired to a wooden base, and other ears joined in an attempt to make it appear as if they were attached seamlessly. He'd done a good job of hiding the wire. And the wire was a good choice, too. Glue would have damaged the flesh of the ear and made it difficult to fine tune his sculpture. Not that fine tuning would do much for it. Basically it was a pile of ears. Nothing inspirational at all in this thing. It was very disappointing. It made me want to kill him even more.

The basement had its own entrance out to the back of the house. I'd left Boomer upstairs on alert, but now I called softly to him. He padded down the basement steps, still huge with the two massive drooling heads.

"Do you think he uses the upstairs door or this one down here?" I asked him. He looked around the room with obvious interest. "If he comes in upstairs, I may move his ear sculpture up there and wait to greet him, but I'll just stay here if he comes in through the basement."

I wanted to provide maximum impact when the guy came home. Sort of like a surprise party of death. If he came in upstairs, moving his sculpture up there would most likely send him into a screaming rage. The fact that I'd touched it, moved his sculpture from his personal area to the foreign part of the house, would be a violation on the level of rape. I would have laid my hands on, ripped from its safe place, the most private part of him. If he came in down here, though, and I was upstairs, he'd see the missing sculpture first and I would lose the element of surprise. If he came in down here, I'd need to think of something to do that would have the same emotional punch.

While Boomer checked the doors, I went through another interior door that presumably led from the finished area of the basement to a utility side that should hold a washer and dryer. No surprise, this was the guy's staging area. I hadn't been sure if he brought the bodies back here or dumped them close to where he killed them. I'd assumed from the lack of front page news that he'd been disposing the bodies in a discreet fashion. No one would notice missing homeless people, but a rash of earless bodies would definitely spur an investigation. The room was clean and smelled of bleach. A variety of useful tools hung on a pegboard over a stainless steel table. Saws, axes, picks, drills. Rolls of poly and boxes of biodegradable garbage bags stood neatly by the table along with several bags of lime and various shovels. I assumed if I looked around the wooded area, I'd find graves. Boomer could locate them easily, but I really had no interest in digging up dead bodies. The most interesting thing in the room was a food dehydrator by the innocuous washer and dryer. This was the tool to preserve his precious ears.

Boomer indicated to me that this guy used the basement entrance the majority of the time. Patting one of his heads in appreciation, I sent him off to the side of the door where he'd be less likely to be noticed as the guy entered the room. Then I turned off the lights and sat down to wait.

I'm not good at waiting. I fidgeted in the recliner, got up and rooted through the fridge, snapped an ear off the sculpture and played with it a bit. I found a steak knife and killed time by stabbing holes in the arm of the recliner. It was getting on past midnight and I seriously thought about turning on the TV, but the light would alert him to my presence. Sighing in boredom, I continued to hack bits of foam and stuffing from the chair arm. If this guy didn't get home soon, I was going to order pizza.

It was close to four in the morning before Boomer alerted me of the ear-man's approach. I'd already drank all the beers and sodas in the fridge upstairs and used the empty bottles to improve the lumpy ear sculpture. Luckily I'd found some ham and cheese and made myself a sandwich, too. I was still starving though. Waiting with anticipation in the dark basement, I heard a dragging noise and a huffing of breath. He must have dragged his victim in some kind of tarp or blanket all the way from the parking area. Now that was dedication.

The guy unlocked the door with familiarity and flicked on the light as he came in. Instead of yelling "Surprise!", I took a bite out of one of the ears I'd impaled on the steak knife and chewed thoughtfully.

"This one needed a few more minutes in the dehydrator," I told him as he stared at me, stunned. "It's a little raw on the inside."

You would think the guy would realize something was off. Normal humans wouldn't break into your house, rearrange your body-part sculpture, hack up your chair, and cheerfully chow down on one of your victim's ears. His emotions clearly took control of his brain in this instance, and I saw the red flush of rage flare up his face. With an impressive, piercing scream, he launched himself at me from the doorway.

The guy had good physical instincts. He cleared the floor space and slammed into me, knocking the recliner backwards with the force of his impact. He'd also been paranoid enough to have a knife, a really sharp knife, on his person. I'd barely smacked the floor and he was slicing at me, stabbing furiously over and over into my mid-section with the knife.

"Bitch, bitch, bitch," he screamed in time with his stabs.

He was heavy, and fast. I couldn't push him off or completely avoid his knife without using energy, and I didn't want to hurt him too much yet. This was going to be fun, and I wanted to prolong the experience even if it meant I got sliced up. Inspired, I grabbed his head and planted a kiss on him, figuring the oddness of having someone he was stabbing kiss him might jolt him back into his brain.

No such luck. He bit down on my tongue and raised his hand to stab my face. Now that was something I wasn't going to tolerate. I blocked his knife with my arm, skillfully wedging the blade between my ulna and radius, then twisted to lock the knife in place. It hurt like fuck, but I'm used to that sort of thing. With my other hand, I stabbed him in the wrist with the steak knife, cutting the tendon and pinning the chewed ear to his skin. This infuriated him further, and he shrieked again, twisting the knife in my arm and grinding it against the bones. Throughout this whole skirmish, Boomer watched with interest from his stealthy position behind the door.

"Boomer, you dumb fuck, get over here and help me!" I shouted at him.

Boomer's idea of help was to lope over and shove a slobbery head in my assailant's face, licking him thoroughly. Great, he liked this idiot. I guess I shouldn't be so critical since I'd kissed the guy. Boomer probably figured affection was the help I was requesting. It did have a positive effect though. The guy took one look at my two headed dog and screamed in terror, scrambling off me and attempting to make a break for it out the door.

Boomer, for once, did something proactive and headed the guy off, blocking the door and wagging his tail in a friendly manner. While I was trying to fix the worst of my stab wounds and repair the chipped bones in my arm, Boomer and the guy did a complicated game of rush-and-block across the basement. Boomer was winning. By the time I was on my feet, he had the guy pinned in a corner and was assaulting his crotch with a very large nose.

"Call off your dog-thing, call off your dog-thing," Earman shouted in a high-pitched, panicked tone. At least he seemed to be regaining use of his thinking processes and some control over his emotions.

"Boomer, hold him," I commanded my hellhound, hoping he'd obey. "And get your nose off of his dick. Don't bite it off or anything." Boomer's other head looked disappointed. "At least not yet. Maybe later." He wagged his tail.

I walked over to the guy and yanked the steak knife out of his arm. He grunted and looked at me warily as blood seeped from the wound. I pulled the ear off the steak knife and

313

DEBRA DUNBAR

proceeded to finish eating it. Hopefully he'd get some clue as to what I was from that very pointed action. He must have made the connection because his eyes widened and traveled from my ear chewing down along my smooth, un-sliced abdomen, and across my healed arm.

"You've been a naughty boy," I told him, waving the last bit of ear in his face before shoving it in my mouth. "Poaching in my territory. Killing off humans that are under my protection. What have you got to say for yourself?"

The guy swallowed a few times, glancing from Boomer to me, then back again.

"I didn't know. I'm so sorry, I didn't know. I'll hunt somewhere else." He was careful not to look me in the eye.

"How could you not know?" I asked. "You seem a meticulous kind of guy. The sort that plans these things out. I'm sure you checked out gang activity and drug territories so you don't run across any other predators. Didn't you notice the big, clear area you chose to hunt in and wonder why they steered clear? You hunt my humans, thumb your nose at me, and when I come here to discuss the situation, you attack me. That sounds pretty disrespectful to me."

"You look like a human," he whined. "Where is the red skin, the horns, and tail? They told me a bad-ass woman owned most of the downtown rentals, but no one said anything about Satan. Look, I don't want any trouble from you. We've got a lot in common. Maybe we could come to some kind of understanding."

The more I spoke with this sniveling idiot, the more pissed off I got. I'd hoped for Ted Bundy and got this bumbling fool. How dare he presume to take what belonged to me, to kill my humans? Worthless sack of shit. And there was the issue of that deplorable ear sculpture. I might be able to overlook disrespect and the attack on my people, but a lack of artistic sentiment was something I could not accept.

"Tell me about your sculpture." I waved a hand toward the lump of ears. I figured I'd give him one last chance to make a poetic statement before I killed him.

He scrambled for words, obviously put on the spot. "Well, they're ears. Like, you know, like Van Gogh or something."

"Yes, well why do you use both ears from your victim and not just one? Why ears and not something else," I prompted.

Was he planning on sending them to a girl he was in love with? Someone whose rejection cut him off from the divinity within himself? Throw me a bone here buddy, I thought.

"Well, because if I take both ears, then I have more ears to make a bigger display. And bigger is better, you know. Because big is…well, big is larger than small. And ears are a cool shape. They have lots of stiff stuff in them, so they don't fall apart when you cut them off, and they preserve well. They look cool."

"Because they look like shells?" I prompted again.

He frowned at his lump of ears on the table. "No, they look like ears. Not like shells at all."

This was going from bad to worse. "And why did you arrange them like this? With the wire, on the wood, in that particular shape."

"Well, I thought that since people pierce their ears, wire would work well. If they weren't pierced, I could easily poke a hole in them. I put a lot of ears at the bottom, kind of like a pyramid with less at the top." He looked at his sculpture as if it would help him better articulate his vision.

"Oh, a pyramid." I finally felt a glimmer of hope. Of course. The dehydrated ears were a type of mummification, displayed as a pyramid in keeping with the Egyptian theme; a process of rebirth, of reuniting with the Ba-soul. Very intuitive.

"Yeah, because then it won't fall over, see? Because it's

wide at the bottom and narrow at the top. So the ears don't topple over with weight."

"And?" Almost there, buddy.

He floundered, searching for the right words. "And. And, because then I can add to the bottom of the stack as I add to the top, so I can have a really tall display of ears and not worry about it falling over and getting dirty or bending one of the ears. Because tall and big is cool."

I was crushed. Just fucking crushed. What had the world come to? I'd been so excited to read about Bundy and that Gacy guy, had such high hopes, and this is what I got. Beavis the serial killer. He wasn't worth any more of my time. He wasn't even worth the effort it would take to kill him.

"All yours, Boomer." I went upstairs, too devastated to stay and watch the fun.

Upstairs, I raided the closets until I found a reasonably sized shirt and put it on over my bloody one with the holes in it. I'd stashed my jacket in the basement, so I headed back down. I was sure Boomer had made quick work of the guy. Sure enough, he'd finished Beavis off quickly, containing the blood and gore to the small corner of the basement where he'd trapped the guy. One of Boomer's heads looked up at me with an expression of doggie guilt, a foot half out of his mouth. The other head was busy crunching up an arm.

"Yeah, yeah, you can eat him. Go ahead and clean up. I'll just grab my jacket and watch TV a bit until you're done."

I watched early morning infomercials to the accompaniment of crunching and slurping sounds. Honestly, it made me think twice about ordering that panini maker the well-manicured woman was urging me to purchase. I hadn't had dinner, though, and I was so hungry that the sounds of Boomer's meal weren't putting me off my thoughts of bacon and eggs. I wondered if that diner a mile or so down on the main road would be open for early breakfast. Either way, I wasn't relishing a ten mile walk back to my car. Boomer looked to be almost done, so I called Wyatt, who had clearly been sound asleep.

"Hey. Come meet me for breakfast. I'm way out of town and really need a ride to my car."

"Hmmm? Where? When? Oh, sheesh it's almost six in the morning. Are you still there? What took you so long?" he asked, shaking off the sleep.

"The guy was out until early morning, so we just waited for him. Wyatt, it was awful. I've never been so bored in my life. And the killer was just terrible, too. Stupid, inarticulate. He couldn't even dehydrate an ear properly. Meet me at that little diner on the way out here, please?"

"Mmmhmm," he mumbled as he hung up. I had a strong feeling he'd drop right back off to sleep and I'd be at the diner all morning by myself. I resolved that if he wasn't there by seven, I'd call him back and make sure he hadn't forgotten me. Wyatt took a while to get going in the morning unless there was sex involved.

Boomer did an excellent job of cleaning up, and we left the house pretty much as we'd found it except for the hacked-up easy chair and the sculpture missing the top ear. Boomer looked longingly at the ears.

"You'll puke if you eat those," I told him. "I'll bet the ones on the bottom have mildewed horribly."

He continued to look at them with one head, and motioned to the door with the other.

"You're fucking kidding me. It's got to be almost thirty miles from our home. You seriously want to come back and eat these ears and the guy's victims?"

Boomer looked at me in reproach. It's not like I'd allowed him to do anything much the last forty years. This was a big part of his nature. I sighed.

"Okay, sweetie. Just don't get caught, and make sure you

don't leave any open graves for people to fall into. Put the dirt back like a good boy."

He wagged his tail in joy. Such a simple thing to bring him so much happiness.

We'd made it almost to the main road when I saw Kitty walking towards us pushing a grocery store shopping cart with various bags and blankets in it. I was surprised she was still around the area since we'd been inside for such a long time. I also wondered where she'd picked up the grocery cart. It was from an old downtown store that had closed over twenty years ago.

"It's done," I told her.

She looked surprised. "Oh, I know. I watched." She glanced down at Boomer, who had returned to his canine, Plott hound form. "Such a good boy!"

Boomer wiggled in response to the compliment.

Kitty dug around in her shopping cart and I saw a small green feline head pop up for a few seconds before submerging back into the blanket.

"Thanks, by the way." She waved at the cat with her hand. "Imitation is the sincerest form of flattery." Rearranging her blanket, she headed down the street with a rattle-rattle of her shopping cart.

"Yeah, well keep away from Batman, if you know what's good for you," I called after her. She gave me the finger without pausing a step, and then vanished from the road, grocery cart and all.

CHAPTER 29

*W*yatt arrived before seven, unshaven with bed head. I was just happy he'd not fallen back asleep and forgotten about me. I'd been hanging out, eating breakfast, and playing Angry Birds while I waited at the diner.

"It's raining, so I stuck Boomer in my truck," Wyatt told me as he slid into a chair and smiled gratefully at the waitress pouring him a cup of coffee. "He was outside trying to hump everyone's legs as they came in or out. Not that I normally notice this kind of thing, but he seems to have a sexual organ that would be more proportionate on an elephant."

Great. This was the kind of thing I'd need to look forward to now that Boomer was unrestrained.

"Thanks for coming to get me. I'd kiss you, but I think my breath is worse than Boomer's. I ate a badly dehydrated ear and I don't think it was washed properly before preservation. It was kind of gritty. And moldy, too."

Wyatt grimaced. "You should have told me to bring a toothbrush and some mouthwash."

I threw a twenty on the table and stood to leave.

319

"Let's just go home and I'll get my car later. Do you think I can get a nap in before I have to kill Sobronoy? Seriously, I'm so tired I'd probably just yawn on him."

"We don't have that kind of luck," Wyatt replied, getting to his feet.

We didn't have that kind of luck. Just a few feet past Wyatt's driveway, Boomer snarled and snapped into his hell-hound form.

"Stop," I shouted, jumping from the car as Wyatt slammed on the brakes.

I held the door while Boomer wedged his massive body out from the back seat. Wyatt threw the truck into park and made to come out also.

"No, no. Just head back to your house and sit tight until I let you know all is okay," I told him.

Wyatt gave me a furious look. "We've discussed this, Sam. I'm not going down a foxhole while you fight this guy. I can help."

"This guy isn't Labisi," I warned him. "We're at a disadvantage here, on the defensive. I don't know where he is, what kind of trap he may have planned. If he grabs you and holds you hostage, he's got me. He's smart enough to have figured that out."

Wyatt hesitated. "Please Wyatt," I pleaded. "This doesn't have anything to do with your skills, or my trust in you. He could be anywhere, and I can't fight him effectively, with deadly force, unless I know you're out of the equation."

"Okay," he said, reluctantly, putting the car back in gear. "I love you, Sam."

"Love you, too." I wasn't lying, for once.

I raced through the tree line beside the road with Boomer right on my heels. Thankfully, the rain was coming down hard enough to mask the noise of our approach. Especially because Boomer sounded like a herd of elephants in this form. The hellhound halted as we reached the edge of the woods before the stretch of lawn in front of my house. He lifted his head, sniffing. I gave him space to do his work and looked around. Nothing. If I hadn't had Boomer with me, if he hadn't been unlocked to his full potential, I would have never suspected Sobronoy was here. My house looked just like I'd left it.

I followed Boomer as he made his way around toward the back of the house. There the cover of the trees ended and I was faced with a long stretch of open fencing between my pool area and the pasture. In the summer, the fence line was hidden by patches of tall, feathery grasses, sunflowers, and zinnias. Everything had been cut down for the winter, and now there was nothing to give me cover. I looked longingly at the barn. Diablo was safely in his stall. I hoped he could use his mysterious Houdini skills to break out if I needed him.

Boomer motioned behind the pool, at a big plastic tub-like bench I used to store the lounge cushions. I'd need to cross the open pool area, clearly visible to him if he was behind the bench. Pulling up my energy, I crept around the right of the pool as Boomer circled to the left. Sobronoy wasn't behind the bench, but his arm was.

I stared in shock. The guy had actually cut off his own arm, branding it deep with his energy as a lure. He'd done his homework, knew I had a hellhound with me. I'd fallen right into a trap.

Before I could react, something huge landed on me, flattening me to the ground and pinning me with its weight, digging long talons into my shoulders. I heard a shriek, then a lessening of the weight, and I rolled to the side, pushing Sobronoy off of me. Boomer had jumped on Sobronoy's back when he'd attacked me and was busy ripping at him with both heads. Sobronoy had assumed the black dragon form

321

that he favored back home. My dog managed to rip off a wing and a chunk of his torso before the demon launched him backward with a shot that ripped his foreleg off at the shoulder. Now I was really pissed. Nobody hurts my dog.

I grabbed the barrette out of my hair and dove at Sobronoy swinging as it transformed. A red gash appeared on the dragon's leg before he leapt out of the way. Sword play is not a skill I have. I hacked at him like I was chopping wood, and he easily avoided my blows. Three swings, and Sobronoy blasted the sword out of my hand, sending it flying through one of my glass patio doors. His next blast took off one of my legs at the knee, and I fell to the ground, totally missing him with the ball of energy I'd launched.

I rolled to avoid his next attack and came to my knees just in time to see Diablo appear from nowhere and kick Sobronoy soundly, launching him across the patio. The horse dashed after him and kicked him repeatedly, trampling him as he fell again to the ground. Sobronoy missed Diablo with two bolts of energy, but hit with the third. Diablo squealed and then vanished into thin air. I don't know if I was more shocked that my hybrid horse could teleport or that he ran away to save his sorry ass.

Diablo's attack had given me time to repair my wounds. I ran at Sobronoy and launched myself at him, popping into a more sturdy form just as I hit him. It was a huge tiger that I'd modified, enlarging it to three times the normal tiger size, and exaggerating the head and jaws. I pummeled him with a blast of energy, and simultaneously bit down on a wing at the shoulder joint, ripping the limb right off his body. Sobronoy screamed, which bought me enough time for another blast before he recovered. Unfortunately, he did recover and shot me so hard it threw me two feet back to crash into a lounge chair.

My tumble with the chair took me out of the line of fire

of two of his blasts and gave me time to gather the raindrops, in puddles all over my patio. I froze them and launched them, little arrows of ice, at Sobronoy as I charged. He fell under the rain of hail and I jumped on him once again. I felt a slap of something on my front leg and jerked, just as Sobronoy activated the portable gate.

"*Glah ham, shoceacan,*" he shouted. The last word came out just as the button bounced on one of my lounge chairs. In a flash, both the chair and the button were gone. I had a moment of amusement thinking of Haagenti's shock when a large lounge chair appeared before him.

Sobronoy was not so amused. He screamed in frustration to have lost his easy way of getting me back to Hel. This was clearly now a fight to the death. We grappled, both of us shooting blasts of energy into each other that tore through flesh and dissolved bone faster than we could repair. Sobronoy, though, had a special skill. Suddenly I was blind and deaf, my energy unfocused and unusable. If I only fought like a demon, I'd be done for, but I knew how to fight like a human. And a tiger. Opening my huge jaws, I wrapped them around his head and crunched. Bone broke, and the squish of brain filled my mouth as I pulverized his head. He jerked in surprise, and I felt his spirit flutter before dissolving in death. As with Labisi, I claimed his store of raw energy as mine, pulling it inside.

I was still deaf, so I didn't hear the gunshot. I did feel the bullet rip through my shoulder, and the next one graze my back. I looked up in blurry surprise. I didn't have to see him clearly. Wyatt was shooting me. Idiot. You'd think he would have made sure which one of us was which before he opened fire. Maybe I'd been stressing that "shoot first and ask questions later" a bit too much. I popped into my Samantha Martin form just as another bullet plowed into my head.

Fuck, I thought as I felt myself falling and coming apart. It's not supposed to end like this.

The body was dying, and I would go with it. Consolidate, I thought for some reason. And I saw myself standing at my kitchen sink, pulling drops of water into globes with Gregory's arms around me, his power pouring through me as he showed me how to freeze the globes. Pull back. I should be able to exist within energy, within an inanimate object, within any matter. This body was dead, but it was still matter. Consolidate. I pulled back, safe within the dying flesh. I was a corpse. Too bad I couldn't seem to figure out how to animate the dead flesh, because that would freak Wyatt out completely. Pay him back for killing me. Unable to do anything else, I recreated my entire form with a pop.

"Sam, Sam," Wyatt sobbed. He was holding me, his face buried in my rain-slicked, naked chest.

I reached up and twisted my fingers in his wet hair. "It's okay, honey. I'm fine."

Wyatt made a choking noise and grabbed me so hard I thought he'd pop my head off.

"I thought the dragon thing was you. I thought he'd murdered you and I just started shooting. I'd already fired when you changed into human form. I killed you. I shot you right in the head."

"I know. It's okay. Really." I pulled loose enough to kiss him. "Honestly. Dar has done worse to me many times. And I did encourage you to be a little trigger happy, so it's kind of my fault anyway."

I knew he needed me to be there, to hold him close and assure him I was okay, but I couldn't comfort him when my dog was injured and in pain. I pulled free from Wyatt's arms and walked over to fix Boomer, who was whining and squirming in a pool of blood with his three legs.

"You were a good boy," I told him as I repaired him.

"Diablo was good, too, even if he was a total shit for running away. I guess I shouldn't expect too much from a horse."

I turned to Wyatt. "We should be safe, at least for a few days. I need to call Dar and then get some sleep before sending this carcass back to Hel."

"Should I stay with you?" Wyatt asked. He needed me, I could tell, but I was just too tired. I'd never get sleep if he was in bed with me. If it wasn't sex, it was his bondage spooning. Later tonight, we'd cuddle and I'd reassure him all was okay. Now I just desperately needed sleep.

"Give me six hours to call Dar and get some rest, and then I'll call you. Sobronoy's elf button went back to Hel with a lounge chair, so we'll need to take this up to Columbia. Maybe we'll get some dinner after I lob his head through the gate."

He hesitated.

"Wyatt, we're fine. I know you're freaking out about shooting me, but it's okay. You're stressed from this whole weekend, and so am I. Trust me, I really, really want to cuddle up with you and have the kind of make-up sex people only have when one has killed the other, but I need to call Dar, then get some sleep. We can talk about this later, please?"

He nodded, kissed me, and headed back to his house. I felt like a total jerk, but I just wanted to wrap this up and go to bed.

Dar was so agitated that I could barely understand him. I wished I'd had slept first and called him after. Maybe then he'd make sense.

"Calm down and speak slowly," I shouted at him.

"Mal, the shit has totally hit the fan. Haagenti is on the verge of an aneurism. Labisi's corpse shows up at Haagenti's place looking like a house fell on it. Then the elves find Busyasta's head on the border of their woods with a 'fuck you' note stapled to it. How did you manage to kill Busyasta? She's five levels up from you. Five."

"I'm sending Sobronoy's head over just as soon as I get in a nap," I warned him. "Has Haagenti been able to recruit anyone else to come get me? I need to know what I'm going to be up against and have some idea of when."

"Mal, no one is really sure where your level is right now. You fucking took out Busyasta! The pros are weighing the risks. None of them is jumping to take this job until they can figure out what your power degree is. And Sobronoy, too? For fuck's sake! There are some lower demons eager to make a name for themselves that Haagenti might be able to recruit, but the heavy hitters are all taking a pass."

Thank the fates for that one. I was grateful everyone thought I'd taken out Busyasta solo. Maybe this would do more than buy me time to get out of this mess. Maybe I could put enough fear and uncertainty into them all to stop this madness.

"Dar, please just lay low for a while, okay? Once Haagenti finds out I kept the sword, he's going to be even more pissed off. I don't want him taking it out on you."

Dar snorted. "I'm under your household, Mal. He has to go through you first, and you killed Labisi, Busyasta, and Sobronoy. Unless you fuck up and show an Achilles heel, I'm fine."

I disconnected and staggered up to bed.

CHAPTER 30

I opened my eyes, sleepy from my nap, and saw an angel watching me.

"What the fuck are you doing?" I asked him.

It was rather disconcerting to wake up to someone staring at you. Rather like that creepy, teenage vampire from the movie.

"Waiting for you to wake up. Why are you sleeping in the middle of the day like this?"

He walked over and sat on the edge of the bed, which was even more disconcerting.

"If you weren't so committed to your corporeal form, you wouldn't even need to sleep. You could get a lot more done."

"I like to sleep," I told him, rubbing my eyes. "I like to dream, and it feels nice to be drowsy and tired with soft sheets and fluffy pillows. Sometimes Wyatt sleeps with me and wraps me all up in a straightjacket of arms and legs. His skin is smooth and warm, and I can feel his breath in my hair."

Gregory's eyes narrowed at my mention of Wyatt. Yep, no love lost there.

"Here's the weekly kill report." He handed me a paper with his swirled writing on it.

I looked at him nervously. "I killed another human last night. Well, Boomer did actually, but on my command. Do I need to do paperwork for that? Am I allowed a certain number of kills as the Iblis? Do I have a maximum?"

He sighed. "Yes, there's a form. You need to justify the kill, and then the Council reviews it at the next meeting to ensure it complies with the regulations. Before you became the Iblis, I had to report on any of your kills as the one who bound you. I'm relieved that you now have that responsibility. I've got enough paperwork to do."

Fuck. I looked at the paper. It detailed each demon killed this past week for violating the treaty, who had killed them, how they were killed, a physical description of them. It was quite a report. Four demons turned to dust. Gregory had killed three. Busyasta's name was at the bottom of the list.

Level four-dot-two-point-eight-six demon, known as Busyasta. Removed by AA One. Raw energy absorbed by sword. Decapitation and transmutation. Violation of treaty concerning trespass in the realm of humans. Violation of statute one-four-nine-five-point-six-three regarding assault on the property of an angel.

Property of an angel. I guess that was me. I looked around for a pen.

"Am I supposed to sign it in blood or something?" I asked. "I'm not really sure the protocol here."

Gregory handed me a pen from the dresser and sat back down on the bed, disturbingly close. I could feel the power flowing from him in hot waves. Again, I thought of myself at the sink, with his arms around me, creating the water globes. Stop it, I thought and shook my head to clear it of the memory.

"Ink is okay for these, although there are some reports

that require special signatures." He watched me sign the document and took it from my hands.

"What happens if I don't do a report on my kill?"

"You'll be reprimanded. If you still don't report, you'll be disciplined." He smiled at me. It was a gloating sort of smile that held a hint of intimacy. "You really don't want to be disciplined. I'll personally take care of the matter, and you know how thorough I am."

"I don't know the forms or the statutes or anything," I told him in frustration. "I can't believe the old Iblis did this sort of thing. I can't see any demon doing this sort of thing."

Gregory's smile vanished.

"What happened to your old Iblis? Do you know? What happened after the banishment?" he asked, his voice strained.

I looked at him closely. He'd fought the guy hand to hand. The Iblis had cut his wings to ribbons, had probably been the one to kill his beloved youngest brother. Even millions of years later, he still should be in a fiery rage over it. He should want to descend into Hel and take off the guy's head.

"I don't know. The sword and the title were lost right after the fall. The vampires said you can't give up the sword, so I assume that it abandoned him or he died. I'm sure he's dead by now," I reassured him. "There are very few demons still alive from the wars."

My words didn't seem to lighten his mood. He sat for a while in silence, looking with unseeing eyes at the kill report.

"Why did they all die?" he asked, his voice flat. "There's no reason that demons shouldn't live as long as angels. Did someone kill them? Do you all go on murderous rampages?"

"Not really. We do sometimes kill each other by accident, or if we have a feud, like this thing between Haagenti and me, but it's not like we're constantly murdering."

I looked at him closely, not sure what he wanted me to say. "We're not really stable beings. Eventually we run out of interesting, new things to do and experience, and we become bored and depressed. The day comes when we just convert out of our bodies and allow our spirit-selves to splinter and disperse into the universe."

Gregory looked horrified.

"You commit suicide?"

"Eventually, yes."

He grabbed my shoulders. "Vow to me that you won't attempt such a thing," he commanded in that arrogant, imperious way of his.

I was perplexed. Why did this bother him so much? I couldn't believe he really cared whether I lived or died. If I committed suicide, it would save him the trouble of killing me.

"I can't make that vow. This is who we are, what we do, and sometimes the call is too strong to resist. It's not a bad thing, really. Not from our point of view."

He looked furious, the hands gripping my shoulders tightened painfully. "Then you will summon me if you feel that you want to do this thing."

That was a really odd command. Was this like some kind of intervention? Was he a sponsor that I would turn to when I was feeling down and blue? And how the hell was I supposed to get a hold of him anyway.

"With a cell phone? How do I call you?" Was I supposed to pray or something?

"Not call me, summon me," he said. "This brand binds both ways. You don't need to know my names, or my titles. You don't need my sigil or anything. Just pull on the ties between us and command me to you. I'm compelled to come to you no matter where you are, or what realm you are in."

Wow, he must have been really angry over the thought of my suicide to reveal that to me. I had the power to command an angel, to summon him to me. What a novel idea. Life just got more interesting.

"Okay, I will summon you if I ever feel like I want to off myself, or if I'm feeling that level of desperation where death seems like a pleasant alternative."

He let go of my shoulders and sat back.

"Is this because I'll kill a part of you too?" I asked, half afraid of the answer.

He looked surprised, as if he hadn't thought of that.

"No," he said before turning away to look down at the paper again.

"Then why? Why do you care?" I pushed for an answer.

He looked at me, his expression unreadable. "I'm simply indulging in reckless fantasy."

I looked back at him. I had no idea what my possible death had to do with reckless fantasy.

Gregory got up to leave.

"See you soon?" I asked.

"Hopefully not too soon," he said sternly, waving a finger at me. He was smiling. "Behave yourself. I've still got a leash with your name on it ready and waiting."

I pretended to look horrified as he vanished.

Clipping the Barrette of the Iblis into my hair, I dialed Wyatt.

"Hey, let's go deal with a corpse and grab some hot wings."

ALSO BY DEBRA DUNBAR

White Lightning Series

Wooden Nickels

Bum's Rush

***

The Templar Series

Dead Rising

Last Breath

Bare Bones

Famine's Feast

Dark Crossroads (2019)

* * *

IMP WORLD NOVELS

The Imp Series

A Demon Bound

Satan's Sword

Elven Blood

Devil's Paw

Imp Forsaken

Angel of Chaos

Kingdom of Lies

Exodus

Queen of the Damned

The Morning Star

* * *

Half-breed Series

Demons of Desire

Sins of the Flesh

Cornucopia

Unholy Pleasures

City of Lust

* * *

Imp World Novels

No Man's Land

Stolen Souls

Three Wishes

Northern Lights

Far From Center

Penance

* * *

Northern Wolves

Juneau to Kenai

Rogue

Winter Fae

Bad Seed

ACKNOWLEDGMENTS

A huge thanks to my copyeditor Jennifer Cosham whose eagle eyes catch all my typos and keep my comma problem in line, and to Damonza, for cover design.

Most of all, thanks to my children, who have suffered many nights of microwaved chicken nuggets and take-out pizza so that Mommy can follow her dream.

9 781952 216268

Debra lives in a littl
her sons and two sl
jogs and horseback
horse between he
super power is 'Ide

CPSIA information
at www.ICGtesting.
Printed in the USA
BVHW07120411072
583500BV00001B